Praise for the novels of Audrey Carlan

"Readers will be gratified to see the sweet relationship between the sisters treated with as much importance as the steamy one between Suda Kaye and Camden. This small-town contemporary is as stylish, confident, and free-spirited as its heroine."   —*Publishers Weekly* on *What the Heart Wants*

"Audrey Carlan has created a gem of a story about sisterhood, love, second chances, and the kind of wanderlust that won't be silenced, reminding us that sometimes the most important journey is the one we take home."
            —Lexi Ryan, *New York Times* bestselling author, on *What the Heart Wants*

"A wonderful story about building a dream and loving your life, home, family, and more."
            —Kylie Scott, *New York Times* bestselling author, on *What the Heart Wants*

"This book pulled at my heart in all the ways! An emotionally charged story of friendship, sisterhood, and love that shows us what it means to fly free."
            —Elise Lee, owner of Away With Words Bookshop, on *What the Heart Wants*

"Sexy, smart, and so unique! I was completely immersed."
                              —Katy Evans, *New York Times* bestselling author,
                              on the Calendar Girl series

"A fast-paced and downright addictive read. I devoured every word of Mia's journey."
                        —Meghan March, *USA TODAY* bestselling author,
                        on the Calendar Girl series

"Carlan's three brilliant and irrepressible ladies' men will have romance lovers looking forward to the next fix."   —*Publishers Weekly* on *International Guy*

"Readers will be intrigued... Recommended."
                              —*Library Journal* on *International Guy*

AUDREY CARLAN

On the

Sweet

Side

HQN

ISBN-13: 978-1-335-91639-6

On the Sweet Side

Recycling programs
for this product may
not exist in your area.

This is a work of fiction. Names, characters, places and incidents are either
the product of the author's imagination or are used fictitiously. Any resemblance
to actual persons, living or dead, businesses, companies, events or locales is
entirely coincidental.

This edition published by arrangement with Harlequin Books S.A.

For questions and comments about the quality of this book, please contact us at
CustomerService@Harlequin.com.

HQN
22 Adelaide St. West, 41st Floor
Toronto, Ontario M5H 4E3, Canada
www.Harlequin.com

Printed in U.S.A.

To Jeanne De Vita, my editor, my friend.
When I felt lost and rejected, you were there.
When I was abandoned by a sister, you were there.
When things felt impossible, you were there.
You are what the sisterhood is all about.

On the

Sweet

Side

one

I would never forget the exact moment my life changed forever. There wasn't anything particularly special about the day. Jasper, my best friend in all things, and I had been celebrating our graduation from culinary school with some homemade donuts at my fathers' place. We'd each planned to stay with our parents until we got jobs as fabulous pastry chefs in the city and could afford a place together.

The ultimate dream—the one we'd been planning since the day we met in kindergarten and had dared each other to eat our disgustingly crafted mud pies—was to one day open our own bakery. We talked about it incessantly. Jasper had two mothers, and I two fathers. Naturally, we were the oddballs on the playground, and we gravitated toward one another as the weird kids with the same-sex parents. Through the years we realized our parents were no different than those in any other happy home. They were strict, loving, supportive and most of all, always encouraged us to chase after our dreams.

We'd been inseparable ever since. Best friends for life and we had the tattoos to prove it. Me with the word *Soul* inscribed just above my elbow on my right arm—my baking arm. Jasper with the word *Mates* on his left in the same spot, so that when we stood side by side, everyone knew we were soul mates. From hobbies, to friends, to our taste in men, Jasper and I shared nearly everything—including our dream to co-own a bakery and do what we love: make everything in life taste sweet.

So it wasn't uncommon for Jasper to have slept on my fathers' couch. We'd gotten drunk on bottle after bottle of champagne while celebrating our graduation with my parents late into the night. My fathers may have been strict over the years, but they loved to socialize, kick off their shoes, dance and drink until dawn if the circumstances warranted. And after six years of an intensive culinary program, complete with two years abroad working under grandmaster pastry chefs, our graduation was absolutely a warranted event.

Which brought me to the moment when it all changed.

Elbow deep in pastry dough, Jasper prattling on about some hot Black guy he'd met recently, I didn't see them at first. I *felt* them. The air in the room changed as if someone had turned off the fan, cut off the AC. All of a sudden the space was filled with tension.

I glanced up as my dad Casey entered the room with two gorgeous women in tow. Jasper kept prattling on, his shiny silver bomber jacket, golden spiked hair and crystal-blue eyes not capable of taking my attention away from the two women standing behind my dad.

One was tall with an athletic build and looked like she'd just walked off the Paris runway. Her long golden hair hung

over her shoulders in perfect beachy waves. Her skin seemed
to glow a tanned bronze as if she'd been lit up from within
by the very sun itself. She wore perfectly tailored white capri
pants, a peach silk tank that complemented her coloring in
ways I'd never be able to achieve without Jasper's instruc-
tion, and gold accessories. Her eyes were a startling icy blue
and rather cold, the exact opposite of the woman standing
beside her, whose hand she was holding.

I tipped my head as I stared at the brunette beauty before
me. She was familiar in a way that would make you tap on
her shoulder if she were, say, on the L train heading the same
direction as you into the city and you couldn't get over how
much she looked like someone you knew. There was a *pull*, a
tether to her, that had me focusing on more detail. She wore
a brilliant, flowing maxi dress in a riot of reds, oranges and
a teal tone that fell beautifully around her curves. Her hair
fell nearly to her waist, a couple inches longer than the hair
of the woman beside her. Her eyes, however, were amber, a
color I recognized instantly.

My heart started to pound and I gasped as the two women
stood in my kitchen looking painfully nervous and maybe
even a little scared.

It was my papa who reacted first, dropping his news-
paper on the table and standing with a flourish. Ian Collins
was the perfect dark to my dad's light. Casey was glow-in-
the-dark pearlescent white befitting his full Irish genetics,
much like my own, whereas my papa was a beautiful mix of
Caucasian, Indian and Egyptian. His skin tone was a rich,
luxurious brown accompanied by espresso-colored hair and
effervescent golden eyes.

The brunette made a startled-sounding noise and placed
her hand to her chest as though the mere sight of my papa
gouged her very soul.

"These ladies were sitting out in front of the house and said they were here to see Izzy." My dad set down the ingredients I needed to finish the donuts I was working on when the blonde finally spoke.

"Um, maybe we, uh, should come back another time?" Her voice sounded strained and uncertain. These two random strangers being in my house, in my kitchen, was odd but she seemed genuinely fearful.

"I'm sorry," I said while wiping my hands on a towel and focusing on the two women. "Have we met before?"

"You look so much like her," my papa whispered, edging closer to the two ladies. "Catori." He raised his hand close to the brunette's face as though he was studying a famous work of art and was completely in awe of it. The hairs on the back of my neck tingled as I watched the woman step back, pulling the blonde with her as tears fell down her cheeks. "Suda Kaye?" He choked out what I assumed was her name as tears filled his eyes.

What in the heck was going on?

"It can't be?" My dad went to his husband and wrapped an arm around Papa's back in a loving, supportive hold.

Momentarily, I was stunned into a daze as I watched Papa's gaze switch to the pretty blonde. "Evie?"

She nodded.

Okay. So the blonde was Evie and the brunette was Suda Kaye. Two names I'd never heard in my entire life.

"Anyone going to tell me what's going on?" I reached out to Jasper, needing my best friend's support, though I wasn't sure why.

"Izzy, baby girl, your father and I have something to tell you," my dad announced to the entire room.

The two women stayed deathly silent until one of them dug through the big purse she was carrying.

"Excuse us for coming without calling. Unfortunately, I have some things I need to give you." The blonde's tone was all business even though I could tell by the tightness in her shoulders that she was incredibly uncomfortable.

I frowned and narrowed my gaze, trying to figure out what was going on while my fathers acted weirder than normal. "Who are you?"

"I'm Evie Ross and this is my sister Suda Kaye. We'll let your dads explain in more detail." She pulled out a stack of pink letters tied with a ribbon and handed them to my dad. Then she removed a folder, and her voice shook when she said, "This is our father's last will and testament…"

My papa winced and looked at Suda Kaye as though she were a living dream he couldn't quite touch.

"And Catori?" my papa asked, a hint of sadness in his tone.

Catori. I'd only known one person in my lifetime with that name. The surrogate my fathers used to conceive me.

"She passed eleven years ago… I'm sorry," Evie responded flatly, though her lips pressed together tightly.

Eleven years ago. I was thirteen.

"This document will explain things." She pressed the file into my papa's hands. "He's left Isabeau quite a lot and his attorney needs to get in touch with her."

The fact that the blonde knew my name was startling, to say the least. Saying it with the words *last will, left Isabeau a lot* and *attorney* had me beyond confused.

"What? Who left me what? And why did you mention my mother's name? There can't possibly be many Catoris in the world."

Suda Kaye pressed her face against Evie's shoulder and cried.

"Why would he do that?" My dad ignored me but looked at Evie with such gentle compassion it made my heart squeeze.

Casey Collins—my dad—had the biggest heart and loved everyone for exactly who they were. My papa Ian was the fiery, super-passionate one. I always teased that Papa gave me his temper even though my lush auburn locks came straight from my dad's genetics.

"Because he loved our mother and the children she bore, regardless of if they were his blood. He wants her legacy protected," Evie explained with a direct, no-nonsense approach as though this was a simple business transaction when it was clear as day these two women were fighting extreme emotions. Suda Kaye was failing miserably to conceal her feelings. I was just trying to figure out why they would have them when it dawned on me what she'd said.

Her children.

As in more than one.

"Her children. Are you saying that you two…" I pointed to Evie then Suda Kaye, who lifted her watery gaze. "Are my half sisters?"

No. Freakin'. Way.

Jasper squeezed my hand as I started to tremble.

Evie looked surreptitiously at my dad and then at my papa, who hadn't taken his eyes off Suda Kaye. The impact of what she was saying slammed into me like the first swallow of a perfect French champagne bursting on your tongue after tasting a pristine ripe strawberry off the vine.

"Catori Ross was your mother, too? Oh, my God!" You couldn't have wiped the giant smile off my face as the possibility of my having sisters flowed through my veins. "You were donor eggs, too? And you found me! This is awesome!" I let go of Jasper's hand and clapped, jumping up and down on the balls of my feet. My mind whirled with excitement. "I'll betcha there's tons of us!"

Evie tilted her head, that cool gaze seeming endless as she

responded. "Not exactly. Like I said, we needed to bring these items and we'll be on our way." She once again reached into her purse and pulled out what looked like a business card, then set it on the counter closest to her. "When, uh, you've had some time, and if you want to, feel free to call that number. It's my cell phone. We'll be in town for a couple more days."

"Where do you live?" my papa asked Suda Kaye, longing coating every word.

Why would he care? I mean, if they were my half sisters through in vitro, technically it would mean I was related to these women. But my biological father was Casey, not Ian.

"We live in Colorado. I'm in Pueblo and Evie is in Colorado Springs." It was the first thing Suda Kaye had said since they arrived.

"Suda Kaye, we need to talk," my papa said, his words a plea before he glanced at me, then Evie. "We all do."

Evie, whom I realized was the communicator in this crowd, nodded and answered, "Yes, and we're open to that, but I think you have something more important to talk about." She lifted her chin in my direction and my shoulders sank.

I looked at the way Papa was shaking, my dad rubbing his back in a soothing manner as though this conversation, these two women, were a dream. Maybe a nightmare.

Oh, no. I squinted and suddenly realized why Suda Kaye seemed so familiar. My papa's skin tone and hair color were not only similar to Suda Kaye's, they were also downright replicas of one another. Still, the smoking gun, the knife twisting inside my heart, was looking into Suda Kaye's watery amber gaze and seeing Papa's unique eyes staring back.

"You're not from donor eggs, are you?" My voice was but a whisper. So small that Jasper stepped up behind me and looped an arm around my waist, pressing his chin to the back of my neck in support.

Evie shook her head solemnly.

"I don't understand," I choked out as Jasper held me close and placed a kiss to my temple.

"You will soon. Thank you for having us. We'll be going." Evie moved to leave.

As they headed out, my papa grabbed Suda Kaye's arm and pulled her into an embrace. He buried his tear-streaked face into her hair and I watched in confusion as his shoulders shuddered with unspent tremors. Suda Kaye shakily lifted her arms and put them around him.

What he said next fileted me from my stomach to my throat.

"I've dreamt of this moment. Every day of my life for the past twenty-eight years I dreamed of holding you. *My daughter.*" He pulled back and cupped her cheeks. "You are stunning. Just like your mother."

"Your daughter?" My body convulsed in shock and I gasped, placing my hand over my heart.

"Babe, let her go." My dad put his hands around my papa's waist and attempted to pull him away.

"I don't want to let her go." His voice was hoarse, a guttural sound I had never heard before. As though someone were literally ripping him to pieces and he could barely speak through it. "Never again. I wish I never had…"

Tears pricked the backs of my eyes and I watched as Suda Kaye pulled herself from his hold and raced out of the kitchen, her steps thudding across the hardwood floors until the unmistakable sound of the door opening and shutting filtered through to us.

My papa crumbled into his husband's hold, sobbing against my dad's neck.

My heart wanted to jump out of my chest, and my arms longed to wrap around my parents, but I couldn't move. My feet were virtually glued to the tile floor under me as I watched uncertainty, sorrow and devastation wrack my papa's proud frame.

"I'm sorry. We shouldn't have come." Evie's voice cracked as she backed farther out of the room.

"No, you definitely should have. Only I wish it was twenty-five years ago," my dad said softly over my papa's shoulder. "We should have pushed harder. We knew it after she left when Isabeau was three months old, but we'd made a promise." His voice was laced with pain and regret.

Promise? What promise? My mother was with us when I was a baby? How could that be? They told me that I was handed to them at the hospital and they never saw my surrogate again. Said she up and disappeared without a trace. All they ever gave me was her name.

Catori.

"Some promises are never meant to be broken," Evie said, a coldness sweeping across her pretty face as she turned and left the room. Her steps were silent. I only heard the hammering of my heart like a steel drum.

For a second I stood there stunned, incapable of moving, of feeling anything. Until I realized that those two women were my sisters.

My *sisters*.

We had the same mother.

A mother they'd known, and I hadn't.

I had a million questions and the answers were walking out of my childhood home. My feet finally moved on instinct and I ran to the front of the house. Evie was gliding down the sidewalk toward the car parked in front. Suda Kaye was already inside, waiting.

"Hey!" I yelled from the top of our little concrete landing.

Evie stopped halfway down the path and turned around. Her eyes were filled with unshed tears, the once icy waters a warm sky blue. Not cold. I could see the mask she'd held in place was gone. The heartache and sadness no longer hidden in whatever emotion she had to set aside to come here and face me and my fathers. She waited as I looked my fill of her features, so different than mine. Yet, the angles of her face, with the same high, rounded cheekbones as mine, her full lips, almond-shaped eyes, all very much what I saw when I looked in the mirror. Except she was golden all over and I was pale, a dark auburn with hazel eyes.

Taking a deep breath, I wrung my hands in front of me, trying to release the anxiety and fear welling up. "When all of this is figured out, in there—" I gestured toward my house behind me and remembered her card on the counter "—I'll call."

"I'll answer." She offered a small, sad smile.

I smiled wide in return and then focused on the woman in the car. Her head was down, hands covering her face as her shoulders shook.

"Will she be okay?" I lifted my chin toward the car.

"Suda Kaye will be fine. I'll make sure of it. It's what sisters are for. We take care of one another," she whispered.

Sisters. Taking care of one another. I only ever had Jasper and my fathers.

"Something to look forward to." I smiled once more and waved before going back inside and shutting the door.

My dad was still holding on to my papa, who had not stopped crying. It was as if his entire world had just come crumbling down at the sight of the two pretty women who claimed to be my half sisters.

"Jasper, this is a tequila conversation," I requested as my papa's shoulders straightened from my dad's arms.

My dad cupped his cheeks, wiped his tears with his thumbs and then placed a brief kiss to his lips. My dad's hazel gaze came to mine. "We'll meet you in the living room for a family meeting."

"Should I go?" Jasper's eyes widened as he held up the bottle of Patrón Silver.

My dad looked at Jasper. "You family?"

Jasper nodded. Because he was. He'd been in my life since we were five. Nineteen years. There was nothing we didn't know about each other.

"Take Izzy and get comfortable. We have a lot to talk about," my dad urged.

Twenty-four years old, and as I looked at my fathers holding on to one another and my best friend's sad smile, I knew that what my parents were about to tell me would change my life forever. Because apparently, my mother had been alive until I was thirteen. She'd been with us for three months of my life until she left. Papa had another daughter. And I had two half sisters. Ones who obviously felt it was important to come meet me in person. Then there were the letters sitting on the counter next to a file that contained the last will and testament of a man I did not know, but who had known my mother. A man important to my half sisters had left me some sort of inheritance.

More than anything, I couldn't wrap my mind around the fact that I'd been living a lie. One carefully crafted by the two people who claimed to love and cherish me above all others.

two

The four of us lounged on the cashew-colored micro-suede couch we'd had since before I graduated high school. Jasper sat plastered to my side, hip to ankle, one of my hands in both of his. Usually, he was boisterous and the life of any conversation. Today he sat in silent support as I stared into the two faces that I loved more than any other.

The two men who had lied to me my entire life.

"Izzy…" My dad Casey balanced his elbows on his knees, his hands held in front of him under his chin. "I… Jesus, Ian. I'm not sure where to start." He shook his head and blew out a long breath.

"The beginning would be nice? Starting with why you lied to me, oh, I don't know, a million times!" I barely sucked back a sob as tears blazed down my cheeks. Jasper squeezed my hand, lifted it to his face and kissed my fingers.

"Baby girl, it's not that we lied exactly," my dad attempted, but then slumped back against the couch. He rubbed his bearded chin and pushed his fingers into his auburn layers. "It's a really complex situation. I lived it and I'm not sure I understand how it all happened anymore."

"So those women are my half sisters?" I asked even though I'd figured out that part on my own.

"Yeah," he sighed.

My papa sat next to his husband, bouncing one of his knees as if at any moment he would stand, grow wings and take flight. Likely chasing after his *real* daughter Suda Kaye.

"And Suda Kaye is biologically Papa's?" I stared at my fathers.

My papa's red-rimmed eyes searched and locked on mine before his face crumpled into an expression of absolute torment. I gripped my free hand into a fist, wanting to jump up and comfort him the way he always did for me growing up.

"Suda Kaye was a happy accident. Not something Catori and I planned." My papa inhaled deeply and I watched as silent tears fell down his smooth-shaven cheek.

"And Evie?"

My papa shook his head. "Not ours. Catori's with her husband, Adam Ross."

"The man that apparently died and noted me in his will." I glanced at the kitchen where I knew the file folder sat, burning a hole in the tile.

They both nodded.

"So Evie is older, by how much? Do you even know?" I accused snidely.

"Sweetheart, don't take that tone. This is hard enough on us as it is." My papa winced as though he just heard what he'd said and knew it was wrong.

"Hard on you? I've been lied to by my parents my entire life. I had a mother. A *real* mother. Not a donor. A woman who already had two kids. One of which is my fucking father's, and I've never met her, or my other half sister."

"Don't curse. It sounds ugly coming out of such a pretty mouth," my dad chastised.

I groaned and looked up at the ceiling, counting to ten under my breath. It was something Jasper and I taught ourselves to do when the bullies at school would make fun of us for having two dads and two moms, and later when Jasper came out officially freshman year of high school—the only openly gay boy in our small school at the time.

"Izzy, I met Catori before I met your dad. You know I dated both women and men in my early twenties. That is, until I met Casey and my heart exploded. I knew then and there that man would be mine for eternity. He was a puzzle piece that I was missing in my heart. It clicked in place and it's been him ever since."

I gritted my teeth. "I've heard this story a million times, Papa. Get to the part about my mother," I demanded.

"Catori and I met when she was separated from her husband. He was a military man and always deployed overseas. Catori was like the wind. A free bird flying from one destination to the next, forever in search of the meaning of life."

I pulled my legs up onto the couch and sat cross-legged. Jasper followed suit but stayed close, a hand clutching my thigh at all times.

"I met Catori at an arts festival in downtown Chicago. Next to you, Isabeau, she was the most beautiful woman I'd ever seen in my life. A hundred percent Native American. Long black hair all the way down to her bum. Lithe, curvy body and a siren's smile that could light up the world. And she did, your mother. Every man, woman and child in her path was mesmerized by her beauty, her laugh, her kind, accepting nature."

I smiled, imagining what she might have looked like when Papa got up and went to our built-in shelving unit. He stepped on a stool and grabbed a marble box from the top shelf. It was about the size of a small shoebox. It had been sitting on that shelf in this house for as long as I could remember.

He opened the box and pulled out a stack of pictures. He handed me the top one. It was my papa, younger by twenty-five years, smiling wide, his dark hair long enough to reach his shoulders.

"Your hair!" I chuckled and showed the image to Jasper. "You looked like an artist."

He smirked.

In my papa's arms was a stunning beauty. The woman he spoke of. Catori. My mother. Black hair with dark eyes to match. Her skin a darker shade of brown than my papa's. Though her cheeks, nose, eye shape and definitely her smile I'd have recognized anywhere—they were the same as my own. Also, the same as the two women who showed up today.

"Catori was part of a belly-dancing crew that was performing in the area. Our eyes connected, we partied, got to know one another and became intimate. She stayed in the city for a month until her dancing group planned to dance their way across the nation, ending in New York. It was a magical month. We lived, we loved, we were carefree. Before meeting Casey, and having you, it was the best time of my life."

His head fell forward and he focused on the ground. "Only we were too carefree. After she left to move on to Indiana, I got a call. She told me that she was pregnant. I freaked out. I was so young. Hell, we were both so young. And I knew what we had was indeed love, but it wasn't the type of love you build a life on. It was kinship. Seeing yourself in another in a way you relate to and enjoy for a time. We could never have been together long-term."

"Then what happened?" I asked, imagining how freaked out my young papa must have been.

"For months we discussed our options at great length. That's when I found out that she planned to go home to her reservation where her one-year-old daughter was being taken care of by her father."

"She left Evie with her dad?"

He nodded. "Catori wasn't like anyone I'd ever known. She was the wind. A free spirit not meant to stay in one place for long. It wasn't her destiny."

"Then she should have taken birth control," I grumbled.

Jasper snorted and then pressed his lips together.

"Be that as it may, she convinced me that our child would be best raised by her and her husband, Adam. They were reconciling or whatever it ended up being, and she wanted to raise the baby with her husband on the reservation. I was barely twenty-three. A foster kid with no family of my own, and no one to turn to for help. I was going to college part-time and working part-time as a mechanic. I lived in a basement of an older lady's home that she rented to me for cheap because I did all the yardwork and took out the trash. I had nothing to give a baby or Catori, so I let her do what she thought was best."

My dad put his arm around my papa's shoulders. "You did the right thing at the time, Ian. She had support. An older husband, a family on the reservation and another daughter."

"Every day of my life I regretted not being a part of Suda Kaye's life. Then a year later I met Casey and he changed my world. Older than me by seven years. Had his shit to-gether when I was still scrambling to make ends meet and finish my schooling. We got together. I moved in with him and within a short time we were married. A year later, when he was in his early thirties, Casey was ready to start a family. Which is when I told him what happened with Catori and Suda Kaye."

My dad kissed my papa's jaw and pressed his forehead to his husband's. "And I understood, but that didn't change the fact that I wanted a child to raise with Ian. Wanted him to have a home and a family the likes of which neither of us had. We contacted an agency and hired a woman who used donor sperm and her own egg to undergo in-vitro fertilization."

"Oh, my God!" I lost my breath.

He nodded. "And it worked, too. Ian and I were so happy. We were going to be a family. A real family. Not just by marriage but with a child of our own."

A swell of sadness coated the air as I closed my eyes, knowing the next part before either one of them could utter the words.

My dad Casey continued. "She became pregnant but when it was time to give us the child in the hospital, she refused to hand over the baby. Said it was her blood and she'd take us to court to keep her child."

"Did she? Take you to court?"

He nodded. "At first, yeah. We'd paid almost twenty thousand dollars between the in vitro and her surrogate fee. None of which we ever got back. The attorney's fees alone to fight after those initial meetings would have been astronomical and stripped us of every dollar we had at the time."

"Which is when I hired a private investigator to find your mother. It wasn't hard. I knew her full name and the name of the man she married. I also knew she lived on a reservation in Oklahoma or Colorado."

"Why did you contact her?"

His expression was tortured. "Because I'd given up my daughter and we'd just lost our chance at having a family. I was angry, hurt, destroyed, over losing that opportunity twice. Catori listened. Consoled me. Was heartbroken for both Casey and me. Understood what it meant for me to give up having Suda Kaye in my life."

"What were you planning?" I asked, holding my breath.

My papa shrugged. "Honestly, I didn't know. I just knew that my husband and I wanted a family desperately and I had a daughter I'd never once seen."

"She owed you," Jasper whispered. "For Suda Kaye. She owed you."

My papa looked at my best friend and nodded once. "She owed me."

"So one day, Catori, in all her glory, shows up at our house with a big suitcase. She walked in, took in the place, went right to Ian, grabbed his cheeks and kissed the daylights out of him. Then she turned around and did the exact same to me." He laughed, scratching at his red beard. "She was fire and ice, the wind and the earth and everything in between. A true beauty the likes of which I have never seen."

"You guys had sex with her!" I stood up and covered my ears. "No, no, no, no, no!"

I felt hands tugging at my biceps and I opened my eyes to see my dad, his hazel eyes twinkling with mirth. "Baby girl, you know women don't do it for me. Besides, your papa and I had committed to each other and *only* each other for better or worse. His days of bedding women were long over."

I frowned. "Then how did I come to be?"

My papa smiled and put his ankle up on his opposite knee, tapping his fingers on his leg. "Catori said after our call she had a dream and she knew what needed to be done. She was going to be our surrogate and donor. Said in her dream she'd given birth to a fire-haired porcelain beauty and the Creator demanded she follow through. Something about karmic debt being paid. I gave her a child, so she gave us one. But there were rules. Hers, not ours."

I sat back down and chewed on my bottom lip. Jasper snuggled up close to my side and pressed his bony chin to my shoulder.

"She said she'd get pregnant, and then go back home until she was showing. Then she'd come back and stay only until she knew the baby was healthy, home and safely with her parents. Then the universe would be balanced."

"And you took her up on her offer."

My papa shrugged. "We were desperate. Only had enough money to go through the in-vitro process once more. If it worked, fate intervened."

"And it did," I said softly.

"And it did. We were never so happy as the day Catori took a pregnancy test and it was positive. Shortly after, she left to be with her daughters as we prepared for our baby. We talked often until she appeared again seven months later, you in her belly. We organized all of her doctor's visits and she stayed in the room that would be yours one day. We had a day bed put in there, the one you slept on when you were out of your crib."

I smiled, remembering the swirling white iron curlicues of the metal head and footboard I used to trace with my fingers as I fell asleep.

"She was so proud to give you life. Said her girls gave her meaning and you were special."

My heart warmed and a sense of peace filled me from within.

"Then she only asked for three things of us in exchange for you."

My mouth went dry and my chin trembled as I waited to hear what the three things were.

"Your name would be Isabeau. She said it means 'God is my oath' or 'pledged to God.' Catori believed it was her destiny to do this and that you were fated to be born. A gift from the Creator. And in her culture, you don't deny God or Fate."

A tear fell down my cheek as I listened to my father tell me my mother believed I was a gift from God. A gift she was meant to bestow on two childless fathers who wanted a family.

"And the other two things?" My voice cracked but I swallowed down the emotions in order to hear the rest.

My papa closed his eyes. "To accept that one day she would be gone from our lives. We were to accept the act for what it was. A gift made by a woman who loved far greater than any other we've ever known."

Dad reached for my papa's hand and held on to it before he looked at me. "The gift that would give back to us our whole lives long."

I sniffed and wiped my runny nose. "And the third thing?"

"To have you know love every day of your life, but to not know of her," my papa whispered.

That had my shoulders quaking as the pain of that admission shot through my veins like burning acid. My birth mother didn't want to love me. Didn't want me to know her.

"Exactly three months to the day, when Catori would normally be up nursing you when the sun kissed the sky, we heard you crying. An angry wail that spoke of your hunger for your morning breakfast. Catori had solely nursed you for the first six weeks. The next six we'd been weaning you on to formula and getting you used to us. That morning you had your first day of nothing but formula. We entered your room, her room, to find her gone. Clothes, toiletries, everything just gone. She'd left us a note." My papa dug through the box once more and brought out a ratty-looking envelope. He pulled out a small piece of lined paper that had seen better days and handed it to me.

Ian and Casey,
Your love knows no bounds. Teach our daughter that gift.
Be well. Be happy. Be a family.
With all my heart,
Catori.

I folded the letter back up and handed it to my papa. He placed it carefully back into the envelope as though it was a treasured correspondence from a loved one. And I guess in their way it was, for Catori Ross gave them me, made us a family.

"And Suda Kaye?" I asked and my papa's eyes filled with tears once more.

"Today was the first day I've ever set eyes on her." His voice was ravaged with pain and grief.

"Why? Why couldn't we all have known each other? Be a family with Suda Kaye and Evie and this—" I waved my hand in the air "—this Adam guy."

"It's hard to grasp, harder to explain, but Catori wasn't meant to be in any one place with any one family. She belonged to the wind, the stars, the earth. She had a hunger inside her that could never be quenched by staying still."

"Then what you're saying is, Evie and Suda Kaye had her love and sometimes had her in their lives, but mostly she left them, too?"

My papa swallowed and closed his eyes. "I don't know their story, but I trust that Catori would never harm nor hurt her children intentionally. She gave up everything to give us you. Perhaps she did the same for her husband, Adam, with Evie and Suda Kaye. We sent pictures of you every so often to a post office box she'd given me once. She never sent pictures of Suda Kaye. That was my cross to bear. I accepted you in lieu of a relationship with her." The admission seemed to gut him as he winced and more tears fell.

"Papa," I choked and scrambled to the floor, putting myself between his long legs and pressing my head against his broad chest. He held me around my shoulders and cried into my hair.

"You are everything your dad and I ever wanted. Everything we could ever dream of." His breath was hot against my neck. "How could I ask for more by demanding access to Suda Kaye after she gave me you? How? I couldn't."

I shook my head and cried into his chest. I cried for him. For me. For Suda Kaye. For Catori. It all seemed so beautiful and tragically hopeless at the same time.

"Just know, my Isabeau, your mother stayed until she couldn't any longer. With the life she lived, it wasn't possible to be everywhere at once, and we all made our choices. Me, when I gave up Suda Kaye because I was young, broke and immature, and Catori giving us you because she was nothing but love and light. If she had it in her to give such a gift to someone she cared for, she set about doing it." He tightened his arms around me. "But don't you for one second believe you weren't wanted or loved. That woman gave up her rights so we could be a family. Gave up her daughter so two men could love their child wholly and completely with every fiber of our being. Left us to be a family, a *real* family. And baby girl, that is beautiful. As heartbreaking as it is, and as much turmoil as we feel now, I'd do it all over again to have you."

My dad hugged us both from the side. "We'd both do it

all again to have you. You're the best thing we ever did and will continue to be that until we take our last breaths on this earth."

"I love you both so much even though my heart is breaking." I pressed harder against my father's chest.

"We love you more, baby girl." My dad rubbed his hand down my back and my papa kissed the crown of my head. I pushed back and he held my cheeks in his big, strong hands. I looked into those amber eyes, the same color as Suda Kaye's, and let more tears fall. I looked into my dad's hazel eyes and saw my own as he shed a tear for all of us.

"I want to know them. Evie and Suda Kaye. No matter what happened twenty-four years ago, no matter what promises you all made to each other, I want to know my sisters. And I want to know who my mother was. Family is family, right?" I looked at my fathers and watched as they wiped their tears away and nodded. I looked at my best friend in the universe and waved him over.

He slid across the floor so fast you'd have believed he just powered down a black diamond mountain on a snowboard. He put his arms around me from behind and held on.

"Family is what you make of it. It's something you build, work on and cherish your whole life long. I want to know them. I think I need to."

Papa nodded. "We'll help in whatever way we can."

three

===

Two months later

Jasper entered my room in a flourish of vibrant colors. I placed the picture frame of me and my fathers on the top of the clothes already packed in my biggest suitcase. Two other cases were on the floor filled with clothes, toiletries, special items and my favorite cooking utensils. A pastry chef wouldn't dare leave behind the tools of her trade when she ventured off into the sunset, even if I had no idea if I'd be baking anytime soon.

"What the hell is this?" Jasper shook a full-size piece of paper right in front of my face as though he was not only angry with me, but also angry at the inanimate object.

I narrowed my gaze and tried to read the flashing words but couldn't. He dropped the item on top of my suitcase and started to pace my childhood bedroom the same way he'd done a bazillion times before when he was in a snit.

"Jas, what is it?" I picked up the document and noticed our school's logo in the top left-hand corner. Jasper and I were not only connected at the hip, we were as close as siblings, too. Twins would be more accurate.

Until now. Because I was leaving. Heading for Colorado for an undetermined amount of time. The goal: get to know my sisters. Find out who this Adam guy who left me so much money was. Learn more about my mother. I didn't exactly know what I would do when I got there, just that I had to do it. And now I had the money to do whatever the heck I wanted.

"It's a statement from school of my account." He stole the paper from my hand and tapped on it angrily. "My mother almost fainted!"

I grinned, imagining Penelope, the petite woman with the corkscrew blond curls and the pixie-like face doing just that.

Jasper glared. "It says, *paid in full.* All forty-seven thousand dollars I still owed wiped clean."

Oh, that was what this was about.

I shrugged nonchalantly, grabbed the paper, crumpled it into a ball and tossed it over his head and into the small wicker basket near my vanity, scoring a perfect three points.

"A shrug? You've got nothing to say about this?"

I shrugged again and snorted while closing up my suitcase.

"You paid almost fifty thousand dollars of my school debt!" He screeched as though he was entirely put out by this miraculous gift.

"Yes, I did." I zipped up the suitcase and yanked on it, but it was so heavy I just left it there for one of my fathers to lift and bring to the car.

"Forty-seven *thousand* dollars!" Jasper again huffed.

"Yep."

"Why?" His tone was soft and filled with awe.

I turned around and stood up. "Because I love you. Because I have more money than I need. Because your mothers worked their asses off to pay for the first twenty thousand. Because a dude I've never met gave me a boon that I never asked for. Because you deserve to be free of debt. Paid off my fathers' house, too. Though they won't know that until I've left, thank God!" I playfully winced. "Now, pick up the smaller suitcase while I take this one." I gestured to the carry-on-size case that held the cooking tools I could not leave behind.

He grabbed the case and hefted it up. "It's heavier than it looks," he grumbled but dutifully led the way out of my bedroom.

I stopped at the threshold and put my hand to the knob, taking in the pretty lilac walls with white trim, my bed with the padded headboard, a dark purple floral comforter and tons of frilly pillows accentuating the design. My whitewashed wooden desk where I studied but mostly drew pictures of cakes and hearts filled in with the names of boys I had crushes on. The little ballerina music box that held baubles and plastic rings from quarter machines I collected as a child. This room held so many good memories. Jasper and I may have been bullied growing up but we both had amazing childhoods. My fathers loved me beyond reason, and I knew it to the core of my being. I never once felt unloved or uncherished by them. I was their whole world and looking at this room they provided for me, the schooling they encouraged me to seek, I was finally starting to realize just how much they loved me.

"Bye, room," I whispered and shut the door, not knowing if I'd ever step foot in it again. I didn't know where this adventure was going to take me or if I'd tuck my tail between my legs and race back home to my parents. Still, I had to do it. Take the plunge. Become my own person. Figure out who I was without the safety net of my fathers' comforting arms.

Find out what the place inside my heart needed. The piece of me that never felt fulfilled. The ache, the twinge of emptiness I'd lived with, ignored, but now felt thrumming inside my veins in a way I knew this choice was the right one. I'd find my answers, on this journey of discovery. I knew it down to my toes this was what I was meant to do.

Jasper led me down the hall and straight out to the car where my fathers were poking around. Three other big suitcases were being loaded into the back of my shiny, new Ford Explorer. It was a huge upgrade from the small Toyota four-door hand-me-down my fathers had given me. This one was brand spanking new, courtesy of the Adam Ross inheritance fund. It was the most beautiful blue-green slate color I'd ever seen.

"Um, Papa, why are you putting more cases into Serenity?"

"Serenity?" He smirked as I approached. His golden-brown skin glowed under the sun's rays. Ian Collins was a handsome man. All of our extended friends thought so. With his darker coloring, devil-may-care smirk and amber eyes, even I knew he was swoon-worthy. Of course, when I was a teenager and Jasper and my friends would talk about it, I'd gag and pretend to vomit at their girlish crushes.

"That's her name." I ran my hand over the sparkly paint and curving metal. "Isn't she beautiful?" I gazed at my new car with extreme delight and sent up a silent thanks to Adam Ross for yet another gift his money had bought me.

My dad chuckled and took the bag from my hold. "This all?" He frowned.

I shook my head. "Nope. The big one is in my bedroom."

He grinned. "Of course it is."

Jasper went to the back and hauled my other case into the large trunk space.

"Again, why are there three more bags in here?" I asked as my papa wedged in another.

"You didn't think you were moving without me, did you?" Jasper blinked and then stared me down.

My heart pounded and my stomach buzzed with excitement. "You're coming with me?" I could barely speak as hope poured through my veins. Having him with me would be better than anything I could ever have wished for. So much so, I never even asked or considered the idea, because he'd be giving up everything.

He scoffed, bum-rushed me and took me down to the grass until we were rolling and laughing like old times. He stopped half on top of me, half to my side.

"You can't go on an adventure without your best friend!" His striking blue eyes were filled with a love and a light so bright I could barely look into them without shading my view.

"But your dreams…to be a pastry chef at a fancy restaurant in Chicago," I choked out, his handsome, androgynous features so carefree and unsoiled.

"I can't live my dream if you're not in it, Izzy. We made a pact. To live our lives together, intertwined as family."

"Family can live in different states," I reminded him, even though I very much did not want to sway him from accompanying me on this journey.

He shook his head and shifted my wild red curls off my forehead. "We're finally free to live how we want. I don't want to live in a city without you. Work in a restaurant where you can't visit me all the time. Meet a man of my own and not go on double dates. Fall in love and not have my best friend there in all things." He scowled. "Wouldn't feel right."

I smiled. "You know that makes us incredibly codependent, right?"

He grinned in response. "Codependent but happy as a clam. I'm cool with that." He lifted his body up and off the ground then reached his hand out to me. "You ready to get on the road or what?"

I took his hand and my best friend helped me up. Just like he always did. Just like I would do for him in a nanosecond if he needed anything.

My fathers finished with our bags, checked the tires and made sure all the lights worked on the brand-new vehicle. I stood in front of my childhood home and stared. Remembering every beautiful memory at once, all made in this place I'd never forget.

Behind me I felt a warmth before I saw my dad's pale forearms wrap around me. He rested his bearded chin on my shoulder.

"Do you know how insanely proud I am of the woman you've become?" His words were thick and filled with emotion.

I held on to his forearms and leaned back against him. "Thanks, Dad."

"You'll call every day until I feel you're safe." His demand brooked no argument.

I smiled. "Dad, it's a sixteen-hour drive. I plan on doing eight hours today, and eight hours tomorrow."

He huffed and squeezed me around the waist. "Just be careful, honey."

I patted his arms. "I've got Jasper."

"That's what I'm worried about," he teased.

"Hey! I heard that," Jasper hollered from somewhere behind us.

"Are you going to let our daughter go so I can get some love in and they can be on their way?" my papa asked.

I turned around and hugged my dad, taking in his fresh water and rich, musky cologne scent before letting go and turning to my papa. He wrapped his arms around me and pressed his face to my neck.

"You are beyond loved, kid," he whispered near my ear.

"I know, Papa, I know."

"We will miss you every second," he continued.

I held on tight. "Me, too."

"You sure you have to do this? What if they're mean?" Always the worrier in our trio.

I grinned and dug my fingers into his shoulder blades. "They're not mean. And you know I have to do this."

"I want to protect you. We want to make sure that nothing ever hurts you." His voice was rougher than normal, showing how deeply my leaving was affecting him.

"You can't protect me from living, Papa. You have to let me go. Understand that it's my time to figure out the world. Learn who I'm going to become. Grow and change."

He nodded but squeezed me tight one last time before releasing his hold. "I love you. Please keep in touch."

"Often," my dad said while sidling up to his husband. "You know we're going to be lost without you."

I shook my head. "Nah, you won't. You have each other."

My dad kissed Papa's cheek. "That we do. Now, go before we lock you up in your room and try to pretend our baby girl is only five years old and hasn't turned into this twenty-four-year-old beauty the likes of which the world has never seen."

"Dad," I sighed, letting his praise fill me up with optimism. I'd need it for the journey ahead.

"Daylight's wasting!" Jasper slammed the door on the passenger side.

"Don't slam Serenity's door!" I hollered and Jasper held up his hands, palm sides out, in surrender.

"Go," my papa said.

I lightly kissed my papa's cheek then my dad's. "I love you both more than the sun, the moon and the stars above."

Then I turned on my sandaled feet and dashed to my new car. I jumped into the driver's side.

"You ready for a new life?" I asked my companion.

He handed me a pair of mirrored aviators and placed a matching pair on his own face. I followed suit.

"Baby, I was born ready."

Three hours in and the questions finally started. I expected them sooner, but Jasper knew me better than I knew myself and he'd been giving me time. We listened to music, stocked up on junk food and got gas. Besides listening to him sing the words to every song on the radio, a weird superpower he'd always had, he didn't speak about what was ahead of us.

"Evie and Suda Kaye were gorgeous. Don't you think?" He turned down the radio.

I nodded.

"I mean, not as pretty as you, but you have that classic porcelain doll Irish-eyes-are-smiling type look. Suda Kaye was one of those super-hot, alluring chicks with her perfect brown skin and dazzling eyes like Ian's. She also has a body on her, but not as curvy. You definitely win in the tits and ass department. And Evie… Damn. She seemed rather cold but dressed spectacularly. Like an ice princess, but I think it was for show." He rambled on but what he said last struck a chord in me.

"She is anything but cold." I remembered her standing on that path, her mask having fallen away, showing the sad, devastated woman she was in that moment.

"Yeah? How you figure?" He turned his body to the side a bit.

Since that day in the kitchen I'd had a couple of calls with my half sisters. Nothing impressive or deeply life changing, but little, get-to-know-one-another calls. I'd heard bits and pieces about their lives and shared parts of mine.

"For one, when they were leaving, I caught Evie outside. I could tell from the expression on her face that meeting us had wounded something deep inside her. Something she was keeping to herself. From the two calls we've had, I could tell that Evie was the leader in a way. Maybe because she's older, but I got the impression that she was super responsible. Had made something of herself already without any help. Also, our mother died when Evie was only nineteen and she took care of her seventeen-year-old sister. That had to harden her."

Jasper nodded. "Have you read any of the letters they brought?"

I shook my head. "No."

"Why not? They're from your mom, right?"

I shrugged. "That's what they said. That she wrote letters for them to open every year on their birthday after her death. If you add them all up, there are about a hundred letters total among the three of us."

"Wow." He stretched his long, slim body, putting his hands over his head and cupping the back of the headrest. "That had to take forever. And to think she was doing that when her body was being ravaged by cancer." He shivered. "Why haven't you read any of them?"

"Maybe because I haven't been ready. Or I'm afraid of what they'll say. I mean, she didn't want to know me. Left me when I was three months old. Went back to the two girls she thought of as her children."

"Izzy, she wouldn't have stayed a day if she didn't want to love and know you. But she stayed, nursed you and made sure you were left in a happy home with a family."

"True. She left me to two men who gave me everything. Everything but her."

He sighed heavily. "I get it. You're pissed."

I firmed my jaw. "I don't know what I am."

"What if those letters explain more?"

"What if you found out that your biological father wasn't your mother's sperm donor? That they knew all along who the man was, but they willingly kept him out of your life. Worse, the man didn't want you to know anything about him…"

"Isn't that exactly the case? My bio dad is Donor number 517. A baby in a cup. Worth a hundred bucks. My mothers picked him based on his description: tall, thin, blond hair, blue eyes—just like my mothers."

It was totally true. Though Penelope was a fairy-like, petite pixie of a woman who was becoming well-known for her knack for photography, and Josie was a tall, ex-supermodel who designed clothes. Definitely where Jasper got his talent for art and fashion design. Both his mothers were beautiful, kind and wildly affectionate. The best aunties ever. Never questioned my relationship with Jasper. Always just understood we were soul mates of the friendship variety.

"It's not the same, Jas," I tried.

"Except it kind of is. Donor number 517 wanted quick cash and didn't care that the result of his seed would amount to a living, breathing human being. Still, it was a gift to my moms. I'm grateful he did it or I wouldn't be here. My moms thank God every night that he made that choice and that they picked him for me. Just like Catori picked Ian and Casey for you. The same but different."

I let out a long breath as I let what he said stew in my mind.

"It's hard to wrap my mind around the fact that she had a child and one day just walked away. How could she do that?

How could she go back to her home and her two other little girls and not tell them anything about me?"

"My guess is it would be pretty hard. Still, she did it and here you are. The perfect woman."

I snort-laughed. "Hardly."

"To me you are." He grinned as he rested his head on the buttery-beige leather seat. "If my dick got hard for a woman, I'd totally nail you down, marry you and fill you full of babies."

I scrunched up my nose and laughed. "Gross. Dude. No. Just no. Do not talk about your dick getting hard in my presence."

"Made you laugh, though." He waggled his brows. "What do you think Evie and Suda Kaye are going to think about you showing up out of the blue?"

"Don't know. I figure I'd wing it. They both claimed any time I wanted to visit they'd be up for it."

"Yeah, but you're moving there. Where are we going to stay if you haven't told them you're coming?"

I shrugged. "A hotel. I'm sure there are plenty of them available until we can find us an apartment or something."

"Well, my moms gave me the money from my grandma's inheritance a year early. I'm pitching in to whatever our living situation is going to be."

"Jasper, that money was supposed to be for you. Not part of my grand adventure. And besides, this trip is being paid for by the Adam Ross inheritance fund."

"He left you that much, huh?"

I nodded. "Paid off my schooling, yours, the mortgage note left on the house—though they only had six years left on their loan, so it wasn't huge. Still, the accountant I hired to deal with it all said I still have close to a million bucks and more with the investments."

"What? You're a millionaire?" His mouth fell open in shock. I knew that look. I'd had it, too, when the accountant notified me.

"Not by choice or hard work," I sighed as the weight of that money added another brick on top of my already tight shoulders.

"Well, my grandma left me enough. I'll be fine for a good while. So I'm chipping in."

"Whatever you say, Jas." I flicked on the blinker to take the exit to the next rest stop. "Lunch?"

"Definitely. I'm starved," he said while shoveling a palm full of chocolate-covered malt balls into his maw.

The man was stick thin and had a four-pack, but ate like a hippo. Overactive thyroid, apparently. He'd been skinny his whole life and would likely die that way. Bastard. I wouldn't have called myself chubby exactly, but I liked food. More so, I liked *sweets*. All sweets. Which meant my body had some serious curves, enough to buy size large or extra-large tops instead of the extra-small my buddy bought in the men's section. And I was perfectly at peace with that. My parents taught me to love the body I was given in whatever size it came and however it aged.

Besides, I've never seen a thin pastry chef. I wasn't sure, but having some extra fluff might have been part of the requirements for graduating from culinary school.

I parked in front of what looked like a small café. It boasted sandwiches, soups and baked goods.

"Perfect. I'd kill for a cappuccino right now." Jasper exited the car and slammed the door.

I got out and hollered, "Stop slamming Serenity's doors! She doesn't like it!"

"I'm sorry! I keep forgetting we're not in your old car. Remember, it took acts of God to close that door."

"Yeah, well, a stiff wind will close this one, so be nice."
I poked at his chest and held open the café door for him.

He pranced through like the queen he was. Jasper looked
like a mix of desert cool and eighties rock ballad groupie,
wearing teal skinny jeans tucked into black ankle boots,
and a flowing, wide, white tunic that made his tanned skin
stand out. None of it should have gone together but all of it
did beautifully.

Me, I was easy. Dark blue bootleg jeans, yellow ribbed
tank, brown leather sandals, an Apple watch so I could track
my steps and a simple silver bangle with a giant turquoise
stone in the center my parents gave me when I turned sixteen.
Sometimes I rocked dangling earrings but not all the time
because they got caught up in my hair. No muss, no fuss, I
called it. My hair was a dark auburn and wild. I was told all
the time that I looked exactly like Drew Barrymore from the
first *Charlie's Angels* movie. My biological dad Casey was incredibly proud of this fact and puffed up with extreme pride
every time someone compared me to the actress. I'll admit
she was really pretty, and I did look a lot like her. Though
at least now I know where I got the crazy hair from. Both
Evie and Suda Kaye had a lot of hair, both with natural wave.
Must have been a feature from my mother's side.

I followed Jasper in and set about getting my bestie a sandwich, though we both instantly spied the dessert display and
went there first, picking out the dessert before our meal.

What's life without a little sweet?

four

"Open it, I dare you!" Jasper shoved the pink envelope in my face.

I batted at the offending envelope as though it was a pesky mosquito then reached for the rum and Coke on the night-stand of our shared hotel room. I took a long gulp while leaning back against the headboard.

Jasper frowned deeply while flipping the envelope over and over. "The envelope only has your name and a number on it. This one says 'Isabeau 18.' Which means it's the first letter she wrote to you since the others seem to follow almost every year after that." He shuffled through the big stack.

"Mmm-hmm. Evie and Suda Kaye told me that."

"And did they ever break the rules and open all of them?" His eyes gleamed with mischief. "We can totally do that if you want," he encouraged.

I shook my head. "No. They told me it was an honor to read one each year on their birthdays. They looked forward to it. Did you know that both Evie and Suda Kaye have the same birthday, exactly two years apart?"

He bounced on his knees a bit on my bed. "If I'd been five minutes later, we'd have the same birthday, too!" He scrunched up his nose. It was a consistent sore spot for my bestie that his mom couldn't wait the additional five minutes to have him.

"At least you'll always be older than me," I teased.

"By five minutes!" He stretched his long limbs out as though he was flying.

"By a whole day!" I stuck my tongue out and he groaned.

He held the envelope up. "We got tipsy like we planned. Now, are you gonna open the damn envelope already? I'm dying of anticipation."

I kicked at his knee with my bare foot. "You open it if you're so excited."

He sat up straighter and his eyes bulged. "You sure? Because once you say go, I'm tearing into this puppy. No holds barred. Hulk style."

I laughed. Jasper was a ball of light and positive energy. Drunk, or in this case pretty tipsy, you could multiply that by a thousand and you'd have the happy-go-lucky, cuddly, sweet, amped-up, wiggling-puppy vibe he had going on.

"Go ahead. Read it to me." I set my head back and closed my eyes.

I heard him tearing open the envelope and unfolding the paper. I didn't dare look for he'd see the fear and anxiety I was hiding behind my uncaring facade.

"Kah…sah…rai…bo." He sounded out a word I'd never heard before and then repeated it. *"Kasaraibo."*

I peeked at him as he pursed his lips. "What's that mean?"

He shrugged. "Don't know. It's the heading, like a name."

"Huh. Well, continue."

Jasper cleared his throat and focused on the paper. I went back to closing my eyes and pretending I didn't care what my mother had wanted to say to me for the very first time. That my stomach wasn't twisting and mixing the rum and Coke like a vortex in my gut. Like my heart wasn't about to pound out of my chest. Like I wasn't scared of what she wanted to say to me.

My mother.

"*Kasaraibo*,
I'm sorry.
    If you're reading this letter it must be an incredible shock to hear from me."

I huffed.

"She got that right," Jasper snarked in a high-pitched whine.

"No comments from the peanut gallery. Just read it straight through," I requested.

He shook his hands out to the sides, fluffed his always-perfect hair and took a deep breath.

"Okay. I'm ready," he said as though he was about to read an audiobook straight into a recorder at an audition.

"Good, now, read it. Start from the beginning again. Please and thank you." I tacked on a wink.

"*Kasaraibo*,
I'm sorry.
    If you're reading this letter it must be an incredible shock to hear from me. I did my best to keep you a secret throughout the years. A treasure that was not mine to behold for long.
    You, Isabeau, were a gift. From the Creator.

A gift that was never meant to be mine.

I am sorry if that truth hurts you. It has ravaged my soul since the day I left you warm, beautiful and snuggled in your crib.

You were meant for Ian and Casey. One man I loved very deeply and one I came to love through Ian and through your conception and birth. Your fathers wanted you more than anything in the world and it was my honor to give them this gift.

I'm sure your fathers have now explained our history and how Evie, Suda Kaye and you came to be.

Do you believe in dreams, fate and destiny, my *kasa-raibo*? It will help you understand that you were wanted and were brought into this world based on love and hope.

Love from your fathers. Love from me. Love from the Creator.

You are here because you were meant to be.

Above anything else that you may think of me, and how I entered and left your life without a trace, know that you were wanted, loved, even wished for.

You just weren't to be mine. It's an unfortunate truth and something even years later while writing this letter I have trouble accepting.

My fate. My destiny was to give you life. To give life to Evie and Suda Kaye.

I was warned at a very young age that I was not long for this earth. My mother died a short time after I had Evie. The same sickness that took my mother young would take me, too. It was to be part of my path. It was written in the stars.

When I had the dream of birthing a fire-haired angel after speaking with Ian, I knew what I was supposed to do. Though doing so, I would be leaving yet another child of mine to grieve. The sickness had started to weaken me even then. I wouldn't dare have another child yearning for a mother. And you had two devoted, loving parents. That was when I made the decision that after I left, you wouldn't know of me. In doing so, I know I took away your knowledge of your sisters, but I truly believed it was the right thing to do for us all.

Now I'm not so sure. And yet, I write this letter in the hopes that you'll never have to read it. Never have to know how much I loved and missed you every day, every waking moment. How I'd look down at my empty arms and wish they were filled with my beautiful Isabeau.

As the years slipped by I got weaker, and my girls suffered, but I knew I'd made the right decision. I checked in on you as much as I dared, staying in a home my husband, Adam, bought for us in Chicago. Watching you play in the schoolyard and at the park with your fathers was a dream come true. You were so ethereal and effervescent. The perfect happy child.

Happy. My Isabeau was happy. And that's all I needed to fill up the emptiness your absence left on my soul.

I have more to explain but not a lot of time. For now just know, my dearest Isabeau, you, Evie and Suda Kaye are my legacy. You three are the beauty I leave behind.

The world is a far better place with the three of you in it.

With all my love and loss,
Catori"

Tears slid down my cheeks so fast I wasn't able to wipe them before they fell to my shirt. Big, dark blobs soaked the fabric in waves of sadness.

"Oh, Izzy." Jasper sniffed, set the letter down and crawled over to me. He reached around my shoulders and tugged me against his thin frame. I snuggled against his chest and bawled my eyes out. Sobbed for a woman I didn't know but wished I had the chance to. I cried for the time I'd never have with her. Tears fell rapidly for a woman who made a difficult decision that maybe wasn't right, but it was honest.

Catori Ross gave me life knowing she was going to die. Paid the ultimate price of bearing a child and giving it away.

"She loved you, Izzy. She loved you so much." Jasper's words shook me to my core.

I nodded. "It seems that way. At least from the letter."

"Woman, that letter was her setting her pain free. Shredding herself in the hopes of finding a way to make you not hate her."

"I don't hate her. How could I?" My voice cracked.

He pressed his head to the top of mine. "Then how are you feeling?"

"Hopeless. Sad. Brokenhearted. Even if I'd only had her for a little bit of time, I would have cherished it, had something to show for it. She stole that decision from me, from all of us. And granted, she did it so she wouldn't hurt me, or Evie and Suda Kaye, but in the end, not having her in my life was worse. I never knew who my mother was. Never heard her voice. Never saw her dance or listened to the stories of her travels, like my sisters did. And worse, I never had my sisters in my life. She kept them from me. Her decision to disappear from my life to protect me, us…is what has wounded me the most."

Jasper kissed the crown of my head.

"I would have liked to know her," I said against his chest.

He inhaled and let out a long breath. "By the end of this journey, I think you will know her. It's what we're here to do. Learn about your mom and make a connection to your sisters. Maybe carve out a new life of our own. Ultimately, even after reading those words to you, I know she's probably watching and kicking herself in the ass for not choosing another way. Still, it was her choice to make—*hers*, Izzy. Kind of like a closed adoption. She gave you to your biological father and his husband, two people who could provide you with a safe, wonderful home and support you your entire life. She knew she wasn't going to be able to do that, and she already had to deal with that brutal fact with Evie and Suda Kaye. I understand why she couldn't bear to do it to another younger child. Especially if she didn't have to."

I thought about his words, the logic behind them. There was definite truth to what he was saying. And yet, it still hurt deep inside. I bucked in his hold and sobbed for all that I'd lost.

The loss of being a part of my heritage growing up.

The loss of connecting with my sisters as children.

The loss of knowing my mother.

Then my best friend held me until I cried myself to sleep.

"Slow ride…ba na…" Jasper played air drums on the dash of my new baby. "Take it easy!" He sang the classic rock song by Foghat at the top of his lungs.

I grinned and focused on the road ahead. After our night of many rum and Cokes and tears galore, we slept in, ate lunch at a nearby diner and then headed out on the road.

It was now close to nine in the evening and we were just entering Colorado Springs. I turned off the radio and handed my phone to Jasper. "Pull up Evie Ross in my contacts and hit Call for me, will ya?"

He did so without question while shimmying in his seat.

The song was badass and I imagined it was still running through his head.

The phone rang and I took a deep breath, not sure if I was hoping Evie would answer or hoping she wouldn't. Either way, I had to take the plunge.

"Hello, Isabeau?" Evie said through the speakers in my car.

"Hi, Evie. Yeah, it's me, Izzy."

"So glad you called. How are you?" Her voice sounded cultured, yet direct.

"Um, well, fine. Actually uh, my best friend Jasper and I are in the area and I know it's late and all that but…"

"You're in the area? Meaning Colorado?"

"Yeah, we've actually just entered Colorado Springs."

"Oh, my goodness! You have to come straight to our home. Where are you staying? Why are you here?" The questions came rapid-fire.

"Um, I, you know that's kind of a hard question and a long story. Though we figured we'd stay at a hotel. No biggie…"

"Absolutely not! You'll stay here with me and Milo. Suda Kaye is going to lose her mind when she finds out you're here."

"Look, I know it's a surprise, we can totally just go to a hotel and then meet up with you tomorrow if you have the time. Or not if you have work or other plans."

"Tomorrow is Saturday, so no work. I can't believe you're here. You must come straight to our house," she demanded yet again. "Let me give you the address."

Jasper put the info into his phone because I didn't know how to use the satellite navigation on Serenity just yet.

"Says we'll be there in fifteen minutes," Jasper announced.

"Fantastic, see you soon!" she said, and then hung up.

"That was unexpected," I stated, biting into my bottom lip.

"Looks like no hotel for us tonight. Where do you think

she lives?" He glanced around the landscape, but it was dark and there wasn't much to see.

I shook my head. "She mentioned on one of our calls that she lives in a secluded area by a lake and mountain on the outskirts of town. Said nature calls to her and her fiancé." Not exactly sure what that meant but I figured it was likely beautiful.

Jasper leaned back with his eyes glued to the phone. "Take that exit there." He pointed.

I followed Jasper's instructions to the letter until we pulled down a long, winding gravel-and-dirt road. We drove for maybe half a mile before we came upon what had to be the most beautiful log cabin I'd ever seen in my entire life. Not that I'd seen many log cabins in Chi-town, but I'd been out in the wilderness with friends over the years. Skied a time or two, but nothing would have prepared me for this splendor.

To the left of the enormous wooden house was a serene, sprawling lake and a mountain in the background. Pine trees were everywhere.

The house was two stories tall with a wraparound porch. Everything was made of wood. Though that wasn't the most imposing thing about the house.

No, that would be the giant Native American man with long, flowing black hair, his locks lifted by the breeze and shooting away from his striking bone structure and imposing features. He stood at the top of a flight of wooden steps with his massive arms crossed over one another. Daunting. Dark. Dangerous. Hot as heck. If he wasn't casually dressed in jeans and a T-shirt, I might have thought he was a warrior who would mount up on his horse and chase us away from his land. Until he smiled wide. A bright white smile against his dark skin that was welcoming and warm. Especially when the tall blonde approached him from behind and cuddled up against his side. He immediately wrapped an arm around her shoulders.

"Holy hotness. Who is that hunk of a man?" Jasper gasped.

I grinned and turned off the car. "Pretty sure that's Milo Chavis. Evie's fiancé."

"Dang, she hit the jackpot with that one." My best friend practically drooled, his gaze never leaving the handsome man.

I opened my door while snickering under my breath and started toward the house. Evie let go of Milo, raced down the stairs and shockingly, threw her arms around me, pulling me against her chest in a tight hug.

"I'm so happy you're here. In Colorado. At my home." She leaned back and put both of her hands to my shoulders. "You're absolutely gorgeous."

I grinned. "Says one of the hottest chicks I've ever seen."

"She speaks truth, *Nizhoni*," Milo said, a smirk on his lips. His long legs ate up the slack between our huddle in no time. He held his hand out to me. "Milo Chavis, soon to be your brother-in-law."

"Isabeau Collins, but my friends call me Izzy." Jasper came up to my side. "And this is my best friend, Jasper Prince."

"Prince?" Milo repeated.

"I know, right? Isn't it fab?" Jasper held his hand out and shook Milo's, then reached for Evie and pulled her into a hug. "My Izzy's sister. This is so cool!" He kissed her cheek and stepped back with a flourish. "Now, you must show us your incredible home. You have your own lake! No one has their own lake," he gushed. "Amazing!"

Milo and Evie chuckled as Jasper walked around us, up the steps—uninvited—and to the left side where he could get a better look at the view. Jasper loved anything water related.

"I'm sorry to just show up out of nowhere like this. You really don't have to take us in for the night."

"Any family of Evie's is welcome in our home. We are honored to have you stay." Milo's voice had a deep bass to it that could comfort or scare the bejesus out of you.

I slumped in relief, my shoulders aching after driving for two days.

"You must be worn out. Come on in. We'll get you set up with some drinks and show you your rooms."

"Rooms? You mean we don't have to share?" Jasper asked in awe.

"He's a character, isn't he?" Evie smiled sweetly.

"That he is. Also, the closest thing I had to a sibling growing up…" I realized too late how that sounded. Evie's lips flattened and a sadness shuttered across her pretty features. "I'm sorry, I didn't mean anything by that. It's just having sisters is new and…"

Evie placed her hand on my shoulder. "Relax. It's okay. Jasper is your family. I get that. I just hope during the time we have while you're here, we'll be able to build our own relationship."

"Definitely," I agreed readily.

"While we're here?" Jasper snorted and trounced to the other side of the porch, probably trying to see whatever he could through the dark and the forest beyond.

"How long are you staying?" Evie asked as we took the steps.

I shrugged. "Honestly, we don't know."

Milo opened the front door and gestured us all inside. The room was enormous with a giant wall of windows to one side boasting a view of the lake and mountains beyond, and a larger-than-life fireplace already lit with a crackling fire that warmed the room perfectly.

"Wow." I gazed at my surroundings. The comfortable environment looked ideal for lounging, with a U-shaped cushy sectional, big, fluffy blankets and pillows everywhere and sturdy wood trimmings surrounding the space. I could see a huge dining room table that would probably be super fun to sit at during Thanksgiving dinner, everyone passing around plate after plate of mouthwatering dishes. I could almost taste the turkey and stuffing now. Which was also when my stomach growled loudly.

"Sounds like someone is hungry. I shall make a meal for you and a dessert for my beloved." Milo's deep voice was soothing as well as direct. The perfect balance of manly yet charming.

"Oh, no, it's okay. We ate." I frowned, trying to remember when we last had a meal.

"We ate at noon, girl. It's nine thirty now. Food from the hands of a Native American god sounds right up my alley." Jasper nudged my shoulder playfully. "Don't ruin my fun. I wonder if they have fry bread." He licked his lips.

"There will definitely be fry bread if Milo is putting something together. We had goulash and fry bread for dinner, which is likely what he's heating up," Evie offered.

"Mmm," Jasper hummed and headed for the kitchen.

Evie grabbed my wrist, holding me back before I started to follow. "Hey, you said before that you didn't know how long you were staying. Is everything okay at home?"

I smiled at her. "Yeah. It's just there's this whole new world I don't know about. Family I didn't know I had. Sisters I barely know and I…" I took a breath and let it out. "Jasper and I finished school and were going to apply for jobs in the city. But after meeting you, getting that huge inheritance from your dad, I don't know. I felt like I needed to be here. To spend some time getting to know you and Suda Kaye. Meeting Milo and Camden and anyone else that is important to you."

"Well, Toko, obviously," she said immediately as though I knew who or what that was.

I frowned. "Toko?"

Her eyes widened and she put a hand over her chest as she swallowed. "Oh, my. I didn't realize we never told you about Toko."

"What does that mean? Who is that?" I frowned.

"*Toko* means grandfather in Comanche. Tahsuda is his name and he's your maternal grandfather."

My tongue almost fell out of my mouth as my jaw dropped open. My hands shook and I clenched them into fists as Evie's admission hit my body first and my heart second.

"I have a living grandparent?" I could barely get the words out, or even believe them.

She smiled wide. "He is going to be beside himself with joy. Well, as much as a stout, traditional elder of the Comanche tribe on our home reservation can be." She wrapped her arm around my shoulders and led me toward their open kitchen. Jasper was on a stool chatting up Milo, who maneuvered his large form around the open kitchen with extreme grace.

"Jas," I said the second I saw him.

He turned and his eyebrows arched high onto his forehead before concern flashed across his face.

"I have a grandfather. His name is Tahsuda."

His eyes widened and his mouth dropped open. "Holy shit. That's huge."

I nodded as his expression morphed from surprise to happiness. "You have a grandpa! This is so cool! Man, this move to Colorado keeps getting better and better. I can't wait to meet my new grandpa." He wiggled in his chair. "Hope he likes pseudo-adopted grandkids."

"Moving to Colorado?" Evie gasped and pressed her hands

to the counter. Her body language was stiff as though she was holding her breath.

"Um, we… Well, yeah. Maybe. I mean, we think so. We don't really have any set plans."

"You're moving to Colorado." The words left her as though they were a prayer. "I'm going to have both of my sisters in the same place." Slowly, tears filled her eyes and she smiled wide. The woman was already beautiful but when she smiled like that, with such unfiltered joy, she was stunning.

"Yeah. We think we might stay, make a life of our own here," I admitted finally.

"Adinidiin." Milo stepped up behind Evie and wrapped his arms around her, pressing his face against her neck. Something silent moved between the two lovers as she closed her eyes.

"Did you hear what she said?" Her voice was small and filled with unchecked emotion. "My sister is going to stay."

"I did hear that and am very pleased." He had eyes only for her.

She sniffed and let a tear fall that she quickly wiped away. "Me, too."

Jasper and I exchanged a look. He shook his head to say I should comment on what just occurred because whatever happened had meant something to Evie. A whole heck of a lot but I didn't want to intrude on such a private moment.

"No more of that." She wiped at both of her eyes, cupped her man's cheeks and laid a fast and hard kiss to his mouth. He barely reached her hips with his massive hands when she moved out of his arms. "Time to celebrate. My sister Isabeau is home. Now we can all start to heal."

I smiled but let her words soak in. *Now we can all start to heal…* As though she and Suda Kaye faced just as much uncertainty and emotional turmoil as I had these past couple months.

Milo winked at me and then presented us with a large steaming bowl filled with goulash and a mound of succulent-looking fry bread. He then placed two glasses of wine before us. After, he poured two more glasses and handed one to Evie.

He lifted his wine and we all followed suit.

"To love, friendship and family…in all things."

I couldn't have said it better myself.

five

—————

Jasper and I tiptoed back up the front stairs of Evie and Milo's home, doing our best not to make a sound even with our bags of groceries bogging us down. It was only six thirty in the morning, but to us, it was an hour later, and we'd crashed hard after Milo's homemade goulash, fry bread and copious amounts of red wine. It was a great evening and exactly what I'd hoped hanging out with my big sister for the first time would be like. So when I got up at five in the morning, I snuck into Jasper's room and woke his snoring ass up. He was all for making a breakfast fit for rock stars and celebrities to give back to our awesome hosts.

"Hope they don't mind we left the cabin door unlocked." Jasper pushed open the door and we both made our way into the quiet house.

We set the bags down and sought about making our feast, complete with homemade pastries with fresh fruit filling and melt-in-your-mouth dough made from scratch. Alongside that we put together a ham, cheddar and asparagus quiche that would give a whopping dose of protein and offer the savory taste buds some satisfaction.

An hour later, the quiche was in the oven and I was whipping up a special yogurt to go with the pastry and fresh fruit. Jasper was frying up some pancetta to place on top of the quiche for a little crunch when it was done.

"What in the world is going on in here?" Evie entered the kitchen wearing a long burgundy satin robe that swished along the sides of her bare feet. Her toes were painted the same color as the robe, and her hair was up in a messy bun on the top of her head. Much like my own wild locks in a wonky ponytail.

Milo entered behind her, wrapping an arm around his fiancée's small waist. His hair was in a long single braid down his back. He wore a simple pair of navy blue cotton pajama pants and a white T-shirt that molded to his broad chest.

My sister was a lucky girl. All that hotness. Fit, huge and rockin' a serious body with a handsome face. Yep, I sure hoped one day I'd have me some little nieces and nephews with those combined genetics.

I gave a jaunty wave. "We're making you breakfast!"

Jasper pulled out the quiche and set it on top of the stove. "A thank-you for not kicking us out into the cold world of Colorado all alone." He smiled.

"Smells amazing. My mouth is watering at those treats," Evie breathed, her eyes widening at the dollop of homemade yogurt dip I added to each of the four plates I set out.

"Coffee's ready," Jasper announced. He brought the quiche to the workstation and expertly cut and dished out perfect steaming triangles.

"I could get used to this, Isabeau." Milo looked at the

plates from over my shoulder, then gave me a peck on the cheek. "Thank you."

Evie grinned and sat her prim-and-proper booty on the stool in front of me. "Should we eat here or at the dining table?"

"Here's good. Then you can easily reach for seconds," I offered.

"Good idea." She pressed her hands to her cheeks and watched while Jasper and I finished plating our masterpieces.

"This looks gourmet," Evie stated as I pushed a plate in front of her. "And I've eaten at the Four Seasons before. This display tops even that."

I grinned. "Your sister and new adopted brother are bakers first, but chefs second."

"Well, technically, we did culinary school first. Then the two of us got a wild hair and wanted to go for the pastry chef program, which took us abroad and added an additional two years to our studies." Jasper chuckled.

"Looks like it was worth it," Milo said, taking a seat next to Evie.

I set a heaping plate in front of him. A big man like that must have a huge appetite. "We love to cook but both of us excelled when it came to desserts. I am a whiz at making intricate candies, pastries and donuts. Jasper takes the crown for his cakes, muffins, fresh bread and ability to come up with new recipes."

Jasper crossed one of his hands over his waist and bowed. "Thank you, my darling. I resemble that compliment."

We all laughed. Jasper and I stood opposite the couple and ate while standing. My favorite part of cooking wasn't just about the blending of flavors and textures, or even the endless options. It was watching people *eat* the food I've made that gave me such pleasure. Knowing that I made something with my own hand that someone enjoyed was an endless high I would never top.

"Jasper, this quiche is everything. The toasted pancetta on top is divine," Evie said before taking another bite.

Milo dipped his fresh pastry into the yogurt and took a massive bite. When he was done, he licked his lips. "You're an excellent cook. I've never tasted a better pastry. Have you guys thought of opening a business?"

Jasper and I looked at one another and busted up laughing.

"Only every day of our entire lives!" I chuckled.

"It's our dream to one day own a bakery of sorts. Something that offers not only baked goods but specialty desserts like tiramisu and homemade candies, alongside cakes, cookies, cupcakes and the like."

"Have you looked into it?" Evie queried.

I finished chewing a bite of cherry-filled pastry. "We have. Our plan before all of this happened was to find jobs in the city as pastry chefs. Get more fast-paced experience under our belts, learn more of the on-the-job business side and then open our own shop one day."

Evie tilted her head and pushed some fruit around her plate. "Well, as a financial adviser, and knowing what you received in Dad's estate since me and Suda Kaye received the same, your dream of owning your own place could start imminently."

I frowned. "What do you mean?"

Milo's lips twitched. "Evie, you're doing it again with another sister," he warned.

"Doing what?" I asked.

Evie ignored my question and turned her head to her man so fast I worried she'd get a neck kink. "That simply isn't true. I have only Isabeau's best interests at heart. If she wants to own and operate her own business, she now has the capital to do just that. And we—" she pointed to his chest and then her own "—are in the position to help her make good choices about her future as it pertains to her finances and goals."

"And you'd be sure to have your sister settled close to you where you can watch over her and know she's happy and healthy and just a short car ride away, no?" Milo stated outright.

She glared and crossed her arms over her chest. "And how is that a bad thing?"

He sucked in a breath through his teeth. "Not bad, *Nizhoni*, but perhaps a little self-serving."

I watched in avid fascination as a pretty pink blush washed over her features and her lips curled. "Wanting my sister to have the life she dreams of is not self-serving." She raised her chin in obvious affront.

"What's *Nizhoni* mean?" Jasper asked, breaking up the tension wafting in the air around the fiery couple.

The question had Evie sighing and her body relaxing. "It's Navajo for *beautiful*." She scowled at Milo. His lips twitched in response.

I brought the conversation right back to her suggestion. "Do you think you could tell me more about opening up our own place and what that would entail?" It was a good idea. I had tons of money now and no idea what to do with it. Jasper had taken a huge leap of faith following me to Colorado. If we truly wanted to build a life here, what better way than to start out working on our dream. There wasn't anything but fear stopping us.

"Well, Milo and I can certainly instruct you from a financial perspective. However, Camden is a business guru. It's how he and Suda Kaye met back up some time ago. He runs a foundation that offers small-business owners financial assistance and mentorship. I'm certain he'd be happy to sit down with you and discuss your ideas once you and Jasper have had the time to work through your idea fully."

"That would be so cool!" Jasper bounced in his outrageous Converse sneakers. They were startlingly bright yellow with black laces he added himself. I called them the "bumblebee" shoes. Today's outfit was what he called surfer-skater chic: a formfitting pair of khaki shorts that hit just above his knees and a ribbed black tank under a Hawaiian shirt in various shades of orange, blue, black, white and khaki. He paired the entire look with a circular pair of yellow-tinted, John Lennon-style glasses that were not prescription—strictly for looks; he kept them on inside and outside. Around his neck he wore wooden tiki prayer beads with a teal tassel.

When he'd come down the stairs to go to the store with me this morning, I told him he looked like a rainbow threw up on him. He told me I needed to exchange my boring-ass green baby doll tee and faded thrift-store Levi's for something that actually didn't disappear into the background. After that comment I put on a pair of silver chandelier earrings with turquoise stones to match my favorite turquoise bangle and a pair of platform rhinestone-studded flip-flops to give myself a little *oomph*. He merely looked me up and down before sighing and shaking his head.

"I spoke with Suda Kaye before bed last night. She's eager for us to come to her store. She works one or two Saturdays a month so she can't leave, but she's dying to see you in the flesh," Evie noted.

I smiled and tucked a loose strand of hair behind my ear. "I'm looking forward to seeing her store, Gypsy Soul. She said she named it after your mom."

"Our mom," Evie corrected, and I felt my cheeks heat.

"That's something I need to get used to."

Evie smiled. "And you will. Being here will definitely help."

"I'm counting on it." I stared into her clear blue eyes and watched as they warmed.

"You'll have to make sure you wear that bracelet when we go to the reservation. My mother always likes seeing women wearing her jewelry," Milo said while picking up his and Evie's plates and taking them to the sink.

I stared down at the turquoise-and-silver hammered bangle bracelet I've worn forever. "What are you talking about?" I held up my wrist. "My dads gave this to me on my sixteenth birthday. It's almost nine years old."

Milo shook his head. "I'm afraid it's far older than that and I'd know my mother's artistry anywhere."

"Your mother?"

Milo nodded and Evie leaned over the counter to inspect the piece.

"May I?" Milo gestured to the bracelet. I took it off and handed it to him.

He inspected the large oval turquoise stone on the front. On each side there were hammered lines of silver. One side had *Free* twisted in the metal as if it was sitting atop the bracket. The other side said *Spirit*. He then turned it over, looked at the inside and smiled.

With his nail he pointed at two letters on one side of the metal. "L.C. for Lani Chavis," he said. On the other side he pointed to two more letters. "See those letters?"

I nodded.

"C.T. Catori Tahsuda. My mother must have made this piece long ago and given it to your mother."

Evie gasped and put her hand over her mouth.

"Then how the hell did I get it?" My words came out in a flurry of frustration. My mother's initials and Milo's mother's initials were engraved on the inside of a bracelet I've had for almost a decade?

"I do not know the answer to that question. I only know that our mothers were great friends as children and then went their separate ways later in life."

Evie held up a hand. "Wait a minute!" She dashed out of the kitchen, her floor-length robe flying behind her like a crimson cape beckoning a raging bull to charge. I heard her feet pounding up the stairs and looked up at the ceiling.

Milo continued to inspect my bracelet. My *mother's* bracelet.

But how?

I hadn't come up with anything logical when Evie entered the room with a large photo album. She spun through the pages faster than I could take in any one thing. Then she pointed.

"Here!" she said triumphantly. "I knew I'd seen that design before. Look, Izzy." She pointed to a five-by-seven of someone I suspected was my mother. I had only seen the one super-small picture of her that my papa had shared with me.

The woman in the image was stunning. A Native American princess if I'd ever seen one. My mother sat cross-legged in front of a brilliant fire pit, a woven blanket stretched out over what seemed to be a desert floor. A little blond-haired girl in a red dress sat in her lap. Next to her was an attractive, smiling Caucasian male with blond layered hair and remarkable blue eyes. My mother was staring up at the man like he hung the moon, her arms carefully locked around the child.

"That's me." Evie pointed. "I was maybe three years old then. Suda Kaye would have been one. Not sure where she was at that time."

From the way the couple in the photo looked at one another, it was clear they were deeply in love. Except if that was the case, why did my mother seek out adventure and leave her daughter only to fall into bed with my papa Ian? And how could Adam forgive her for falling in love with my papa and having his child? So many unanswered questions.

"Do you see it?" Evie asked, gesturing to the photo.

"See what?" I narrowed my gaze and focused on the image of a happy family.

She pointed at the wrist that was tucked around the baby's middle. On it was the very bracelet that I now had in my hand. I held the piece up to the picture, taking in even the tiniest detail and nuance. "It's an exact match." I had to agree.

Evie smiled. "Looks like Mom left you a piece of her, after all."

It definitely seemed that way and I had no earthly idea how I felt about that fact.

I added calling my fathers later this evening to my to-do list to get to the bottom of this conundrum.

Evie grabbed my and Jasper's plates. "How about you two check out the property with Milo while I get dressed? Then I'll take you to see Suda Kaye. Oh, and I almost forgot." She walked over to a box of envelopes that was sitting on the counter. She rifled through them and pulled one out and then handed it to me.

"An invitation to our wedding. We're doing it at the reservation. Very small and intimate. Only family and a few very close friends." She beamed.

"Wow, thank you. I'd love to attend."

Jasper hooked his elbow with mine. "And I'll be your plus-one. Wedding on a Native American reservation with men who hopefully look like him." He pointed to Milo sipping his coffee. "Yes, please. Sign me up for one of those!"

Milo coughed and set his coffee down, shaking his head.

"Do you know of any gay or bisexual Native American hotties?" Jasper asked point-blank.

Evie chuckled. "I'm gonna leave you guys to it."

Milo's eyes widened and he stared holes through her, which I interpreted as him not wanting to be left alone with my gregarious bestie.

Jasper went right over to Milo, gripped his biceps, then petted them like a cat. "Don't worry, I don't bite…" He winked at Milo. "Much."

"Evie, you leave me with him, and I cut off all my hair," Milo stated flatly.

"You do that, and you will find yourself with no sex for the first year of your marriage while you're growing it back!" she tossed over her shoulder while laughing and taking the stairs up to the bedrooms.

"Jas, leave Milo alone. He's not used to your brazen brand of crazy just yet. You have to work that in slowly, like watching a soufflé rise to the perfect height. You don't go whole hog with the heat, or you'll burn it and that sucker will fall flat."

Jasper petted Milo's bulging biceps once more and tsked. "Pity. So, so pretty." He looked up at Milo, who had a straight face and a stern expression plastered across it. "Back to the Native American hotties at the reservation. Know any?" He beamed.

"No," was Milo's one-word reply.

"Would you tell me if you did?" he hedged.

"No," Milo repeated again, and I burst out laughing.

Milo and Evie's property was magical. There wasn't another word that could be used to describe it. Nothing but trees, mountains, animals scurrying around and the crystal-clear lake lapping at the shore. The entire place was a natural oasis of colors, fresh air and sunlight sprinkling through the trees.

I rested my head against Serenity's leather passenger seat while Jasper drove, thinking about the beauty we'd witnessed. Milo chose to stay behind to work on a few things around the house while Evie jumped in the back of my Ford Explorer and directed us to Pueblo. I think he'd had enough of Jasper's shenanigans.

"Your home is amazing and the land absolutely magnificent," I shared while watching the landscape go by.

"We'll have Milo build a bonfire tonight and we can make s'mores while sitting by the lake. The water is pretty cold but it's fun to go stargazing at night. We have a paddleboat you can use, too."

"Sounds awesome. At some point, though, Jasper and I need to find a place of our own."

Evie nodded. "We'll check the local listings. You'll have to decide whether Colorado Springs or Pueblo or any of the areas in between are to your liking. In the meantime you are welcome to stay with us as long as you want."

"I think Milo might have a few words to say about that." I glanced at my best friend.

"What? He's insanely hot. His muscles were just asking to be petted. I can't be held responsible when I see a man that gorgeous just standing there being all broody hot and not touch. It's not in my nature to let an experience pass me by." He shrugged.

Evie leaned toward the front seat from the center spot where she was buckled in and set her hand on his shoulder. "I forgive you. If you think he's beautiful with his clothes on, you'd be struck stupid if you saw him naked. The man's body is a work of art."

Jasper sighed heavily. "All the good ones are either taken

or straight. Colorado better show up with the homosexuals or I'm going to be disappointed. I'm almost twenty-five years old and I want a man who will be just as crazy as me, love my Izzy like a sister—because we don't do separate for long periods of time—have some cushion for pushin' and love to eat. Oh, and to fuck. I want a man that's got it going on like Donkey Kong. And I am not referring to the game." Jas snapped his fingers to accentuate his point.

Evie cracked up and I snort-laughed.

"You guys have been together for a long time?" she asked.

"Since we were five. And he's right. We don't like to be apart for too long. Hence our ultimate plan of owning a shop together. This way no matter where our future lives take us, we'll be a part of one another's lives every day. Or most days anyway."

"That's what I've always wanted with Suda Kaye. For her to be around all the time, just a short drive away. All I've ever wished for was a family of my own. To set roots down and live a happy, beautiful life filled with my family—my sisters, husband and children. Lots of them."

"I don't know a lot about what happened, but you mentioned briefly that Suda Kaye had been gone for a decade until somewhat recently?" I asked.

She nodded and then sighed. "Yeah, but we can talk more about that another time. Can I tell you a secret?" Evie blurted dramatically and rather unlike her cool and calm demeanor. I started to believe that side of her was only for people she didn't know. The ones she did know—or at least me and Jasper—she'd been warm to. Quite a difference from the woman who showed up on my doorstep with Suda Kaye in tow, all badass business ice princess.

"You can tell us anything."

"We're like a vault," Jasper insisted.

Evie bit into her bottom lip. "You know how me and Milo are getting married in a month?"

I nodded.

"We're going to try for a baby right away." She covered her mouth with the tips of her fingers and bounced her knees excitedly.

"Oh, my God. That is awesome!" I breathed.

"Nieces and nephews! We are so here for it, sister!" Jasper added.

"Definitely. Babysitting for sure!" I promised.

Evie grinned. "I can hardly wait. Though it's scary because Milo was married before. He actually got married very young to a woman who'd gotten pregnant."

"Meaning he did the responsible thing," I guessed.

She nodded. "They weren't exactly a love match, but Milo was committed to her. Tragically, they ended up losing the baby."

I reached out my hand and took hers. "Must have been hard on him. However, that doesn't mean it's going to happen to you."

She squeezed my hand. "I know, I know. It's still scary, though. Not only do I want this because I've always wanted a family of my own, but it's a big deal for Milo, too, and I want to be everything he could ever want or need."

"Honey, you are. You absolutely are. That man looks at you as though you were the sun, moon and the stars above."

"Thanks."

"Listen, one thing my dad Casey always said was you can't worry about something that hasn't happened yet. You have no control over something like that anyway. It's all in God's hands. So don't fret or worry until the problem is right in front of you. Right now, and after you get married, the part you know how to do, the *trying* part, focus on that. Everything will fall into place as it's supposed to."

Evie nodded and interlaced her fingers. "I appreciate that, Izzy. I'm scared but I'm also excited. And hey, my mother had three perfectly successful and healthy births. Genetics and family history, I have in my favor."

"Exactly."

"Pull up to the curb over there. See the sign for Gypsy Soul? That's her shop." Evie pointed to a storefront on a quaint, lively street.

There were people out everywhere carrying different-size shopping bags, going in and out of the many storefronts.

"Dang, this place is hoppin'." Jasper put on his blinker and found a parking space not far from the front of Suda Kaye's boutique.

I scanned the many storefronts and noticed the one right next door to Gypsy Soul had a for-sale sign. I squinted and saw the original silk screening on the door and the words *Candy Shop* peeling away.

"This used to be a candy store?" I asked Evie.

She glanced at the store that shared a wall with Gypsy Soul. "Yeah. From what I understand a woman owned it for decades but didn't have the family support to keep it going. I think she tried to sell it but the entire place needs an overhaul. Suda Kaye had to completely redo her entire store. The building owner is quite a pest." She tipped her head to the side. "Though the location is undeniably great for foot traffic." She spread her arm wide toward all the people milling around.

"Interesting."

Jasper looked through the windows. "Looks beat up, Izzy. Would need a lot of work."

I cupped my hands around my face at the window and

peered inside. There were dust and cobwebs and broken-down displays littering the space. There was an old oven in the back that looked like it needed to be retired about twenty years ago. It looked like it would be a fire hazard for sure. Still, the size was right. The location perfect and right next door to my sister Suda Kaye. And if I wanted to truly get to know these women and the life they'd lived with our mother, I needed to be close. This was definitely close.

"It has good bones, though." I kept looking, imagining a big display case running in an L shape. The back could have those super-cool, old-fashioned saloon doors separating the kitchen from the main area.

Jasper, just like me, was still staring. "An L-shaped display." He repeated my exact thoughts and I grinned.

We stepped back and I looked up at the sign. "It could work."

He pulled out his phone and took a picture of the number on the sign. "Doesn't hurt to give it a gander."

Evie hooked her elbows with mine and Jasper's. "Come on. You're gonna love Gypsy Soul."

six

Entering the store was like entering an Impressionist painting. Splashes of color and textured fabrics were everywhere. Lana Del Rey's soothing music filtered around the room, which absolutely flowed with the hippie, dippy, trippy and multi-diverse wares. From flashy, slinky dresses to graphic tees and jewelry, to leather belts and bags with fringe, and a full wall of denim in every color of the rainbow. The entire space was a feast for the eyes.

"That's it. This is where I want to live," Jasper stated seriously, his eyes bugging out as he took in the massive amount of unique and interesting things for sale. "We've driven sixteen hours in the last two days and we finally found paradise," he whispered. "And, baby, it's beautiful."

I laughed out loud and that was when I noticed Suda Kaye behind the long wooden display. Her head came up and her caramel-colored eyes zeroed in on me. "Oh, my God! Izzy, you're here!"

She ran around the counter and catapulted into my open arms. She swung me from left to right while squealing loudly. I held on tight and soaked in her warmth. I swore I could feel a tether of connection weaving around my form like vines of ivy. Her earthiness and joy mixed with my excitement and soothed something inside me I hadn't known was hurting.

Suda Kaye pulled back, cupped my cheeks and kissed me on the forehead. "My goodness, it's awesome to have you here in Colorado and in my store!"

I grinned. "It's great to be here."

Suda Kaye smiled beautifully and then looked at Jasper from head to toe. "And who is this fabulous pillar of fashion fierceness? Loving the look, by the way."

Jasper grinned wildly. "Her best friend. Soul mate. And brother from another mother. Now soon to be your brother from another mother as we're planning to move here."

Suda Kaye's mouth opened and closed. Her eyes filled with delight and came back to focus on me. "Did he just say you are moving here? As in Colorado? As in Pueblo?"

I bit into my bottom lip and shrugged. "It's part of the plan for now. We'll have to see how it goes. But yeah, we're definitely staying for a long while."

Suda Kaye clapped her hands and bounced on her feet. The maxi skirt she wore tinkled and chimed as she did so.

"Hey, she might move to Colorado Springs, so don't get too excited," Evie pouted.

"What's all the screaming? You okay, brown eyes?" a deep voice said from somewhere behind Suda Kaye, but I couldn't see who it was with the displays in the way.

Brown eyes? Camden, maybe?

Suda Kaye turned around in a flourish, the tinkle of her skirt going along with her movements cheerily. "Kyson, you have to meet my sister, Isabeau." She reached out and dragged

someone from behind her over to us. The tall man maneuvered around a large display and I lost my ability to breathe.

Time stopped.

My heart rate pounded.

My skin prickled.

My mouth went completely dry as Suda Kaye ushered the
most gorgeous man to our huddle.

His blue eyes locked on to my hazel ones. I could barely
take in all of his beauty at once. I didn't want to miss a single speck of his perfection.

The cornflower blue of his irises was framed by thick,
pitch-black lashes that curled up just so. The rounded cheekbones and strong jaw currently had three, maybe even four,
days of scruff. His bow-shaped bottom lip was paired with
a lovely, heart-shaped top lip, both looking plump and utterly kissable. I wanted to kiss those lips on sight, not even
knowing the man who was attached to them. They were
that magnificent.

His nose was far from perfect, but it was stunning on him.
Normal in size but with a bit of knot at the bridge, showing he'd likely broken it in the past. Still, that imperfection
added to his good looks. Even though his face was a show-
stopper, his hair was a thing of brilliance. Dark brown with
some hints of a natural caramel tone running through it as
though he might spend some time in the sun. It had lots of
wave and curl, combed up and off his forehead even though
the back and the sides were a little overly long. He could have
used a cut, but I wouldn't dare. No, I'd rather have my fingers running through those locks of love, preferably while
in a romantic clinch.

He wore a black T-shirt and a pair of jeans that had seen
better days but were definitely well loved, much like my own.
Only he filled his out to the max. His thighs stretched the

durability of the denim the same way his broad chest tested the cotton of his tee. He wasn't as big as Milo, though I didn't think many men were, but he was far from small. More like Henry Cavill during his time as Superman.

"I said hello. My name is Kyson." The bow-shaped bottom lip I had locked my eyes on stretched out across his face, the heart-shaped one flattening with the movement.

I blinked a few times and then frowned. "I'm sorry. What?"

He laughed and I felt the rumble push through my chest and down my body. He held out his hand. I took it and held his gaze with my own.

"It's good to meet you, Isabeau."

"My, uh, friends call me Izzy," I finally croaked out.

"Hmm, friends." His lips twitched and I was rapt, watching them.

"This is my long-lost half sister. And it sounds like she will be moving here. Isn't that great!" Suda Kaye announced.

Kyson's eyes slid up and down my form and I swear I felt my nipples pebble and my back arch, wanting to get closer.

Before he could respond, Jasper stepped in front of me and held out his hand. "Hey, hunk-a-licious. I'm Jasper. I can tell from the way you're eyeing up my bestie that you're all about the ladies, and she's definitely single, but if you know anyone that looks like you, or is even half as hot as you, and is into dudes, you let me know." He hooked a thumb toward his own chest.

Kyson took my friend's hand and shook it. "Nice to meet you, Jasper. And, uh, thanks for the compliment. I think," he chuckled.

"Oh, it was a compliment. As you can see, my best friend is drooling like crazy at all that is you…" He waggled his finger up and down in front of Kyson.

I covered Jasper's mouth from behind. "So rude and embarrassing. Shush," I said loud enough for all to hear.

He nodded his head and I let his mouth go.

"Fine. I'll just be over here looking at all this fab-u-lousness!" He sashayed over to a display case that had a variety of sunglasses and scarves.

I turned back to the hottest man on the planet, realizing that Evie and Suda Kaye had disappeared from our little huddle, leaving me alone with Kyson. "I'm really sorry about that. He's extremely forward and has no filter. Though to be honest, that's actually a good thing. You always know where you stand with him and he's genuinely loving and the best friend a girl could ever have."

Kyson crossed his arms over his chest as though he was settling into my blathering. I had to clench my teeth to avoid focusing on his large biceps as they bulged and flexed.

"I, uh, well…yeah." I waved my hand. "Isabeau. The new sister. I'm sorry if my friend offended you."

"No offense taken." He smiled, and my knees quivered. "And I quite like the idea of you drooling over me." He gave me a saucy grin.

I'm pretty sure my face looked as starstruck as I felt by his comment because, after I didn't respond for a full thirty seconds, he laughed heartily. I watched him avidly and allowed myself to swoon from his attention.

"How's about since you're new here, I take you out, show you a little of what might be your new digs?"

Stupidly, I blinked again, waiting for my brain to catch up with his words. "Like on a date?"

His lips pursed with what I knew to be mirth at my dorkiness. "Yeah, Isa, like a date."

Isa.

Not one person had ever called me Isa. Coming from his

rugged, beautiful mouth in that deep, gravelly tone, my heart leaped, and goose bumps appeared on my skin.

"If you're worried about me being a stranger and you being safe, your sisters can vouch for me." He moved to gesture to the girls.

I shook my head. "I, uh, yeah. That never entered my mind." Probably because nothing entered my mind except why such a perfect human would be interested in an unemployed drifter from Illinois who should probably stop eating copious amounts of her own baked goods. Plus, we'd just met. After thinking on it for a few seconds I realized he was probably just being a nice guy. Offering to take the sister of a friend of his out to see the area. Maybe nice guys in smaller locales than Chicago did that.

"You really don't have to do that. I'm sure Suda Kaye and Evie will show me around so I can get the lay of the land."

He frowned. "I'm not following."

"Just saying, you know, you don't have to be the nice friend of my sisters' and take out the new girl to try and make her feel welcome."

He smirked and coughed behind his hand while looking around, perhaps to see if we were being watched or listened to. "Isa, I'm not playing at anything. I don't feel bad that you're new in town and am not jumping in like a boy scout to be chivalrous. I'm asking a gorgeous woman out on a date. A date between a man and a woman. A date that I hope ends in a knockout kiss that sweeps you off your feet so I can ask you out on another one."

"I wha, um, you, uhhh," I blurted, not being able to form a coherent sentence to save my life.

"And I see I've rendered you unable to speak." He chuckled.

"Holy shit. You are more forward than Jasper!" I accused with a smile.

He shrugged. "If it gets me what I want, I'm fine with that. Did it work?"

I furrowed my brows in question. "Did what work?"

"Are you going to go out on a date with me?"

I nodded before I could say the words.

"Let me see your phone." He held out his hand.

"Okay." I reached around to my back pocket and pulled it out.

He engaged it, typed in it for a bit and then I heard another phone ring. He pulled his out of his back pocket, hit a button and then put it back. "I'll call you later to confirm. I've got a few jobs this week that will tie me up, so this weekend or maybe early next week after work? I try to get off by four most days since I work so early."

I bit into my lip and watched his eyes dilate. He shook his head. "Very nice to meet you, Isabeau."

"Same to you, Kyson," I breathed like a lovesick teenager who'd just been asked out by her year-long crush.

He reached for my hand and then squeezed it before letting it go. "I'm outta here, brown eyes," he called over his shoulder.

"Later, gator! Thanks for fixing the lights!" Suda Kaye hollered from the display stand where Evie and Jasper stared at me with wide eyes. The three of them were huddled conspiratorially.

"Call you soon," Kyson promised as he moved around me.

"I look forward to that." I smiled and watched his tight buns move in those faded jeans.

The door shut and a plethora of squeals, cackles and catcalls from three different voices entered my dreamy brain, breaking me out of my hot-guy stupor.

Did that just happen?

"Get over here right now and tell us everything," Jasper demanded on a gush of air.

I had a bit more sway to my hips as I went over to tell my siblings about Kyson asking me out on a date.

"Mine's burnt. Man, this sucks." Suda Kaye pouted while evaluating her crispy marshmallow. Not only had the thing caught fire, it turned totally black, too. "I'm terrible at roasting marshmallows. I always forget to keep an eye on them."

I giggled at her super-sad face.

"Aw, sweets, take mine. I like 'em the color of tar and coated with black ash," Camden lied and kissed the side of her face. One of his arms was already wrapped around his wife, and a sweet smile licked at his lips.

Her entire face lit up like a little kid sitting in front of her birthday cake with ten candles glowing. "I love you so much right now," she announced, handing him the obliterated marshmallow and stealing his perfectly browned one. She immediately plucked at the top layer of crispy goop with her fingers and plopped a blob into her mouth.

His eyes focused on her mouth and I felt the heat from his gaze even more than the bonfire before us. When she moaned and opened her eyes, he swooped in for a rather indecent kiss. So much so I looked away and focused on Evie and Milo. The two were cuddled up, Evie sitting on the ground on a blanket, her back to Milo's front, his back against a large log. The two of them seemed content to just stare at the fire and soak in the four of us spending time with them.

We'd had a blast today at Suda Kaye's store. I ended up leaving with at least three outfits and a hoard of new jewelry. None of which she let me pay for. She said it was because she missed all of my birthdays, she felt like she had a lot of presents to make up for, and my new duds and the accessories were nothing compared to what she wanted to bestow on me. She also finagled me into posing in the outfits that Jasper put together so she could use them on her website to promote the store and its inventory. This was when Evie announced the entire lot was a business tax write-off in the advertising category. Whatever that meant. I didn't know anything about tax write-offs and business expense buckets and the like. That was not something I remembered my culinary school spending much time on. Though if I were to open a store with Jasper, I imagined we'd need to figure these things out. Maybe take some classes or speak to a tax person to see how detailed it all was.

"Such a sucker for a pretty face," Jasper announced jovially.

"Guilty." Camden laughed and ran his hand through his chin-length sandy-blond hair. It fell perfectly in wavy locks around his beard-and-mustache combo. The man had it going on. Even sitting on a log in a pair of slacks with his dress shirt unbuttoned at the neck and collar, tie removed and sleeves rolled up his muscular tanned forearms, he looked incredibly sexy and not even a little out of place next to his bohemian wife. Maxi skirt that jingled when she walked due to the little gold discs dangling from a layer close to the hem. A tank top and an oversize blousy shirt that she'd tied in a knot at her hip, one shoulder falling off to expose a tasteful amount of her toasted brown skin. She was the belly-dancing flower child to his business mogul GQ appeal.

"Hey, Cam, we actually wanted to discuss some business ideas with you. When you get a chance, of course. Maybe Jas and me can set up a time to meet with you or your foundation?" I asked out loud.

"Are you looking to go the route Suda Kaye did with the foundation helping to bankroll your business startup?"

I shook my head. "No. Uh, you know that I got the big

inheritance from their dad, and Jasper and I discussed it a little bit with Evie and Milo. We are interested in starting up our own bakery. Either in Pueblo or Colorado Springs depending on the price and the place."

Suda Kaye's eyes widened, and she stood abruptly. "Holy moly! The old candy store next to Gypsy Soul is empty. It will need to be completely gutted and redone, but you totally have the capital now." She bounced on her feet and her skirt jingled prettily. "And guess what else! It comes with the apartment on top of the store."

"What apartment?" I looked at Jas and then back to Suda Kaye.

"Gypsy Soul has one, too. I had mine renovated, but it actually didn't need much. I know the old gal that used to own the candy shop lived there, so it can't be in too bad of shape. Then you'll also have a place to live. And one of you could totally live in my old apartment above Gypsy Soul!"

"No, we couldn't do that..." I started.

"Oh, yes, you can, and you will. You don't have a place to stay. Now you do. Only problem is that there's only a queen mattress, but there is a couch. So one of you could have the bed and the other the couch until your other apartment is ready. And it's super nice! Ready to go with all the essentials. You can move in tomorrow!" she breathed as though she could hardly contain her excitement.

"This isn't a bad idea. That building is a prime location for a bakery and of course, having the apartment above does help us out a lot, Izzy," Jasper added.

"The owner is an ass, but he'll give you a screaming deal if you tell him you're renovating it. Once all the businesses are fully up and running the guy will likely raise the rent, but it's already really low for what you'll get. You can have the property manager add a restriction on raising the rent the first two years like I did. And you saw how busy my store was. Imagine twice that if you're a bakery. People love to buy treats while they shop."

"We will also be doing specialty cakes for weddings and birthdays, call-in orders, boxes of homemade candies, fresh bread. Oooh, maybe Milo will teach me how to make traditional fry bread. It was by far one of the best things I've ever put in my mouth. And that's saying a lot…" Jasper grinned manically.

Milo covered his mouth with a suspicious cough that sounded a lot like laughter.

"Jas…" I warned. "Keep it clean."

He curled his lips and made a silly face at me. "You're no fun."

I laughed and focused back on Camden. "Evie mentioned maybe you could help us go over things. I mean, I understand if you're too busy. We're new to this family and I wouldn't want to take advantage or put you out in any way."

He scoffed. "Why would me giving you business advice be taking advantage? I'm happy to help my sister-in-law get her feet wet in the business world. And if Evie and Milo are willing to chip in on the financial side and with recommendations, I'm sure we could get the two of you up and running in no time. How about we meet up at the end of the week? I'll have my assistant call and set up a time for the two of you to come meet with me at my office."

"That would be amazing, Camden. Thank you."

He smiled and it notched his handsome business-surfer vibe up a thousand degrees.

"In the meantime, I want the two of you to make a list of the things you want to offer in your business. How many people will be working with you? Guesstimate on how much you want to make and any employees you'd want to have…"

"I think it would just be me and Jas in the beginning until we got really comfortable. Right, Jasper?"

"Definitely. We make all the decisions and set it up how we want before we add anyone else into the mix," he agreed.

Camden nodded. "Makes sense. You also need to start thinking of your bakery's theme. What sets it apart from others? What makes it special? What are you going to offer? What do you think you want to charge for those items? Also, you'll need to look at equipment. What are you going to need to purchase appliance-wise? Then of course there's the location. If you choose the space next to Gypsy Soul, you get the benefit of the apartment on top. That's a big plus since you both don't have living arrangements for the foreseeable future. You'll need to name it, and think about vendors you want to work with for the packaging materials, your supplies of milk, eggs, butter and the like."

My mind was blown.

"Wow. There's a lot that goes into this." I lifted my hand and brought my thumb to my mouth to worry the nail there.

Jasper instantly grabbed my hand and glared. "No nail biting. You're not alone in this, Izzy. You've got me, and your sisters and brothers to help guide us. We'll do our homework and make lists. Tons of lists. You love lists."

"I do love lists," I whispered.

"Me, too!" Evie beamed, obviously appreciating something we had in common.

"And, sister, I just opened my business last year. I know a ton and would be happy to have you and Jasper hang out at Gypsy Soul and talk through some ideas. Take some notes about things you'll need to be aware of. Maybe I'll have more to add so you'll be ready for your meeting with Cam."

"Also, guys, we can meet twenty times if that's what it takes. There is no limit to my help. I can also connect you with Turner Brothers Construction. They did Suda Kaye's store and it was done well, quickly and under budget. We can trust Kyson to do right by you."

"Kyson?" I asked, my cheeks flaming instantly. Thankfully, the bonfire was pretty hot and I didn't think anyone would notice the change.

"Yeah, he's a good guy. Once I got his lips away from my wife," Cam grumbled.

"Honey, it was just a kiss…" Suda Kaye rolled her eyes dramatically.

"It was a full-on make-out session. I know what I saw," Camden fired off, a hint of irritation in his tone.

"Wait a minute, you dated Kyson? The guy I met today?" I asked, my stomach clenching and my heart pounding even more wildly.

"Um… I wouldn't call it dating," Suda Kaye said, though the way she said it made me believe she was downplaying it.

"Only because I made my move. Otherwise, who knows? You might be shacked up with Kyson right now."

I'm pretty sure that was the moment that my eyes almost bulged right out of my head and I felt as though someone had punched me in the stomach.

"That is not true in the slightest," she groused, her voice rising. "Kyson's all about a fun time, no strings attached."

"Oh, really?"

"Yeah," she said nonchalantly at the same time Evie said, "Suda Kaye!"

Suda Kaye turned her head from her grumpy husband and then realized what she said. "No. I mean, I don't really know him that well. I…uh, ugh! What I meant to say is he's a super-nice guy. I wouldn't have let him ask you out if I didn't think you'd have fun going out with him."

"You're going out with Kyson Turner?" Camden asked.

"Damn, one day at work and I miss everything happening in my wife's family."

"Well, that settles all. I'm definitely not going out with him now! He's kissed my sister." I scrunched up my nose and made a gagging sound even though my stomach was twisting violently, and my heart had plummeted to the pits of despair.

Man, I'd really liked him. I'd dated a lot of good-looking guys over the years. I mean I'm not horrible to look at, but I never had instant chemistry with any of them or dated anyone who had such charisma. Not only had he already made out with my sister, he was also a no-strings-attached player. Those were the worst of the worst in my book. They just wanted to get in and get out. I was so not down for that. It wasn't that I was a prude or judgy about what people wanted to do with their bodies, but I wanted to spend time with a guy. Get to know him before I became intimate. Which was also why I had a strict six-dates-to-sex rule. Sure, we could get hot and heavy before then, but I never broke that rule. Seeing as I was still single, it clearly hadn't served me well, but it definitely weeded out the douchebags who just wanted to get off and move on to the next piece of ass.

"No, come on, Izzy. Give the guy a chance. It was a year ago, for crying out loud, and it was one single kiss. It happened and then it was done. No harm, no foul. I have zero problem with you dating him because like I said, he's a really good guy. And besides, he does the best renovation work and he's truly loyal and honest about his intentions. I think you should definitely talk to him at the very least."

I shrugged. "I don't know. We'll see."

"That means no," Jasper announced to our group.

"It does not," I sighed.

He nodded. "I've known you almost my entire life. If you say the words *we'll see* it means it's not happening."

I frowned and shrugged again. "How's about we talk about something more interesting. Evie, Milo, tell us about your wedding next month. I'm excited it's on a Native American reservation. I've never been on one."

"Well, there's this incredible spot, just past the rez, that leads up to the bluffs. You can see the horizon for miles and miles. We'll be getting married there," Evie said, dreamily looking into the fire.

"Sounds magical. Tell me more."

seven

———

Sitting cross-legged in one of Evie's spare rooms, I tugged on the ribbon holding all the pink envelopes together. I'd moved the first one to the bottom of the stack. The next one had *Isabeau 19th Birthday* on the front in beautiful, elegant penmanship. I took a deep breath, opened the envelope and unfolded the pink parchment paper.

My little *Kasaraibo*,
Since we never spoke in person, I feel my letters to you would be best spent sharing more about my side of your heritage, including information about me, your grandparents and your sisters. Starting with your grandmother. Her name was Topsannah Tahsuda. She was the most beautiful woman inside and out. Her heart, mind and touch were as pure as snow. Like me, she was not long of this earth, dying even younger than I will be when the cancer inside me has won.

My mother was an excellent cook. Taught my father everything he knows about Native American cuisine because she knew she was fighting her own losing battle. She wanted him to be able to take care of himself, me and her grandchildren, sharing the food she loved. She also had a talent for sewing. I was always amazed at how she could make intricate, woven, Navajo-inspired blankets, many of which I'm sure your grandfather still has. My mother also had a unique and very special gift, something she shared with my father: the ability to read the stars. Let him tell you the story of meeting and finding his soul mate. It's a tale I hope you'll tell your own children one day. Though it will be better coming from him.

Anyway, she read in the stars that she would not live long. When I was born, she saw the same. Thankfully, your Toko has read the stars for all three of my children. You will all live long, glorious lives. However, that does not mean you won't have strife and many sacrifices ahead. That, my darling girl, is unavoidable. We all have to sacrifice for the people we love. You were my biggest sacrifice.

Your grandfather is Tahsuda. When our people were required to secure official birth certificates from the government, the tribe's people had to pick their last names. My father refused. He told them repeatedly, "I am Tahsuda." When pressed, they ended up just putting his first name twice. He is not the type of man to let anyone demand anything of him. He is an elder in the Comanche tribe and highly respected. Mom's family was Navajo so me and you girls are both Comanche and Navajo. Your Toko is a man of honor, loyalty and wisdom.

Since my parents knew I was not meant to live a long

life, they encouraged me from a very young age to experience all that life had to offer. I didn't want to live out my days on the reservation like my mother had. I wanted to feel the sand beneath my toes at the edge of the sea. I wanted to belly dance with the sisterhood until my feet hurt. I dreamed of seeing the world and all its glory and I did. But all of this beauty came with great price. I sacrificed time with Evie and Suda Kaye. In order to live, I had to leave my girls to be raised mostly by my father. Sometimes I deeply regretted my time away. At other times I knew my girls were loved, fed, sheltered and taken care of. They would have their time to live and I knew when I passed, I'd have my experiences and their love to guide me through eternity.

Which is how I'll end this letter to you, my fire-haired daughter. If you learn one thing from me, let it be this.

Take chances. Love deeply and freely. Rewards are in the risks.

With all the love I have within me,

Catori.

I folded up the letter, put it back into the envelope and moved it to the bottom of the stack. My grandparents knew Catori was going to die young. They encouraged her to spread her wings and see the world, ensuring she didn't miss out on any of her dreams.

I thought about her advice again, letting it roll around in my head.

Take chances.

Love deeply and freely.

Rewards are in the risks.

If Catori were here right now, what would she say about

this crazy idea I had of starting a new life and getting to know my sisters?

Take chances. I grinned and bit into my bottom lip before whispering aloud, "She'd approve a hundredfold."

And what about opening the bakery with Jasper? Dumping in tons of the money her husband left me to fulfill my dream? *Rewards are in the risks.* "She'd probably throw her hands up and cheer the same way Suda Kaye did," I murmured to myself.

My phone buzzed with a text. I rolled over to the side and snagged it off the nightstand. Butterflies took flight in my stomach as I read the message.

Kyson: How does Thursday night dinner and a walk around town sound?

The last bit of advice. *Love deeply and freely.* "Catori would absolutely go on the date with Kyson," I sighed. Regardless of her advice, I didn't know if it was a good idea to go out with a man who had made out with my sister. I mean, sure, she's married and super happy with Camden, but my seeing him was bound to be weird. And what about girl code? Didn't it break some type of cosmic sisterhood rule?

Still feeling uncertain, I decided to get another thing off my mind by pulling back up my phone, finding my papa's cell and hitting Call.

It rang only twice before my papa Ian answered. "Izzy! How are you, baby girl?"

I smiled and tugged at a loose string on my sleep shirt. "Hi, Papa. I'm good. Just woke up not long ago."

"You still at Evie and Milo's?" he asked conversationally.

"Yeah, but not for long."

"Oh? You found a place already?" Leave it to my papa to

be worried about my finding a home to settle into. Since he'd grown up bouncing from one foster home to another, he was huge on making a space your own as soon as possible. He believed it connected to your goals and happiness, and gave you a great sense of pride to know where you were going to lay your head at night.

"Actually, Suda Kaye has a studio apartment above her store, Gypsy Soul. Jas and I will share the studio for a little while."

"That doesn't sound very stable, honey. Are there no apartments or houses available for rent?"

"We did look, but this is free and ready now. No having to worry about putting Evie and Milo or Suda Kaye and Camden out by staying in their spare rooms, ya know?"

"Yes, I understand that, but a studio apartment is small. And I know you and Jasper are used to sharing space, but you'll both eventually need alone time. You know how tense the two of you can get when you spend every waking minute together…" He let the reminder fall away, probably knowing I was a big girl and could handle my own relationship.

"This I know. But guess what?" I changed the subject a little.

"What? I like hearing that excitement in my girl's voice." He chuckled.

"Jasper and I have decided to kick our dream of owning our own bakery into high gear. We're going to do it here. Well, actually, probably in Pueblo, in the empty store space right next to Suda Kaye's boutique."

"What?"

"Yeah! I can hardly believe it. We've been talking about it nonstop for two days." I filled my papa in on everything planned to date and how much help my sisters and their mates were giving us. "So basically, we decided to just go for it!"

"Just go for it…" He repeated my own words, though when he said it didn't sound pleased.

"Papa, why aren't you excited? You know this is my dream."

He sighed and cleared his throat. Was he crying?

"I'm happy if you're happy, baby. You know that. All your dad and I ever wanted for you was to live out your dreams. It's what we worked so hard for. And here you are, doing it."

"Thanks, Papa."

He laughed drily. "I just wish you weren't doing it over a thousand miles away where your dad and I can't participate or cheer you along the way good parents should."

My shoulders sank, my excitement disappearing in a flash. That was the hardest part about my decision to be where my sisters lived. They were here, but my fathers were in Chicago. The longest we'd been apart was the eighteen months Jasper and I did our schooling in France and Italy.

"You know we'll come home for important things. Or have you come visit. And the store we're looking at has another studio apartment on top of it. Jasper and me will both have our own spaces, but we'll share the business together."

"It sounds amazing, Izzy. Truly wonderful. I honestly couldn't be happier. Casey's gonna freak when I tell him your news."

"So you're okay with the fact that I'm setting up shop in Colorado and not Illinois?"

"Sweetheart, you have to go where your heart leads you. If you want to get to know your sisters and have them in your life, Colorado is the best place to do that. Sure, your dad and I will miss having you close, but children grow up. They leave the nests. It's hard, of course. We love you more than anything in the entire world. But that love doesn't change based on where you live. It's unconditional and yours until we take our last breaths."

His words had me tearing up. "I love you, Papa. So much it hurts sometimes."

"That's how love should feel, baby. Don't ever settle for a man who you don't love with your entire being without knowing you've got that kind of love in return. When you share that special connection with the right person, you'll be able to share that love with your children. God willing," he added, not being shy at all about his desire to have grandchildren one day. Then again, he'd never been shy about his desire for me to procreate. My entire life he'd commented on things with, "When you have your own kids one day, Izzy," or, "Just wait until you have a child. Your whole life has more meaning." Yada yada.

"I know, I know."

"I have to get back to work, honey. Mrs. Caravali's rosebushes won't cut themselves," he teased.

"Wear your hat and tons of sunscreen. I don't care that your brown skin never burns. There's still a serious risk for skin cancer, and being a landscaper with his own business, you need to protect yourself!"

"Jeez, you sound just like your dad," he admonished. "I will protect myself. And I'm excited for you, baby girl, and can't wait to hear more about your business startup as you progress. I want regular updates."

"You got it, Captain!"

He chuckled. "You doing okay? Getting to know your sisters?"

Holy crap. That reminded me why I called in the first place. "Yes, but actually something odd happened yesterday."

"What?"

"They recognized the bracelet you guys gave me for my sixteenth birthday. They claim it was Catori's."

"It was your mom's. She left it sitting next to that note I shared. We held on to it until you were old enough."

I let out a long breath. "Why didn't you tell me?"

"She didn't want us talking about her. It was the only way we thought we could honestly give you a piece of your mother without breaking our promise to her."

For a full minute I didn't say anything. I understood that Catori had had her reasons for staying away, but damn it to hell in a handbasket. I wished she'd made a different choice. I wished I'd had the time to know her. Really *know* her. Spend time understanding who she was, even if it was short-lived.

"Izzy?" Papa asked.

"Yeah, I'm here." My eyes were leaking, tears running down my cheeks before I even realized I was crying.

"Baby girl, I'm sorry we lied to you."

"I know. I get it. I really do. It's just, facing all of this, getting to know these amazing women, learning about the woman my mother was…" My throat tightened and I swallowed around the cotton coating my tongue. "It's a lot."

"Baby, it would be a lot for anyone in your position. Understand that there is no right way to feel. You are entitled to experience this however it comes and feel whatever flows through you. Just be honest. Talk to me, talk to Casey, to Jasper, your sisters. Don't bottle it all up or eventually, one day it's going to explode. And that mess is far harder to clean up than accepting the truth about your emotions as they come. Your dad and I will never judge you. We've made a lot of our own mistakes, even some with you. There is no right way to raise a child, but we did the best we could. We are so damn proud of the woman you've become. Any time you want to unload on us, you do it. Okay, honey?"

More tears. More sniffles. More dry throat.

"Yeah, Papa. Thanks. I will. I promise."

"Okay. Now, your dad is going to be pissed he missed you today, so call him tomorrow and give him some Izzy goodness."

"I will. I love you. Tell Dad I love and miss him, too."

"You got it. Bye for now."

"Bye for now," I repeated.

I took a deep breath and let it out along with a hundred pounds of tension that was sitting on my chest.

I was entitled to my feelings. And as much as I could fall into a well of unhappiness at the choices my biological mother had made, it wouldn't change the outcome.

Yesterday was in the past.

Today was the present and I needed to treat it as the gift it was.

It was also the day we would see the candy shop with the property manager, and that was exciting. Hauling my body out of the seriously comfy bed, I looked in the mirror over the vanity.

Wild, red bedhead curls fell down over my shoulders to the middle of my back. Pearlescent skin the same as my father Casey. Bright hazel eyes that looked even more green due to my tears. A smallish button nose. Almond-shaped eyes with thick, rust-colored lashes. A smattering of freckles across my nose and cheeks that I thought looked attractive even though a lot of women tried to cover them up. My skin rocked and always had. My dad taught me to protect my skin as though we were at war with the sun and I followed that advice faithfully. My lips were a good size, very pink and cherublike. At least that was what I've always been told by the guys I dated. Though my body...yeah, curves for days.

I turned from side to side checking myself out. Nipped-in waist, wide hips and large boobs. I felt like I had more boobage than Evie and Suda Kaye put together. Though I'd never had a single complaint from the men I took to bed. My stomach wasn't exactly flat—rounded but not overly so. Unless I wanted to work out like a demon—because I'd have to in order to look anything like what society thought was toned and fit—and never eat my desserts—which I lived for—I had to accept what the good Lord gave me. And until I stood next to my gorgeous sisters, I'd never doubted myself. Never found myself lacking. Just comfortable in my own skin.

Again, I looked at myself, this time with a shrewd eye, trying to see what Kyson saw. All in all, I liked what I saw, was comfortable with my body. If a man wanted to be with me, a chef, a *baker*, he'd need to like a woman with some cushion for pushin' as Jasper always said. He, too, wanted a man with meat on him, even though he was super trim with a naturally athletic body. He had a four-pack and didn't even work for it. The bastard.

I hummed to myself, whipped off my pajamas and set my outfit for the day on the bed. Jeans, check. Tank, check. Flip-flops, check.

I grabbed my robe and put it on so I could hit the hall bathroom and get my shower out of the way before I made breakfast for Evie and Milo again. This time I was thinking a fancy French toast with powdered sugar, hot maple syrup and a special hot fruit drizzle.

After showering, I left my hair to air dry and moseyed back to my room. On the bed was a completely different outfit than what I had laid out. Seemed I had a dressing gnome sneak into my room, assess my outfit and declare it unworthy.

I strained to hear the sounds coming from the house. In the distance I heard some pots and pans clanking. I shook my head.

Jasper.

I removed my robe and dug through my suitcase for a pair of panties and bra. Matching, of course. Lacy and sexy as all get-out. It was the one thing I spent any money on clothing-wise. I learned it from Jasper's mom Penelope. She had always been the motherly type figure in my life. Teaching me and Jasper how to paint our nails, take care of our faces. She even helped me out with the whole womanhood and puberty issue. But the one thing she said every woman should do for herself was fill their drawers with pretty underthings. Penelope believed that it made every woman feel sassy, sexy and feminine.

I'd taken this advice and invested in beautiful underwear. Her advice worked. Each day when I donned my undergarments, I felt pretty and liked knowing I had something beautiful and sexy hidden away, only to be seen by me, unless I invited a suitor to see them.

Once I got the pale peach matching set on, I evaluated what Jasper had picked out for me today. A darker pair of wide-legged jeans. A belt made of multicolored pieces of interwoven leather that we'd picked up at Gypsy Soul. My tall wedge sandals that did actually go really well with the jeans. And a flirty white blouse that had ruffles at the short-capped sleeves. Next to the shirt lay a slew of gold-and-silver bangles and a pair of gold-and-silver chandelier earrings. He even added a huge statement necklace of twisted silver-and-gold vines that turned into leaves that I would have never thought to pair with this blouse, but looking at it then…it rocked.

Evil genius.

Quickly, I got dressed and made my way downstairs where Jasper was washing fresh fruit. He eyed me from top to toe. "Beautiful as ever."

My lips quirked. "Mmm-hmm. I was thinking of making our fancy French toast today. What do you say?"

His eyes lit up. "Perfect. I'll just cut these up and start heating them." He gestured to the strawberries and blackberries we'd picked up yesterday.

"I'll get the egg wash going."

For the next thirty minutes we worked side by side, a familiar dance we had perfected over the years, especially when working in a kitchen together. We complemented one another so well, instinctively knowing what the other was best at, being each other's sous-chef on different things, filling in for the other, handing one another the appropriate utensils and spices when needed.

"What do you think about doing a color theme of coral, peach and cream for our bakery?" he asked while stirring the fruit and sugar over a low flame.

"Add in some gold touches and I think it's brilliant."

"Oooh, gold touches would be so extra and elegant! I can already see the colors weaving together."

I grinned. "What do you think about Sweet and Sassy for the name?" I added while pouring the vanilla into the egg mix.

He curled his lip to the side. "Sounds like a clothing store."

"Hmm, true. Sweet and Salty?"

"That has merit." He nodded but didn't seem excited. We both needed to be excited about the name of our bakery.

"The Sweet Life?" I offered while adding in salt, cinnamon and a touch of nutmeg.

"Too much like that sitcom with those dudes Zack and Cody."

"Ah, right. Hmm," I said, heating up the griddle.

As I was soaking the thick slices of French bread Jasper had already cut, and laying them out on the griddle, Evie entered the kitchen. This time in an ethereal royal blue satin robe. Her hair down around her shoulders. Her eyes were a stunning bright sky blue due to the reflection off her robe, making her seem more like a queen entering her throne room, rather than my big sister coming down for breakfast made by her houseguests.

"Ooh, what is that heavenly scent? Something on the sweet side this morning?"

On the Sweet Side.

I smiled huge and spun around to Jasper, who held the fruit spoon in the air, juice dripping down the wooden handle.

"On the Sweet Side!" We both screeched at the same time like tween girls having heard their favorite pop band perform live for the first time.

I got chills. "Oh, my God!" We both started laughing and dancing around. I held up my hand and he gave me a whopping high five.

"Thanks, Evie!" I came around and pulled her into a tight hug, shaking her from side to side. "You just helped us name our bakery."

She jerked her head back, confused but still smiling. "I did?"

"You did, lady." I went over to stand next to my bestie, hooked an arm around his shoulders and looked at him. We both turned our heads, stared into her baby blues and said the name again.

"On the Sweet Side!"

eight

When Jasper and I arrived in Pueblo, Suda Kaye was already standing outside, talking to none other than Kyson Turner and another woman I assumed was her property manager. I pulled Serenity into a parking spot close to the store. Before I got out, Jasper grabbed my hand.

"Okay, no pressure. This may be the one, this may not be. We'll know it when we see it," he confirmed.

I inhaled fully and let it out. "Definitely. We'll know it when we feel it."

"Now, put on some gloss because hunk-a-licious is out there and I want my girl looking sexy, sassy and sweet enough to eat!"

I ground down on my back teeth and narrowed my gaze. "No. I'm turning him down."

He had his fingers curled around the door handle with the door pushed open a few inches before he slapped it closed and turned to the side. "Excuse me? You're what?" He cupped his hand in a circular motion around his ear. "I couldn't possibly have heard you right. For a second there I thought my Izzy was turning down an insanely hot guy, one who has a good job…no, one who *owns* his own business, seems to be into you and again, is seriously freakin' hot."

"He made out with Suda Kaye," I whined and slumped into the supple leather of my driver's seat.

He jerked his head as though he was winding up for a serious lecture.

I put my palm up in front of us. "Don't even…"

He grabbed my hand and held it in his. "Your concerns are bogus, and you know it. Suda Kaye gave you the okay. Actually, she wholeheartedly wants you to date this guy. She's practically hooking you up with him. They're just friends. Look at the way he's talking to her—if he was into the bohemian goddess, he'd be getting into her space, making a point to touch her. He's doing none of those things. Though damn, he sure looks good with that tool belt around his waist, a clipboard in his hand, that pencil behind his ear." Jasper licked his lips. "Izzy, you have to go out with him. Single women everywhere would jump at the chance to go on a date with a man that looks like Kyson Turner."

He was not wrong. I studied Kyson through the windshield. Long legs encased in a pair of black worn Levi's. A white T-shirt that hugged his muscles like a second skin. I could even see the indentations of what must have been a ripped stomach. The man absolutely took care of his body, but I imagined that was pretty common in his industry. Hammering things. Nailing things. Lifting, squatting. My heart rate picked up as I dug through the random items in my console and grabbed my lip gloss. I flipped down the visor and applied a peachy shine.

"There's my Izzy. Now, come on. I'm excited to see the space." He pushed open the door and slammed it behind him.

"Dude, stop slamming my girl's door!" I followed him out of the car, making a point to show him how easy it was to simply shut the door on my new car.

He held up his hands. "Okay, okay, I'll try to remember. Sorry, pretty baby." He patted the hood and I grinned.

The second we hit the sidewalk Suda Kaye jumped up and down and bum-rushed us. "I'm so excited! Are you guys fa-reak-ing out or what?" she squealed.

"Suda Kaye, what's Kyson doing here?" I whispered as she hooked her arm in mine and the other in Jasper's and led us toward the man who had his Ray-Ban sunglasses focused dead on me. I noticed his head tilted down just a smidge, but it was enough to know he was checking me out.

"Well, if you choose to renovate, he'd be the best to work with. Cam told you that last night. So I figured we should just have him here right out of the gate and give you a good, solid guesstimate of what renovations will cost. If it's too far over your budget, then he'll be the best one to tell you. He's honest and won't take you for a ride."

"He won't? Pity. I was kinda hoping he'd take her for a ride. Woman needs to get herself some. Been too damn long as it is." Jasper blatantly vomited my personal business out there.

"Shush!" I growled as we approached.

"It's true."

I groaned under my breath and then plastered a smile on my lips as Kyson took off his sunglasses and clipped them into the collar of his tee. "Isa, looking as lovely as when I saw you last."

"Kyson." I lifted my chin to him and then held my hand out to the property manager and introduced myself.

"Pleasure to meet you," she said, and spun on a spiked heel and headed to the door. She opened it and gestured for us to enter.

"I'm going to let you guys have your time. I'll be over here. Come by when you're done and tell me everything." Suda Kaye pulled me into a super-fast side hug then did the same to Jasper. "Good luck!" She held up two fingers that were crossed over one another.

Kyson let us both enter before he pulled up behind me and whispered in my ear, "You haven't responded to my text."

"Because I haven't decided if I'm going to go out with you or not," I answered.

He grabbed my biceps and tugged me over to the side. I watched Jasper go deep into the space and I turned around, my sass already at the surface. I was certain Jasper wanted Kyson and me to have a minute alone, the brat.

"Hey, we're here for business. This is important to me," I griped.

"I know. That's why I'm here. However, that doesn't change the fact that our date is very important to *me*, and I was hoping you'd give me an answer."

I put a hand to my hip. "I will, when I'm good and ready. No sooner."

His gaze slid to the hand on my hip and then his lips quirked in a half smile. "Hard to get? I see I've got the sassy Isa on my hands."

"Excuse me?"

He grinned. "I like a challenge. We'll talk after," he said decisively. Moving around my form, Kyson reached for the pencil behind his ear and held up his clipboard.

The property manager stood near Jasper, waiting patiently.

"Okay, show us what you've got," I announced with a clap of my hands and more bravado than I felt.

The property manager took us through the main space first. It looked very similar in size to Gypsy Soul but Kyson said it was actually ten feet wider, which was ideal since we planned to have some tables and chairs for people to sit and eat their treats if they so desired.

"Wiring is a problem." Kyson pointed up to the ceiling and then to the sockets in different places. "You'll need entirely new electrical. None of this is up to current codes." He marked something on his clipboard.

"Here's the kitchen. As you can see, it's pretty rough." The property manager pointed to the broken-down countertops and the beat-to-hell small oven.

Jasper cringed as he opened the metal door and peered inside. "How did she manage with all of this old equipment? It doesn't seem like it would even hold its temperature let alone be able to make a wide variety of candies."

"Over the years the original candy shop owner started offering fewer and fewer homemade items until finally it was just over-the-counter candy. I don't think she even baked any of it herself in the last five to ten years, but she had some extended family working here until she died. It's been empty since Suda Kaye moved into Gypsy Soul," the property manager clarified.

"We'll need multiple ovens with the ability to release the heat. Multiple refrigeration units and everything in between," I announced, scanning the space.

Kyson moved along the wall and inspected each socket as well as the stained ceiling tiles that looked like they used to be in an office building—not ideal for a bakery. "I'd suggest we tile the entire room for safety, cleaning and comfort."

I nodded.

"You'll need to show me what appliances you are considering for your business so I can determine the needs for the structure, electricity and setup. Though the place has been a bakery for years, so it should be able to withstand the demands. It's also plumbed well." He pointed to several drains in the floor. "Means you can hose this all down each night and keep it really clean."

Off to the side of the kitchen were three different doors. One was metal with a reinforced bar Kyson had to push to release the lock.

"Fire door and exit." He opened it and we noted a small parking lot and several large Dumpsters toward the back.

"Those are only used for these buildings and there are three parking spaces per business," the property manager announced.

"Cool, so we don't have to take up a potential customer spot on the main strip," Jasper said and she nodded.

Another door looked like it was attached to a massive freezer. I watched Kyson open it and peer inside before he disappeared behind it.

I went over and dipped my head around the door and was surprised to find a pretty wide and rather long refrigeration unit. Sturdy metal shelves lined the space neatly.

"This is amazing," Jasper gasped.

"Does it work?" I directed my question to Kyson.

He fiddled with something behind the door and all of a sudden, we heard something click. Cool air shot from the vents in the floor and ceiling.

"Yup, but I'd like to leave it on so we can determine if it runs smoothly, gets to the appropriate temperature we set it at and stays that way." Kyson jotted something down on his clipboard.

The property manager nodded. "Leave it on. I'll tell the owner that I have potential tenants who need to know if it works properly or not."

"If it does, that will save a ton on equipment, Izzy," Jasper noted.

I walked out of the unit and to the other door. "And this?" I asked, pulling it open. It looked like it led up a flight of stairs that I imagined went to the apartment.

"You were interested in renting the apartment on top as well, correct?" the property manager asked.

"Yes, but this door goes right into the kitchen. Even if we didn't want it, the landlord couldn't rent it to someone else and allow them free access to our business space," I noted.

She grinned. "I've heard that before. From your sister, actually. The owner will lock the door and leave it unoccupied if you don't want to rent it, but if you do, it will be tacked on to the business rent for a really decent price. We worked it out a year ago with Suda Kaye's agreement, so it won't be hard to ensure you get a fair price."

"Cool. Can we take a look?" I asked.

"Yep, follow me." She hoofed her small booty and tall heels up the stairs. Jasper followed behind her and I gestured for Kyson to go up ahead of me.

"Ladies first." He grinned.

I squinted, pursed my lips and pointed to the stairs. "It's the twenty-first century. Men are allowed to go before women up a flight of stairs. In fact, I insist." I harrumphed and that bit of my sassy self from earlier made an appearance once again.

He moved close to me, casually put his hands on my biceps and turned me around before leaning into my ear from behind me. "If you think I'm not going to take the opportunity to watch your stellar ass and long legs move up those stairs, you're crazy, honey. Better hurry, they're waiting."

I was just about to respond when Jasper whooped and

clapped. "Izzy! Come up here right now! You've gotta see this!"

Once more, I glared at Kyson. He smiled wide and chuckled. "Fine!" I spun around fast and dashed up the stairs, winded once I hit the top. I leaned my hand against the wooden door frame as I caught my breath.

I could not believe what I saw.

Jasper's eyes were the size of lemons. His entire body practically vibrated with happiness.

"Oh, boy." I looked around at the antique furniture filling the space. Curved arms and fancy crushed velvet material the likes of which you'd see in a castle, definitely not on top of a run-down bakery. The walls were something else: shimmery gold wallpaper striped with fuzzy burgundy fleur de lis.

The property manager seemed shocked as she turned in a circle, a horrified expression on her face. "I… I was told that whatever was in the place was left for the renters to have. We knew there was some furniture left but I was not expecting it to have this much. I can talk to the owner about getting it all removed. And the wallpaper… My God…" She held her hand in front of her face.

I felt a warm hand curl around my hip and one cup my shoulder. Kyson ushered me into the space.

"Fuck." He said only the one word. And it was enough.

My gaze flew to Jasper. This was not good. I could see it on my bestie's face; he was about to lose his mind.

And then he exploded.

"This is my new home! It's everything, *everything* I ever wanted," he breathed. "Izzy, I must have it. I have to live here. You know me. You *know me*! It's meant to be." His form continued to tremble as his excitement grew.

Kyson squeezed my shoulder. This time I shivered at the

familiarity with which he touched me. "Your boy has a couple screws loose."

I couldn't help it. I burst into laughter. I took in the antique furniture, the pattern of one chair a myriad of woven flowers in bright reds, golds, teals and oranges. It was gaudy. It was god-awful. And my best friend in the entire world was in love with every inch of it.

He fluttered from piece to piece then pointed to one that looked like it was a love seat with a wooden end table attached. The feet were made of a heavily carved, curved, glossed wood almost reminiscent of a claw-foot tub. "This is a design from the Victorian era. My guess, late eighteen hundreds. Technically, it's not real, but still antique by our standards. It's a knockoff but it's at least sixty years old!" He gushed. "In Queen Victoria's era, these used to be in the homes of the rich and fabulous. They'd sit and take a phone call looking regal and sophisticated." He plopped his ass rather daintily in the seat and opened the drawer. He grinned wide. "And here is where you took notes." He pulled out a pad of paper and a pen. "So cool!"

"Oh, sweet mother..." I groaned.

"What's happening here?" Kyson's breath feathered light against my ear.

I swallowed and tried to ignore it, focusing on Jasper. "He's in furniture and apartment heaven."

"You're kidding," he admonished. "I can taste the dust mites on my tongue."

I shook my head and watched Jasper prance, yes *prance*, to a velvet couch. "And this beauty, this one's real," he said with such awe in his tone it was like he was getting every single one of his wishes and hopes handed to him at one time. "It's sage green, tufted antique from the nineteen twenties. I'm sure of it." He sat in it and stretched his arms out along the putrid-colored fabric. Calling that thing sage green was being kind. It was a sickly pea green, in my opinion, but you couldn't deny the look on Jasper's face. He loved it.

"Jas…" I warned. "Remember what we said in the car?"

His gaze flicked to me. "Yes, and I remember saying last night that if this place is it, this place is it. The apartment proves it. It's meant to be mine."

"Honey, you don't know that. Let Kyson ensure this place is not going to fall into the empty showroom below."

"You like this?" the property manager asked, total shock in her tone.

"Like? No, honey. I *looooooove* this." He made the word *love* last for five syllables.

Kyson chuckled and moved about the room, checking the sockets and the lights, tapping on the walls at random. He went to the small kitchen and turned on the faucet. Thankfully, there were newer appliances, but no fridge. Odd… They'd taken the fridge but left several antique pieces behind. My guess, they didn't know what they had. Maybe it was lucky that my best friend was an antique freak. He loved anything old as dirt except his fashion. He proudly wore every era and mixed and matched as he deemed worthy and fashion-forward.

"All I'm gonna say, Izzy, is if there is a claw-foot bathtub, you know what that means," Jasper breathed.

I closed my eyes and quietly said a prayer. I didn't pray that there wasn't one; I just prayed that if this was the place for us, he'd get what he wanted and so would I, in a building and location that didn't cost an arm and a leg and a year to renovate.

Jasper entered a door that led to a tiny hallway. On the right was a bedroom. Thankfully, there wasn't any furniture but there was more crazy wallpaper, this time a silver-

and-black print. Much to his delight, there was a chandelier dangling from the center of the room.

"Oh, my God, oh, my God, oh, my God," Jasper chanted with his fingers to the sides of his cheeks.

If the antique furniture didn't seal the deal, that chandelier did. He'd be happy as a clam with that thing hanging over his bed. Something sparkly and pretty he could gaze at while resting in his bed or being banged by his next partner. Me and my best friend didn't judge people for their sexual proclivities, or care one way or another about each other's desires. We loved who we loved. We liked who we liked. We were raised by homosexual couples. It's just part of our lives. With that being said, my bestie loved girly things. And just like all the women I knew, myself included, we liked men who were bigger and broader than we were. Having a chandelier in his bedroom would absolutely suit the man he was. And who was I to deny him his heart's desires? He dropped his entire life to be with me and follow a path completely opposite of what we had planned.

The longer I thought about it, the more I realized I owed him this happiness. If this apartment made him love his new home here, I should be championing it, not working against it.

"If you want this to be our place and this to be your home, Jas, I'm here for it. We just need to make sure we can afford it, okay?"

He licked his lips and sucked the bottom one into his mouth so it disappeared. "I really want it, Izzy."

"I know, baby. Let's see what the property manager says..." I trailed off when she yelled super loud, obviously realizing she could hook us, "Claw-foot bathtub with shower! And it's so cute!"

Jasper's eyes twinkled. Actually lit up as though his bright and pure soul was glowing from within.

I laughed and tilted my head to the side. "Go check it out."

"Eeeeeek!" He raced by me, shaking his fists in front of him the way an eager baby did when it was excited about a new food or toy.

I sighed when I entered the living room. Kyson was making notes.

"How's the bathroom?" I asked.

"Perfect condition. There were more upgrades to the apartment than the business. Everything up here is top-to-toe fine." He looked around and cringed. "I mean, for people who like this sorta look. Definitely not what I did in Suda Kaye's place."

"She had you renovate the apartment above her shop?"

He nodded. "We gutted the kitchen. New cabinets, granite, appliances—the whole nine. The rest of the space was fine. Did some updating to her bathroom but it's smaller than this place. Since there's ten more feet in width in the business below, add that to the length and you've got a full bathroom and small bedroom as you saw. Hers is one open room, aside from the bathroom."

I shrugged. "I don't need much."

"Actually, I have another idea and we'd need to chat with Suda Kaye about it, but it might be cool and it's definitely safer for you moving between buildings."

"What do you mean?"

"Let's go downstairs and I'll show you," he said.

I followed him down but hollered to Jas that we would be downstairs checking things out, not that he cared. The man was a kid in a candy store.

We made it down the stairs, through the kitchen and over to the front of the space.

"This wall is shared with Suda Kaye. We could tear through the wall here, and it would end up in her stock room. Out of the way, but easier access for you to get to your apartment without having to leave through the back or front door, go into her store and then up to the apartment."

"Okay, I guess. I mean, it's not really a big deal to me."

"You will feel differently when you need to show up at six a.m. and it's still dark outside."

I pursed my lips and thought about it. He wasn't wrong. The back didn't seem scary in the daylight, but it could if I was by myself. A woman could never be too careful. At least that was what my fathers drilled into me at a young age.

Kyson walked over to the space near the open windows. "Now, expand your mind a little. If we opened up this wall between the bakery and Gypsy Soul, maybe two doors wide, you could come and go easily. The door to your apartment is actually closer to the front. Though it's kind of hidden since she's painted it the same color as the dark walls."

"Wouldn't that be weird? Having our spaces connected?"

He lifted a shoulder. "Would it? I mean, you'd have more time to go back and forth and chat, but also her patrons and yours could come and go between the stores. Meaning, you might catch some of hers and she yours. When they're standing in line to get a dessert, they might see a purse or dress they like. And her customers will smell your goodies and maybe get hungry for a treat."

"Wow. That is pretty brilliant." I tapped on my chin as I thought about being able to easily gab with Suda Kaye or dash up to my apartment for whatever reason.

"We'd have to discuss with her, but I'm guessing easier access to her long-lost sister will make her happy. There's also the issue of suggesting it to the building owner, which is why I brought it up now. We could make that part of negotiations if this is truly the place you want. And as long as the space can be easily repaired if one or both of you leave and he has to lease again, you can put it in writing that you'd be willing to fix the breezeway if needed."

"Sounds like you know your stuff."

"I've been doing this a while." He smiled.

"Oh, yeah?" I said, but it came out breathy.

He stepped closer to me, lifted his hand and cupped my neck with his big, warm palm. "Yeah. There's a lot I would like to tell you about me, things I could show you even…"

I held my breath as he dipped his head closer to my face. "Really?"

His eyes lit up. "Yeah, if you agree to go out with me Thursday night, I'll tell you anything you want to know."

I closed my eyes and pressed my chin to my chest.

He squeezed my neck. "What are you afraid of?"

"No strings. No attachments. Just fun. That's what you wanted with Suda Kaye, right?" I took a chance telling him the truth.

He dropped his hand and I missed its warmth instantly. "You're not Suda Kaye. And a lot has changed in a year."

"You made out with my sister. And now you want to date me. Said to my face that you wanted to kiss me."

"I do. Very much so." He took another step closer and I lifted my head to stare into his cerulean-blue eyes. They were dreamy, watery pools and I wanted to wade into them.

"And what about Suda Kaye?"

He frowned. "What about her? We kissed…once. I'm not gonna lie and say it wasn't good. It was. At the time it was fun. She's a cool girl with a quirky Janis Joplin vibe I like. I went for it. Cam went for it. He won. I didn't even try to stand in their way. They were meant to be—I could tell the second they got back together. And, Isa, I was perfectly okay with it. There were no expectations. But if I get my shot to kiss a beautiful woman and the time is right, I'm gonna take it and enjoy that experience for what it is. A great freakin' kiss with a beautiful woman who I'm now friendly with. That's it. No more, no less. Are you going to let that one experience color the opportunity for something that might be magic between us?"

"Magic?"

"Honestly, I don't know. The second I laid eyes on you, I wanted to get to know you more. I haven't felt that feeling in a long, long time."

"A year ago…with my sister."

He sighed. "Not exactly. There's something else. Something I want to explore. And I'm asking you to take a leap of faith and go out to dinner. I'm not asking you to jump in my bed, sweetheart. Dinner. A stroll. Who knows? We may find we don't suit each other at all and that's okay. If so, you'll get a nice dinner and a friend out of it. What's the worst that could happen?"

My nerves tingled and butterflies took flight in my stomach. I knew what I had to do.

"Okay."

"Okay?" He tilted his head and focused on me. "As in, okay you'll go out with me?"

I nodded. "Thursday. Should I dress up?"

He grinned wide. "You can wear what you want but I planned on a nice place. A dress on those curves would not go unappreciated."

I giggled. Yep, like a little girl. "You're on."

He leaned forward with his hand curled around my hip and pressed his lips to my cheek. "I'm looking forward to spending time alone with you."

It took everything I had in me not to shiver but I didn't

want him knowing how much his nearness affected me. I heard feet clomping down the stairs. I stepped back and Kyson reversed a full two feet, bringing his clipboard up in front of him.

"In order for me to give you a good idea of the cost, we need to discuss what you plan on doing with decor, and the sizing of the ovens and additional equipment my team will need to put in place. However, the biggest expense is going to be the wiring, and the kitchen tiling and cabinetry. The space is better off than I thought it was, especially for what you're planning on using it for." He handed me his clipboard and it showed a series of expenditures for wiring, tiling, labor, paint and some empty spots for the expenses depending on the ovens.

"I'll need to get onto the roof to check out the exhausts and other things once I know what your equipment will entail. Can you send me over detailed information about the ovens, sinks, fridges and anything else you can think of?"

I nodded.

"Now, what were you thinking for this space?" He waved his arm in the emptiness before us. I went over the L-shaped display, the saloon doors, our color scheme, and he reminded me about storage and shelving and other things that would be important.

Once Jasper was done drooling over the apartment, we agreed to go over to Suda Kaye's to chat privately and check out her apartment.

We told the property manager we were definitely interested and would be in touch. Since the place hadn't been bitten on in a year, things were looking good. We hoped we could score it and all of the furniture in the apartment for a song.

Now I had a potential business location, a name and a date for Thursday night.

Colorado was turning out to be one of the best decisions I'd ever made.

nine

―――――――

"Suda Kaye, I swear to God, you think my booty is the same size as yours! No, Evie's. She has a tiny bum. Me, I've got serious junk in the trunk and it's not squeezing into this speck of fabric!" I grumbled as I shifted my body left and right as the napkin-size dress clung to my voluptuous tush.

My sister narrowed her gaze with her head tipped to the side and focused purely on my ass. "Huh. They really said one size fits all…" She frowned.

"And you believed it?" I finally pushed the damn dress down my thighs and let it fall to my ankles. There was no way on God's green earth that I was getting the thing back over my boobs. It had been hard enough shoving it past them the first time. "One size has never in a million years fit all," I huffed.

"That's bad advertising. I'm not going to buy from this seller." She pouted prettily and I shook my head.

I flung the dress onto the bed. A bed that was now mine,

in an apartment I was now renting from my half sister that sat above her boutique. I dug through the various items and found a pair of wide-legged, low-waisted black trouser slacks. They had a large cuff on the bottom and screamed sexy sailor business chic.

"Oooh, those are hot." She moved around the bed and grabbed a shimmery tank in a deep eggplant. "This will look amazing with it."

"Will it fit these?" I cupped my double Ds. Suda Kaye was stacked. She might be a D-cup herself, but Evie was barely scratching at a B.

She sighed. "Yes, Izzy, I've been in this business a while now and I'm very familiar with these brands. I just wanted you to try that one dress on because it looked sexy as all get-out in the catalog and they had a curvy girl in it. False advertisement to the extreme. I'm going to make a complaint." She flopped onto the messy, clothes-covered bed as I slipped on the trousers.

They fit like a dream. I turned around in the mirror and Suda Kaye whistled. "Your ass looks awesome in those," she breathed.

I grinned and ran my hands over my tush. "It does, doesn't it? Woo-hoo! We've got a winner." I glanced at the clock. "Shoot, he'll be here in twenty."

"Crapola!" My sister grabbed the top and tossed it at me, and I tugged it over my head. It fell into a cowl neck, framing my cleavage nicely. "Excellent!" She popped up and grabbed a bunch of sparkly bracelets and a pair of matching dangling earrings.

I put them on, yanked out my loose bun and shook my hair. I'd done the full hair treatment today, making sure my waves were well-defined and had it going on. My dark auburn locks fell over my shoulders.

"You are so beautiful, Izzy. Mom would gush over your beauty. She always pointed out redheads when we had our time with her." She stared off as though she was remembering something. "We'd be at the park and she'd see a mom with red hair and her redheaded daughter and point. 'Look at those pretty girls. I sure love redheads. So unique,' she'd say." Suda Kaye smiled. "Now I know why she was fascinated with redheads," she murmured sadly.

"Hey, it's okay, you know. To feel weird about all of this. Me being here. Living in your old apartment. Moving to Colorado and invading your life…"

Suda Kaye jumped up and grabbed my hands. "It's not weird at all. It's like getting a new piece of my mom I never had. And then of course there's Ian…"

I smiled softly at her. "Have you two been talking?" I asked.

She nodded. "It's a little strained because he wants so badly to know everything about me right now and that's kind of impossible. Especially from a distance. Though Cam said he'd take me to Chicago so we could get to know him and Casey a little better. Or we could host them here, which I figured would be more fun for you."

"My papa is love personified. If he commits to you, he's loyal for life. And from what he told me, you're this huge mystery that he already loves with his whole heart but doesn't know how to earn that love in return. It's hard for him because he was raised in foster care. He never had a family until my dad Casey and me. He wants to pack the last almost twenty-nine years of what he missed of your life into one month. Want my advice?"

She nodded.

"Just give what you can. Be honest with him. Tell him it's weird for you to try and give him the years he lost but want to look to the future and focus on the years you have ahead of you."

"That's good advice," she whispered. "I mean, it's not like I don't want to get to know him. I want that more than anything, but he always seems so eager for any little tidbit of information. Never wants to talk about himself, just learn everything about me. Sometimes I feel like I'm being interviewed for a job." She laughed.

I chuckled. "He can be intense. Just remember it's all wrapped around love. And of course, if it gets too much, you talk to me and I'll get on his case and set him straight." I grinned.

She smiled and pulled me into her arms. "I'm glad you're here. It's so easy being around you. Caring about you. Like we've always been sisters."

My throat dried up and my nose tingled with the anticipation of tears, but I pushed them down and hugged her back. "I'm happy to be here, too."

There was a knock on my door. "Shit! He's here." I dashed around Suda Kaye and into the bathroom to spritz my hair so the curls stayed, then layered on the lip gloss. I also didn't have my heels on. "Will you get the door?" I hollered.

"On it!" she said from right behind me, her hands stretched out with a pair of my strappy heels. They were amazing. Four-inch platforms with a wide, two-inch strap that ran across the toe, and rounded-off metal studs punched into the leather, making them look not only sexy but dangerous as well.

I stood in front of the mirror and took in my appearance. Sultry, dark eye shadow, pink highlighted cheeks, a peachy mauve gloss that made my lips look juicy and a little wet. My hair was wild but in a way that said daring and sexy, not hoochie and unkempt. I turned from side to side and decided, *this was me*. He either liked what he saw or not since I had no plans of changing. Not for a man, not for anyone. Something I think my mother would approve of greatly as she lived as the woman she wanted to be, in the short number of years she had.

Taking a full breath, I opened the bathroom door and saw Kyson, ass to a stool in the small kitchen area. He looked distinguished in a pair of dark gray slacks and a pristine white dress shirt open at the collar, which gifted me a good gander at his tanned neck. He was head down, eyes to his phone, when I took a couple steps into the room. Suda Kaye was gone.

I smiled as his head lifted and his gorgeous blue-eyed gaze met mine. My breath caught in my throat, but I swallowed it down, put my hands out to the sides and spun around in a jaunty circle. "Will this do for dinner tonight?"

His gaze turned white-hot. "Come here, Isa."

Isa.

I closed my eyes. Man, I loved it when he called me Isa in that deep, growly timbre.

When I made it to him, he stood, curved one hand at my neck and one at my hip, then dipped his head. For a mere moment I thought he was going to kiss me and was surprised at my disappointment when he spoke instead.

"You are an out of this world beauty. And honey, you could be wearing a paper sack and I'd still think you were the most stunning woman I'd ever laid my eyes on."

I gasped and stared deeply into his eyes. I put my hand to his chest. "You're joking…"

He shook his head. "Not even close. You'll learn when I'm being funny and when I'm holding on to my restraint with everything I have."

"Restraint?"

"In not taking your mouth and seeing exactly what the lip gloss tastes like on my tongue. I can smell it and just that is making my mouth water."

My eyes widened and I lost my ability to speak.

He grinned, leaned forward and pressed the side of his scruffy cheek to mine. I inhaled, smelling the woodsy and earthy cologne that had a hint of citrus to it, and clung to his form as he invaded my space. I shivered as I felt his breath caress my ear. "Never doubt you're a beautiful woman, Isa. I can tell you every man that sees you walk by will be wishing they were me."

His cheek rubbed along mine and he laid a soft kiss at the corner of my mouth. I could just move my head and he'd be there, right *there*. Close enough to kiss. And I wanted to; oh, boy, I wanted to, yet I had to get my hormones under control. Sure, there was an attraction there, but I wasn't just out for a good time. I'd had Mr. Good Time, more than one of him, in fact. Even though they were fun, they were not what I wanted long-term. Kyson, he had bad boy written all over him, though it was his sweet, forward, unfiltered nature I was attracted to. That and his ridiculous body, pretty eyes and the way he filled out a pair of jeans better than any model I'd seen. He was smokin' hot.

He grinned smugly as he ran his hand from my neck, to my shoulder and down my arm, until he grasped my hand. "You ready?"

I nodded and reached out and grabbed the small purse that I'd left on the counter.

"I was going to take you to a swanky joint, but I figured you'd been in town only a few days so a pub would be a lot more fun. They have awesome steak, seafood and pasta, too, but it's a livelier atmosphere. Nothing too stuffy."

"I'm not a stuffy kind of girl. Lead on. I can find a good

time in just about any environment and I'm a chef. You can't be a chef and be a picky eater. At least that's what my fathers say."

"Fathers?"

I took his hand, laughing, and let him lead me out my door, which I locked, and then followed him down the stairs. "I'll tell you at the restaurant." We entered Gypsy Soul and saw Suda Kaye at the register, ringing up a customer. "Bye, Suda Kaye." I waved.

"Bye, sis! Have fun!" she hollered.

When we got outside Kyson opened the passenger door to a white work truck with a big square Turner Brothers Construction logo on the side. The inside of his truck surprisingly smelled and looked clean. Even the floor had vacuum lines as if he'd run it through the car wash.

I smiled. "Did you just clean your car for me?"

He folded into his seat and put his seat belt on. "Yep." He answered right away, no bullshit. "Didn't want your outfit to get all dusty. My job is pretty dirty, but this is my primary vehicle. So even though I did clean it for you, it's something I do regularly."

His honesty was astounding and welcome.

"Though I thought about picking you up on my bike."

My eyes widened. "You ride a motorcycle."

He nodded. "Have for years. Love the open road. It's something I share with my brothers and my pops. He's a member of the local motorcycle club. They own a garage in downtown Denver."

"Are you a member of this club?" I rolled my mind around the word *club*, trying to remember if motorcycle clubs were more like gangs. I watched *Sons of Anarchy* for a full season and hoped that was pure fiction because those dudes were scary. Good-looking, but still frightening, and it seemed like they were always getting in trouble with the law.

He shook his head. "Nah. One of my brothers is. Pops is deep in the club. Vice president. My brother Vincent has his eyes on being in that role one day."

"And you?"

"Honestly, don't have the time. Between my business and uh, other things, I can't commit to something that involved. They're a brotherhood. Most of them work together, ride together, spend a lot of time at the clubhouse carousing and having a good time. They even do a lot of charity work. We're friendly with each other, but it's not the same. They are a family of brothers. Would eat, bleed and die for one another."

"Makes sense. And you said brothers plural?"

He lifted his chin as he pulled into the parking lot of a restaurant called Bryant Brews & Grill. "Lincoln and I work together. He owns twenty-five percent of Turner Brothers and is working up to owning fifty."

"Is he like you?"

He grinned and shook his head. "Actually, no. In looks, a little. Personality, absolutely not." He pulled into a parking space maneuvering the big, four-door work truck as though it were a small, two-door sports car. "Actually, he's got a tough personality."

I tipped my head, unhooked my belt and turned to the side. "How so?"

"Suda Kaye calls him grumpy. And it's probably good we get this out of the way now, in case there's an issue. When Suda Kaye had me renovating, there was a little scene where my brother misinterpreted our relationship. Then Cam entered the picture and Lincoln got a little mouthy. Cam fired him from the job and rightfully so."

"Yikes. What'd he say?"

He shook his head. "It doesn't matter. It was a year ago. But what does matter is that he'll be working on your bakery. He's a good guy, and a very hard worker. Fast. I trust him implicitly. We have a few guys working with us, but they're already on other jobs. My preference is to work with my brother on jobs that are more intricate or personally important to me because we have the same work brain. And for you, I want the best."

I smiled wide, reached out a hand and placed it on top of his where it sat on the seat. He interlaced our fingers. "That's sweet. I've got no problem with a grumpy construction guy. I can deal with most people."

He licked his lips and I watched, fascinated. "You're not my concern. You see, Linc, he's uh, not into the ladies, if you get my drift."

"Oh," I said.

"Yeah, and uh, Jasper is a wildcard."

I frowned, thinking that he was about to say something hurtful about my best friend, who was admittedly a wildcard as he put it, but he was the best human I knew. I tried to pull my hand out of Kyson's, instantly feeling my blood heat.

He gripped my hand and shook his head.

"If you're about to insinuate something about Jasper, we should just end this right here…" I started to defend my best friend.

"Isa, honey, you've got it all wrong. What I'm trying to say is that he's Lincoln's type. Wild. Forward. A bit feminine."

"And this is a problem because…?" I was lost. Totally. Had no idea where he planned to go with this line of conversation.

"Linc might hit on him. Repeatedly. Things could get uncomfortable," he said with a serious sigh.

I stared into his handsome face, noted his worried gaze

and burst out laughing. It rolled through me like a tidal wave and sounded exceptionally loud inside the cab of the truck. I laughed so hard I pushed at his chest and then fell forward until my head rested against his neck and even then, I kept right on laughing my butt off until I couldn't breathe.

He held on to me tentatively at first, then rubbed his hand up and down my back. "Uh, I'm guessing this is not something I should be concerned with?"

Eventually, I pulled my head back, flipped my hair out of my face and dabbed at my watering eyes with my knuckles. "Lincoln making Jasper uncomfortable by hitting on him. That's rich. I can't wait to tell my fathers that. It will have them rolling on the floor!" I half laughed, half hiccoughed, trying my best to get myself under wraps and failing miserably.

Finally, I shook my head and pressed my hand once more to his chest. "Don't worry about Jasper. If he doesn't want your brother's attentions, he will let it be known. I am not at all concerned about it. And if they hit it off, rock on. Jasper's been griping for months about not having a man in his life. If your brother digs him, and Jasper likes his attention, cool. More power to them."

Kyson grinned. "You're a pretty easygoing woman, Isabeau. I like it. A lot." He left it at that and opened the truck door. He came around the front before I even had my purse from the floorboard. He opened my door for me and held out his hand so I could steady myself while getting down from his tall truck.

He led me into the pub, which was hopping for a Thursday night. He must have made a reservation because the hostess led us straight to a more private section in the back that was cordoned off from the buzzing open bar. The main space had sports on the TV and multiple family booths in the large opening. Smart business to have an option for the couples wanting some space from the rowdy crowd or the happy families.

We sat on opposite sides of the booth and scanned the menus. I noted the grill actually sold the beer they made. "I have a quirk," I announced while pressing the menu to my chest so I could see Kyson. "If I go to a restaurant for the first time, I usually order whatever is the chef's special and definitely order the local beer, wine, or spirit that they make in-house."

"I've actually tasted the Bryant Brew, and it's amazing. Porter Bryant is a good guy. Owns the place."

"Wait… Bryant? Like Camden?"

He smiled. "They're brothers. Thought it might be nice to take you to one of my favorite places that also has some ties to your family."

"Awesome!"

When the waiter came back, Kyson asked him to tell Porter that we were here, and then we both ordered the house brew and the chef's special without even asking what it was. I liked surprises and I liked food. My palate was vast. There was very little I wouldn't eat or at the very least try, and not many things I didn't like. Which had worked great for my parents because they were total foodies, too.

"Tell me about your fathers, plural. And why you're a long-lost sister to Suda Kaye and Evie."

I went over the main details. That Catori was basically an egg donor and surrogate for my fathers, who were married and deeply in love. I was raised without the knowledge of who Catori was my entire life, at her demand. I also explained that I hadn't known I had sisters, and that my father Ian was Suda Kaye's biological father so all three of us, me, Suda Kaye and Evie had the same mother but different fathers.

"It's as fascinating as it is twisted up. That had to be hard on you, learning about them due to your stepfather's inheritance."

"Huh. I never thought of Adam Ross that way, but I guess if I had known him when he was alive, that's exactly what he'd be."

"You would have had three dads!"

We both chuckled and it lightened up the heaviness of what I'd just shared.

"And how are you adjusting to your first week in Colorado?"

I shrugged. "So far, so good. I mean, I can't really complain. I've got my best friend in the world with me. We're opening up our dream bakery. I was given a bucket load of money to do it and I'm getting to know two amazing women who I genuinely like and would be friends with even if we weren't related."

"Has to be hard, though, leaving your home and your parents?"

I traced the edge of my beer bottle and flicked at the label until there was an edge I could shred. "Yeah, it is. But I've got a lot of support. I miss my dad and papa, but kids grow up and leave. We have to—otherwise we'd be mooching off our parents our entire lives."

He chuckled. "This is true. I definitely still count on my mom for a lot more than I'd like to."

"Such as?" I questioned and was surprised to see his expression change from jovial to blank in a second flat.

Before I could ask what that was all about, our food arrived. We both looked at the steaming plates of steak with sides of pasta and huge, juicy-looking prawns in a cream sauce with some grilled asparagus on the side.

My lips tilted up and I lifted my fork. "See, you took a ride on the wild side and look what gifts were bestowed. That is, of course, if you like steak and prawns."

"Hell to the yes, I do. I've never even seen this on the menu," Kyson said with awe.

The waiter smiled and pressed his hands together. "It isn't. The chef found out you wanted to know what he was making and felt inspired to make you something he fancied. This was the result," he chirped after setting down a bottle of red wine we hadn't ordered and two glasses. "Enjoy!"

"Apparently, the chef wants us to pair the wine with the meal." I grinned.

Kyson poured us each a glass and we dug in. All conversation ceased until we'd both gotten a good quarter of our food into our gullets.

"Damn, this is probably the best meal I've ever had." Kyson wiped his mouth with his napkin.

I smiled around a mouthful of creamy, delicious pasta. "Mmm-hmm. Just wait until I cook for you. I'll blow your mind, baby," I teased.

His gaze jetted up to mine and his eyes flashed with desire. "I'll be looking forward to having my mind blown... amongst other things."

My mouth dropped open in shock and then his eyes widened, as he must have realized how what he said sounded.

He lifted his hand and waved. "No, Isa, I didn't mean it that way..."

Kyson looked miserable as I began laughing almost as hard as I did in the car. "You should see your face. Freaked you way the heck out!" I taunted and cut another savory chunk of perfectly cooked steak and plopped it in my mouth. "You're so easily riled."

He shook his head. "Normally, I'm not."

"Well, chill out. I'm not easily offended, especially when I know a person's intentions."

"For that, I am grateful." He smirked.

We finished up our meal, chatting a little bit about our families. I told him my dad was an architect and my papa owned his own landscaping business. I already knew his dad worked at the auto mechanic garage the motorcycle club owned, and his mother was an accountant, who worked free-lance from her home. My guess was that his mom did his books for Turner Brothers, but he never clarified why he felt his mom did a lot for him and I didn't pry. I found out that he owned his own home and had been in business for six years. Also, he shared that he was thirty and had graduated college at the University of Colorado with a business degree. Of course, I shared bits and pieces of my past as well as de-tails about my culinary degrees and my time abroad learning under people my industry considered masters.

After finishing our food, we left our table and headed to the bar area where he introduced me to a game I'd never played before called shuffleboard.

"This is so fun!" I squealed and pushed the blue circular disc down the long, sand-covered table. It smacked right into one of his red discs. Mine pushed his off and over the side of the table to the cubby area that meant it was out or fouled.

"You *would* think it's fun since you've been kicking my ass." He came up behind me and pressed his front against my back and reached around me with one of his discs, keep-ing me wedged in place and incapable of moving. Not that I wanted to, because the hot guy pressing up against me was well…pleasurable.

He leaned his face over the crook of my shoulder, put one of his hands on my hip and squeezed as he lined up his move to take out one of my discs.

"Um, I'm not quite sure this is how you play?" My voice was deeper, sultrier, than I intended.

He nuzzled my neck and inhaled before placing a kiss there that ended with a featherlight tongue touch. "I think this is *exactly* how to play the game, Isa."

I reached around to put my hand over his on my hip and leaned back against him. His face was close to mine, in easy kissing distance. I licked my lips and he watched me do so, leaning closer until we almost touched.

"Hey, Kyson!" I heard a man's voice approaching.

Kyson turned his head automatically and the spell was broken. Dammit.

He let me go and reached out a hand. The tall, dark and—it had to be said—handsome guy shook his hand and clapped him on the shoulder. "Haven't seen you in here since you came with Hope. What was that, at least a few months ago? Brother, you can't go that long before visiting."

Hope.

Kyson stiffened at the mention of her. I assumed she was a woman from his recent past.

My heart sank but I straightened my spine and moved around Kyson and waved at the good-looking guy who resembled Camden, except his hair and eyes were dark to Cam's light.

"You must be Isabeau. Good to meet you. I'm Porter. The entire fam has heard so much about you from Suda Kaye. She's been gushing about your beauty and how sweet you are for the past couple months."

I smiled and shook his hand. "Aw, that's nice of her. And you have a great place here, Porter. The food was to die for."

Kyson wrapped an arm around my waist and tugged me to his side in a rather territorial move I wouldn't have expected. "And she'd know as she's a chef," he said with a hint of pride.

Porter rubbed a hand over his unshaven jaw. "That's right. Cam mentioned you were a chef, but he said you were focused on desserts if I remember correctly."

I nodded. "It's my passion. I'm actually opening up a bakery with my best friend right next to Suda Kaye's store. Kyson here will be doing the renovation."

"I see that. And it looks like he's also mixing business and pleasure," he jabbed good-naturedly.

My cheeks heated as Kyson responded, "Hey, when a stunning, smart and sweet redhead enters your sphere, you toss out any archaic rules about not mixing business with pleasure and take a shot at the opportunity in front of you."

I gripped his biceps and leaned my head against him, wanting him to know I liked what he said about me and appreciated that he shared his feelings.

"Can't blame you one bit. I'm just sorry I didn't meet you first." He winked at me and I laughed. "I'll send over another round of brews on the house."

"None for me. I'm driving. Safety first, man."

He nodded.

"None for me, either." I prodded a finger at Kyson's very hard chest. "Have to keep my wits about me," I teased.

Kyson waved Porter off and smirked. Once again, I wanted to kiss those beautiful lips. They were mesmerizing.

"I'm thinking we should uh…" He licked his lips and I swear I could feel the physical ache between my legs. I may have even whimpered a bit, something I had zero control over. "Take the, uh, walk downtown."

I grinned and pressed my body in front of his. He casually wrapped his arms around my waist and held me close as I looked up into his face. "Who's having trouble speaking now?" I stretched up, curled my hand around his neck and right at the last minute kissed his jaw. "Dinner was awesome. Thank you."

His nostrils flared and he ran his hands up and down my back. "We better go."

"I'm ready whenever you are." And I was more than ready. For him. For what could happen when we were finally alone.

Ready to break every single one of my rules.

ten

Kyson followed me up the stairs to my new studio apartment. We'd parked in the back and entered Suda Kaye's store from there. Once I unlocked the door I gestured to the space with a lift of my chin. "Would you like to come in for dessert? I baked homemade chocolate chip cookies today. Was planning on giving you some to take home as a thank-you for taking me out."

He grinned and nodded. "Sure, for a little bit."

The heat between us cooled off as we'd walked up and down Main Street. Kyson was an excellent host, pointing things out, showing me the places he liked to eat at and others he thought I might like to shop at. He'd held my hand the entire time and that alone had me swooning. It had been a while since a man I liked romantically held my hand, keeping me close and whispering little jokes or teases in my ear.

Beyond the restaurant where I'd almost kissed him twice, he'd been a perfect gentleman, not pushing for more physical intimacy other than enjoying a nighttime stroll down a pretty street with a woman he'd taken out on a date.

At that moment, though, his gaze came to mine and heated. The fire we banked on our walk started to spark and sizzle between us. I held the door open so he could lead me into the space and watched his sexy-as-all-get-out swagger ramp my desire up to scalding.

Suda Kaye's apartment was smaller, but far nicer than Jasper's in my opinion. The kitchen had been fully renovated so the granite countertops gleamed against the glass pendant lights that hung over the bar as I flicked them on. The couch was a three-seater and very comfortable, though I wanted to get a lounge chair and some of my own throw pillows and lay down rugs that would give the space a little bit more of my personality. Maybe I'd hunt around the local shops we'd seen tonight to see if I could find any wall hangings that struck my fancy. Add a lamp or two. Normal things anyone would want to purchase in order to make a space their own.

Of course, the first thing I'd unpacked were my personal cooking supplies. I'd absolutely need more pots and pans but what was there would be sufficient for now. Jasper and I would order extras for both of our homes when we put in our supply order for the bulkier items.

When I opened the fridge to see about drinks, I felt Kyson come up behind me and wrap his arm around my waist. He nuzzled his chin at the side of my neck and goose bumps trailed down my arms at his touch.

"Isa, I'm not hungry." He trailed his nose along my neck, and I stretched it out to the side, giving him better access. I closed the fridge door and allowed myself to enjoy his warmth and presence against my back.

"I thought you wanted dessert?"

He hummed and I felt the timbre of that sound shoot straight down my body and curl my toes.

"Not hungry for food, sweetheart." He turned me around to face him and stepped forward until my back was flat against the fridge, his body plastered against mine. He curled his hand around my neck, lifting my chin with his thumb.

I stared into his eyes. His pupils were dilated and I lost my breath at the sheer desire coating those baby blues.

"Relax, baby. Just *breathe*..." He encouraged me in that low tone that made my heart pound and my nipples throb.

I shook my head. "I can't," I said breathily.

"Why not?" He ran his nose along mine in a light caress and I trembled in his arms.

"I want you too much," I admitted.

"Christ," he said before he slammed his lips down over mine.

I opened immediately, allowing him inside, glorying at the rich, heady taste of him. He held my head tipped to the side and took the kiss impossibly deeper, flattening his tongue along mine, flicking against the tip, teasing me by licking in and out the way I wanted him to repeat on me in other, more *private* places.

For a long time we took from one another. One moment he led, the next I did. The hand at my hip ran down and cupped my tush, pulling me higher and tighter against his body. I could feel the long, hard, rigid length of him against my stomach and it broke something open inside me. My skin felt hot, too hot. I wrapped my arms around him and tugged at his dress shirt where it tucked into his pants, fumbling until I got my hands on bare, warm, male skin.

He growled into my mouth and pulled us away from the fridge, hiking me up by the ass until I wrapped my legs around his waist, and he carried me out of the kitchen and to the bedroom. Once there, he brought me down by putting a knee to the bed and easing me carefully onto the soft surface.

His lips finally left my mouth and went straight for my neck. He licked the length from shoulder to ear and then nibbled there until I sighed. I put my hands back under his shirt and shoved it up as far as I could go. He got the hint and straddled my form up on his knees, while I watched. His eyes were all over me as I panted, waiting for him to remove each button, glorying at the new skin revealed with each release. To my displeasure, he also had one of those white ribbed tank tops on, adding another layer that needed to be removed. I reached out and yanked at it defiantly.

"Off," I demanded.

He grinned. "You first, honey."

Without even thinking twice I curled my fingers around the glittery tank, heaved my torso up and pulled the offending piece of material over my head, tossing it off the side of the bed. I was left in a dusky gray lace bra, my breasts heaving, nipples erect.

In what felt like a second flat, he lifted his tank and tossed it over his head, too, giving me only a moment's view of his broad, muscular chest before his face swooped down. He cupped both of my breasts with his hands and kissed me in my cleavage.

He pulled down one bra cup and thumbed the nipple until I cried out. "You have magnificent breasts, baby," Kyson said, awe coating his words before he swirled his tongue around one tip and then sucked…hard. I arched my back, curled my hand around his neck and fed more of my breast to him. I tunneled my hand into his thick hair and closed my eyes, letting the extreme pleasure flow in ribbons of ecstasy with every flick of his tongue.

Kyson moved to my other breast and gave that one as much time as the first until I was a gasping, throbbing mess of need.

"Please, Ky," I moaned and dug my nails into his shoulders while he sucked relentlessly at my nipples. My legs were restless, running up and down the sides of his, my center aching for something, *anything*, just more. More of him. More of whatever would feed this burn inside me.

He lifted his head and gifted me the sexiest grin I'd ever seen on a man. As though he were a kid in a candy store, and I was his favorite treat.

"Baby, I'm a serious breast man, but I'm eager for a taste of something else sweet." One of his eyebrows cocked and the corresponding grin melted me to liquid fire instantly.

My heart pounded and the little wanton woman hidden inside me came out cheering when he palmed my breasts, tweaked both nipples simultaneously and ran his tongue between them, over my rounded stomach and straight to the edge of my trousers. He unbuckled the clasp with his teeth.

With. His. Teeth.

I'd never seen that done before, but the man was a master at it. Fast and skilled, he had the button undone and the zipper down with his nose nuzzling my lace panties.

I lifted my hips and he tugged at my trousers, bringing them just far enough down my thighs so he could put his mouth on my soaked panties, and he did. He pressed his nose and mouth right where my clit was and sucked at the fabric. I held on to his hair and lifted, trying to get more, to take all he was offering.

Out of nowhere an annoying, blaring sound clanged from his back pocket.

"Fuck!" he growled and rested his cheek against my pubic bone and breathed deep. Air left his mouth and stirred the exposed skin of my hips. The alarm went off again.

"What is that? A call?"

He shook his head and pushed off me until he was on his knees. He brought the phone from his pocket and hit a couple buttons, then to my absolute shock, backed away from my body until he was off the bed.

"Isa, baby, you're gonna hate this but definitely not more than me. Honey, I gotta go." His beautiful, muscular shoulders slumped at his admission.

There I lay, the cups of my bra pushed under my giant knockers, breasts flapping in the breeze, his saliva cooling on the tips as he spoke and…he had to go. My trousers were pushed down over my hips, my panties wet not only from our activity but from his mouth, and *he had to go*?

"Go? I don't understand." My once heated skin cooled as if I'd been blasted with an avalanche of snow.

He closed his eyes, curled his hands into fists and swallowed as though it was taking extreme effort not to jump on the bed and go back to what we were doing. Which would have been my vote and the absolute right choice.

"I'm sorry, I can't. I gotta get home. I didn't expect for things to get this outta hand…" His words were tortured as was the expression on his handsome face.

I frowned, lifted my hips and pulled my trousers back up. I rolled over so my back faced him as I covered my chest. I sidestepped off the bed and saw my robe dangling on the counter of the bureau. I grabbed it with shaky fingers and tucked my arms into it. Behind me I could hear Kyson shuffling around for his clothes.

"Isa, seriously, if I really didn't have to go, wild horses wouldn't be able to keep me away from you. I just… Shit, I can't get into it right now. It's my alarm, meaning it's eleven and I have to get home. I'll uh, explain later…"

I spun around, lifted my chin and held the robe lapels up

at my neck to ensure every horrified naked inch of me was covered. "You'll tell me later? Why not now?"

He shook his head and put his arms through his dress shirt, the discarded tank twisted in one of his fists. He left the buttons open so I could still see his golden chest on display. My mouth watered at the sight of the smattering of dark hair sprinkled across his pecs and running a line down the center of his cut abdominals where it got thicker, dipping into his pants. I had very much hoped to see the rest, free of his pants, and run my fingers through all that beautiful fuzz but no, he had to go.

"Is it me? Did I…do something wrong?" My bottom lip trembled, and he stomped over to where I stood. He curled a hand around my cheek and lifted my jaw.

"You are by far the most perfect woman. Never doubt that. Every kiss, every touch of your hand, set me on fire, baby. I'm burning for you." His gaze held mine and I could see the sincerity, but it was in direct conflict with his actions and that did not make sense.

"Then why are you going?" My words were small, wounded.

He sighed and closed his eyes, pressing his forehead to mine. "There's still much to learn about me. And I hope to share those things, but right now I can't. I'm already late. I *have* to go…"

I nodded, trying to hold on to the emotions that were ready to burst free in a deluge of tears and uncertainty the second he left.

Until he dipped his head and kissed me—hard, fast and with enough of his tongue that I started to lose myself in him again, and then he regrettably pulled away.

"Can I take you out this weekend? I have to work Friday and Saturday but how about Sunday brunch?"

He was asking me out again. So I definitely didn't do something wrong; he just really had to go. I just wished he'd tell me why instead of leaving me to my own devices, which will ultimately lead to a full freak out and the consumption of a gallon of Ben & Jerry's ice cream. Cherry Garcia was the best at soaking up sorrow and heartache, and I had a brand-new gallon in my freezer.

"Only if you let me cook for you," I said, not believing my own response. What in the heck was wrong with me?

He grinned and shook his head. "Definitely not like any woman I've ever known. Thank God." He kissed me briefly. "Sunday brunch here works perfect. I'll make sure we're not interrupted." I pursed my lips. "Thank you for a great evening, Isa," he murmured before letting me go and heading for the door.

"Oh, wait…"

"Baby, I really gotta go," he said again, his voice strained.

I dashed to the kitchen counter where I had a Tupperware tub filled with large, chunky, chocolate chip cookies. "I made them for you," I whispered, and he smiled, taking the tub.

"My sweet Isabeau. Thank you, honey. Now lock this behind you. I'll text you tomorrow and we'll decide a time for Sunday."

I followed him out the door of the apartment and watched him head down the stairs. Suda Kaye's door to the back had an auto-lock mechanism so I didn't need to follow him out. When he hit the bottom, he turned and waved. "I had an amazing time. Best date I've been on."

"Me, too." I wiggled my fingers and stepped back into my apartment, shutting the door and locking it. I rested my back against the door and tried desperately to wrap my head around the past ten minutes.

What in the world had just happened?

★ ★ ★

Jasper pushed an overflowing cart down the aisle at Bed
Bath & Beyond. We were shopping for towels, linens, house-
wares and everything else we'd need to start a new life in our
new homes. We were mainly shopping for Jasper, since I had
what Suda Kaye left. The kitchen and bathroom in his place
were completely empty. When we first moved in a couple
days ago, I'd given him some of what Suda Kaye had so he
wouldn't be missing any essentials. Now we were loading up.

"I don't understand. The man had you half-naked, panting and willing." Jasper reiterated what I'd told him.

"Mmm-hmm," I agreed.

"And you were breaking your six-dates-to-sex rule for
him, and he got up when things were getting good and
just…left."

My stomach twisted into knots. "Yep."

"And he gave you no indication he wasn't into what you
were doing?"

I nodded and leaned my arms over my cart and pushed
it next to his while we walked down the linens aisle. Definitely not the most fun part of the store, which was why
we'd tackled the necessities first. Because the second Jasper
and I hit the cookware all hell was gonna break loose. We
loved buying kitchen items and could easily spend a full day
in that section alone.

He pursed his lips and stopped his cart, putting a hand
at his hip, his long fingers curling around a pair of sienna-
colored jeans. On his feet were kick-ass motorcycle boots
that I very much wished were in my size in the event I could
wear them when riding on the back of Kyson's motorcycle.
If I ever got the chance.

My shoulders slumped farther toward the cart. I hoped I
got the chance.

Jasper wore a black stretchy tee that had a big white diagonal stripe slanted across the front that molded to his athletic, lean, yet still muscular build. His frosted blond hair was in a faux hawk and in one ear was a long, dangling silver arrow earring. As always, he looked fabulous and he knew it.

"If a guy I was into was shirtless, his pants undone and I had my mouth over the cotton of his secret treasure, there would be no way in hell I'd be torn away for any reason," he stated rather dramatically.

I shrugged and even that movement ached. "Maybe he's just not that into me. Maybe he thinks I'm a hoochie who gives it up on the first date and now isn't interested."

Jasper guffawed and made a snort-like noise. "Puh-leeze. Every man that looks at you thinks you're the cat's meow. Babe, I keep telling you this. You're ridiculously gorgeous with a body that doesn't quit. Men like that type of thing. I know this. I'm a man. Albeit a gay man but even I know when a woman is all that and a bag of chips. A person would have to be dead to not find you incredibly appealing inside and out. Please, please, please, don't even go there because, honey, it vexes me."

That time I made a snorty noise. "Vexes you?"

His face lit up. "I've been reading one of the old romance novels on the bookshelf that was left in my place and the hero uses words like *vexes* and *arse* and *fortnight*. It's fabulous. I'll give it to you after I'm done. I need to find out if Lord Hemingford nails down Countess Beatrice and they get their happily-ever-after."

I laughed. "Either way, I don't know what to think, Jas. I've never been in this predicament before."

He nodded and started to push his cart again over to the bathroom section. I yawned. Borrrrriiiiingg. Me, I just picked the first thing that caught my eye, which was a seahorse-shaped liquid soap dispenser. It was a rainbow of colors and I thought it was funny. I put it in my cart along with two yellow towels, two bright blue and two rose-colored ones. I figured why not be bright and cheery. It was a bathroom.

Jasper, however, spent a good, long time assessing every possible theme and then mixing them up, creating the perfect collage of colors, materials, shapes and sizes that would not only be interesting to look at when you were taking care of your bathroom business, they would also show how much attention to detail he gave to his belongings.

I looked down at my lonely seahorse and boring towels. Maybe that was my problem. Kyson found me boring and uninteresting.

"There's also the issue of the mysterious Hope that Camden's brother Porter mentioned in passing. It's entirely possible that he's dating several women and I was just one in a line of them. It's not as though we agreed that we'd only date one another. We're nowhere near that type of commitment."

Jasper frowned and tapped at his chin. "True. I guess it could be possible, but then again it could be that the mysterious Hope is his sister or a friend that he likes to have casual dinners with. You don't know until you ask. Why didn't you ask?"

I lifted a shoulder. "It felt intrusive. If he wanted me to know about this woman, then he'd have told me. Porter didn't say the name conspiratorially or try to hide it in any way."

He pointed a jaunty finger at me. "Exactly. Which proves my point that it's likely not another woman he's seeing but someone who's just currently in his life."

"Like an ex," I surmised pitifully.

"Like an ex," Jasper repeated instantly and then winced. "Boooo. It actually could be an ex. That scenario does not fit into my 'happy hunk-a-licious Kyson for my bestie' world so I'm going to immediately kick that option to the curb."

I laughed and it perked me up a little from my foul mood. "I guess it's that it was embarrassing. I mean, here I was bearing all, *literally*, and he left me high and dry."

"Sounds like he left you wet and wanting." Jasper snorted.

"Jas!" I fired off and looked around to make sure that no one else was in hearing distance of our conversation.

"It's true."

"Be that as it may, I don't want you spreading that around willy-nilly. I'm already mortified."

He nodded.

"Well…?"

He sighed. "Well what?"

I groaned. "What would you do if you were me?"

Jasper tipped his head to the side and then walked over to me and put both of his hands on my shoulders. "Izzy, I'm not you. You're sweet and soft and kind. Your heart is bigger than anyone else's I know. Me, I'd blow him off. Find another hot guy and strut that man around in front of his face, showing him exactly what he left hanging out to dry."

I closed my eyes and the misery took over once again. "I really like him. Really, really, *really* like him."

His glossy lips pitched into a deep frown before he brought me into his arms. I wrapped mine around his waist as he spoke softly. "If you like him that much, you give him the benefit of the doubt. You said he sounded sincerely sorry and he'd explain at a later date. Let him. See if what he says fixes everything." He pulled back and grabbed a wayward lock of my hair between two of his fingers and eased it behind my ear. "Just don't get your hopes up, babe."

I inhaled full and deep and then let it out slowly. "Okay. That's good advice. I'll do that."

And just as he smiled and dipped forward and kissed my nose, my phone buzzed, announcing I had a text. I tugged the phone out of my small purse that I'd set on the kid seat in the cart and checked the display.

It was from Kyson.

Isa, looking forward to making things up to you at brunch. What time would you like me to be at your place? X Ky

Jasper must have noticed my smile and suddenly shaky hands because he nosed his way over and read the text from over my shoulder with zero qualms about invading my space or privacy. His mouth split into a huge smile.

"Looks like someone wants a better taste of my girl's charms," he teased.

I grinned and nudged his shoulder, the heaviness slipping away and excitement taking its place. It was Friday. I had two days before I'd see him again.

"Now we just have to make sure you make a meal that will knock his socks clean off. And his shirt. And his pants. Definitely his pants!" He waggled his eyebrows and I burst out into laughter. "I'm thinking we hit up Gypsy Soul for a new outfit, too."

"I have so many clothes now. Too many."

Jasper made a *"Pfft,"* sound. "You have a tenth of what I have, and I've been here a week and one day, the same as you. I don't have enough clothing, which means you have the bare minimum."

"We just picked up three outfits and I got another new one for my first date yesterday."

He shook his head and put his arm around my shoulders. "Izzy, Izzy, Izzy, have me and my mom taught you nothing? In order to feel your best, you need to look your best. If you want to hook hunk-a-licious Kyson Turner, you need to make the effort. And a sinfully sexy outfit will do just that."

I rolled my eyes. "Whatever." I could already feel my pocketbook going up in flames living above and working next door to a boutique.

"Don't worry. I spied the perfect outfit when I was in there yesterday."

"You hanging out with my sisters while I'm not there?" I nudged his shoulder playfully.

"Of course. What else am I supposed to do when you're gallivanting off into the sunset in a white quad cab work truck with Colorado's most handsome hunk?"

"Oh! I forgot to tell you something!" I blurted with unconcealed excitement.

He leaned forward and lowered his voice. "Is it juicy? Tell me it's juicy."

I grinned. "Well, Kyson…"

"Yeah?" He leaned his ear closer to my mouth.

"He has a brother. Actually, he has two brothers."

"Okay, and how is this juicy?" His brows knit together.

"One of them is gay and available." I mini-clapped, my enthusiasm getting the best of me.

He jerked back a few steps as though he'd been Tased. A hand over his heart. "You're kidding? All of that hotness in a blood relation that is also gay?"

"Definitely. And better yet…"

He waved in front of his face, cutting me off. "I don't know if I can handle *better*. My heart is already about to pound out of my chest, and I haven't even seen the man, but I've seen and drooled over Kyson. Any blood relation has to be hot as hell."

I nodded. "Kyson admitted he was worried because he believed that Lincoln would find you his type."

Jasper gasped and then shook his head and lifted his chin. "Well, of course he would, my darling. I'm everyone's type," he said with false smugness. "Tell me more."

I decided not to tell him the part that Camden fired him from the job because he got into it with him and Suda Kaye. It didn't really matter anyway.

"The only thing I know is that Suda Kaye called him Mr. Grumpy. I guess he's got a chip on his shoulder."

That admission did not deter my bestie in any way. He simply shrugged.

"Also, Kyson said he was worried he'd annoy you by hitting on you. Repeatedly." I snickered, loving every minute of that possibility, and hoping it came to fruition.

Jasper grinned wickedly. "Good thing for him I like a man who knows what he wants and goes after it. Especially if what he wants is *moi*!" He pointed to his chest.

"Figured you'd find this information yummy!"

"Looks like I'll be dressing to impress on Monday in order to take a gander at Mr. Grumpy, brother to hunk-a-licious."

"Just remember, this is Kyson's brother and one of our renovators. We have to be good."

"Oh, honey, you know me. If anything, I'm *always* good." He bumped my cart with his. "We got what we need. Let's move on to Heaven, otherwise known as cookware."

I laughed and pressed on. My heart much lighter, my stomach no longer twisted up. I was excited about brunch with Kyson and what that would entail. "Yes, let's."

eleven

A knock came at my door right after I'd just added the final dash of chopped parsley on top of the poached eggs I'd finished for the eggs benedict. The hollandaise was prepped and ready to heat. With a smile, I eased the dish into the oven to keep the eggs, ham and bread toasty warm. I'd already finished the fresh apricot, spinach, romaine, crumbled feta and almond salad to go with it, as well as the balsamic and olive oil dressing I put together to drizzle over the greens. I'd even prepared a raspberry lemon tart for dessert that paired amazingly well with the dry champagne I picked up.

Another knock and a muffled, "Isa, babe, it's me," came from the other side of the closed door.

I rushed over on bare feet. Even though this was a date, it was in my home. It wasn't a fancy dinner; it was brunch. Which, in my limited experience, wasn't cause for a full dress-up regardless of what Jasper claimed. If Kyson wanted to date me, he was going to get *me*. Isabeau "Izzy" Collins.

An easygoing chick who loved to laugh and enjoyed the hell outta life. I didn't want Kyson to see me pretending to be someone I'm not. Being dressed to the nines had its place and I liked doing it for special occasions, but I wanted a man who liked me as I came.

The only concessions I did make were to put on some light makeup and pull my crazy hair half up so it was out of my face while the back fell all the way to my bra strap in loose, curly waves. I wore a simple black tank top dress that molded to every one of my curves and fell to my ankles. I added a long silver chain that held a dangling quartz crystal I'd picked up at an arts festival outside Illinois. On my wrist was my mother's bangle and a long, wide silver ring that went from my knuckle to the webbing of my fingers.

Simple. Easygoing. All me.

I opened the door with a smile and received one in return. Kyson was dressed much the same as I'd seen him prior to our date. Faded jeans. A deep emerald-green short-sleeve shirt that buttoned up the front but was still casual enough to wear out to lunch or the beach. On his feet were a pair of brown suede somewhat dressy lace-up shoes that showed he put the right amount of effort into his attire.

He entered my place, putting a hand around my waist and dipping his mouth right to mine for a light kiss. It startled me so much I began to back up as he approached, but realized that was stupid and allowed the brief touch of lips.

"You look good, babe. Love your hair wild anytime but pulled back away from your face gives me a great view of your pretty hazel eyes," he said and then proved it as he spent a good thirty seconds admiring them.

I couldn't help the beaming smile I gave him. "Brunch is ready. I hope you're hungry."

He inhaled and his eyes heated. "Starved."

I patted his chest and stepped back to find he'd been holding his arm behind his back. With a flourish, he presented me with the most stunning bouquet of wildflowers. The bright orange, blue, purple, deep red and soft pink flowers were tied in a wonky bow with yellow satin ribbon.

"Cut these from my ma's yard this morning. She's got the greenest thumb and her garden is the best I've seen around." He held them out to me. "Figured you'd appreciate flowers I chose and cut for you instead of the standard bouquet I could easily pick up at the store."

"Wow, these are incredible." I pushed my nose into the bundle and breathed deep. Lovely. I took in his happy smile, stretched up onto my toes, put my free hand to his shoulder and showed him how much I liked them with a sweeter, much wetter kiss than we'd started with. The kiss went crazy the moment I touched my tongue to his. Those powerful arms I liked so much wrapped around me, so I had no choice but to wrap both of mine around his neck.

He kissed me as though I hadn't seen him in a month, and we'd been together for years instead of having first kissed me only three days ago. When he was done, he pecked my lips softly and rubbed his nose along mine in a silky caress. I inhaled his earthy leather-and-citrus scent and sighed at the contentment I felt being in his arms.

"Damn, woman, you can kiss." He grinned.

I was certain my cheeks were flushed and my eyes a bit dazed as I steered the conversation to something safer. "So uh, your mother grew all of these in her yard?"

He nodded. "I'll show it to you sometime. I keep tellin' her to submit pictures of it for those home-and-garden contests, but she won't. Ma's sweet and likes the focus of attention to be on the ones she holds dear. Me, my brothers and uh, all of our family members."

I lifted the flowers and inhaled their floral scent once more, letting it soak my senses, reminding me of picnics in the park with my fathers growing up. I sure missed them.

"Well, they are lovely. I'd like to see her garden and meet her sometime."

He smiled back and my knees felt a little weak.

"Food smells amazing. What do you have planned?" He followed me to the kitchen and sat on one of the stools at the bar.

"A feast for the senses. I hope you like eggs benedict." I brought the flowers into the kitchen and found a beat-up vase in the cabinet above the fridge. Looked like I'd be adding a vase to my list of things to find in town.

He shrugged. "I don't know. Never had it."

"Really?" I gasped and brought the flowers and the vase to the counter and noted the ends were already cut at a slant. I added the flowers to the vase and filled it with water. "These are beautiful."

"Nothing compared to your beauty, Isabeau."

My cheeks heated even more, and butterflies fluttered in my stomach. "You are quite the flirt today."

He cocked his head to the side and put his elbows on the countertop, clasping his hands in front of him. I'd already set out the new placemats Jasper and I picked up, along with my set of matching silverware. Suda Kaye was definitely into recycling. A lot of her stuff was mismatched to the extremes, but I wasn't about to complain. I'd decided to simply replace what I wanted to and ask her if she'd like it returned or boxed up and donated when I was done with it.

"I have a lot to make up for. Especially with the way I bailed a few nights ago." His tone dropped and I could tell from his body language that he felt crummy about what had transpired.

I clenched my teeth and took a breath while stuffing my hands into the pot holders in order to retrieve the main course. Once I set it on the counter, I turned on the stove and started heating the hollandaise, whisking away to ensure it didn't burn and kept its creamy consistency.

"It's none of my business but I will admit to feeling rather embarrassed by the whole thing," I answered truthfully.

He sighed and he did it deeply. "If I didn't have to go, I wouldn't have. I hope you understand that is the God's honest truth, seeing as I'm right back here now, exactly where I want to be."

I nodded. "Mmm-hmm."

"What's the *mmm-hmm* mean in this context, honey?" He interlaced his fingers together and leaned his clean-shaven jaw on top of them. I hadn't noticed he'd shaved when he entered. It did not take away from his allure in the least. Shaven, scruffy, I'd guess even a full beard and he'd still set my heart pounding and my lady bits tingling.

I took the pot off the heat as I got the plates out. I shrugged. "Just that I'm not the type of girl who does that on the first date." I chanced a look at him and watched his lips twitch.

"And what type of girl are you, Isa?" His voice dipped to a more sexy, deep-throated rumble that I had to work hard to ignore or my wanton side might have made another appearance.

"The type that has a strict six-dates-until-sex rule!" I admitted with a hint of frustration in my tone.

Kyson tipped his head back and laughed heartily. "Six dates to sex, eh? That was not the vibe I got from you the other night, sweetheart."

I groaned under my breath as I served him double the portion of eggs benedict than I did for myself and covered it in the creamy sauce. Once I'd finished that I reached for the salad and took up the tongs to sift the brightly colored greens, making sure I got just enough of the feta, almonds and apricots into the matching bowls I'd set next to the plates.

"Honestly?" I asked as I dropped the tongs into the larger salad bowl and curled my fingers around the bullnose edge of the countertop, needing to get my concerns off my chest.

"With me you can always be honest." His voice was low and serious.

"You make me want to throw all caution out the window with your sexy self." I waved my hand up and down, gesturing to his body and face. "The body, the smile, gorgeous eyes, thick, silky hair, and the way you look at me…drives me nuts. I feel like I'm constantly in a state of want around you and it's annoying because I've never been like that in my entire life! Not with anybody." I ended on a huff, letting it all hang out.

He grinned and pursed his lips. "If you expect me to see a problem with this admission, honey, you're talking to the wrong guy. I'm as hot for you as you are for me. You have no idea how bad I want to run my hands all over your body. The curves, your sultry voice, those plump lips and high cheekbones. Jesus, woman, you have a face of an angel and a body made for sin. And that's nothing compared to the sight of your wild hair alone making my dick hard."

I gasped and covered my mouth with a now shaking hand.

"Yeah, so if you're expecting me to be sorry that you get hot and bothered around me, you're gonna have to think again. Now, what I will say is, I'm willing to work with you on this six-dates-until-sex rule."

"I'm reinstating the rule," I fired off instantly. "The other night was a fluke. A one-time deal and look how bad that turned out." I swallowed down the nerves coating my tongue.

"You mean to tell me you think after the other night—me

having my mouth on you, almost tasting the sweet between your thighs, having already tasted your skin and mouth— that we need to take a step backward on the intimacy?" His eyebrows rose toward his hairline.

I frowned. "Think? No. I know. If you want to continue seeing me, I'm not going to be a *wham, bam, thank you, ma'am* woman in your life. I'm telling you I wasn't in my right mind. Now I am. And this is only date number two, so if you want to get in there with me again, you'll put in the time and effort."

He grinned. "What about a barter? A compromise. Say half the time. I think that's fair?"

"What!" I scolded him while taking up the dressing. "Date number three is next. That's no time at all!" I frowned.

"Four?" He countered instantly.

I growled low under my breath and drizzled the balsamic over both salads. "This is a rule. Meaning it's not open for negotiation," I placed his plate and salad in front of him.

"Bet I can make you break your rule," he stated with an arrogance I'd not seen on him before. And like everything else, it was sexy as all get-out. Dammit.

"Feel free to try but I'm convinced this is the right path. For me." I set my plate in front of the empty space next to him and he looked down at the feast before him, then back up at me. "Eat up. It's nice and hot."

He smirked and cut into the eggs benedict first. "Okay, honey, I'll play by your rules, but you mark my words. You're going to be begging to break them before the six dates are up." His confidence was also insanely attractive, but I kept that to myself.

I smiled wide and put my hand out for him to shake. He took it in his. "Deal."

"This is going to be fun, babe. So where do you want to go on our third date?"

★ ★ ★

I strolled along the aisle of wedding dresses, picking through them alongside Evie and Suda Kaye.

"And he agreed to this six-dates rule?" Suda Kaye asked, positively scandalized by the fact that I was making a man that could have been Henry Cavill's double wait to seal the deal. "How does that work for you?" She pulled a huge fluffy dress out of the line and held it up in front of Evie then shook her head. "Too princess," she surmised and shoved it back.

"Kaye, not all women hop into bed the first night. She had a momentary lapse of judgment and doesn't feel right about her actions. And besides, some people like to get to know a person before becoming intimate. There's nothing wrong with that," Evie added delicately.

Suda Kaye scowled but even on her it was cute. "What better way to get to know a guy than to sleep with him? If he sucks in bed, move on. He's not marriage material. You don't want to be saddled with a bad lover for the rest of your life."

I couldn't help but see her logic. She made a lot of sense. "In the past I've been burned by guys who just wanted to sleep with me and then move on to the next best thing. I'm over that. College basically burned me out on sex for the fun of it. I want a man in my life. A relationship. Someone I can go out with, build a life with. What you and Cam and Evie and Milo have."

Evie grabbed my hand and squeezed it. "You will find that. I'm certain of it. If it's not Kyson, then it will be another man. Though if Kyson is willing to put the work in, that says a lot about his character."

I chuckled. "Yeah, but he thinks he's going to get me to break the rule. He tried bartering for half the time."

Suda Kaye shimmied her hips. "I just knew that guy was a smart one." She pointed at me. "I want in on his bet."

Evie rolled her eyes then pulled out a simple sheath dress that would have looked great on a woman twice her age. "This is pretty." She showed us both.

Suda Kaye and I exchanged a glance before we both looked at Evie and shook our heads.

"Evie, I'm getting the feeling you're into simple, sleek and elegant. I'm sure there's a way to do that without being too mature," I shared a little hesitantly.

"Absolutely. That's a grandma dress, sissy." Suda Kaye stated her unfiltered opinion flat out.

The three of us kept looking. Evie's wedding was three weeks away and she didn't have a dress to wear. They were doing it on the bluffs at the Native American reservation, where I would also meet my maternal grandfather for the first time. I was beyond excited and terrified at the same time.

"What's Milo wearing?" I asked.

"Oh, it's going to be so perfect. He's wearing black jeans, black cowboy boots and a white dress shirt with a new black blazer. He'll have a handmade bolo tie his mother is making and plans to have his hair braided down the center. On each side, they've chosen to weave in these amazing feathers. One of the Navajo tribeswomen makes these amazing decorative headpieces that fall in line with their tradition. One of the elders will be marrying us in full celebration attire. I cannot wait!" She pressed her hands in a prayer position at her chest.

"It's going to be epic!" Suda Kaye added. "Now we just need to find the perfect dress."

Evie's shoulders slumped. "I'm not into any of these. They're too church wedding, or princess-like. Too much fabric and satin."

As she and Suda Kaye picked through the next section, I spied a cream-colored slip of fabric across the store in the cocktail attire section. I went over to it and pulled it out.

The dress had the tiniest spaghetti straps at the shoulders that fell into a triangle bodice. The front was set in a soft fabric with small beads woven over the cups and rib cage in a dainty, elegant design. There was a satin ribbon that tied at the waist about an inch thick. The skirt draped all the way to the floor in loose chiffon. It would look amazing against a desert backdrop and still be elegant, unique, simple and stunning. All things I've come to learn about my big sister Evie.

I brought the dress over and stood behind my sisters, who were pointing at another dress. Evie's lips were turned down. She was not enjoying herself, and today was supposed to be all about fun. However, when you've looked at a hundred dresses, tried on ten and nothing has caught your eye, I could imagine it would feel daunting and frustrating. I wasn't trying anything on, and it wasn't my wedding day, but I was already in need of a stiff drink and a burger.

"Ladies…" I tried to interrupt.

"Just give it a try, Evie, come on," Suda Kaye encouraged, pushing a dress in front of her.

Evie shook her head. "If I hate it on the hanger, I'm going to hate it on me."

Suda Kaye groaned. "You don't know that until you try it on," she bit out through clenched teeth.

"Guys!" I spoke up and both of them turned their heads.

Evie's eyes settled on the dress that I held up and instantly widened, softened, then filled with tears. She reached her arms out, one to take the hanger and the other to hold the dress by the waist and inspect it closer up.

"My goodness, I've never seen anything more beautiful," she whispered.

Suda Kaye grinned huge, came over to my side and put her arm around my shoulders, hugging me close. "Our baby sister is about to save the day methinks." She wrapped her other arm around my chest and leaned her head on my shoulder. Her hair smelled of cherries and I committed it to memory, never wanting to forget this moment.

"I'm going to try this on right now." Evie held the gown aloft as though it were priceless.

I swirled around to face my sister and put both of my hands up in the air. Suda Kaye high-fived me with both of hers. "Should we say a little prayer?" I joked.

"Good idea!" she agreed.

Suda Kaye interlaced our fingers and tugged me closer. Then she pressed her forehead to mine and closed her eyes. I did the same, not knowing what to do, but followed her lead.

"Momma, if you can make this dress be the one, we'd be eternally grateful. Evie deserves to feel like a queen on her wedding day and the dress is the most important part. So help us out, will ya?" she spoke in a whisper, but I found it funny and chuckled.

"Yeah, what she said!" I added and Suda Kaye giggled.

"Thanks, Mom. We miss you and love you," she added. "Amen."

"You pray to Catori?" I asked when she was finished.

She nodded avidly. "All the time. She's hanging around us, so I know she's listening, guiding us along the way. Probably why we found out about you, actually."

I stepped back and crossed my arms over my chest protectively. "What do you mean?"

"In our culture, when a member of the tribe passes, they are set to rest on our lands. Then a fire is built to help guide the spirit to its final resting place. Mom was adamant she did not want her spirit to move on. Not yet. Only Toko knows when the time is right." She shrugged as if this wasn't a big deal.

"You're basically telling me that our mother's spirit has not left this earth even though she's been dead for over a decade?"

She nodded as if this information was all the same to her.

"I'm not sure I like this." I felt uncertain and a little weirded out.

Suda Kaye smiled. "Relax. It's not like she's watching you in the shower or when you masturbate or have sex." She made a gagging noise. "But I know Mom pretty well and she'd watch over all of us when we need it. She's why I'm back in Colorado and ended my wandering."

"What do you mean?"

"One of the letters. The one on my twenty-eighth birthday last year told me to go home. From the second I landed to every step I took after I felt her close. Her essence seems to be carried in the breeze. And ever since I came home, I've never been happier. We lost Adam, but we gained you. More happiness."

"And how would I know what the feeling of her essence is if I didn't know her in person?"

She smiled softly. "You'll know. You'll feel it. Either way, that's why I pray to her. I figure if she's hanging around, making sure her girls are happy, safe and protected, she'd want to nudge us in the right direction."

Before I could continue the discussion Evie came out.

The woman was a vision.

A golden goddess. She wore the dress as though she were an angel walking on a cloud, not a woman trying on a cocktail dress.

Suda Kaye covered her mouth with both hands and stared at Evie. "Oh, my God. Sissy, you look magical."

Evie swished the bottom skirt layers from side to side and stepped up on the riser. My eyes could barely handle the beauty before them. This was it. The most perfect dress for a stunning woman.

Tears fell down Evie's cheeks and she tried to blot them with her knuckles. "This is the one. I'm going to marry the man I've loved my entire life in this dress and become his wife." She smiled so huge even as more tears poured down her cheeks.

Suda Kaye bounced up and down and raced up onto the riser and pulled Evie into her arms. The two of them burst into happy tears while I watched. Then Evie turned her head, opened her arm and said, "Baby sis, get over here!"

My heart exploded with love and acceptance. The sensation of belonging was so acute it flooded through my veins as I stepped up on the riser and was embraced by these two amazing women. Tears shimmered in my eyes as I was held by my sisters.

My sisters.

They were no longer two women I was getting to know. They were people I now loved, cared for and adored in a way I hadn't felt for anyone other than Jasper. I wanted to be a part of their lives forever and knew in that moment, forevermore, I would be. These ladies had been through so much growing up. Having a mother and father who'd rarely been present. Living their early adult years separated from one another and going through the painful yet necessary process of finding and rebuilding their lives together. Expanding that to include the men in their lives. And now me.

Since the first day we met I never got the feeling they didn't want me in their lives, and that had only been proven through the love they showed me this past week. It was as if I was always a missing part of this duo, now a *trio*, and I couldn't have been more pleased.

"I love you both," I whispered where our heads were pressed together.

Blonde. Brunette. Redhead.

Three sisters.

United for life.

Committed to the sisterhood we were building.

"I love you, too, Isabeau." Evie lifted her head and cupped my cheek.

"What's not to love about you, Izzy?" Suda Kaye beamed, tears in her eyes.

"My sisters." I choked out the words. "The best gift I've ever received." I looped my arms tighter around the two women and held on. "Thank you, Mom," I whispered into our huddle. Using the word *Mom* for the first time in reference to Catori.

Out of nowhere, in the center of a department store, no open windows in sight, I felt my hair lifted by a soft breeze that smelled vaguely of bergamot, patchouli and the earth.

twelve

———

By midweek the bakery construction had shifted into high gear. I'd already met with Camden twice to hash out the decisions we needed to come to in order to make smart business choices for our start-up. Between Jasper and me, we divided and conquered. He worked on getting supplies and building relationships with the vendors, as well as researching and meeting up with the companies to determine the appliances we would purchase. I took up the administrative side by setting up bank accounts and working with the graphic designer on our logo and other promotional materials we would need in order to officially launch. I'd even had a meeting with Mayor Browning to set up a ribbon-cutting ceremony, which would also bring the local press.

Bright and early on the first morning of construction, Kyson and Lincoln showed up. To say Lincoln wasn't the most perfect man for my best friend was putting it mildly. He was grumpy as hell. The exact opposite of my bestie's jovial and extroverted personality. Still, the second those two met it was like an explosion of instant sexual tension.

Much to my delight, Jasper did what he always did with people who didn't want to like him. He pranced around and made a nuisance of himself every chance he got. Lincoln was not deterred by this behavior in the least. And Kyson had not been lying about Lincoln's taste in men. Right out of the gate it seemed that he appreciated every inch of my fantastically loud and fashionably adventurous bestie. At the end of day one, Lincoln had stomped over to where Jasper was picking through a catalog and slapped the book shut, demanding to take him to dinner.

Jasper put up a fight by looking him straight in the eyes, crossing his arms over his chest and answering with a flat no. This reaction seemed to be a new challenge for Lincoln because as I watched surprise flit across his handsome, rugged, manly features, there was also a determined gleam in his eyes that spoke volumes.

Me, I'd made a point not to get involved. I wasn't going to wade into this firestorm because honestly, I had my own hot Turner brother to deal with.

It was Wednesday evening and I hadn't actually seen Kyson since he'd taken off around lunch. This wasn't unusual since he owned most of Turner Brothers Construction and needed to check in on his guys at other jobs, or meet with customers somewhat frequently.

I looked up from the list of to-dos I was going over in the kitchen area when the man himself entered. I smiled.

"Isa, babe, have you eaten today?" Kyson leaned against the doorjamb.

I sat across the room at the ugly, battered butcher-block counter we were removing and replacing with all new stainless-steel countertops.

Jasper exited the big refrigerator unit, which thankfully did in fact hold its temperature and worked amazingly well. Thank God. "She hasn't eaten anything since the cupcakes we bought from a bakery across town this morning. Gotta taste our competition." He waggled his eyebrows.

"Well, yeah, and because cupcakes," I answered with a secret smile. Jasper snorted. We never needed a reason to eat cupcakes. Ever.

Kyson lifted his chin toward me. "Wanna take you out. I'm craving pizza and beer. You down for that?"

I grinned and nodded my head. "Of course. I love pizza. I'm from Chicago where the best pizza in the entire world is made. Besides, I could use a beer or three," I admitted on an exhausted sigh.

Kyson and I hadn't met up for an official date since our Sunday brunch three days ago, but we'd seen one another daily and texted. It had actually been nice seeing him work, being able to chat with him about inane things. Aside from that, I'd found his mind was filled with unique and innovative ideas on the renovation process and how we could better provide customers an experience while they were in our bakery.

"Sounds heavenly," Jasper groused. He came over to me, wrapped his arms around me from behind and pressed his face to my neck. "You have the best boyfriend," he sighed.

At hearing the word *boyfriend* I sat still as a mouse about to be pounced on by a big, fat cat. My gaze instantly went to Kyson, who didn't seem fazed in the least at the title Jasper announced; nor did he correct him. I felt it prudent to ignore the comment and just let it go. For now.

"Glad you're hungry, pretty boy, because we're going with 'em," Lincoln commanded as he entered and leaned against the wall close to Kyson.

Jasper let me go and put his hands to his hips with a dramatic flourish. "If you think you can demand me to go anywhere with you, you're crazier than I thought."

"Crazy enough to be chasing after the prettiest man I've ever seen, with a mouth that fuels my fantasies, even though half the time I want to gag you and tie you up until you'll do what I say. That type of crazy is about right. Now, get that fine ass in gear and get it seated on the back of my bike."

"Oh, snap. He told you!" I taunted, because he absolutely had.

Lincoln might have had a stick up his booty and a cranky personality that drove my bestie up the wall in a good way, but he also had an excellent work ethic. He was always on time, very thoughtful and direct when communicating with me and almost as hot as his brother. The family genes were strong in these two with their dark hair, light eyes and big, muscular bodies. Then again, those bodies could have come from the manual work they did—which Jasper and I had been doing, too. Watching Kyson and Lincoln lift, hammer and nail things made us both need a cold shower at the end of the night.

"A bike? As in a motorcycle?" Jasper gasped, awe clear in his tone.

Lincoln's lips twitched, showing he actually did have some humor in him. "You like motorcycles?"

"I like hot guys who ride them," Jasper admitted breathily. I could tell he was excited by this new layer of Lincoln. Not only was the guy persistent when it came to flirting and asking my best friend out, he also rode and owned a motorcycle. Jasper had been obsessed with guys who rode bikes since *Sons of Anarchy*. Opie was his favorite character but alas, Jasper had never dated a guy who actually rode a bike. This was a big plus on Lincoln's side.

"How's about you, Isa?" Kyson grinned. "You dig guys who ride bikes? Picked mine up after that last job." He smirked.

I jumped up from my stool and put my hands into the air, cheerleader-style. "Heck, yeah!" I went over to Jasper and pulled him into a hug. "We're going on double hot-guy bike rides! This is so fun!" I squealed.

Jasper jumped up and down. "Colorado is the best!" He whooped and then screeched, "Bucket list!" Then we high-fived like the children we were in our zealousness to ride on the backs of real motorcycles.

I spun around and pushed my hair out of my face. "We are *so* ready to take a ride on the wild side."

"Jesus, you two are nutty," Kyson chuckled.

Jasper licked his lips and his gaze set on Lincoln, who had the sexiest smile locked on his face. "Um, do you ride a Harley?" Jasper's question practically dripped with excitement.

"Knock me a kiss on the cheek right here and I'll tell you," Lincoln demanded rather boldly, pointing to his cheek.

My mouth dropped open. I left Jasper's side and made my way to Kyson. He looped his arm around my shoulders and brought me into a hug, dipping his head. "How's about *you* knock me a kiss? Been days since I've had that mouth, and I'm *thirsty*, baby," he whispered against my lips.

I mewled and pressed my hands to his chest, lifted up on the balls of my feet and gave him a kiss. It started with a little peck but turned into a deeper, wetter, delicious kiss I didn't want to pull away from. Unfortunately, we were in mixed company, so I pulled back. Kyson nibbled on my bottom lip for a second, as if he was loath to leave it, and ran his hand down my back and cupped my tush. "Damn, woman, you got the most perfect mouth."

I smiled with said mouth and bit into my swollen bottom

lip and snuggled into Kyson's warm chest. I looked at Jasper, whose face was pinched into an expression of being put out by Lincoln's request.

"I can wait all day for my kiss, Jasper, or you can hurry it up and give me what I want so I can give *you* what you don't even know you *need*. Then we can go eat."

Jasper narrowed his gaze and did a model-esque walk over to stand in front of Lincoln. Linc did not move his sexy self from the wall, even when Jas put his hands to both sides of Lincoln's head. Instead of kissing him on the cheek, he went right in for the gusto. His mouth moved over Lincoln's, who barely got into the change of events and had pushed off the wall to grab hold when Jasper catapulted back, pecked him a couple more times and pranced around his form toward the front of our bakery.

Lincoln groaned and put his hand to his lips to touch them. "That man is going to be the death of me."

Kyson hugged me tight to his chest. "I actually think that man is going to bring life to your world. You deserve some happiness, Linc. It just pranced out in a poof of color after kissing you stupid." He laughed.

"Oh, my God! They both have Harleys!" Jasper hollered from the other room, nowhere near hiding his glee.

"Come on, babe. Let me and my brother take you and yours for a ride."

Riding on the back of a motorcycle with my front plastered to Kyson's back was intoxicating. The wind in my hair, the darkening horizon in front of us and the open road and the rev of the engine between my thighs were beyond pleasurable. It was downright Nirvana. I never wanted it to end.

The guys must have known we were into it in a big way because they gave us a full thirty-minute ride. If I didn't think I would have killed myself, I would have busted out my phone and taken a picture of Jasper. The smile on his face, the contentment he had with his cheek pressed to Lincoln's back, his arms wrapped around the much larger man, made my heart jump for joy. No man on this earth deserved happiness more than Jasper Prince.

He not only gave love, he also was love. Pure. Honest. Beautiful love. The way all people should love one another in my opinion. It was a gift. His gift. I was just thrilled to be one of the people he shared it with. And secretly, I hoped maybe Lincoln could end up being one of those people, too.

Kyson followed Lincoln's bike into a parking lot. There was a line of bikes parked right in front of the shack-like building on the outskirts of town.

When Kyson parked and put his feet down to steady the bike, I tugged off the helmet he'd made me wear and let the rest of my hair fall free and wild, just the way he told me he liked. I wore jeans, a black tank that said "Bad Ass" in hot pink glitter across the boobs that I'd picked up in Suda Kaye's shop, a pair of dangling silver earrings, my mom's bracelet on one wrist and, luckily, a pair of black leather wedges. I wasn't one hundred percent biker babe, but I felt as though I could pull it off.

Jasper, on the other hand, was not in the least.

"Are we at a biker bar?" I inhaled and waited until Kyson turned his head.

"Yeah, babe, they have the best beer and pizza around. See that pizza joint attached?" He pointed to the building next to the bar that seemed to have a breezeway connecting the two. "You can get whatever you want from inside the bar, too. Also, I can try to kick your ass at pool since you kicked mine at shuffleboard last week."

I grinned then looked at my best friend, who was still

hugging Lincoln from behind, eyes closed as though he was sleeping and having a peaceful, pleasant dream.

Lincoln looked at me and winked but didn't make any moves to get up. Guess he was content with my best friend plastered to his back.

Yay!

I kept my delight to myself. "Um, how do I get off?" I frowned and looked down at all the hot metal near my feet.

"Put your hands on my shoulders and then swing your leg around and off. Can you do that?"

I chuckled. "Without eating road? Maybe, but I wouldn't count on it." I was sorta teasing, but mostly I was worried I'd face-plant after I slipped and fell off or burn my leg on one of the pipes.

As I was considering my options, checking both sides before making my grand exit, Kyson stood up, turned his torso around and plucked me at the waist. He lifted me up and off the bike as though I weighed as much as a child. I most certainly did *not* weigh anything remotely close to that of a kid.

My surprised squeal brought Jasper out of his motorcycle trance.

"My pretty boy likes to ride. This pleases me greatly," Lincoln growled, and I'm not gonna lie, I, too, felt a little shiver at his sexy alpha words.

"Oh, I ride, and do it *very well.*" Jasper's statement sounded a whole heck of a lot like a promise.

Lincoln obviously agreed when he said, "Looking forward to experiencing that...soon."

Jasper pursed his lips and flounced off the bike like the queen he was.

Punk. How'd he do that without even thinking about it?

"Izzy, was that not fabulous!" Jasper's clear blue eyes lit with joy.

"Absolutely amazing."

Jasper and I spent a few minutes hashing out our favorite parts, nattering on like little girls until finally, Kyson broke our huddle with an ear-splitting whistle.

"Hungry, sweetheart? And you needed a beer an hour ago, remember?" Kyson smiled and held his arm out.

I promptly dashed over to him and he put his arm around my shoulders. Jasper took his time as was his way. The moment he got close to Lincoln the man instantly grabbed my best friend's hand.

I grinned at the possessive move, and Jasper's face showed a hint of disbelief before he shook it off and interlaced their fingers.

Aw, my bestie and his hot, grumpy guy.

I looked up at Kyson to find he was watching me watch them. "Thank you for the ride. It was awesome."

"Happy to give that to you, Isa." His voice was a sexy rumble that flowed through my body in a pleasurable wave, straight down to my toes.

I beamed up at him and he gave me a quick peck on the lips, then led me to the door, which he held open for me and our duo behind us.

The place was filled wall-to-wall with leather-clad bikers. Beers were flowing. The pizza smelled out of this world and looked it from what I could see at a couple tables nearest to the door. The last thing I noticed was that all eyes were on us.

Kyson lifted his chin to the bartender. "Round of beers for me and my girl and my brother and his date," Kyson announced as if it was all the same to him. He clearly was a regular here because the bartender nodded, and one of the waitresses waved him over to a table she was clearing.

I watched as the eyes of many rather rough-looking dudes noted our approach. I turned around and found that Lincoln had let go of Jasper's hand so he could wrap a large arm around my best friend's shoulders.

This ownership move was not lost on my best friend. And in turn, I was happy to see that Jasper wrapped his arm around Lincoln's waist.

Kyson held out my chair and I was just about to sit when a massive, bearded biker came up behind him, wrapped his arms around his chest and tugged him off his feet in a death-defying arch of his masterful frame.

At first, I thought Kyson might lose his mind, turn around and punch the guy but instead, he laughed hard and spun around the second his feet touched back down.

"Pops!" Kyson went into the bearded man's arms and clapped him on the back several times.

"Ky, what are you doing here? Thought you were taking out the pretty redhead you told me and your mom about. That's why your ma's back at home and not sitting on my lap shooting the shit with the fellas."

"Wanted to take my girl for a ride on the bike and treat her to the best pizza in town. No better place than here."

"Damn. Ain't that the truth." The older man laughed as I took in his appearance. He wore a white-and-black bandanna around his head, and long, dark hair shot through with gray came out of the back and fell down his chest. And when I say long, I mean it went past his shoulders. His long beard came to a furry point somewhere near his sternum. It wasn't full ZZ Top-style, but definitely close. He had on a black T-shirt with the image of a skull on fire on the front. Over his shirt he wore a black leather vest that had a patch on it noting him as the "Vice President."

From top to toe the man was biker cool with a hint of danger. He made the guys on *Sons of Anarchy* look chill in comparison.

"Pops, meet my girl, Isabeau Collins." He let his father go and gestured to me.

I smiled wide and waved from across the table, feeling a little shy meeting his father for the first time in a pair of jeans and a tank I'd worn all day while running around and working in the dust at the bakery.

The man took me in from top to bottom. "Wow." He grinned. "Boy, you are in trouble."

Kyson chuckled. "Don't I know it. Had me twisted up the second I laid eyes on her."

"That I can believe. Straight from heaven. Hope she sins like the devil." He winked at me and patted his son's back then gripped his neck as though he was proud of him.

Strangely sweet.

"Dad." Lincoln stepped up and opened his arms.

"Jesus Christ, I got two out of three of my boys in one place on the same night and I didn't have to wrangle your ma into cooking for that miracle to happen." He hugged Lincoln and clapped him on the back.

"Got someone I want you to meet, Pops," Lincoln grumbled—pretty much the only way that man always spoke it seemed. He gestured to Jasper, tugging his hand and pulling him close.

Jasper looked nervous from his frosted, spiky blond hair down to his combat-booted feet. Today's outfit spoke for itself. His pants were a neon yellow swishy material that made noise when he walked. Drove me crazy until I got used to it. He paired that with a tight-fitting white T-shirt that had a Canadian flag on it. Jasper was obsessed with all things Canada. His mothers loved taking quick flights from Chicago up to Toronto for family trips and he'd been in love with it ever since. His shoes of course were red combat boots with black laces. Nothing matched in the conventional sense, but on him, it somehow looked incredibly fashion-forward.

"Hi, Mr. Turner. It's nice to meet you. I'm Jasper Prince." Jas held out his hand for the man to shake.

"Prince?" His father grinned and took in my best friend. "Sounds about right."

I held my breath because we were in a biker bar filled with rough guys who looked like they could cave your skull in with one punch, but also because my bestie was a little overly fabulous, which could rub scary biker dudes the wrong way.

"Razor." The man took Jasper's hand and shook it.

"Um, razor?" Jasper queried.

"My name, son. Razor," he repeated.

"It's my father's road name. All club members have a road name," Lincoln said. "He's sworn us to secrecy on his real name." He smiled.

Lincoln actually *smiled* and it was beautiful. Made him five times more handsome. Still, my guy was way hotter.

Jasper looped his arm around Lincoln's waist and looked into his face. "Will you tell me what it is?" Jasper batted his long eyelashes. The little flirt.

And right in front of everyone, including his dad, Lincoln swooped in and kissed my best friend in a barely decent but brief kiss that had some definite tongue action.

My gaze jetted to Razor's only to find him grinning like a loon. Kyson came over to my side and snagged my hip, maneuvering me closer.

"Your dad is cool about uh, all of this?" I nodded to Jasper, who was now looking at Lincoln as though he'd hung the moon just for him. My best friend may have been playing hard to get for all of three days but if the look on his face was any indication, he was now besotted with the grumpy Turner brother.

"Linc's been out for a long time, babe. And my father would never put up with anyone treating him poorly for his preferences. That includes the club. If they have issues with people loving who they love, they show those men the door. Being a biker is all about being loved by your brothers, living wild and free. You can't put limitations on that kind of thing. Doesn't fit what they're about. In the club you'd live, bleed and die for a patched brother. Doesn't matter who they take to their bed or who they have on the back of their bike."

"Cool," I breathed and meant it.

"You kids have a good time and when you're done eating, bring your dates over for a round of drinks and pool on your old man, yeah?" Razor slapped the tabletop in front of us.

"Sure thing, Pops," Kyson said, and Lincoln just lifted his chin in assent.

Once we were all seated, Kyson and Lincoln went right into ordering food as the waitress set down four cold beers.

"Your dad seems super nice," Jasper noted.

Lincoln smiled. "He's a good guy. Loves his boys, his wife, his brothers, beer and his food. Lives the life he wants to live and is happy doing it," Lincoln shared.

I put my hand to Kyson's thigh and gave it a squeeze.

"Do you uh, think maybe we could go to an event at the club house?" Jasper's eyes widened, and he bounced a little in his chair.

Kyson and Lincoln both laughed.

"I want to come, too! Oh, and we can invite Suda Kaye and Camden. She'd love every second of it. Cam would go just to make his wife happy. Though I'm not sure Evie and Milo would enjoy a biker event, but we could see." I was rambling and imagining hog roasts and cookouts and girls in skimpy attire hanging off wild biker dudes like arm candy.

On this Kyson and Lincoln burst into raucous laughter.

Kyson hooked me by the neck and brought me closer. "Baby, you can't just go inviting yourself to a motorcycle club event. That shit is invite only."

Both Jasper and I frowned.

"But I'm sure we could get Pops or Vince to let us bring the two of you to one of their family barbecues. Though at night, those turn rather obscene."

"I can totally handle obscene," I whispered. Jasper heard me and announced, "Me, too!" rather loudly.

The two men shook their heads, smiles on their handsome faces. "We'll see. Depends on how date number six goes." Kyson's crystal-blue eyes heated, giving me a red-hot, smoldering look.

I licked my lips and imagined all the things I wanted to do with my hot motorcycle man in a much quieter, more private place.

"For the record, this is date number three. And you bet your life I'm counting."

That had me giggling.

"Oh, he told you," Jasper taunted then sipped his beer with a pinky finger out like a princess would.

"What are you counting?" Lincoln asked.

Jasper turned toward Lincoln and opened his mouth. I reached over and clamped my hand over his pretty face. "Don't you dare."

His brows pinched together, and I waited for a moment until he nodded. I let him go but shouldn't have.

"Why in the world would you not want me to tell Linc about your six-dates-to-sex rule?" he blathered.

"I can't believe you!" I swore, then grabbed my beer and sucked back half in one go.

"Six dates until sex?" Lincoln's face contorted right back into his resting grumpy face. Then it was as if the lightbulb went on and he turned to Jasper. "You don't have this stupid rule, do you?"

Jasper tipped his head back and laughed so hard I thought beer might come out his nose. "Hell, no!" He bit into his lip.

"That's good because I sure as hell am not waiting six dates to have you. Brother, you're a saint," he said to Kyson.

Kyson chuckled and I blurted, "Hey!"

Lincoln continued, focused on me. "Izzy, you are damn lucky you are my brother's dream woman because that kind of blue balls could kill a man!"

I scrunched up my face and was about to filet Lincoln with my sharp tongue when Kyson saved the day with his next words.

"You see this woman? Not only is she my dream woman, she can cook, she's gorgeous, intelligent and the little I've had of her body is topping every fantasy I ever had. I'm happy to get to know all of her mind and soul before I get to know every inch of her body."

I preened on a, "Thanks, baby," then proceeded to give my guy my mouth. He took what was offered and kissed me harder and for a lot longer than I would have normally allowed at an establishment, but I didn't care. We were in a gritty biker bar with tons of rough guys around who probably did a lot worse with their own women.

Besides, Kyson thought I was his dream woman. With every minute I spent in his presence, I was beginning to believe he very well could be my dream man, too.

thirteen

"Date number four was amazing, Ky," I breathed against his lips and then kissed him, sucking on his tongue then flicking the tip of his with my own.

We'd gone out to a movie and then had incredible Thai food at a little place out of the way. He'd taken the bike and by the time we got back to the bakery and made our way inside, I jumped him. My hormones were going wild. So much so, I pushed him up against the wall in the open main area before we ever reached the entryway they'd cut in the wall leading from our bakery into Suda Kaye's boutique.

The kiss was so feral, Kyson lifted me up by my ass and walked me over to a folding chair that was sitting near a workbench and took a seat.

The moment I was in his lap, I rubbed my center for all I was worth against the rigid length behind his jeans. The friction was dizzying and exactly what I needed.

"Jesus, woman, you are something else," he whispered

against my neck while his fingers tunneled into the back of my hair and gripped tight at the roots. A prickle of pain zipped through my scalp and morphed into arousal when he slanted my head to the side and took my mouth in a deep kiss I quickly got lost in. His other hand ran up and down my bare thigh and underneath the flirty skirt I'd worn for our date. Once he gripped my ass, he lifted his hips and ground me down on his steely erection.

"Baby," I gasped and arched my body, getting as close as possible. "Please," I begged.

He grinned and sank his teeth into the space where my shoulder and neck met. His hand left my hair and trailed up my inner thigh, shooting streaks of pure fire along my nerve endings. I was sitting astride his lap, my entire focus on the hand creeping up my leg.

"Let's see how much you want me," he murmured against my skin then cupped my sex with his large hand. "Damn." He rubbed along the outside of my panties as I thrust against the pressure. "Soaked."

I jerked my hips, searching for something, *anything*, to give me more.

He didn't disappoint, maneuvering his thumb against my clit, swirling the fabric and his thumb in a dizzying circle that was just what I needed to make me cry out.

I ran my hands from his shoulders down his muscular chest, going straight for his belt.

He shook his head and grinned wickedly as he tsked. "No touching, sweetheart. Just enjoy what I make you feel."

"But…"

My retort broke off when he dug his hand inside the front of my panties and slid his fingers against my flesh, sinking two of them inside.

Heaven.

I lost my ability to speak, my entire focus on the walls of my sex stretching around those two talented fingers.

My head fell forward to land against his forehead as he pulled those fingers out an inch and thrust them back inside, going even deeper than before. I cupped his head and threaded my fingers through his luxurious hair, holding him to me. My mouth was inches from his as he manipulated my sex beautifully.

His eyes were a startling dark midnight blue when filled with lust; his pupils pitch-black and enlarged.

"Ride those," he growled between his teeth, his nostrils flaring as the smell of sex filled the space around us.

"Baby…" I mewled, then lifted up and slammed my hips down as he requested. Ribbons of bliss wove through my veins.

"Fuck, yeah," he murmured. "You're so hot, wet and tight. Can't wait to sink into you. And once I do, I'm never going to stop, Isa. I can already tell. You're going to be an addiction. With your sweet fucking mouth, wild hair, big tits and this wet pussy… I'm never going to get enough. Never, baby," he breathed, every filthy word ratcheting my arousal higher and higher.

I cried out as he ground me down and widened his legs. My thighs were stretched impossibly wide across his lap, my center open indecently for the taking. And, boy, did he take his fill. Plunging his fingers in and out in a relentless rhythm created to draw me to the pinnacle of release.

My entire body was burning. Long underused muscles were screaming and filled to the brim with unreleased tension as he kept at me.

"Can you take more, my Isa?" His tone was rough, as though he'd swallowed a box of craggy rocks.

I shook my head, not even knowing exactly what I was

responding to, but I definitely wasn't certain I could take anything *more* than what he was already giving me.

Kyson rubbed a third finger alongside the first two and wedged it inside me, making a triangle shape that stole my breath when he eased it in. His thumb came up and circled the throbbing knot of nerves begging for attention as he pierced me deep with three thick fingers.

I tipped my head back, letting out a soundless cry and bounced on his fingers, greedily stealing every ounce of pleasure he was doling out. Positively wanton in my need for release.

Eventually, I was chanting, "Yes, yes, yes," over and over as he locked an arm around my hips, slid his fingers along the front wall of my sex and tugged down as though he were pulling a fire alarm.

It was *alarming*. It detonated the swirling intense heat building at the base of my spine and splintering out like a spiderweb of electric pleasure through every single nerve ending.

His mouth slammed over mine as I convulsed in ecstasy, my body succumbing to the sensations, allowing endless waves of euphoria to coat my form in pure bliss.

I shook in his arms and he held me through it, kissing me soft and sweet, swirling his tongue over mine in featherlight touches that sent shivers racing down my cooling skin.

Throughout it all, he held his hand still, locked inside me, until I finally came down enough to lift my head and look into his eyes.

"That was intense," I whispered rather vulnerably.

He smiled softly and eased his hand out of me and my panties.

"One of the most beautiful things I've ever seen is watching you catch fire for me, Isabeau." His voice was a low rumble like the thunder before a storm. "Thank you for that gift, honey."

I kissed him as tears pricked at the backs of my eyes. For a long time I sat in his lap and kissed him. Swirling my tongue along his lips, nipping them teasingly, getting used to his taste and what made him sigh. I was connecting with him on a physical level I'm not sure I'd ever had before with other men I'd been in relationships with.

Kyson was different.

Unusual.

When he touched me, I lit up. My attraction and desire for him was so far beyond anything I'd ever felt, it scared me. I could so easily lose myself in this man if I wasn't careful. Though part of me believed that maybe we were both supposed to do that—lose ourselves. My parents did. They loved one another in a way that I revered. People could write books about it. That kind of intensity, respect and commitment to one another...it was special. One in a million. Maybe a billion.

Hell, maybe Kyson was my one in seven billion.

The man who was made for me.

My soul mate.

Not that I believed cosmically we were given only one person who would match with us. I truly believed there could very well be many people on this earth we were meant to have in our lives for different reasons. Jasper was meant to be in my life, too, share it until we were old and gray. I knew that with my entire being. It was the same with my parents. And now my sisters were starting to be something I cherished and knew I would until the day I died. Perhaps Kyson was that man for me. The person I was meant to love romantically. Share my day to day. Come home to at night.

My parents taught me to never settle for anything less than what would fill my life with joy and happiness.

After I'd kissed Kyson so long my lips felt bruised, I pulled back. "Should we take this party somewhere more private?" I bit down on my bottom lip, knowing exactly what I was suggesting. My rules be damned.

One side of his mouth turned up. "I'd like that, baby, but I gotta get home. Besides, there are things we still need to learn about one another…and something that I need to explain before we go any further."

I frowned and curled my fingers around and through his soft hair. "But what about you?" I gestured my chin down to his lap where the hard ridge behind his jeans had not gone down in the least.

He smiled. "I like that you want to take care of me but if I get your mouth on me, or sink inside you, I'll not want to leave, and we'll definitely not talk."

I grinned and nipped at his scruffy chin. "Talking is overrated. Action is where it's at." I ran my tongue around the seam of his lips once more.

"Dammit, baby, you steal my words and make my mind go blank but really…" He was cut off by the sound of bodies coming through the back door.

I locked my arms around Kyson's shoulders and was about to jump off when two figures came barreling toward the door leading upstairs.

I gasped loud enough for the dark figures to enter the light. Which is when I saw Lincoln, his big hands to my best friend's ass, holding him aloft. Jasper's legs were wrapped around Lincoln's waist much the same way mine were wrapped around Kyson.

Jasper grinned at my position and I grinned at his.

"Don't mind us, we're uh, just getting back from our date," Jasper gushed.

"Mmm-hmm." I nodded. "I can see that. Your legs broken?"

Jas smiled wide and waggled his brows. "Too tired to walk. You know how it is. Riding on the back of that bike and all."

"Brother, what are you doing here?" Lincoln asked, allowing Jasper to slide down his body but kept him close when his feet touched down.

"Walking Isa to her door," he responded deftly.

"Yeah, I can see that with you sitting with her in your lap and her skirt around her waist. Cute purple panties, Izzy. Though I prefer something more in the boxer brief variety myself." Lincoln ran his nose down Jasper's ear and neck.

I shoved my skirt back down around my legs, covering myself, heat flushing my cheeks and neck.

My friend shivered then boldly announced, "And what about commando?"

Lincoln stood stalk still. "You telling me there's nothing under those skinny jeans?" he grumbled low in his throat.

Oh, boy. This was about to get heated.

Jasper smirked at me then turned to the man who still had his arms wrapped around him. "Guess you're gonna have to find out now, aren't you?" He spun around and sashayed toward his apartment door.

I watched as Lincoln's hands clenched into fists and he stood still, breathing deeply. It was obvious he was trying to rein in his control. I found it wildly interesting and couldn't wait to quiz Jasper about it later.

Oddly, Lincoln lifted up his arm and looked at his wrist. "Brother, it's eleven fifteen." He tapped on the face of his watch with a finger before heading up the stairs after Jasper.

Kyson jerked up and I stumbled off his lap rather inelegantly.

"Shit, Isa baby, I gotta go." His tone was off the charts worried.

I frowned. "What? Again with this? Why?"

He shook his head. "Told you we needed to talk, but now I don't have the time. I'm late as it is." He cupped the nape of my neck, tugged me forward and laid a hard and fast kiss to my lips. "Babe, had the best time. Plan to have more of it."

"But… I don't understand." My mouth continued to move but no words came out. I was truly speechless.

"Honey, I can't explain right now, but you'll understand soon. We'll talk tomorrow. See you in the morning, yeah?" His gaze held mine and I nodded my head as my shoulders slumped.

"Sure thing. Whatever works, Kyson. Go. You're late," I stated flatly.

He sighed deeply, turned on his kick-ass motorcycle boots and left me standing there. Usually, he'd walk me up to my place and make sure I locked the door before he left. Obviously, there was something happening that was making him late. For what? I didn't know. I sure as hell planned on finding out tomorrow.

No more secrets.

No more bailing on our dates when he had me all hot and bothered.

No more. I'd had it. Tomorrow, for better or worse, I was sitting him down and getting to the heart of whatever it was he was hiding.

Unfortunately, tomorrow came with the delivery of the big appliances. A huge truck pulled up in front of the building in the center of the road right at six in the morning instead of 2:00 p.m. when they were supposed to arrive. Thankfully, Lincoln had stayed the night with Jasper and was Johnny-on-the-spot to handle the team and get all the equipment in place.

Much to my irritation, Kyson was nowhere to be found.

For the next few hours Jasper, Lincoln, the three guys from the delivery company and I painstakingly dragged in each piece. Then we had to ensure that the wiring, exhausts, electrical connections, heating and cooling units were all a go. The silver lining was that we'd already stripped and tiled the entire space where the equipment would go so we wouldn't have to move it all again.

By noon Kyson walked in with a white bag and a drink carrier, looking distractedly handsome. A frown marred his features, and his eyes were dead-set on Lincoln. Me, I was still reeling from last night. I desperately wanted him to look at me so I could skewer him with my laser glare and demand to have our talk, as well as find out where the hell he'd been this morning.

When he entered the kitchen area he looked around then his frown turned upside down. "Excellent. They arrived early. I was worried they'd be late, and it would put off the grand opening."

I put my hands on my hips and Jasper wiped sweat from his brow. "Dude, why are you not on the floor on your knees groveling after the crap you pulled last night," he demanded on my behalf.

Kyson jerked his head back as though Jasper slapped him.

"Pretty boy, don't get involved. You don't know what you're talking about," Lincoln warned.

Jasper circled his head and glared at Kyson. "I know my girl went to bed alone. I know my girl didn't get a wink of sleep as shown by the ugly blue-and-purple smudges under her eyes, which I also know was because hunk-a-licious left her ass hanging in the breeze. A-gain! Then you prance in here looking all hot and brooding while we've been to hell and back getting this equipment in here."

"Jasper, stop. Kyson, I need to speak to you," I requested.

"What's this about you not sleeping and me groveling, babe?" His words came as a warning not as a question. "I've been on a job since first light. A job where one of my best guys fell off a seventeen-foot scaffolding and broke his back, several of his ribs and his pelvis. My phone stopped working sometime in the night and I couldn't call any of you. I had to borrow a phone just to call the goddamned ambulance and Frank's wife!"

"Fuck!" Lincoln cursed.

Kyson didn't stop. "So excuse me if I wasn't here to deal with your appliance delivery. But I knew you had Lincoln, not to mention the men who were sent to deliver and help install the items." He tossed the bag on the beat-up counter we'd yet to remove and set the drinks down more softly, yet liquid still splashed out and onto the counter. "Picked up lunch after I spent the last few hours in the hospital consoling Frank's wife and kids." He shook his head and ran his hand through his hair. "You know what, I don't need this shit. Not today. Not ever," he sneered and stormed to the back door. He shoved it open so hard I heard the jarring *thunk* of it hit the brick wall on the outside before it slammed shut.

"Kyson!" I called out and started after him.

Lincoln stopped me with a hand around my biceps. He shook his head. "I'll go. When he's like this, his temper can be bad. He'll lash out and say shit he doesn't mean."

"I don't care. He needs me!" My heart squeezed and my chest felt like a vise was around it. I wanted to go to him, soothe his hurts and apologize for being such an ass. Even though I still needed to get to the bottom of what had been happening between us, I should have given him the benefit of the doubt and let him explain why he kept disappearing on me when things got heated.

"Let me go first. I'll cool him down, get him to see reason and talk him through his pain over Frank." He gritted his teeth. "Frank's a good man. Married, three kids all under the age of ten. Needs this job. Fuck, this has got to be hurting Ky. I'll let you know when he's calmer."

Since I didn't know Kyson's moods just yet, I nodded. It was the only thing I could do.

Lincoln bolted out the door but not before grabbing Jasper's hand and giving it a squeeze. That was sweet. I wanted that for my best friend. Then again, I wanted that for me, too.

"Izzy, this is not your fault. Heck, it's my fault for attacking him the second he entered," Jasper said with genuine sadness.

"No, you were just trying to protect me. I get it. I'd do the same. And we had no idea what he was dealing with. Now I just feel like a tool and I don't know what to do or how to fix this. I mean, what if I've ruined everything between us by not trusting him to share whatever it is that was so important to him?"

Jasper wrapped his arm around my shoulders and led me into the main room. The space was finally taking shape. All of the old bakery furniture and displays had been gutted and removed. Wiring hung from different spots in the ceiling that the guys had prepared before they plastered it and set the lighting. The walls had been stripped of the old siding and was now primed a pristine white.

"Let's look at our samples again and put some on the wall to make a final decision. We can start painting tomorrow if we do." He urged me toward the table that had all the paint chips and small sample paint cans sitting next to them.

For the next half hour we debated the merits of leaving the bakery white, versus painting it pink or peach. Eventually, we decided on peach walls we'd accent with words painted in gold to inspire patrons to eat our treats. Words like cupcake, cookie, donut, sprinkles, delicious, tasty and sweet.

We were cackling about the word *titillating* when the door behind us opened and a little brown-haired, blue-eyed girl of about five or six entered all alone.

Jasper and I looked at one another and then back at the girl.

"Are you the cookie lady?" she asked and smiled brightly. Her pigtails swayed as she looked at me with big eyes. She was quite possibly the cutest little girl I'd ever seen.

"Hi, sweetheart, where's your mama?" I asked softly.

She pursed her lips then twirled in a perfect circle on her pink Converse and stopped as though she was winded. "I don't have a mama. I have a daddy, a Pop, a Nana, an Uncle Vince, an Uncle Linc." She grabbed one of her pigtails and spun it around her finger. "And a whole bunch of uncles at the bike house." She beamed.

Uncle Vince. Uncle Linc.

"So are you?" she repeated.

"Am I what?" I walked over to her and crouched down to her level.

"The cookie lady. Daddy said that the prettiest woman with fire-red hair made cookies for me. I ate them all. Can you make me sugar cookies with frosting? Those are my very favorite." She licked her lips as if she was imagining herself eating one right now.

"What's your name, sweetie?" I asked again.

She smiled as the door opened behind her and Razor, Kyson's dad, entered.

"Girl, I told you to slow down. Your pop can't move that fast in his old age!" he teased. Razor picked the little girl up and put her on his hip as though he did it regularly, then tickled her belly.

She howled with glee. "Pop-Pop, is this the cookie lady?"

He nodded. "Yep, peanut, this is Isabeau. Daddy's girl-friend," he said as if it wasn't the biggest freakin' news of my entire life. Aside from finding out I did in fact have a mom, and two sisters and had inherited a fortune from a man I'd never met of course. So it wasn't the *biggest* news exactly, but it was pretty freaking crazy.

I opened and shut my mouth but all that came out was, "Wha, wha, wha…"

"Hi, sweetheart. I'm Jasper."

She waved at Jasper. "Hi, Jasper." Then her eyes got big. "Ohhhhhh, you are the boy my uncle Linc likes!" She clapped her hands and grinned. "I heard my nana talking all about a boy that Uncle Linc loooooveeeeesss and his name is Jasper," she confided.

Jasper stepped closer. "Loves, huh? Tell me more, precious?"

"Jas," I whispered, my heart pounding out of my chest.

"Izzy, honey, is Kyson or Lincoln here? Nana has a bad case of the flu. Came on after she picked up our peanut from kindergarten. By the time she got home she was sweatin' and burning up with a fever. She called me to take care of my granddaughter but I'm working on a bike that has to be done by me and me alone. She doesn't want her getting sick. You understand, yeah?"

I nodded numbly, my eyes glued to the little girl. Her eyes were the exact same shade as Kyson's; her hair, too. She didn't have the same nose or mouth, but the girl was definitely a Turner.

"Of course. No matter what, we can take care of her.

Kyson and Lincoln are out back. One of their men got hurt…"

"Who?" he asked.

"Someone named Frank, but I don't know him…" I let the words fall away as I continued to stare at the child. A marching band could have paraded down the street and my attention would not have been swayed from taking in the tiniest detail of the little girl and comparing it to her father.

"Shee–it. Frank's one of my brothers. He okay? The club will want to know if they don't already," Razor grumbled and set the girl down.

I shrugged. "I honestly don't know."

"Where's the boys?" he demanded gruffly.

"Out back." I hooked a thumb in the direction he needed to go.

He immediately addressed his granddaughter. "You be good for Izzy, okay, baby? Pop-Pop's gonna go talk to Daddy and Uncle Linc, but I'll make sure Daddy or Uncle Linc come and get you soon."

She nodded then spun around in a circle, watching her yellow dress flutter out as she did so.

"You got her?" he asked.

"Yeah, definitely," I answered on autopilot.

He beat feet to the back of the room where the kitchen was and disappeared.

Jasper's eyes widened and he put a hand to his chest, his face set in shock.

I didn't know what to think or feel but I had a little girl that I just promised I'd keep an eye on while Razor gave more bad news to my man.

My man.

The man who didn't tell me he had a daughter.

I closed my eyes for a moment, allowing that hurt to burn through my system before I felt a little tap on my hand.

I looked down at the stunning little face. She really was a beautiful child.

"Do you have any more cookies?" she asked, swishing her skirt from side to side, one of her sneakers up on a toe that she was wiggling back and forth the way kids did when they wanted something.

Did I have any cookies? I always had cookies. I was a baker. Desserts were life. In fact, I had two different types of cookies in tubs in my apartment and a full cake on display on the counter.

"I do, but you have to answer one question and then we'll go to my place and get some. Okay?"

Her eyes lit up and sparkled, making her even cuter as she nodded avidly.

"What's your name, little miss?" I asked and tapped her nose.

"My name is Hope."

Her name was Hope.

The exact name that Porter mentioned when Kyson and I went on our very first date. It wasn't another woman he was hiding or an ex-girlfriend. It was a child. He had a daughter. And if she was in kindergarten, she had to be five or six. Kyson and I had been on four dates and spent the past two weeks working side by side and he'd never bothered to mention he had a daughter.

"Hope is a beautiful name. Do you know what it means?" I took her hand and led her toward the curtain that separated our renovation from Gypsy Soul.

She nodded and took my hand.

"Daddy says Hope is a feeling and it means good things to come."

I swallowed the dryness in my throat and held back the emotion swirling to the surface. "He's exactly right." I just hoped it meant good things to come for Kyson and me, because this was a huge fork in the road. And I had no idea which way things would go.

For Kyson, or for me.

fourteen

===

"You live here?" Hope spun herself around and around on my kitchen bar stool.

I pulled a plate from the cupboard and set it down on the counter. "I do."

"But there are no walls? It's like one big room." She stuck her tongue in the side of her cheek as she assessed my place, clearly finding it odd.

"Yep. It's called a studio apartment. Lots of big cities have studio apartments."

"Why?" Her little brows came together.

I smiled at Hope and removed the lid from both the cookie tubs. Unfortunately, I didn't have sugar cookies with frosting, but I had snickerdoodles and peanut butter.

"Have you had peanut butter before?" I asked, making sure she wasn't allergic to peanuts. She nodded so I placed a fat one on the plate and added a snickerdoodle. "Well, cities have a lot of people in them. Which means you need to have a lot of apartments. A studio allows a person to have everything in one smaller space."

Her lips opened into an "oh" but her gaze was glued to the two cookies as I pushed the plate toward her. She licked her lips.

"Milk?" I asked.

"Yes, please!" she chirped happily then picked up the peanut butter and took a bite that was far from kid-sized.

I chuckled and went to the fridge. "Slow down, the cookie isn't going anywhere."

She chewed and nodded.

I poured her a small glass of milk and set it next to her plate.

When she was finished with her first bite, she took a big gulp of milk, leaving a white mustache along her upper lip.

"You make the bestest cookies ever."

From a child, that was a high compliment. I leaned forward, resting my elbows on the counter, and focused on her pretty face. "Thank you. You know your dad is helping me and my friend renovate our bakery. Soon, I'll have all kinds of desserts available for you to choose from."

Her eyes got big. "I love desserts. It's the best part of the day. Nana allows me a treat every day after school though hers are from the store. Not as yummy as this one, but don't tell her because she'd be sad."

I winked. "Your secret is safe with me."

She sniffed the snickerdoodle and inspected it top and bottom. "Smells like cinnamon."

"That's because it's made with sugar and cinnamon. It's called a snickerdoodle."

"Snickerdoodle! That's a silly name!"

"It is but it tastes divine. Try it," I encouraged.

She took a cautious small bite then smiled. "The doodle is good!" She chomped down on more.

"I'm glad you like it." And I was glad. This precious girl was Kyson's daughter and simply by sitting with her I could see was happy, well taken care of and sweet. Made me very curious about her mother since Kyson not only hadn't mentioned Hope, he hadn't shared about his ex, either.

"What other things can you make?" Hope asked.

"Just about anything. I'm a chef and a baker. I went to school for both. Kinda like college for cooks."

"Oh. My daddy went to college, too. He builds and fixes things. Sometimes it's a house, a big building and one time it was my school!" she stated with pride and awe.

"Is that right. What was broken at your school?"

She wiped her mouth off on the back of her hand and I realized I hadn't given her a napkin. I pulled off a square from the paper towel roll. "Sorry, sweetie. Here you go." I handed it to her and she wiped her mouth again.

"One of the classes had a ceiling that crashed in from the big rain." Her eyes were bugging out of her head as she held her arms out wide and arched her little body backward, showing me this event was clearly a big deal.

"You mean during a storm?" I asked, and she nodded. "Was anyone hurt?"

Hope shook her head and picked up the peanut butter cookie. She seemed to be eating them both. One bite then to the next and so on. "No, it happened at night. The principal was very sad, but the class just moved to the library and then Daddy and Uncle Linc fixed it real fast."

"That's good to hear. And what does your mother do?" I asked nonchalantly even though I felt a wave of heat flow through my veins, making my hands and the back of my neck felt a little clammy. Digging for information from a child was a crappy thing to do, but I couldn't help it. I didn't understand why Kyson wouldn't just tell me about Hope from the first date when we were getting to know one another. And if not at that point, then by the fourth date at the very least, or one of the many days we saw each other while he was renovating my business.

"I don't have a mommy anymore." She frowned but then took another bite of her cookie.

Oh, my God. Was Kyson a widower? And here I was making this little love talk about the mother she'd lost. I gritted my teeth and clenched my hands.

"You don't?" I put my hand over my heart as my chest became tight.

She shook her head and chewed slowly, looking around my space as if she wasn't really comfortable talking about it.

I felt like a jerk for bringing up something that might not be my place to know. "I'm sorry to hear that, sweetie."

Hope shrugged. "It's okay. I don't remember her anyway." She traced the edge of her milk cup, a bit of melancholy having come over the child before she looked up at me, smiled and said, "Can I have some more milk?"

"Of course you can. Would you like one more cookie?" A kidney. A cake. Whatever would make her smile with pure happiness at this point I was willing to give.

Her blue eyes sparkled with excitement. "Yes, please. I think a doodle cookie."

I chuckled. "A snickerdoodle," I clarified and pulled the biggest one from the tub. If it ruined her dinner, it would serve Kyson right for not telling me about her in the first place.

"Yes, that one." She spun around in a circle then stopped when she made a full three-sixty back to her plate.

I'd just refilled her milk and given her another cookie

when there was a knock at my door. Then Kyson's solemn face appeared as he opened the door, entering without waiting for me to answer. I inhaled a full breath at the sight of a broken man I'd come to care for very much. His gait was slower as he approached us, shoulders slumped as though he were carrying a pile of bricks on his back. But it was his eyes that worried me. They were raw and filled with sadness.

"Hey, bug, whatcha eatin'?" He tugged on one of her pigtails.

"Doodle cookies! They are so yummy, Daddy."

The side of his mouth tipped up into a half smile, but I could see the effort it took when it didn't reach his eyes. "Looks good. Isabeau is an amazing baker." His gaze came to mine, the blue orbs searching my face.

There was so much in that one look.

A plea for time to explain.

Acknowledgment that he'd screwed up.

An apology.

It was all right there before my eyes. I could choose to wail, scream, complain, moan and groan, or I could listen, bide my time and hear him out. Determine my feelings after he'd explained why he'd kept such an important part of his life a secret.

For him, and because little ears were present, I pressed my lips into a soft smile, saying without really saying anything at all that I'd give him the time he needed. "Any news on Frank?"

He sighed deeply. "Lincoln and Pops checked in with his wife. His injuries are serious, and it will be a long road to recovery. The club will descend on the hospital and they won't know what hit them when thirty burly bikers show up and demand to see their brother."

"Yikes. Though I imagine all that support will be good for his wife and kids."

Kyson nodded and then ran his hand through his hair and let out a long sigh. "Isa, I'm sorry, I can't… I don't even know how to start right now."

I shook my head and went over to his side; the pain he was feeling filled the small kitchen area like a thick fog. "It's okay. We'll talk later."

"We will? You're not running for the hills?" There was a hint of hope in his tone that I couldn't bear hearing without touching him.

I cupped his cheek. "Running is not exactly my thing."

He shifted his face and kissed the center of my palm. "What is your thing?"

"Eating. Cooking. Baking. I don't even think I own running shoes." I pursed my lips together.

"You wanna meet my daughter, baby?"

I grinned wide. "Kinda already did that."

He closed his eyes. "Hope, Daddy wants you to meet a very important woman in his life." He looped his arm around my waist and turned us toward his kid.

Hope frowned and tipped her head to the side, looking exactly like her father when he's studying some building specs.

"But Daddy, I already know the cookie lady is your girlfriend. Do you have another girlfriend?" Her mouth dropped open and she shook her head, looking positively scandalized. "Nana says boys can only have one girlfriend or boyfriend they like at a time. And Pop-Pop said she was your girlfriend."

Kyson chuckled and then tugged me tighter to his side. I rested my hand against his chest and sighed into the contentment I felt. We had a lot to talk about. A lot of things to go over. We were still new and there was much we didn't know about one another. And yet, his having a daughter was not something that would put me off being in a relationship with the big lug. It was hiding her I didn't agree with and didn't understand.

"No, Daddy does not have any other girlfriends. Just Isabeau." He ran his nose along my cheek.

"Whew. You could have gotten in big trouble for that." She bit into her third cookie.

"Absolutely!" I playfully made a mad face until Kyson laughed. "Though you can call me Izzy, little miss."

"Izzy. I like it," she said through a mouth full of cookie.

I grinned. "I'm glad, sweetheart."

"Now that my two best girls have met, I think our next date should be the three of us. What do you think, Hope?"

She nodded ecstatically.

"Isabeau? Would you be interested in having dinner with me and my daughter tomorrow night at our house?"

My heart started pounding and butterflies took flight in my stomach. "I'd love to. Do you cook?"

"Kinda have to, babe—have a child that needs to eat real food. She can't live on pizza and burgers, as much as she'd disagree." He chuckled and the sound made the air seem lighter.

"I so could! I love pizza and cheeseburgers!" The pitch of her voice climbed to a rather screechy timbre that could pierce straight through to your eardrum if you weren't ready for it. Something I'd have to get used to.

"Cool it, bug." He laughed. "How's about your dad makes tacos?"

"Awesome," she breathed. "Daddy makes the bestest tacos."

I smiled. "I haven't met a taco I didn't like. How about I bring the dessert?"

Hope wiggled her bum on the stool then spun around in

a much faster circle than she had before her dad was here. Perhaps the third cookie put the hyper meter over the top.

"Careful, bug, you don't want to hurt yourself," he warned.

"Will you make frosted cookies?" Hope asked me while ignoring her father.

"If you want. I can also make a cake, pie, tart, donut, whatever you like."

"I love frosted cookies but Daddy says they are too sweet. I don't understand how. Daddy's favorite is lemon and chocolate desserts."

"Then I'll make you frosted cookies and your daddy a lemon tart. And you can taste test both and decide which one is better. How's that sound?"

She lifted her hands into the air and cried, "Hooray!"

Kyson snuggled close to my neck and laid a kiss there. "Spoiling my daughter already, I see."

I shrugged. "She's cute and thinks I make awesome cookies."

He groaned under his breath. "Can I call you later tonight? I need to check in on Frank and my mother. Plus, this one needs to get home to do homework, bath, dinner and bed."

"Aw, man. But I like it in Izzy's one-room house. Everything's colorful and she has treats."

I grinned. "I'll send you home with some cookies for you and Daddy to have after dinner. How's that sound, little miss?"

"Awesome." She made the word sound twenty letters long for how far she dragged it out.

"I owe you, Isa. More than just an explanation," he admitted, his tone low and solemn, proving he knew just how much he'd hurt me.

"Yes, you do."

"Call you tonight after I get her settled in bed?" There was an eagerness to his tone.

"I'll be here. And if you need someone to pick her up after school tomorrow and bring her back to the bakery so you can work, I'm happy to do it. The bakery needs you far more than it needs me. Besides, I could take her to Gypsy Soul to meet the girls."

His brows pulled together. "You barely know her and you're willing to help us out of a bind. Are you for real?" He said it with so much wonder it made me sad that he didn't have a person in his life to share these burdens with aside from his family. Which is also when I realized I could so easily see myself in that position.

I turned into his arms and looped mine around his waist, looking up into his exhausted and haggard face. He needed food, a good night's sleep and a break from today. Unfortunately, he wouldn't be getting that any time soon. He had responsibilities. Mostly in the form of a small child who needed him for everything, a burgeoning business, a fallen worker and friend, and a girlfriend he had to make amends with. At least that last one I could do something about.

I lifted up onto the balls of my feet and placed a light kiss to his lips. Behind me I heard a little girl giggle and smiled against his mouth.

He smiled fully for the first time since I'd seen him enter the bakery kitchen earlier.

"Last I checked, I was as real as it gets," I teased.

"Ain't that the truth." He pressed his mouth to mine hard and fast before pulling away. "Come on, bug. We gotta get you home and on to homework."

Hope jumped off the stool, grabbed her plate and milk cup and walked it around the bar and over to the sink where she set both items.

"Excellent manners. Who taught you that?" I asked, grabbing the cookie tubs along with a new empty one. I put more than half of each kind in the extra takeaway tub so they could have a mixture of both options.

She smiled. "Nana says a lady always has good manners."

I closed the lid, tapped her nose and crouched down to her level. "Your nana is a pretty smart woman."

She nodded avidly.

"Do you want to come here and help me bake those frosted cookies and the lemon tart tomorrow while your daddy and uncle Linc work on my bakery? We can go to the store after I pick you up and get all the ingredients we need. What do you say?"

She lifted her arms up, spun in a circle and cried, "Yay! So fun!"

I chuckled and opened my arms.

Hope went straight into them and I hugged her tight, glorying in receiving such a reaction from Kyson's girl. She smelled of cinnamon from the cookies and apples, which I suspected was her shampoo.

I let her go and Kyson took her hand. I held out the Tupperware filled with cookies and he took it from me.

"Call you later, yeah?" He walked his daughter over to the door and opened it. She let him go and started down the stairs while singing "The Wheels on the Bus." Already on to her next adventure.

"Yeah," I said to Kyson with a smile. "Bye, little miss," I called out and waved.

Hope got to the last step and jumped to the floor and let out a peal of laughter.

Kids were awesome. Nothing but joy and innocence. If I could bottle that up and sprinkle it on a cupcake I'd be as rich as Betty Crocker.

"Isa," Kyson called out as he was halfway down the steps. "Thank you."

"It's all good," I said in response.

He shook his head. "It's not, but it will be. I'll make sure of it. Later, baby."

"Bye." I waved again, then turned around, entered my apartment and pressed my back to the door.

Kyson had a child. A beautiful little girl named Hope. No, an amazing, sweet, bright child who'd obviously not been raised with a mother in the picture. Looked as though Hope and I had more in common than caring about her daddy. I looked forward to learning more.

fifteen

=====

At nine that evening I'd just gotten myself cuddled into my bed, back against the headboard, legs crisscrossed and Catori's stack of letters piled in my lap when my cell phone rang.

I took a deep breath and glanced at the phone that I'd tossed on the bed before I got comfy. The screen said, "Kyson calling."

Once I shifted the letters to the side for later, I picked up the phone and whispered, "Hey, did Hope go down for bed okay?"

He chuckled. "You've spent a half hour with my child and you're already asking about her well-being? Jesus, Isa, stop being so damn perfect."

His comment had me laughing. "I can't help it. She's really sweet, has great manners and I enjoyed her company today. And I'm looking forward to tomorrow. I'm sure we'll have a blast."

"See? Perfect."

I laughed harder. "No one's perfect."

"I definitely learned that lesson the hard way," he grumbled.

"Sounds like you have experience. Want to be more specific?" We really did need to get his secrets out into the open so we could move past them and carry on enjoying our time together.

"Dammit, Isa, I wish I was there, able to have this conversation with you in person, hold you in my arms so I can see and feel how you react instead of trying to guess your thoughts over the phone." His tone was genuinely frustrated at our distance, which sent a warm feeling through my body.

"How about you start from the beginning and I'll be honest with you about my thoughts and feelings."

He huffed. "Not something I'm used to experiencing. Honesty from a woman, that is. Most especially Hope's mother, my ex-wife."

"So you were married? I kind of gathered from the bitterness in your tone that it wasn't the best of experiences?" I guessed.

"Actually, at first it was the opposite. Veronica was my world. Met her my senior year in college. We hit it off instantly. Fell hard and fast for her. She had just started college when we got together. Was a freshman and worked at the local coffee shop I used to visit. By the time I graduated, and she was a sophomore, we were living together in a small place near the college. I went straight into working for a larger construction and restoration company and learned the ropes while she finished her degree. By the time she graduated college, I was ready to start my own business and my life with her."

"What was she into academically?" I asked.

"Finance. Which was awesome because in the beginning she was instrumental in helping me get financed, set up with a bank loan and knew how to invest my savings and loans the best way possible. We felt like a team."

He sighed and just the sound hurt my heart.

"I'm not exactly sure when it all changed with Roni. The same year she graduated and went straight to work for a big corporation in C-Springs, we eloped. Everything was awesome."

"Why do I feel like I'm at that part in the movie where everything goes crazy and flips upside down?"

He chuckled. "Because that's what happened. Though it wasn't one huge thing that went wrong. It built up over time. By our first anniversary Roni was pregnant with Hope. We were both ecstatic. Sure, she'd just started her career and was only twenty-three to my twenty-six, but we were happy. Living our best lives, working, loving one another and then we were building a family of our own. Life was great. At least I thought it was."

The sorrow in those last words were heartbreaking. I wished more than anything that I could wrap him up in my arms and hold him tight as he revealed something that was obviously very painful for him. "Then what happened? You had Hope…"

He coughed and took a deep breath. "Yeah, shit started to get strange shortly after she gave birth. She was acting erratic, depressed, sad all the time. Tired. Angry."

"Postpartum depression?" I gathered.

"Yeah, at first. I eventually got her to go to the doctors. They set her up on some heavy-duty antidepressants but even after six months when she was back to work and Hope was in day care during the day, she didn't bounce back to her old self. The woman was lively, energetic, fun and was excited about being a mom when she was pregnant. Each day I'd come home from a really long day at work to find Hope crying on a blanket on the floor, or in her crib while Roni would just sit there staring at her daughter. Sometimes she'd be crying with her. Sometimes she'd be devoid of any emotion."

"My God, that's horrible. Something was obviously really wrong."

"Yeah, but she claimed it was work and being a new mom. I was a first-time dad running a brand-new company and working myself to the bone to make it successful. What did I know about women who were overworked and overwhelmed with postpartum depression? Nothing, that's what."

"You couldn't. Don't beat yourself up," I shared softly.

"Easier said than done. When Hope was about a year, the day care called and said Hope hadn't been picked up by Roni and it was already an hour after the scheduled allotment."

I clenched my teeth and wrapped myself in my comforter, scared of what was to come.

"Veronica had disappeared. The first of many times I'd experience over the next two years. Sometimes it would be a week, sometimes two, then months would go by."

"What happened?" I choked out the words, afraid to hear what might come next but needing the entire story.

"At first, she got hooked on the quick fix antidepressants in extremely high dosages. Then she'd go to the doctor and claim she had severe back and neck pain so she'd get pain medication. Once the doctors caught on to her prescription drug addiction, she started to drink. Only I didn't figure any of this out because she was stellar at hiding it. Until of course she started disappearing. Which I later found out were full manic breaks where she'd lose herself in the drink, drugs and whatever else she could get her hands on. She almost bankrupted us with her addictions."

"Oh, Ky, I'm so sorry. That had to be awful to witness from a woman you devoted your life to."

He sighed deeply again. "Yeah. A couple times the family and I were able to get her into recovery programs. Supposedly, she kicked the pill-popping habit, but the drinking just got worse and worse. Almost as if she was substituting her other addictions with booze."

"And what about Hope during all this?"

"Honestly, she spent most of the time with my mother. Veronica's parents live in Kansas City, Missouri. They would come out to visit once or twice a year and we'd go out there but those trips slowed down when we couldn't plan around Roni's disappearances. I had no idea what to do. Here I was with a toddler who missed her mother. Needed her mother."

"And you needed your wife," I said gently.

"By that time the love I had for Roni died. Every day she chose her addiction over Hope and me, it got worse."

Tears filled my eyes, but I sucked in a breath, trying to hold them back. He didn't need me to be a sobbing, emotional mess while he was sharing his story. He needed a strong woman to listen to him.

"Understandable." I swallowed down the desire to get mad and hurt on his behalf.

"I don't know about that, but by the time Hope was three, Veronica had lost her job and been in and out of two different extremely costly rehabilitation programs, neither of which worked long-term. I sat her down and told her I wanted a divorce and I wanted full custody of Hope with only supervised visits allowed to her."

I sucked in a harsh breath and covered my heart that was beating like a drum in my chest. "And what did she say?"

"She lost it. Screamed the house down, scared Hope, broke things and stormed out. That was the last time I saw her. Three years ago."

"You're kidding? You haven't heard from her since?" I wasn't able to hide the shock in my tone.

"My brother Vince has seen her a few times. Always three sheets to the wind and hanging on the arm of some douchebag in a seedy bar. Vince does the delivery of the high-end bikes, cars and the like that the club garage fixes. He hasn't seen her in our area for a long time. When he makes deliveries, he pops in for a drink here and there and that's when he's seen her. Mostly in Kansas City. Her parents have also seen her a couple times when she's come to them to ask for money."

"Has she come to you?"

"No. She'd already put me into twenty thousand dollars' worth of debt before she bailed on me and her daughter. I don't think she'd dare come back for fear of my response. It took two years of working myself until my fingers bled and refinancing our house in order to pay it off. Only this last year was I finally in the black."

"You've been through a lot. More than most. And yet you're still driven, hardworking and a great father," I responded. "You should be proud of yourself for what you've achieved, Ky."

"Nah. There are a million single parents out there trying to do what's best for their kid and to give them a good life. I did what any parent would do in the circumstances."

I shook my head even though he couldn't see it. "Not true. You rallied. You provided a good life for your daughter. Anyone who meets that little girl can see she's happy, loved and well taken care of. I hope you know you're doing an amazing job with her, baby." I lowered my voice because it felt like a private, special moment. Something we were sharing just between the two of us. Him giving me some of his insecurities, and me showing him they're unfounded.

"Thanks, honey. Still, I should have told you about Hope."

"May I ask why you didn't?"

He groaned. "Honestly, it started off as self-protection. I didn't want to meet another woman and share my life. I'd just suffered through the last six years of dealing with a woman who destroyed me and the life we built. So at first, I only hung out with women when I was feeling the need for intimacy."

I chuckled. "Mr. Hit it and Quit it."

"Truth?" His voice was low and sexy.

"Always, baby."

"Yeah, that's exactly what I did. Not the first year when Roni left us. That year I avoided any romantic or physical connection with the opposite sex and focused solely on my kid, my business and paying off Roni's debts."

"Makes sense. I'd be put off men if the same happened to me, too."

"When Hope was around four, I started to date a little. It didn't feel right. I still wasn't ready to share my world. Definitely not my daughter. So if I met a woman I liked and she felt the same, we'd hook up. Did that for the past two years."

"Then what happened?"

"Haven't you figured it out? I met you, baby," he stated rather directly.

I gasped. "You haven't dated anyone seriously since your ex-wife?"

He laughed heartily and the sound filled my soul with joy. "One woman I had a great time with. Felt there might be a connection and met up with her a second time. Told her I had a child and she made it clear she wanted no part of that type of baggage."

Instantly, my blood boiled. "What a bitch! Hope is not baggage. She's awesome! I can't even…"

"Cool it, honey. It's fine. She wasn't the woman for me. After that experience I promised myself that until I was certain a woman was right for me and fit into the life I led, I wasn't ever going to introduce her to my kid or even talk about her. Hope didn't deserve a parade of women coming in and out of her life when she'd already been abandoned by her mother."

"Oh, Kyson…" I sniffed as the tears came back and anger leeched out. "You're such a good man and father. Putting your girl first in all things. It's commendable and I hope you realize it because she truly is great."

"Yeah, she is. Best thing I ever did in my life. Doesn't change the fact that I'm sorry I didn't tell you about her sooner. I had to leave at eleven those nights we were out because the teenager next door that I have watching Hope has to be home by eleven-fifteen or her mother gets salty with me. I can't lose her as a babysitting option and honestly, it never felt right telling you about Hope when I had you half-naked or we'd had a hot-and-heavy session."

I held the phone tighter to my ear so I could hear every nuance of his breathing. "I get it, I really do. I still wish you would have been forthcoming, but I understand why you weren't."

"With you, Isa, you're already more than I could ever hope for. I haven't felt anything this good in a long time. As the days kept sliding by, I started to worry that I'd lose you once you found out. And even though it's only been a few dates and a little over a couple weeks, it would have killed me to lose you. I wanted to hook you deep. Keep you as all mine for as long as I could."

"I wish you were here. If you were, I'd hold you close, kiss you hard, look you in the face and tell you your daughter only adds to your appeal. And you're pretty damn appealing to start with, Kyson Turner."

"Damn, now I want to kiss you."

"I want that, too."

"Tomorrow we're going to make up for this lack of kissing," he demanded.

I chuckled. "You say the time and the place and I'm there, baby."

"Hope liked you." He changed the subject and for that I was grateful. Too much sadness for one night. I was ready for the ease that Kyson had brought to my world lately.

"I liked her, too."

"She talked about how pretty you were the entire way home. Says she's going to have fire hair when she's older just like Izzy. Also, she claims she's going to be a famous baker and work in your bakery so I need to hurry up and finish it up so she can get to work."

That had me cracking up. "Guess we'll see how she does tomorrow. Make sure to send me all the details about picking her up."

"We'll discuss it in the morning after I drop her off and come to work at the bakery."

"Oh, that's right. I'll see you in the morning." I played with a lock of my hair. "What's on for the rest of your night?"

"Wiped, baby. Gonna grab myself a beer, surf the TV for something mind-numbing, take a shower and crash early. You?"

"I'm going to read one of my mother's letters, then read a

few chapters of this romance novel that Jasper found in his apartment."

"Your mother's letters? What do you mean? On our first date you said you never had any contact with her."

I could feel the butterflies picking up in my stomach as I fingered the stack of letters. "When Evie and Suda Kaye showed up out of the blue to my childhood home almost three months ago, they brought me a huge stack of letters that my birth mother had written to me when she was ill and close to the end of her life."

"Whoa, that's heavy."

"It is. Not something I ever expected. My mother was never on my radar at all. I'd been raised to believe she was only an egg donor and surrogate, which wasn't the truth."

"Damn, Isa, learning all of this had to be a shock."

I nodded and continued. "According to Evie, when she and Suda Kaye were teenagers, our mom came home and moved them to Pueblo. She spent the next few years with them and when they were at school or helping her with her illness, she'd write letters. She ended up leaving each of us a stack, one to open every birthday. I'm playing catch up since the letters start when we're eighteen. I'll be turning twenty-five later this year and have only read numbers eighteen and nineteen."

"You're going to open up the letter she wrote you for your twentieth birthday," he surmised accurately.

"Yeah," I breathed. "It's hard. I like reading them and getting to know my mother. Her name was Catori, by the way."

"Beautiful name. Like Isabeau."

"Thank you." I picked up the letter and tapped it against my lip. "It's just strange learning about her. I went my whole life not knowing I had a real mother. Not knowing I had sisters. It makes me angry, but also incredibly sad that she felt she had to make the choices she did. I would have rather her been in my life even from afar, knowing she was chronically ill, than not at all. You know?"

"I do. For the last couple years, I wanted that for Hope desperately. But it doesn't mean Catori didn't love you. Based on what you've said, it actually means she loved you very much."

"It would have been nice to hear her say it, even just once to my face."

"Baby..." he whispered.

I swallowed and swiped at the stupid tears that I didn't realize were running down my face until they dripped off my chin.

"I'm fine. Honestly. I'm used to it. I actually feel really hypocritical about my feelings surrounding Catori."

"How so?"

"Because I had amazing parents and a childhood filled with nothing but support and love. My fathers doted on me like their most prized gift. They gave me everything I needed and worked hard to give me a lot of what I wanted. Evie and Suda Kaye might have had Catori and Adam, but it wasn't regularly or even frequent. It was whenever their father was on leave and when their mother was ready to flutter back into their lives. That had to be way harder than having two devoted parents your entire life. And still, now that I know about Catori, I feel her loss as if it's always been a part of me. It's ridiculous and doesn't make any sense."

"I don't believe that's true, Isa. You're entitled to miss something you've never had because it should have been yours in the first place. All kids deserve to have devoted parents. It doesn't take the place of wanting to connect to the woman who gave you life. It's okay to be upset. It's okay to feel deeply about all of this. It's a lot to take on in a short amount of time."

"You think?" I stuttered.

"I do, sweetheart. Don't feel bad because you're missing what you didn't have. It's natural. There's nothing wrong about wishing you had someone in your life. I wish Veronica could have gotten her shit together and could be a mother to Hope. Sometimes I still wish she'll turn things around, because one day it's going to really bother Hope. I can see it happening. She's already started asking why she doesn't have a mommy because she's in school with other children and they often talk about their moms on the playground or in class."

"Poor Hope."

"Yeah, and poor Izzy. Baby, you were abandoned by your mother. She may have had her reasons but it's not that different from Veronica bailing on Hope because of her addiction. It's abandonment any way you look at it and that brings about a lot of strong feelings."

"But I'm gaining so much... Evie, Suda Kaye..."

"And you should have had them in your life the entire time. Ian should have been able to connect with Suda Kaye. I don't care what the agreement was. It doesn't change how much being left behind hurts. I feel that every time I put my daughter to bed at night and she prays that her mommy is safe and happy wherever she is. It's not okay. And it wasn't okay for Catori to do that to you, either. So be mad, baby. If you want to yell, yell. If you want to cry, cry. But don't ever disregard your feelings as being ridiculous. They are real and you deserve to have them however they come about."

"If you keep being so awesome, I'm going to fall in love with you. Then you're going to have to deal with having your counters filled to the brim with baked goods, and you're going to lose that washboard stomach, because my treats are *that* good."

He chuckled and I felt it rumble through my entire body

and settle in my toes. "Good problem to have, Isa. A woman that stays. A woman that wants to be with me and my kid and serve us up delicious treats made by her own hand? Twist my arm already. A gut is nothing. I'll add more crunches to my workout routine. Don't you worry, honey, I'm all about any treats you want to bestow on me and my girl."

"Thank you for being honest with me tonight. I'm sorry about Veronica," I whispered as if speaking louder would break the soul sharing we had going.

"I'm sorry about Catori. Though I gotta say, letting it all go and giving it up to you took a lot of weight off my chest. I feel like I can breathe better, baby. You do that for me. You help me to breathe."

I smiled so huge my cheeks hurt with the effort. "I'm glad. Get yourself a beer. I'm going to read my letter, probably have a good, long cry and then read some smutty historical romance."

"Okay, baby. If the next letter upsets you, call me. I'll be up for a while. Don't want you feeling hurt while you're all alone."

I grinned. "Remember what I said about being too awesome…"

He laughed heartily and then yawned.

"Go to bed, Kyson. We'll talk tomorrow. Thank you again for tonight."

"Any time, Isa. And I mean that. You're the only person outside of my brothers and parents that I've shared any of that with. You've got the same from me, yeah?"

"Yeah, Ky. And, honey, having it feels good."

"All right, baby. See you tomorrow. Sweet dreams."

"You, too. Bye."

He hung up and I sat back against the headboard with my eyes closed. Everything we talked about ran around and around in a dizzying circle in my mind until eventually, I shook my head and picked up the next letter.

"What advice do you have for twenty-year-old me, Mom?" I asked out loud and opened the letter.

My dearest *Kasaraibo,*

Today you are twenty. When I was twenty, I was giving birth to your sister Evie. I'd traveled the states with a belly-dancing group and ended up on the East Coast. I met Adam Ross at nineteen. He was on leave with the military for three months. He's older than me by eight years. I broke off from the belly-dancing group and spent some of the best three months of my life with Adam.

I was enamored with him. He was everything I never had in my life. The light to my dark. Just like my Evie. Everything about him was golden, from his hair color to his heart.

We spent the first month traveling the East Coast together. Soaking up everything we could in the short time we had. One day in Atlantic City, we threw caution to the wind and got married at a little chapel overlooking the ocean. It was spontaneous. Nothing like the strong, respectful, consistent soldier he later became.

For two months we lived in pure married bliss. Which is also when I became pregnant. He went back to his base a married man. I went back to the reservation and my tribe a married woman who was two months pregnant. When Evie was born, he was able to go on leave again. We gloried in the precious gift that I bore. When we were together, we lived and we loved to our fullest. Celebrated every moment we had with one another and our daughter. Never took for granted the time we had. It was all precious. Always.

And that is what I want you to know, my Isabeau. That during the time I had with you, I never wasted a moment. Those three months imprinted on my mind and my heart. There wasn't a day that went by I didn't think of the perfect angel I left behind.

My wish is for you to find a mate that connects so clearly to your heart and soul that it doesn't matter how much time you get together. Whether it's intermittent the way Adam and I were, or for a short time the way Ian and I connected. Or whether it is for a single year, like the time I had with you growing in my belly, and the three months after. One of the most beautiful years of my life. A grand purpose. Something I will always be grateful for, to the Creator, to your fathers and to you. May you find a love that spans time…

I know it's possible, for that's the way I have always loved you.

Catori.

I let out a deep breath as the tears once again fell down my cheeks. My body shook as I realized with every letter I learned more than I ever hoped to learn about the woman who gave me life. It was beauty and pain all wound together in pink parchment and the desperate words of a dying mother who had abandoned her daughter.

Without a second thought I picked up the phone and hesitated for a single moment when I pulled up my recent calls list.

I skipped over Jasper's name and clicked on Kyson's.

He answered on the first ring.

"You okay, baby?" His tone was anxious, worried.

"No," I whispered as more tears fell.

"Talk to me."

And for the next two hours we lay in our beds and talked about life. Me about my mother. Him about his lost hopes and dreams for his marriage and his daughter. We were both emotionally exhausted but neither one of us wanted to let the other go. I closed my eyes and fell asleep to the sound of his deep breaths, my phone still connected to his.

sixteen

═══

The coffeepot glugged along as I rubbed my scratchy, tired eyes. I slept hard after the long talk with Kyson. Even though I was tired, I felt refreshed. Ready to take on the future in a way that the possibilities seemed endless.

I yawned as there was a knock at my door.

Jasper. Probably got up late and didn't bother to make coffee, knowing I didn't leave the house to take on my day without two cups of liquid caffeine rushing through my system.

I covered my mouth when I let out another yawn, dragging my half-asleep booty to the door.

Another knock sounded against the door.

"Okay, okay, Jas. Jeez Louise, hold your horses already," I griped as I unlocked the bolt and opened the door with a flourish.

Jasper was not behind the door. Kyson was. Looking incredibly fine in a pair of worn Levi's with all the faded areas highlighting the best spots. Right then it was his strong, trunk-like thighs that had all my attention. What I didn't realize was at the time was that he was sizing me up, too.

I wore a small pair of boy-short undies, a camisole tank top that left my suddenly erect nipples very visible behind the thin cotton and my hair down and ratty from a night of hard sleep.

"Jesus! You answer the door like that? Baby, we gotta talk about this. But first..." he growled. Before I could even respond, he reached for me.

Honestly, I was still stuck on his muscular thighs when he gripped my hips, pushed me back, kicked the door shut with his construction booted foot, hooked a hand at my nape and pressed his lips to mine.

He went straight for the tongue action, licking against the seam of my lips until I opened my mouth and invited him in. Which I did the second my brain connected with the feel of his body against mine. He kissed me hard and deep. I wrapped my arms around his neck and tunneled my fingers into the long, dark layers of his silky hair.

He moaned against my mouth and sucked my tongue, then pulled back and nipped at my bottom lip. I groaned at the tiny pinch and repaid him back with a nip of his supremely curved top lip. Before I knew it, he'd led me across the room until the backs of my knees hit my bed and I started to fall.

Kyson caught me and eased my descent, but I wasn't alone. No, he stretched his fine-ass body over the top of mine and kissed the living daylights out of me.

His hands roamed along my waist, hips and up to squeeze my breasts. I arched, wanting more of his touch.

Kyson pulled back from the drugging kisses he was giving and pressed his forehead to mine, his breath labored. "Tell me to stop."

"Why would I do that?" I lifted my hips and rubbed my core against the erection behind his jeans. Absolute bliss.

"Isa, if you don't tell me to stop, I'm not going to be able to," he warned.

I lifted my upper body to press against him and ran my fingers down his long back until I reached the hem of his shirt. I curled my fingers around the cotton fabric and yanked it up to his neck. "Off!" I demanded.

"Baby… I'm trying to do the right thing here." He ran his nose along mine, nipped at my bottom lip, then soothed it with his tongue.

"So am I."

"It hasn't been six dates." One of his hands slid up my side and he cupped my breast, swiping his thumb along the nipple over the fabric then pinching the tip until I moaned. "Fuck!" He groaned, plucking at the peak until I was so hot and bothered, I cried out, ribbons of pleasure rippling through me, priming my sex for his entry.

"Please, Kyson, I'm dying over here." I hooked my leg over his thigh and used the friction of his body to grate along my throbbing core.

"I don't have a lot of time to give you, especially after yesterday." His words were a throaty growl, as though he was just as raw and ragged in this moment as I was. He pressed his lips to the space just under my ear and kissed his way down the column of my neck until he reached the top of my camisole. With his teeth he dragged the material down, then used his fingers to prop a breast out the top. It was graphic, needy and completely caveman-like, and I was all about it.

His mouth was burning hot as he took the abused tip inside and swirled it with his tongue before sucking rhythmically until I was breathless.

"Fast is good. Let's go with fast," I breathed.

He lifted up, letting my breast go with a final plop as he got to his knees. "Top off. Now, Isa."

I grinned, gripped the edges of my top and pulled it up and over my head, tossing it to the side. "You, too," I returned.

He backed off the bed and I swear I was having a moment of déjà vu. Only this time, there was no stopping us. His daughter was at school and his partner probably already downstairs getting to work.

Kyson yanked his T-shirt over his head then bent over and untied his work boots before toeing them off along with his socks. I shoved off my boy short panties at the same time and lay back completely buck naked, taking in his masterful broad chest, tight washboard abs and nipped-in waist. The man's body was insane. Stupid, ridiculously, crazy hot. Something no man should be granted for fear it would make smart girls everywhere dumb as a rock the second he bared it.

His light eyes darkened at the sight of my completely naked body and I bit down on my bottom lip, shivers of excitement racing through my veins. I had to clench my fingers together so I wouldn't reach for him.

"Just as I thought. Your body is perfect…*everywhere*."

On that statement I brazenly opened my thighs and let my knees fall to the sides, showing him everything.

I watched as he took in my sex, and then zeroed in on the hands I couldn't keep to myself. I ran them over my large breasts, teasing the peaks until I sighed before moving down my stomach, my thighs and lower in a featherlight caress. "Hurry, baby…" I whispered, not at all hiding the need in my voice.

He stood utterly still but his nostrils flared, and his eyes went even darker with lust as he clenched his hands into fists and licked his lips as if he was imagining touching me the way I was touching myself.

It was the hottest thing I'd ever done or seen in my entire life.

While I teased myself, he undid his jeans and pushed them and his underwear down to the floor, then kicked them away.

His erection was high and proud. Thick and long. My mouth watered as I watched him curl his large hand around the base of his shaft and give the length a luxurious stroke where he ran his thumb around the wet tip.

I swallowed against my dry throat, reached out my arms and called to him, "Come to me, please."

His corresponding smirk turned into a predatory grin.

"Not before I get my taste. Been waiting a long time to have your sweetness on my tongue, and I'm taking my fill," he said as he grabbed my ankles, tugged my body to the edge of the bed, fell to his knees and pressed his mouth to my center.

I cried out, my fingers going straight for his hair as I lifted my hips toward his mouth.

He groaned long and deep, licking me from top to bottom and swirling his tongue around and around in dizzying circles that made me pant and my clit throb to the same beat as my heart.

As I'd come to find with all things Kyson, he was a master at this, too. Just when he drove me to the pinnacle, he'd back down, lick me softly and place gentle kisses all over my thighs and pelvis until I'd start squirming again. Then he'd bring out the big guns by flattening his tongue and using it to drive me crazy as he teased, nipped and sucked, holding my thighs wide open, forcing me to take every ounce of pleasure until I skyrocketed so high I exploded against his tongue.

He kept at me until the aftershocks left and he built up the excitement and arousal all over again. I tugged on his hair and he lifted his face. That smirk I adored was back in place. Me, I'm sure I looked like I'd been through a tornado, but I didn't care.

"Get up here," I demanded and for once he complied without hesitation.

I wrapped my hand around his length the moment I could reach it. He grunted as I stroked it up and down and ran my lips and then my tongue along his strong neck so I could taste him.

"Isa, I don't have a condom…"

I smiled against his skin then bit down on the base of his neck, lost to my desire to mark him, take him in my body, claim him as my own.

"IUD, honey. I'm protected and it's been a long time. Been tested since the last time. I'm clean. You?"

"Jesus." He took my mouth as I swirled my thumb around the pearls of moisture seeping from the tip of his cock.

He settled his hips between my thighs and let my mouth go to look into my eyes. He cupped my cheek. "I'm clean. You can trust me, baby."

"I do. I trust you, Kyson. And you can trust me. I'd never lie to you." It was not only a promise but also a commitment.

He closed his eyes and nodded.

When he opened them there was so much hope and light in them, I lost my breath. He centered his length against me. As he eased inside, he dipped his mouth to press his lips against mine. "I believe you," he whispered and then took my mouth in a soul-blending kiss.

Kyson kissed me as he retreated and thrust inside my body over and over again. Each thrust better than the last. Each kiss deeper than the first. It was magnificent. A dance only the two of us knew.

When I couldn't take the duality of his depth inside my body and his tongue in my mouth, I arched my neck and soared, allowing him to manipulate my form and find his own pleasure as every nerve ending sizzled and my sex locked around his length in a viselike grip.

"Fuck, baby, it's so good. Never been this fuckin' good." He groaned loud and long against my ear, the layers of his hair tickling my nose and lips as he held on, pumping wildly until his release overtook him and his large body shuddered against mine.

For a few minutes after, he slowly eased his length in and out as though he was coming down from the highest high and needed to pace himself, walk instead of run.

Eventually, his hips stilled, and his form became heavy against mine. I wrapped all four of my limbs around him, locking him in place and just felt the beauty of his weight in my full embrace and the measured deep breaths he released against the feverish skin of my neck.

I held on until he slid to the side, disconnecting us intimately but not physically. I snuggled against his chest, pressing my lips to the warm skin against his heart.

He curled one hand around my butt cheek and the other around the hand I placed on his chest.

"Isa, that was…" He let out a long breath. "I don't even know what that was. Phenomenal doesn't quite cut it, but it's close."

I buried my face against his chest and chuckled, then gave a saucy bite to his pec.

"Though I gotta say, I won the bet," he stated triumphantly.

I frowned. "Bet?"

He looked down as I lifted my upper body. He curled his hand around the back of my head for leverage and took my mouth in a deep kiss before letting me go. "I broke your six-dates-to-sex rule. And honey, I am not sorry. Not even a little bit." He grinned like the cat that got his cream.

I pursed my lips and glared. "It was basically six dates." I semi-lied. Thinking it felt like we'd been seeing one another forever.

He laughed. "How you figure? By my count, we had four actual dates. You caved. Admit it. I'm charming and you think I'm awesome enough to possibly fall in love with me." He squeezed my ass cheek and I had to ignore the flutter of arousal the small move wove through my sated body.

I pouted and glared. "Pretty much four official dates, a ton of calls, texts and days spent working side by side."

Kyson shook his head. "Babe, just admit I won."

"No, because you didn't." I held up my hand, checking off dates as I went. "There was the day we met. The day you checked out the bakery we spent some time together. The first date, which kinda counts as two in one since you came to my place afterward. Then there was the biker bar, and the Thai food place where we got hot and heavy in the bakery before you dashed out to relieve your babysitter. And then of course today."

"This morning was not a date, babe. I came for a good-morning kiss and I lost my mind because my woman answered the door in her underwear looking sleepy cute and completely fuckable. No man could withstand that kind of pressure."

Oh, I liked that he saw me as cute and fuckable when I'd just woken up. "Fine, you win." I sighed in defeat because he was right. The brat.

He rolled me over and kissed me thoroughly before he pulled back. "Linc is probably pissed."

"Don't care. We had a really rough day yesterday and shared a lot. This was a natural progression. I'm glad we have this side to us now. I think we both needed the connection. It was time."

He traced the balls of my cheekbones, my eyebrows and then my bottom lip before he smiled and pecked me on the lips. "It was definitely time. And I can't wait to do it again. Depends on how quiet you can be tonight when I make you tacos. Now, do you think I could steal a cup of joe on my way downstairs to get back to work on your bakery?"

I looped my arms around his neck, stretched up and ran my teeth across his jaw, then kissed it better. He was delicious. Better than any dessert. I could just gnaw on him instead of all the desserts I baked.

"You can have anything you want," I said and meant it. The man had dug so deep into my life in such a short time there wasn't much I wouldn't willingly give him if it would make him happy.

He grinned. "I like that my woman gets happy and generous when she's had a couple of orgasms. This bodes well for my future. I'm thinking Hope and I will get a shot at some fantastic breakfasts once I've awakened you with my mouth, fingers, or cock."

My eyes widened and my clit throbbed as visions of sleepy morning sex with Kyson before making my small family breakfast filled my mind.

A dreamy sigh left my lips and I smiled.

"I like it even more that the idea of making a family breakfast after morning sex has you beaming with the prettiest light in your eyes." He kissed me sweet and slow. "Gonna work to keep that light in my life, Isa. Mark my words. This is only the beginning."

The administrative office at Hope's school was super nice and accommodating. Kyson had already cleared me for picking up Hope that morning, so I only needed to give them Hope's name and my ID.

One of the office ladies directed me to Hope's classroom and I stood at the door. They still had a few minutes, but I watched as Hope lifted her arms in the air and followed the teacher doing a series of stretches. Every time they changed position, the teacher would ask a different child how to spell a small word. Hope was asked to spell the word *bell* and got it on the first try. I wanted to clap for her like her own personal cheerleader. Instead, I took a picture of her when she smiled after getting the answer right. Quickly, I fired off a text of the pic to Kyson.

When the bell rang, all the children raced to a series of wooden cubbies that had their names on them, then stood in a line at the front of the door. Hope saw me standing out against the opposite wall and waved liked crazy.

I smiled and waved back until the teacher released the children one at a time, making eye contact with the person picking them up.

The second Hope reached me she hugged my side and then grabbed my hand and tugged me toward the exit.

"I can't wait to make treats with you, Izzy. It's going to be so fun. I told my teacher that my daddy's new girlfriend was so pretty and baked the bestest cookies in the whole world."

I smiled down as she prattled on.

"Do you think we could make some for my class?" She breathed as if she'd used up all her breath with her first burst of conversation.

I chuckled as we walked out, and I led her to the car. "We'll see what your daddy says."

"He'll say it's okay. He says you make the bestest cookies, too. Daddy let me have two more last night, but he ate four! Can you believe it! Four!"

It was nice to hear how happy she was and that they enjoyed the treats I sent home with him. After the treats he gave me in bed this morning, I'd pretty much bake or cook anything the man wanted.

I didn't notice a super-skinny brunette leaning against a tree next to my car.

I clicked the unlock button on my key fob and leaned down and pointed to my car so Hope could see which one was mine.

"Hope?" the woman called out when we got about fifteen feet from my emerald baby Serenity.

The two of us turned toward the thin, rather gaunt, tired-looking woman. She was beautiful with brown hair and brown eyes, but the girl needed to eat a burger, or fifty of them. With cheese.

"Do you know this woman, honey?" I asked Hope.

Hope tilted her head and stared at the woman then shook her head. "Nope!" She jumped up and down and then jetted toward my car. "Come on, Izzy, I want to go to the store and get the frosting!"

"Little miss, we're making the frosting not buying it, remember? We'll get the ingredients for it." I turned back around, and the woman was staring at Hope in a weird way I couldn't read, but didn't like.

"I'm sorry, do I know you?" I asked politely, knowing that I'd never seen that woman in my entire life.

"No, uh, no. I know Kyson, and uh…" She lifted her chin. "Hope. She must not remember me."

I shrugged. "Sorry. Kyson's at work. Would you like me to give him a message?" What I thought was stranger was the fact that she was at Hope's school instead of locating Kyson by phone or at his business.

She frowned and then picked at her dry lips. "Who are you?" she asked.

I squinted. "I'm Isabeau, Kyson's girlfriend."

The woman huffed. "Of course. His *girlfriend*. That's rich. Another little woman to take care of his prized possession."

I jolted my head and then took a step back. "I'm not sure who you are, or what you want, but I'd prefer if you not approach me again. If you want to speak to Kyson, you can look him up on your own. The company is…"

"Turner Brother Construction. I know. I know *everything* about Kyson Turner. Far more than you ever could. Tell him I said hi and I'll be seeing him." She sneered acidly, making her once pretty face look shrewd and hollow. Then the woman looked at my car where Hope was patiently waiting inside but bouncing up and down in her seat, so maybe *not so patiently* though she was still being good.

She waved at Hope until Hope waved back good-naturedly through the window.

I ground down on my teeth, my protective instinct kicking in as she started to walk away.

"Who should I tell him came calling?" I hollered.

The woman smirked and called out, "His wife."

My stomach dropped. Kyson Turner's nightmare was back in town. I inhaled fully and let it all out in a long, slow breath. I repeated the pattern a second time until I felt calm enough to drive. Then I got into my car, checked the mirrors, made sure Hope was safely buckled into the booster seat I borrowed from Kyson and motored off toward the grocery store.

The instant we pulled up to the back of the bakery in what I now considered my parking spot, I was met by Jasper prancing out the already open back door. I opened the car door and he breathed, "Tell me every detail!"

My mind instantly went to the freaky conversation I had with Veronica, Kyson's ex, not the fact that Jasper would want to know about this morning's roll in the hay since I hadn't showed up for work yet that day.

"There really isn't much to tell. I mean, she didn't do or say much of anything. Just freaked me out by showing up out of the blue," I said robotically, and Jasper frowned.

Jasper's brows pinched together. "Say what?" He cupped my cheeks and focused on my eyes. "You sick or something? I want to know about this morning with Kyson. What are you talking about?"

I shook my head and Hope exited the back, cutting off his line of inquiry.

Jasper's gaze went to Hope. "Hey, little lady." He took in her outfit from head to toe. "Looking snazzy in your purple dress and yellow Converse. I especially dig the yellow bow in your hair. I approve."

She smiled wide and it melted my heart. Then she put her hand on her hip and curved a finger around her chin as though she were Tim Gunn from *Project Runway*. She looked at Jasper rather speculatively, taking her time to assess him from his shirt down to his glittery slip-on boat shoes.

He struck a pose and waited on her verdict.

"I like your red pants, but the shoes are silvery, and your shirt is black. It doesn't match."

He pointed to the silver chain belt hanging down around his hips. "Silver," he said and lifted his chin.

She tilted her head and nodded. "I approve." She used his exact words.

"Excellent." He bowed, and she bowed back.

How the heck did Jasper already have a language with a child he'd met only once before and briefly at that? Never

mind. He was Jasper. He connected magically with all be-
ings young and old. It was his superpower.

"I hear you're baking with my Izzy today?" he queried.

"My daddy says that she's *his* Izzy. Nana says a person can
only have one boyfriend. I'm sorry you didn't win her." She
shrugged, came to his side and took his hand. "But you still
have Uncle Linc, right?"

Jasper narrowed his eyes at me. "So you're Kyson's now,
hmm?"

"Apparently." I winked.

"Information is not coming at the speed in which I expect
it. If this continues, we're going to need to bunk up again,
bestie," he warned.

"Then how would you bunk up with Lincoln?" I teased.

He frowned. "Hmm, this is a good point. No bother.
Soon, we'll see each other for the entire working day, and I'll
get my information fresh, not like the day-old bread I bring
to the homeless shelters. Speaking of, I found one not too
far from here. They'll give us a tax write-off for our contri-
bution. Evie was thrilled with this."

"That's great, Jas. Really." I hooked my arm with his and
he led us both inside.

When Kyson's gaze met mine from across the room, he
whispered something to Lincoln and then made his way over.

Hope intercepted him. "Daddy, Daddy, we got all the stuff
to make frosted cookies and lemon tarts!"

He hauled her up and onto his hip then gave her a smack-
ing kiss on her cheek. "That's wonderful, bug. Why don't
you go and say hi to Uncle Linc so I can have a quiet word
with Isabeau, yeah?" He set her back down on her feet.

"Okay, Daddy." She spun around in a circle and then
dashed to her uncle.

Kyson came to me and cupped my cheek. "You're unhappy. Why?"

I bit into my lip. "We need to talk privately."

"Is this about this morning?" His tone was wary yet still trusting.

I shook my head. "No, baby, that was perfect, better than perfect. I need to tell you what happened at Hope's school."

He frowned and then led me into the kitchen and back to the corner. "Lay it on me."

"Veronica is back." I bit down on my bottom lip and waited for him to say or do something. Maybe explode into a million pieces. Cry. Yell. He did none of those things. His brows pinched together, he put his hands to his hips and simply looked at me.

"Come again?" he said so low and deep I had to strain to focus on the words.

"Your wife showed up at Hope's school. I don't know how or why. After insulting me, she told me to tell you hello and that she was back. No, she said his wife was back. Are you still married to her?" I choked out as the tidal wave of emotion threatened to close off my throat altogether.

"Fuck, no! When I asked for a divorce she disappeared. Had to wait two full years of her abandonment for the judge to award me an uncontested divorce. Been free and clear just over a year. Though I suspect she may not realize that."

"Okay, good," I said softly.

He tugged me into his arms and held me close. "I'm sorry she freaked you out, baby."

"Me, too. Though she didn't really approach Hope. That was all I cared about."

"Thank you for protecting my daughter, Isa."

I trembled a little in his arms. "I'd never let anything hurt her, Ky. Never."

He pushed a lock of hair behind my ear and traced the side of my face until his finger was just under my chin. "I know. You're a good woman with a pure heart. Don't worry about this. I'll talk to my brothers and Pops. He'll get his club to ride out and find her."

I swallowed and nodded against his shoulder. "What if what she wants is you and Hope back?" I wasn't able to keep the jitteriness and fear from my tone.

His arms tightened around me and I savored the feeling. "Not gonna happen. Don't worry about anything. We don't know what she wants yet. I'll figure it out and then we'll hash it out together, yeah?"

I leaned back and looked into his soulful eyes. After what we shared last night, and physically this morning, we were connected. Really connected in a way that wasn't going to be easy to break. I closed my eyes and nodded, having faith that what we were building was strong enough to handle any storm that might come our way.

He kissed me deeply before pulling away. I followed his lips, taking another smaller kiss for myself, feeling greedy with the need to be close.

Kyson smiled and I sighed. Just that smile let me know it was all going to be okay. Because he would make it okay.

"Go make cookies with my daughter, baby."

"Okay, honey. We'll be ready when you're done."

"Looking forward to feeding my woman and my girl tonight. Let's not let anything take that joy away from us."

I cupped his cheeks and kissed him again. "I trust you."

He hooked my shoulder with his strong arm and turned us toward the main area of my shop. When we entered arm in arm, Hope looked up from where she was standing, put her hands in the air and cried out, "Cookies!"

seventeen

"Tell us every single detail, and don't leave out any of the sexy parts," Suda Kaye demanded, holding her wineglass as though it was a cup of warm soup, right at the edge of her lips. Her amber-colored eyes twinkled, reminding me of my papa Ian. She had his exact coloring and eyes, even a bit of his quirky smile. My heart squeezed at the thought. I needed to touch base with my parents again. It had been a week or so since I'd last chatted with either of them.

After yesterday's sex, meet and greet with Veronica, cookie baking and an excellent dinner made by Kyson, we'd hung out and watched a movie until we knew Hope was asleep. Then he'd made slow, quiet love to me. It was beautiful, mind-melting and filled my heart with such love I was afraid I'd slipped right past thinking he was awesome and worthy of falling in love with him, right into definitely, probably *in love* with him. Present tense.

He treated me like a queen. Worshipped me so many times

I was barely able to crawl out of his arms and drive home—
though he didn't want me to leave. When I explained that
I didn't want to confuse Hope by being there in the morning, especially since we hadn't been together very long, he
conceded. Only with the compromise that we'd spend more
family time together so that Hope could get used to me being
around. That way, we'd move into spending the nights together much quicker.

Today Hope was with Kyson's dad at the club, being doted
on by some of the old ladies. Apparently, the old ladies were
the top of the female hierarchy in the club. This meant that
none of the desperate women who hung around were allowed on premises. Since Hope was with Razor, I was free
to spend the day with my sisters and Jasper.

The three of them woke me up at noon—I hadn't gotten
much sleep the night before—and dragged my booty out
of bed, into the shower, then into a super-cute outfit Jasper
picked out.

We were at Suda Kaye and Camden's ranch house, sprawled
on their comfy sectional, drinking wine as though it was our
job. All four of us took off work today because Suda Kaye
demanded a girls' day, Jasper included of course.

"Kaye, she doesn't have to share the intimate parts," Evie
scolded.

Jasper frowned. "Speak for yourself. My Izzy doesn't go
light on details. At least she never used to. Not with me.
Until suddenly, she fell head over heels in love with hunk-
a-licious and the cat got her tongue." He pressed his lips together and zigzagged his head dramatically.

"Fine. Let me just say this. Kyson is brilliant in bed. With
his mouth, his fingers and his huge dick. Does that make
you feel better?" I narrowed my gaze at Jasper.

He shrugged. "More details."

"You want girth, length, to know that he drives me insane when he uses the tip of his tongue in a swirling motion right…" I started to point at my lady bits when Evie stood up and put both of her hands out in a stop gesture.

She shook her head, her blond waves falling over her shoulders. "Nope. Stop right there."

Suda Kaye tossed a throw pillow at Evie and hollered, "Heck, no! Do not stop there. I was getting an awesome visual!"

Jasper started to fan his neck. "Day-um. Sounds like my Izzy is being taken care of in the bedroom. Not to mention his brother is super skilled. Must be a family gift. Though it's about freakin' time she had a man rock her world."

I preened and sipped my third glass of wine. "He's awesome, you guys. Loving, sweet, gentle when I need it and then turns that all around and becomes greedy, possessive and bangs me like he'll never get the chance again." I tipped my head back against the couch, the wine swirling in my stomach warmly. "He's amazing," I breathed, visions of the things he did to me last night and yesterday morning rolling around my mind like a high-powered hamster wheel.

"Righteous!" Suda Kaye whispered.

Camden entered with two new bottles of wine, one in each hand.

"I vote Camden best husband ever!" Jasper called out with glee at the sight of the wine.

Camden's lips twitched as he went over to his wife and refilled her glass. He leaned down and took her mouth in a kiss that was relatively decent, but I totally caught the tongue slip before I averted my gaze.

"Thanks, handsome," she said with a smile.

"That is wonderful, Izzy. I'm happy things are working out for you and Kyson. He seems to be a good man. But why didn't he tell any of us about his child?" Evie sat back down and picked up her wineglass.

Camden sat his butt on the back of the couch behind Suda Kaye. "I knew about her. I'm actually surprised you girls didn't. Sweets, you remember when we had drinks and appetizers with Peyton and that woman he was dating for a bit? Sheila or something. Kyson was in a booth with his folks and his daughter having dinner."

Suda Kaye tapped her bottom lip and then her eyes widened. "Yeah, but Cam, that was ages ago. It never dawned on me to ask who the little girl was. And besides, when he came over to say hello, he said he was alone."

Cam shrugged. "The girl is his spitting image. Plus, Porter had mentioned at Sunday dinner a couple months back that he'd seen Kyson and Hope."

"Again, you didn't say it was his daughter. You said the name Hope. I figured it was a chick he was dating or a friend with benefits," Suda Kaye responded.

"Look, it doesn't matter. Kyson has a daughter. She's beautiful and I love spending time with her. I'm not at all afraid to be with him, knowing he has a kid." I defended my man even though I didn't need to. His reasons were his own and all of them had to do with protecting his daughter.

Evie pulled up her legs into the couch and turned more toward me. "Does it worry you, the stuff you mentioned about her mother? And her coming to the school yesterday? What is that all about?"

I shook my head. "I don't know. She made it clear she was back in town. I figure she'll connect with Kyson whenever she's ready to talk to him."

"What did Kyson say about that?" Jasper asked and reached for my hand.

I took it and let out a sigh. "We didn't really talk more

about it. He said he was going to have his father's motorcycle club brothers look for her around town. Then when he finds her, I guess he'll approach."

"Are you afraid that she wants Kyson and Hope back in her life?" Suda Kaye asked.

"Of course. I'm nervous about that, but I don't think he'll go back to her. She hurt him deeply, and the fact that she gave up on her daughter and abandoned them both..." I shook my head. "She'll never get his affection the way she used to have it again. Though I know he'd like for her to be in Hope's life if she's healthy and rehabilitated. I'm just not sure what that will look like. My plan is to simply be there for him in whatever way he and Hope need."

Evie nodded. "That's a smart plan." She sipped her wine and then added, "Will he be coming to the wedding next weekend when you get to meet Toko for the first time?"

I let out a long breath and Jas squeezed my hand. There was a lot to unpack with that question. The mere mention of my grandfather had my palms sweating. I'd never had a grandparent before. I wasn't sure how to act, what to say, and on top of those things, he was an elder in the tribe. I knew next to nothing about my Native American heritage, not that I'd taken the time to quiz the girls.

"Honestly, I don't know. He said his mom should be able to watch Hope, but four days is a long time to be away from his daughter and his business. I was thinking maybe he could come the night before the wedding instead of staying for the whole long weekend. That way he's not gone as long."

"Whatever works for you is fine with me. And of course, Jasper, Lincoln is welcome to come. It's not going to be a big event. The ceremony will be us standing at the bluffs, one of the elders marrying us and then a small party in front of Toko's home. The food will be made by Milo's family. At my count, including Kyson and Lincoln, we'll have fewer than fifteen people. We'll marry at sunset over the bluffs, drink amazing wine and enjoy traditional Native American cuisine."

I licked my lips and frowned.

Jasper sat up and tugged on my hand. "Tell them," he urged.

"His tone leads me to believe this is for all of you to hash out." Camden rose from his seat behind Suda Kaye. "I'm going to order a couple pizzas."

"Thanks, honey." Suda Kaye kissed her husband and then we all watched his fine ass walk out of the living space and into the kitchen.

"He's so good-looking..." I tried to change the subject.

Both Evie and Suda Kaye shook their heads but it was Jasper who spoke first.

"You can't keep your fears bottled up, Izzy. It's not healthy. Think of all the toxins coming straight out of your pores as big blackheads and pimples." He shivered. "You don't want that."

I smiled awkwardly, sat up and grabbed my wineglass, taking a couple big gulps of liquid courage.

"Izzy, we're family. You can tell us anything..." Evie reached across the couch and curled her hand around my knee.

I inhaled full and deep and then swallowed. "I'm scared to meet Tahsuda." I said it superfast to get it out before I chickened out.

Suda Kaye frowned. "Why?"

I shrugged. "I've never had a grandparent before. I've never had any family before aside from my dads and Jasper's mothers. They were the closest things I had to a mother figure growing up. They taught me about my body, my cycle, hormones…everything. Our two little families had all of our holidays and birthdays together. It wasn't traditional, but it was filled with love. I have no complaints."

"Okay, then. What would make you afraid to meet Toko?" Evie asked gently.

The room felt suddenly like the furnace had been turned on. I grabbed my shirt and flapped it against my chest, trying to get some air.

"Wow, you're really bothered by this?" Suda Kaye asked with genuine concern. She moved to a spot on the floor closest to Jasper and me, reaching out to put her hand just above my knee. "Izzy…talk to us," she encouraged.

Evie scooted down the couch so her knees were touching mine and she could put her hand to my other leg.

"I… What if he doesn't like me? What if he doesn't see anything of Catori in me?" Tears hit the backs of my eyes, and my nose started to tingle.

"No, oh, my word. Toko will love you. He won't like you. He will fall absolutely *in love* with you," Suda Kaye promised, tightening her hold on my leg.

"How do you know? He's never met me. Does he even know I exist?" I barely got the words out.

Evie smiled and it was like the sun coming out on a dark day. Effervescent. "Izzy, Toko knows about you. He's always known about you. I've spoken with him. He would have been here the very next day after you arrived had I not told him to hold off."

My eyes widened and I shrank in on myself.

She smiled softly once more. "And that is why I told him to wait. That reaction right there. You were just getting your footing. Getting to know us. Finding your path. Building your business with Jasper. I didn't think it was a good idea to add another family member on top of all that change."

I nodded. "You were right. I would have freaked out, made Jasper get back in the car and we would have headed to Mexico."

"Hey, Mexico was an option? When? Where was I?" he teased, wrapping his arm around my back. "Izzy, you are the kindest, sweetest, most easygoing woman I've ever met. You are the epitome of all the good your fathers instilled in you. Then I look at your stunning sisters and I've never seen you more at peace. It's like a part of you opened up and is shining so brightly it's hard to look at you for fear I'll go blind."

"Jas," I choked out.

"Everyone sees it, honey. You glow all on your own here. I think that's what your grandfather will see. It's what I see in all three of you. Not to mention, girl, your wild, crazy hair." He pointed a finger at Suda Kaye and then at Evie. "Bingo! It may not be brown or gold or black like the other women in your blood, but, baby, it's fire red and all *you* while still being a part of *them*."

Evie reached up and held a lock of my hair. "It's soft and silky just like Mom's."

"And you have her smile. The exact same smile. And the cheekbones, girlie, all three of us got them direct from Mom who got them from our Toko," Suda Kaye added. "Besides, he's an elder and a very spiritual man. He will know his blood granddaughter on sight. I swear. You're going to make his year. Maybe even his decade."

I sniffed as a tear fell down my cheek. "You think?"

Suda Kaye took my hand and held it. "I don't think, I *know*. Toko will absolutely adore you the same way we do. More so because you're of Catori."

I smiled.

Evie squeezed my thigh. "Just tell him you're excited to

learn Comanche and you're in like Flynn." She crossed her fingers over her heart and grinned.

Suda Kaye burst out in laughter. "That's not a bad idea. He's super proud of his heritage."

"And that's another thing. I don't know anything about being Native American. I didn't even know *I was* Native American until you ladies showed up. It wasn't ever something my fathers talked about."

Evie shrugged. "So we'll bring you up to speed on the basics. The rest you'll experience in real time. No one is expecting you to all of a sudden be this long-lost member of the tribe. And besides, there are other tribes living on the reservation that Toko's on. And technically, our grandmother was Navajo and Comanche, but somehow Toko likes to pretend we're all a hundred percent his descendant." She shook her head. "It's pretty funny."

"And besides, I'll be there. Remember our pact?" Jasper held up his pinky finger.

I hooked mine with his.

"We're never alone as long as we have each other," we said at the same time.

He pulled me into a hug, and I held on to my best friend in the whole world and knew, no matter what happened, I had him. He'd be there through it all because he already had been, and he always would be.

"Aw, man, now I want a secret pinky pact," Suda Kaye pouted.

Evie chuckled and reached her hand out, pinky extended. Suda Kaye linked hers around Evie's.

"What's the pact?" she asked eagerly.

Evie pursed her lips. "Uh, sisters for life?"

Suda Kaye scowled. "Lame. We're already sisters by birth."

Jasper leaned over and linked his over theirs. "Izzy?"

I followed his gesture and linked mine over all three.

Jasper looked at each one of us. "Friends till the end..." he said.

Suda Kaye smiled and called out. "Yay! Friends till the end!"

Each one of us called out the phrase and we lifted our arms up into the air and then let them go, all of us giggling and falling backward.

"I think we need to drink to that," Jasper suggested.

"Good idea, friend." I grabbed my glass and each one of us held them aloft.

"To the family we choose. And to Evie and Milo getting married!" I squealed with Evie, Suda Kaye and Jas as each of us clinked our glasses. We shifted the conversation to Kyson and Hope, to Toko, to the details surrounding Evie's small wedding.

The night was perfect. Pizza arrived and we chowed down while we did some serious damage to Cam and Suda Kaye's wine storage. She didn't care. She said her hubby was über rich and to drink up...so we did.

eighteen

===

Hope poured fresh-cut basil into the sauce pot. She was the cutest thing ever, pushing her little tongue into the side of her cheek while putting all of her focus on spreading the basil around the pot.

"Excellent work, little miss. Now you can pour in the oregano." I pointed to the small bowl that held the cut-up herb.

"Maybe our little Hope will be a chef like Uncle Jasper and Izzy." Jasper set the parsley he'd just chopped in front of her on the counter before kissing the crown of her head.

She gifted him the biggest smile. "Will you let me work in your bakery when it's done, Uncle Jasper?" she asked him.

He nodded. "I'm having Uncle Linc build you a step stool just for the job. I'm going to teach you how to expertly swirl frosting on a perfect cupcake." Jasper winked.

Hope grinned and reached for the parsley. "Do I put it in now, Izzy?" she asked, her excitement filling the room. I had her set up at the counter closest to the stove so I could work and watch her at the same time. Jasper fluttered around the kitchen doing bits and bobs here and there. Filling drinks, adding more snacks to the overflowing counter of food we already had out, playing the perfect host when it was Kyson and I who'd invited everyone over. It was his way. He always made himself useful, wanting everyone in his environment to be happy and feel welcome.

Across from us, Evie, Milo, Suda Kaye, Camden, Lincoln and Kyson were playing a round of Left, Right, Center with some poker chips at Kyson's six-seater kitchen table. Suda Kaye introduced us to the game and because it didn't take a lot of thought, especially when imbibing, everyone enjoyed it thoroughly.

The past few days had been a whirlwind of fun and immensely good times. I'd been watching Hope all week while Kyson's mother recovered from the flu, and he and Lincoln worked steadily on the bakery. Hope and I had spent a day with Evie and with Suda Kaye, and a lot of time just being girlie. I took her to get her nails done, and I allowed her to choose colors for both of us. So now I had yellow painted toes and hot-pink fingernails. Another day Jasper and I took her out shopping for more school clothes since Kyson noted she'd been growing out of everything.

I'd never seen a more thankful man when Hope and I came home with an entirely new wardrobe. Courtesy of me and Uncle Jasper, which he'd since been coined, much to his extreme joy. After finding out he'd earned a title, he went a little bonkers in a store called Justice that apparently was little-girl heaven. The two of them hit it off, especially when it came to fashion. I just enjoyed seeing them happy.

I hummed, enjoying the sounds of my new family having fun as I sautéed onions, green peppers and garlic, readying it for adding the tomato sauce and tomatoes I'd already stewed. Kyson came up behind me, wrapping his arm around my waist, plastering my back to his front where he then pressed a warm, thrilling kiss to my neck. He inhaled. "Smells good, baby."

"Spaghetti sauce always does," I murmured.

He bit down on my neck playfully then soothed it with his lips. "I wasn't talking about the sauce, Isa."

I shivered and he chuckled.

"Oh, man, we forgot the fresh sourdough bread," Jasper grumbled from where he was digging through the remaining bags we brought over from our grocery-store haul. "We cannot have spaghetti without garlic bread. It's sacrilege," he whined.

Kyson laughed and patted me on the ass. "I'll run out. There's a store close."

"I'll go with you. Need to pick up some more beer." Lincoln stood up as he'd just been taken out of Left, Right, Center by Evie, who whooped and hollered every time she won a poker chip.

"And wine! More wine, please!" Suda Kaye blurted, rolling the three dice, putting her hands in the air and screaming, "In your face, baby!" To Camden, whom she just kicked out of the game.

Camden chuckled, curled a palm around his wife's neck and kissed her silly. When he was done, she had a dreamy look on her face.

I laughed and shook my head.

Kyson tunneled his hands into the back of my hair and turned my head so I was facing him. He kissed me full and deep then pulled away, tugging on my bottom lip. "The things I'm going to do to you tonight…" he warned and

I sighed. He smirked, kissed me soft and let me go. "You got Hope, baby?"

"Always."

He grinned. "Perfect woman."

"Don't I know it!" I teased back.

He grabbed his keys from a basket at the edge of the kitchen counter. "Come on, bro," Kyson called out and Lincoln gave Jasper a kiss goodbye and told him to be good.

To which Jasper called out, "I'm always good! You know that better than anyone!"

Both men left chuckling and I continued to instruct Hope. For a child her age, she paid a great deal of attention. Maybe she would be interested in cooking as a career one day. Either way, I planned on teaching her whatever she wanted to learn.

"Okay, little miss, time for you to stir all of the ingredients together," I said.

She got off her stool and I moved it in front of the stove. She stepped up and I wrapped my arm around her waist, keeping her a good distance from the hot burners.

"Now, you have to be very careful when you're in front of a hot stove. It could burn you. Always be aware of where your body is and where your arms and hands are. You don't want to accidentally reach for something and touch the hot pot with your arm. It will hurt."

She nodded and backed into my front, keeping her distance.

I held the spoon with her as we stirred the huge batch of sauce we'd made. I wanted Kyson to have extra left over in case I wasn't here to make dinner tomorrow. Not that I'd been anywhere else the past week. Kyson felt that the more I was there, the better, and he'd made it clear he wanted to have dinner nightly as a family.

I wanted to give Hope some time to really get used to me, but also have quiet time with her dad. As much as it concerned me that we were seeing too much of each other, Kyson did not feel the same. He believed they'd had enough time without a woman in their lives and there was no reason to go slow in this relationship.

"You're doing a great job, Hope." I allowed her to stir the sauce by herself but hovered my hand over hers to ensure she didn't accidentally move the wrong way or lose balance.

"I like cooking with you," she said.

I smiled and kissed her cheek. "I like it, too, little miss."

Her small cheeks got pink when she grinned. "My best friend Selena cooks with her mama all the time. She says they make tamales from scratch. What does *from scratch* mean?"

"It means homemade. Like we're doing with the sauce."

"So I can tell Selena that I made spaghetti sauce from scratch with my new mommy, too!" Her voice was filled with excitement while my heart stopped beating altogether.

Jasper laughed and broke into our conversation. "Just wait until your new mommy teaches you how to make candy from scratch. You'll be the talk of the school!"

I nudged his shoulder so hard he sidestepped and had to grip the counter to catch himself from falling. I glared at him, my mouth feeling tight and my skin hot. His face turned beet red and he frowned. He knew he'd stepped over an imaginary line and I could see he'd just realized his error.

"Oh, will you, Izzy? Teach me how to make candy?" She breathed with hope in her tone.

I closed my eyes and took a breath, trying to calm down from the *my new mommy* discovery. Kids said crazy things all the time. It didn't mean she really understood what she was saying. Definitely something I planned to bring up with Kyson so he could explain things to her in his way.

"Of course I'll teach you how to make candy," I agreed, adding candy to the ever-growing list of things Hope wanted me to teach her to make.

"I have to pee," Hope declared loudly so I let her go and she skipped out of the kitchen down the hall.

I turned to Jasper.

He held his hands up. "I'm sorry. I got carried away. It won't happen again, I swear." At least he looked properly contrite.

"We have to be careful. We don't know what the future will hold and I don't want to upset her if things take a bad turn."

Jasper looped his arm around my shoulders. "Izzy, it's not going to go bad. You and Kyson are perfect for one another. I've never seen you this happy. The man exudes pride every time he's near you. His daughter loves you and you love her. What could go wrong?"

As if he'd conjured the devil himself with his words, I heard Hope's voice from the other room talking to someone.

"Can you watch this?" I gestured to the sauce. "I'm gonna check on Hope."

"Pffttt, in my sleep." He waved me off.

I entered the hallway and was going to head to her room when I heard a woman's laughter from the direction of the front door. I made my way to the front and noticed the door was open and the screen closed.

My heart started pounding as I saw an adult's dark brown head next to Hope. I dashed forward and the screen door slapped against the frame when I plowed through.

"Izzy! Look at what I got." She jumped to her feet and

held up a brand-new Barbie doll. Wrapping paper littered the porch around her checkered Converse.

The woman stood and turned around.

Veronica.

"Hope, come here." I reached for her hand and tugged her to my side.

She pushed the toy toward my face. "Look! The nice lady said the doll looks like me and she does!" She squealed in delight.

I clenched my teeth and glared at Veronica.

"Little miss, Uncle Jasper needs help with that sauce. His arm is probably getting tired of stirring, waiting for you to come back."

Her eyes widened and she hugged the toy to her chest. She twirled around and looked at Veronica. "Thank you, Roni! But I have to go. Uncle Jasper needs me!"

"Goodbye, sweetheart. See you soon!" she said sweetly, and I wanted to kick her right in the lady parts.

When Hope was out of earshot, I stepped onto the porch and shut both the wooden door and the screen behind me.

"What are you doing here?" I growled, not hiding the anger pouring through my question in the least.

She sneered. "Technically, this is my house. My husband. And my daughter. Really, I should be asking you what you're doing in a married man's house playing mommy to my daughter!" Her words dripped with a poisonous venom.

"How dare you show up here like this. Did you wait for Kyson to leave?"

She smiled and shrugged her shoulder. "I wanted to see my daughter. There's nothing wrong with a woman wanting to see her child."

"It's been years, Veronica. You can't just show up out of the blue and bring a toy and expect everything to be okay.

That's not how things work when you abandon your child!"
I tried to keep my voice down but apparently, it didn't work.

Out of nowhere I felt a large presence behind me.

Veronica looked up and I turned my head to see Milo standing behind me with his arms crossed and his black hair down around his shoulders. He looked like a Native American warrior from a hundred years ago, come to save the day.

"Leave." He bellowed the single word.

Veronica took two steps back as the hair on my neck stood up in response.

"You can't tell me to leave my own house," she mocked and crossed her arms over her chest, copying Milo's stance.

"I can. I have. Leave before I make you leave," he warned and began to make his way down the four steps that led to the sidewalk where Veronica stood.

She took another two steps back and I smirked.

"Who are you anyway?"

"Uncle Milo," he said clear as day, and my heart pitter-pattered while I literally swooned where I stood. Milo wasn't much for speech but when he did speak, he meant every word he said.

"Hope doesn't have an uncle Milo," she scoffed.

"She does now. Leave." He took another step down.

I stayed where I was and hoped that Kyson and Lincoln would show.

Veronica squinted and her lips twisted into a snarl. "You can't scare me away from my own home and daughter!" she cried out.

"Leave!" he thundered and took the final two steps down.

Veronica jumped and scampered toward the beat-up Honda Civic that had a primed back passenger door with no paint.

I came up behind Milo and put my hand on his shoulder right about the time that Evie came traipsing out the door.

Veronica's gaze flitted to the tall, golden beauty and frowned. Evie came up behind me and wrapped her arm around my waist.

"Izzy, you're trembling." Evie pulled me to her side. "Milo, what's wrong? I heard your voice shake the windows all the way from inside."

Milo didn't speak, just lifted his chin toward Veronica, who was scrambling to get into her car.

"Tell Kyson he hasn't seen the last of me!" she screeched and I winced at the sound.

"Who was that?" Evie asked as the car started up and pulled away, leaving black skid marks in front of Kyson's house.

"That was Veronica."

"She just showed up out of the blue?" Evie choked out the words and I nodded. "What in the world would possess her to do that?"

I shook my head. "I don't know."

"I do not like this woman. Her eyes show her soul is black," Milo stated as he continued to stare in the direction that Veronica disappeared.

Evie linked her elbow with mine. "Come on, let's get inside. Hope needs you."

Her words broke me out of my stupor, and I nodded. "Let's go. I want to feed my family."

Later that night after everyone had left, Kyson tugged off his shirt by lifting his arm behind his head and yanking it off in that manly way that made me drool.

I licked my lips and watched my man pace as I sat on the bed cross-legged fully clothed.

"You're spending the night," he stated in a way that was more of a demand than a suggestion.

"Honey, I don't know if that's a good idea. Hope made that comment earlier..." I tried to remind him of the discussion we'd had.

He stopped midpace, put his hands on his hips and stared me down, making me lose track of what I was about to say. I couldn't help but check out his muscular chest and cut abs. I wanted to run my tongue down every ridge. Maybe twice. Okay, three times.

"Isa, we're done with this. You are in Hope's life and if I have any say, you're going to be in her future. Forever, baby."

I clenched my hands into fists. "What she said about me being her new mommy concerns me. And then Veronica showed up. Maybe it was a sign," I blurted.

I'd told him everything that happened before and after Veronica arrived. We'd agreed to enjoy the evening with family and talk about it when Hope was in bed. Hope was now in bed and I was freaking out.

"It was a sign that you are meant to be her stepmother. Veronica is unstable if she thinks she can show up at Hope's school and here at home, waiting for me to leave so she can get her moment to pounce. Fuck, no. Not okay. My number hasn't changed. If she wants to talk to me and be reintroduced to Hope, she needs to do it the right way."

I nodded my head but fiddled with my fingers. "Honey, I'm not her mother. As much as I love her, and baby, you have to know I do, I, too, want what's best for her. I didn't have a mother. I know what that's like, and if Hope can have even a slim chance at a real relationship with her birth mom... I don't want to get in the way of that."

Kyson let out a long sigh and then came over to the bed

and sat next to me. He took my hand and wrapped both of his around it, resting it on his thigh.

"I get what you're saying. I would love for Hope to have the Veronica I knew and loved. The woman I married all those years ago. Unfortunately, history has not shown her to be stable. I need to know that she's off the booze, pills and anything else she might be into. Veronica is not trustworthy. Until I've seen her and evaluated what's going on in that head of hers, I don't want her near Hope. You did the right thing making Hope go inside and keeping her safe."

"And what about the things Hope said? About me being her new mommy?" My voice shook with emotion. I wanted so badly to be that person for Hope, but I didn't know that it was my place. We were still relatively new. Anything could happen.

"Isa, I think Hope understands that you're the woman in her dad's life. You've brought her into your family, taking her to spend time with Jas and the girls. She hasn't had that. None of my brothers have ever brought home a woman to spend time with the family. Neither have I, as you know. So Hope is picking up on what she's getting with you in her life. Someone who dotes on her, teachers her things, takes her shopping and to get her nails done. Her life has only gotten better since you've been in it. And baby, all those things you're doing with her is what all her friends' moms are doing with them. It's a natural progression and one I'm not at all against."

"But it's too soon."

He shook his head. "Isabeau, it's not. Don't you feel it?" The question came in his low, serious rumble that made me shiver and tremble. The same one he used when he was lost to his pleasure in bed with me.

"Feel what?"

He smiled softly and squeezed my hand. "Don't you feel what we're building here, baby?"

I bit down on my bottom lip. "I'm afraid to hope. It's so soon."

"No, it's just that it's right. We're building a life together, honey, and it's beautiful. Fuckin' amazing. Everything I wanted to have my entire life. A woman that was made just for me. A family. My business. My daughter happy with aunts and uncles everywhere, showing her love. Time with my brothers and parents all together. I have that with you. And Isa, it's only going to get better."

I swallowed down the fear and anxiety prodding at me. "How can you be so sure?"

He let go of my hand and lifted his to curl around my nape. He shifted his face so we were almost nose to nose. "Because I've never loved a woman the way I love you. It's as though you're rooted deep into my life. I never want to lose you. I'm in love with you, Isabeau, and I know you love me. It's in your eyes every time you look at me. Every time you smile at my daughter. Your love shines so clearly anyone can see it."

Tears hit the backs of my eyes and one fell down my cheek. He swiped it with his thumb. "I do love you, Kyson. So much. And I love Hope with my entire heart. All I want is for us to be a happy little family. And I want a future with you so badly, it hurts. But I'm scared."

He pressed his forehead to mine. "What are you scared of?" he whispered. "Tell me your fears, baby, and I'll fight every last one of them until you feel secure in our love, in where we're headed together."

Kyson waited, nose to nose, while I breathed deeply and got myself together enough to speak. "I'm scared you and Hope weren't meant to be mine."

He cupped my neck with both his hands and looked deep into my eyes. "Then it looks like I'm going to have to convince you." He grinned and then took my mouth in a soul-merging kiss.

Kyson took his time convincing me I was his. By the end of the night, when I was curled around his warm body, my cheek pressed to his bare chest, his fingers running through my hair, I fell asleep, content knowing I was exactly where I was meant to be.

nineteen

Warm hands skimmed over my stomach and up my rib cage, pushing my sleep tank up and over my breasts. Kyson's hands covered both my breasts as his thumbs teased the tips.

I woke slowly, blinking my eyes open just as his mouth covered a nipple and sucked. I lifted my legs, pressing the soles of my feet to the bed, and hugged the sides of his waist with my thighs, cradling him over me.

He grumbled around my erect tip. "Good morning, baby." He flicked the peak with his tongue and sucked hard enough to warrant a low moan from me.

I hummed and tangled my fingers into his silky hair, glorying at the pleasure, arching into his mouth as he devoured first one breast and then the other.

My sex throbbed and heat seared through my veins. I lifted my head and ran my tongue along the length of his neck, appreciating the salty, warm, rich taste of him first thing in the morning.

One of his hands left my chest and ran down my body so he could cup my bum. He ground his naked length against my core until I sighed a needy, "Please."

He grinned against my breast and ran his mouth down to my sternum and lower.

"Want you, Ky," I breathed, squeezing my thighs against his waist and yanking my top the rest of the way off, tossing it aside.

"Mmm," he hummed as he inhaled against my panties, rubbing his nose up and down the heart of me. "Want to eat you first." He curled his fingers into the side of my panties and tugged them down my legs.

"You, too." The words turned into a moan when he covered my center with his mouth and twisted his tongue inside. "Turn around for me." I sighed as he sucked on that bundle of nerves that made me arch into him. He was so skilled I had to try hard not to come too quickly. The man was a master at going down on me, but I was hungry, too, and dizzy with lust. I wanted nothing more than to please him the same way he was pleasing me.

"W-want you in my mouth," I stuttered as he sucked hard at my clit, sending ribbons of fire to lick at my insides and swirl low in my belly, readying for one helluva release.

He groaned, got up on his knees and straddled my form backward. His feet faced the headboard, and his head hovered over my sex. He centered his long, thick cock right over my face. I could still smell the woodsy hint of soap from the shower we took after he made love to me last night.

My mouth watered and I lifted my hands, gripping on to his hips to keep him steady as I took just the tip of him into my mouth. He groaned low in his throat as I swirled my tongue around the knobbed head. I was getting into a rhythm of sucking on him, taking an inch more at a time with each plunge, then releasing, when he drove two fingers into my sex and locked his mouth over my clit. I cried out but it was muffled by his length pushing deep into my mouth. He touched the back of my throat and I relaxed, breathing through my nose as I allowed him to thrust in and out at his will.

He was lost to his desire, thrusting into my mouth in jagged, uncoordinated movements. I loved making him like this. Losing his mind to the pleasure I was giving, and what he was giving me in return.

I used my nails, dragging them down his muscular thighs until he lost it, thrusting so deep, I gagged; my eyes teared but the pleasure-pain of the move had me lifting my hips and forcing him to take me as deeply as I was taking him.

He did not disappoint. He growled around my flesh, held my thighs open wide and pinched my hot button at the same time he added a third finger.

I came in a glorious rush of endorphins and sizzling nerve endings, mindlessly thrusting my hips and sucking his cock like it was my favorite treat. I loved every second of it.

"Jesus, Isa." He lifted back up and off the second my hips stilled. He spun around above me so quickly I didn't even know what was happening before he had me flipped onto my stomach where he yanked me up to my knees, centered his length at my willing entrance and drove in to the hilt.

Thankfully, he covered my mouth because the cry that left me was animalistic and surely would have awakened Hope, even if her bedroom was on the other side of the house.

"Damn, woman, you make me crazy," he growled and powered his hips in and out at a relentless pace.

I curled my fingers into the bedding and pushed back, *giving* as much as *taking* the pleasure my man was doling out.

He let go of my hips and curled over my back. His chest

was covered in sweat when he rested it against my own slick skin. He whispered in my ear, "You're gonna give me another one, Isa."

"Baby." The single word fell from my lips on a needy sigh. His length continued to pound that perfect place inside that made me absolutely wild. Still, I held out, wanting him with me this time. Wanting to explode together.

"Give in, Isa." He brought one of his hands up to my breast and plucked at the tip. My sex locked around his length with every twist of his fingers while I panted.

"I can't." I pushed my hips back and stretched my neck out, reaching for something. For what, I didn't know. All I knew was I never wanted this bliss to end.

His hand moved from my breast, down my stomach to where we were joined. His fingers found the throbbing nerve and teased the tight knot while growling, "You will," into my ear.

The room started to blink in and out of focus as stars glittered in my peripheral vision. Kyson was literally making me see stars.

"Isa." He swiveled his hips and brought those wet fingers he'd used on me up to my mouth where he pushed them inside. I gloried in the combined taste of us.

"Fuck, my woman is the hottest thing I've ever seen." He hauled me up to my knees, still connected, plastering my back to his front while I wrapped my arms behind his neck loosely.

He curved a palm around my jaw, easing my chin toward his face, and took my mouth in a searing kiss. He was so deep I could barely breathe, but I didn't care, because it was him and me and everything right in the world.

Kyson moved with complete control over his massive, muscular form, snaking his other hand down toward my stomach and then between us. He pulled his mouth from mine and panted as he cupped me between my thighs, still powering in and out in almost furious, bone-quaking movements.

"Feel us, baby. Feel our love," he ordered.

I covered his hand and separated my fingers around his length as he pierced me over and over. I rested my head against his neck and lost myself to the beauty of our joining. Drugging thoughts of how I was going to receive this pleasure for the rest of my life covered me like a tranquil breeze over my heated skin.

"Love you, Isabeau. Love you so damn much it hurts not being with you every day, right here in this bed."

I closed my eyes as his words coated my soul in nothing but his love.

He picked up the pace, I arched into him, locked my arms around the back of his neck and lost myself. My soul, everything I ever was, and everything I ever would be, to this man. The man I loved.

We were one.

Unending.

Forever intertwined.

He tipped his head back, held me tight, his hand cupping my sex possessively as he groaned, sinking his masterful body back onto his calves and taking me with him as jet after jet of his powerful essence flooded me. He pressed his forehead to the back of my neck and panted, sucking in large bouts of air as he came down from an incredible high.

I covered his arms, the one that came around my waist locking me to him, the other still cupping me carnally.

"I love you, too," I whispered.

He set his mouth against the back of my neck and kissed me there.

"Do you feel it now, baby? All that we're building?" he asked, the sweat cooling in the morning air around us.

"Yes," I admitted without hesitation.

"You still scared?" he murmured.

I shook my head. "No. Not if I have your love."

He let out a long sigh that cooled my sweaty neck. "Fuck me, the perfect woman. I had to wait thirty years to have the woman for me. Went through hell and back to earn this moment, right here with you."

I grinned, tilted my head back and looked into his glorious blue eyes, loving seeing the way he saw me. As something to cherish. To adore.

He kissed me sweet and slow, detangling from my body. "Shower together?" he asked.

I shivered at the thought of another round of sex in the shower.

Kyson chuckled, curled his arms around my form and lifted me into a princess hold. "Come, let me clean you up."

"Mmm." I leaned my head against his chest and let him carry me.

He set me on my feet next to the shower, which he turned on and set the temperature to steaming.

"What are you thinking about?" Innuendo was clear in the sultry way he asked.

"How I'm going to have a blast making pancakes for you and Hope this morning. I'm thinking my magical blueberry and oat with a cinnamon drizzle on top."

That had Kyson laughing out loud. "I fuck her silly. Make her come hard, twice, and instead of thinking about me and more sex, she can't wait to feed me and my kid." He shook his head. "Babe, your priorities are whack," he said playfully.

I harrumphed and crossed my arms over my chest as he

stepped into the now steamy shower stall. It was big enough for two but not huge.

I stepped in and moved toward the back and pursed my lips. "They are not! I need to feed my man and his daughter. This is what I love to do!"

He grinned and soaped his beautiful body up, rubbing his hands down his wet chest and lower around his sex.

I licked my lips and watched in rapt attention as his hands moved over his magnificent form.

"If you keep looking at me like that, woman, I'm going to request you get on your knees so I can feed you something else."

I blindly shut the shower stall door, looked right at his face and went down to my knees. "I'm pretty hungry, baby, and you didn't let me finish earlier." I licked my lips again in a salacious move I didn't even know I had in me.

"You like to finish?" He cocked one of his eyebrows toward his hairline, asking the question all men want to know.

I crooked a finger. "Come here and find out."

He stepped closer, his once again hard cock hovering in front of my face. He was beautifully formed. Maybe above average in length and girth, though I found the best part was the fact that he knew exactly how to use it.

I flicked my tongue against the wet tip. "But when I'm done, and you're done, I'm teaching Hope how to make pancakes."

Before he could respond, I took him into my mouth.

He finished, then finished me off a third time with his fingers and then I made my new little family pancakes.

Hope was circling her entire mouth with her tongue, trying to reach all the syrup and butter that had made its way all over her face. How children got so messy eating the exact same food as adults was a mystery to me.

She finished the last bite and then took her plate over to the sink where she set it down.

"That was yummy, Izzy."

I grinned and prodded a bite of pancake with my fork. "It's because you helped make them."

She grinned wide and puffed up her little chest at the compliment.

"Hey, bug, why don't you come sit on Dad's lap so we can talk, yeah?"

Hope frowned and scrambled over to Kyson where she crawled up his leg and sat sideways on his lap. He curled his arms loosely around her so she wouldn't fall back but could stay close while he spoke to her.

"You remember that lady that came to the house yesterday and gave you a toy?"

Her clear blue eyes lit up and she nodded avidly. "Yes! She brought me a mermaid Barbie that looks like me! I didn't have one like her. She's beautiful. Like a rainbow and her tail lights up! Can I take a bath with her today? Please, Daddy! Please?" she asked in a rush.

He nodded. "Sure, bug, but what I want to know is, what did the lady say to you? Did she tell you her name?"

Hope nodded. "She said it was Roni. I thought it was funny because it sounds kinda like a boy name, Dad. But I didn't tell her that. I swear!" Her eyes got big as though she might get into trouble.

He cupped her cheek. "What else did she say, sweetheart?"

Hope looked up at the ceiling and bit her lip as though she was truly thinking hard about the conversation she had with Veronica yesterday.

"Oh! She said she was a long-lost family member. And

that she just came back and was excited to see me. And um, that she was your best friend and mine, too. Which I said was wrong because Selena is my best friend."

Kyson's jaw locked tight as I watched him react to what Hope was saying.

"Okay. Anything else?"

She frowned and grabbed a lock of her hair and played with it before she shook her head. "No, just, um, that I would see her again soon and she'd bring me another mermaid Barbie. Then I could have them swim together in the bath. Wouldn't that be cool, Daddy?"

Her innocence was breathtaking.

"Sure, baby, two mermaid Barbies would be very exciting. But let's get back to what's important, why I wanted to have this talk."

Hope nodded and focused on her dad. He took in a breath and let it out slowly.

"What I want to remind you is not to talk to strangers, honey."

She frowned. "She said she was family."

"Have you seen her before?" he asked, his voice rising a little at the thought that she might actually remember her mother.

Hope shook her head then nodded. "Yep, I did. Once at school with Izzy, right?" She looked at me to back her up.

"Yes, honey, that's right. We did see her at your school."

She smiled.

"Okay, bug. I understand why you opened the door for someone you thought you had seen before, but you can't be opening the door at all, okay? Let me or Izzy or any adult take care of that. Even if it's Nana, you ask first. I need to know that you're safe at all times, yeah?"

Her little lip trembled. "Am I in trouble, Daddy?"

He shook his head. "No, bug, you're not in trouble. I'm just reminding you of what the rules are. If someone comes to the door next time, what are you going to do?"

She ran her fingers down the long lock of hair she held. "I get you or Izzy."

Kyson nodded and smiled though I could tell it took him some effort. "Exactly. We just want to make sure you're safe, okay, baby?"

"Okay, Daddy. Can I go play now?"

"Wash up first." He picked up her hands and loudly sniffed her fingers. "Smells like syrup!" he teased and then pretended to nibble on them. "I didn't get my fill. I need more syrup!" He gobbled at her hands, making her squeal and kick her feet until she scrambled off his lap and down the hall to the washroom. The peals of her laughter filled the room with joy.

I went over to Kyson. He pulled me into his lap and pressed his nose to my neck. "I hate that she showed up the way she did. I hate that I don't know where the hell she is so I can talk to her first. I hate that she's back even though I still hope that she's well and has found peace."

I ran my fingers through Kyson's hair, dragging them along his pressure points in the hope of soothing the ravaged state his mind was in. I, too, was worried about Veronica re-emerging in Kyson and Hope's life. The woman had a forked tongue but maybe a scared recovering addict was hiding behind that bravado? Maybe she just needed support?

"Whatever you need, honey, I'll give it to you. Just tell me what I can do to make this better."

He pressed his face between my breasts, and I kept up the head massage.

"You're doing it. Being here. Going through this with us." He wrapped his arms around my form and held on. "Just your presence is enough to help me get through this."

I leaned over and kissed the crown of his head. "I'm not going anywhere."

He sighed and I held on until Hope came screeching down the hallway. "Who wants to go to the park!"

Kyson laughed, lifting his head as I smiled down at him.

"Me!" I called out. "Dying to go to the park!" And I kind of was because that was one thing I'd never had the opportunity to do—take a child to the park and watch them enjoy it. "Come on, honey, let's grab a blanket, pack a lunch and have a picnic in the park with our girl."

I didn't realize what I said until Kyson shifted back and grinned. "Our girl?" he reiterated.

I held my breath and then nodded.

He smiled so wide it made me lean forward and kiss it, teeth, lips and all.

We showed up at Hope's favorite park around noon. I severely underestimated how long it took to get a six-year-old ready to get out of the house. Not to mention packing sandwiches, cutting up fruit, prepping drinks and ensuring we had some fun things with us. We brought a Frisbee, a jump rope, bread for the ducks, sunscreen and hats.

Finally, Kyson found the perfect spot under a huge shady oak tree closest to the play equipment. That way we could lie about while Hope went for the toys, but still be able to keep her in sight.

I lay on the blanket on my stomach, sunglasses over my eyes, gazing at Hope, who was dashing up and down this castle-like structure with another girl around her age. She was happy, winded and free as a bird. I enjoyed watching her long brown hair float in the breeze and I dreamily imagined another little girl with red hair toddling after her big sister.

A heavy arm fell over my lower back as Kyson nudged my shoulder with his nose. "What you thinkin' about?"

I grinned. "You don't want to know."

"Try me."

"Hmm…"

"Seriously, tell me what you were thinking about? No secrets, baby." He reminded me of what we'd agreed upon.

"I was thinking about how happy and free Hope looked."

"And?" he encouraged.

"And how maybe one day it might be nice to see a little red-headed girl chasing after her big sister," I admitted rather boldly.

Kyson hummed and bit down on the ball of my shoulder until I squeaked and laughed.

"Not a bad visual. I'd love to give Hope siblings. Always wanted a big family. Things just got…derailed when Veronica lost it."

I nodded. "I never had a big family until now, so it's always been a dream of mine."

Kyson rubbed his chin over my shoulder. "How many you want?"

I pursed my lips and watched Hope run, waving her arms in the air like an airplane. "If they were like Hope, I'd take as many as you wanted to give me."

He chuckled against my arm. "She's pretty special but I'm thinking maybe two more."

"I could live with two more. One girl, one boy?" I queried.

Kyson shrugged. "Don't care how they come just as long as they are healthy."

Before I could respond, his phone rang in his back pocket and he groaned playfully. Then his brows knitted together as he stared at the screen and barked, "Turner?" into the phone.

He listened a moment and then jumped up to standing. I rolled over and sat up, watching him as his body went ramrod straight and his muscles twisted at his forearms, making the veins bulge.

"How dare you come to the house, to the school, without calling me first. Have you lost your mind? No, that happened when you up and left over three years ago!" He grated into the phone.

Oh, no. He was talking to Veronica.

Kyson's form got tighter and his shoulders climbed up toward his ears, his jaw so firm it looked like he could chomp down on glass with zero problem.

"We are not married. The judge granted me a divorce a year ago. No, I have the papers with the judge's name signed on the bottom to prove it. You also lost your parental rights. You see, you can't up and disappear from a toddler's life and expect to walk back into it and still have a claim."

He listened for a minute and then roared, "You abandoned her!"

I stood up and checked on Hope. She was now on the swings. She waved at me and I waved back. Then I got close to Kyson and put my hand on his back. Instantly, the tension seeped out, his shoulders came down and he let a long breath of air out of his lungs.

"You want access to Hope you're going to need to go through me. None of this showing up unexpectedly."

I could hear a whisper of a response but didn't know what she'd said.

Kyson spoke through clenched teeth. "I want proof you're clean before you ever step foot in front of my daughter again. No, she's *my* daughter. Not ours. I'm the one that's been taking care of her the past three years. Hell, I did it before you disappeared for good. Now, if you want to have a relationship, you're going to have to prove to me that you're clean, your heart is in the right place and you genuinely plan to stay in her life. I'm not going to put her through meeting her birth mother and wishing you were a part of her life if you just end up disappearing on one of your benders again."

I rubbed my hand up and down his spine, being there the only way I knew how.

"First step, you and I meet. We'll talk. You'll tell me why you came back and what you've been up to. The truth, Roni. Not some bullshit lies you made up. I don't care how ugly it is or what you had to go through to get to the place where you suddenly want to be back in your daughter's life."

He shook his head and laughed harshly. "No. You and me are done. Dead. My love for you died the day you walked out on our child the last time. There's no going back." He groaned and ran his fingers through his hair as though he was beyond frustrated. "No. I got a woman in my life. A woman I love. A woman I plan to have in my life and Hope's life forever, so don't even try to go there. I'll call you back next week when I've had time to think on meeting up with you."

I put both of my hands on his shoulders when he barked out, "Fuck, no. You wait until I call. I need some time to think about you being back and how I'm going to address that with Hope. Until then, you can wait." He pressed a button on his phone and then roared up into the trees. Years of frustration and anger leaked from his system in a tumultuous burst of emotion.

Hope stopped swinging and ran across the sand and over the grass to where we were. "Daddy, you okay?"

He clenched his jaw and crouched down. He opened his arms and Hope went straight into them, looping her arms around his neck. Kyson picked her up and held her close, dipping his head to her neck and breathing. I watched as all the frustration and hurt seeped out of him as he held his girl. She was amazing, just holding on, not saying anything.

When he sighed and pulled back, he took in his daughter's face. "You're the best little girl in the whole world. You know that, right? How much Daddy loves you?"

She smiled and nodded avidly. She cupped both of his cheeks. "What's the matter, Daddy? Someone make you sad?"

He frowned and shook his head. "I'm okay, bug. You hungry? Isa made you an amazing peanut butter-and-jelly sandwich."

Hope grinned and glanced my way. "Did you cut off the edges?"

"Of course!" I patted her back.

Hope kicked her legs and Kyson put her down. "Let's eat!" She hustled to the basket. "I'll get it all out."

I got close to Kyson until he pulled me into an embrace. His body trembled for a full minute as whatever emotions were left from his call leaked out of his body and he calmed down.

"You keep me sane, Isa," he murmured against my skin.

I curled my hand around his neck and kept him close. "Then I'm doing my job."

He nodded.

"You'll get through this. Hope will be fine. And I'll be here to help in any way I can."

I could feel him swallow against my hold. "Just don't leave. No matter how hard it gets or what happens from now until whatever shit she's going to pull plays out. Just don't leave. I couldn't take it, baby." His words were guttural as if they were peeled from his very soul.

I closed my eyes and locked him in my hold. "I won't. I love you. I love Hope. I'll never abandon either of you. Not ever."

twenty

Jasper drove while I fiddled with the stereo a hundred times, checked my phone another zillion times and stared blankly out the car window. The three-hour drive to my grand-father's reservation was pure torture. It left far too much time to build up all the reasons why I was scared of meeting the man Evie and Suda Kaye revered. The first of which being his daughter chose to abandon me and keep me a secret from my sisters our entire lives.

All over again I was pissed at Catori.

If she hadn't left the way she did, what kind of life could I have had?

If she hadn't made my fathers promise not to speak of her, I would have had a mother.

If she hadn't kept my sisters from me, I would have known their love sooner.

If she hadn't kept my only living grandparent from me, I wouldn't have felt uncertain about my place.

If she hadn't abandoned me, everything would have been different.

I felt so deeply for Hope and Kyson in that moment I could hardly breathe. Every nuance of Kyson's fear was now my own as Jasper pulled my car up behind Evie's Cayenne, which was behind Camden and Suda Kaye's vehicle at the gate of the reservation.

Kyson and Lincoln planned to drive up on Saturday morning as the wedding was scheduled for just before sunset. My guy didn't want to leave Hope for four full days, much to his mother's irritation. The woman had finally kicked the flu to the curb and was ready to see and spoil her grandbaby. Still, Kyson decided two days was enough and I agreed with him. Not knowing Veronica's plans, and due to her pop-up visits, it was safer having Hope close. Plus, it gave him and Hope time alone to bond without me. Of course, Kyson didn't think this was necessary, but I did. She'd had her dad alone her entire life. She probably wanted some special time with him, and I wanted her to have that. Mostly because I had no intention of backing away from their lives, rather ingratiating myself further in the fold as time went on.

Kyson agreed, though he worried about me meeting Tahsuda without him, as he knew that I was nervous. I explained he and Lincoln could attend the wedding on Saturday, spend all day Sunday with the family and head back home on Monday. And besides, I had Jasper. Regardless of all of this, I was a grown woman. Not all challenges needed to be faced with your man at your back. Sometimes you had to take those leaps of faith on your own and let fate play out.

This one was a fear I had to conquer on my own.

Jasper trailed behind my sisters and their men until we reached a one-story home, off the beaten path but close to where the mountains started to rise in the distance. As if we'd planned the move, each car separated and pulled in front of the home one after another.

Standing rock solid was a large, barrel-chested man. Skin the color of the earth. Black hair separated down the center, waving like a flag against the breeze. His face was weathered and showed his age but did not take away from the fierceness or the wisdom in his gaze. He wore a red-and-black poncho, his hands clasped in front of him. Several thin pieces of beaded leather were woven around his neck, a single turquoise inset in the center of his throat. Before I could even put my hand to the door handle, I watched Suda Kaye race from Camden's car like an arrow shot from a bow. When she reached the man, he opened his arms and she slammed into him. He didn't so much as need to take a step back, he was that solid. He wrapped her in his arms and held her close, dipping his chin to the top of her head. He closed his eyes, and his lips moved. I imagine he said something special, something private. A secret the two of them shared due to years of familial love and acceptance.

"Come on, Izzy, let's go meet Grandpa Tahsuda." Jasper squeezed my hand while I stayed seated in the car, perfectly still. Afraid to move. I watched as Evie walked up to our grandfather, jumping up and down on the balls of her feet in a display that was so far from her normal cool and calm exterior, I wouldn't have believed it if I didn't see it with my own eyes.

Jasper opened my door just as I heard Evie squeal, "I'm getting married, Toko!" Then she threw her arms around the man. I held my breath as he took her into his embrace, held her head with her cheek to his heart and closed his eyes.

I shook, my knees knocking together like a game of marbles. Jasper led me toward the dark figure. He let go of Evie, and his coal-black gaze lifted to meet mine. For a full thirty seconds I did nothing but stare at the man. A wave of love so powerful and strong blasted against my body, making my heart pound and my vision blur.

My grandfather.

My blood.

My family.

He lifted his arms out toward me and said one word. *"Kasaraibo."*

I broke down. Tears fell to my cheeks as Jasper led me straight into the arms of the only living grandparent I had.

"You are finally home," he said in a low rumble soaked to the brim in awe. "The missing piece of my heart."

My lips trembled as he cupped my face and wiped my tears with his thumbs, which fell in rivers over his hands. His dark gaze took in every feature as though he was memorizing it. His lips twitched as he lifted his hand and hovered it over my hair in a rather delicate caress for a man so intimidating.

"Fire," he whispered, gesturing to my hair. "Ice." He traced the pale skin of my cheek with a single finger. *"Isabeau*, the Creator's gift."

My grandfather thought I was a true gift from God. I choked back a sob and held my breath, not wanting to break this moment or forget a second of it.

"I will give many prayers of thanks for the gift of you. My grandchild is home. This makes me complete. We will celebrate."

He pulled me against his chest, and I locked my arms around him. Finally, I couldn't hold back the sobs tearing through my body, needing to make their way out. I lost it. I let it all go and gave it to my grandfather. The fear, the hurt, the sorrow of not having had this all these years, on top of breathing in the treasure that this moment was. All of it. Regardless of how it came to pass, Toko, Evie, Suda Kaye,

Camden, Milo, they were all such a blessing. A gift from Catori to me.

"What does *Kasaraibo* mean?" I choked out between the body-jarring emotions spilling out all over the desert floor and at this man's feet.

I felt him kiss the crown of my head. "*Kasaraibo* is Comanche for *angel*. As my Catori believed you were a gift from the Creator, meant to bring joy, love and understanding to the world."

My mother and grandfather not only thought I was a gift, they also believed I was an angel. I cried harder.

Tahsuda opened his arms wide once more and suddenly, I felt two bodies squish up against me. "My *Huutsuu*, *Taabe* and *Kasaraibo* in my arms. I am happy. It is a good day."

I grinned and lifted my head to see my sisters smiling wide, but their eyes were closed as they pressed close to our grandfather and me.

"We have much to celebrate," he whispered over our heads. I felt his grip get tighter. "My girls are home."

I had never felt more at peace than I did in that moment, cuddled to the man who ultimately created the woman who gave each of us life. And while we stood there in Toko's arms, the sun shining at our backs, a breeze flowed over us, smelling of bergamot, patchouli and the earth.

Jasper wiggled his booty to the music playing inside as he brought out a bottle of insanely delicious wine. Apparently, it was Toko's favorite and made by Native Americans. I learned today while cooking side by side with my grandfather that he was very proud of his heritage. Our people were born to this land far before the Europeans came across the pond, and everything Toko did was in support of Native Americans. Right down to the wine he enjoyed.

"Here you go, Grandpa." Jasper bobbed his head while holding out the glass of wine. He'd taken to calling Toko Grandpa. I asked him why he didn't call him Toko as it didn't seem to bother him when Camden called him the same. Milo, however, addressed him as Elder Tahsuda. Jasper said he felt like it was mine to have with my sisters.

Toko pressed his lips together but the right side lifted with a hint of what I've come to see was his way of showing amusement. *"Ura,"* he said in Comanche. "Thank you," he repeated in English.

Jasper handed my glass to me.

"Ura." I glanced at Toko to ensure I enunciated it correctly and he nodded, his chest lifting a bit.

"Teach me something beautiful in Comanche," I requested and sipped more wine.

Toko set his wine down and picked up the piece of wood sitting in a basket with a bunch of metal hand tools. Currently, the piece was formed into the shape of an owl sitting down, its wings at rest. Though it didn't have a face yet.

Jasper clapped and leaned against the banister surrounding the cozy porch.

Toko pointed at Jasper. *"E-haitsma,"* he said.

"E-haitsma," I repeated.

"Very good, *Kasaraibo.* You speak excellent Comanche."

I grinned wide and sat up straight, pride licking at my spine. "What does *e-haitsma* mean?"

Jasper put his hand on his hip and struck a semiserious fashionable pose. "It means your best friend is fabulous. Isn't it obvious? *He's. Hot. Ma.*" He twisted the word into exactly what worked best for him. "You got some great taste, Grandpa." He lifted his wineglass in salute. "I am pretty hot."

Surprisingly, Toko tipped his head back and laughed full

and deep; the sound rumbled straight through my body and out the soles of my feet.

"My new grandson of the heart is funny," he murmured, and both Jasper and I lit up like a Macy's parade on Thanksgiving.

Me because he liked my best friend and Jasper because he wanted everyone to like him.

"The word means *good friend*," Toko answered.

"Well, I am that. Anyhoo, I'm going to let you two catch up and see if I can wrangle Milo and Camden into taking off their shirts and arm wrestling." He waggled his eyebrows dramatically.

"You'd have better luck getting Suda Kaye to make the request," I hollered as he opened the door. Suda Kaye would be all over that plan. Always interested in a new experience.

"Oh, good idea! Have fun!" he tossed out before letting the screen door slam.

Toko and I both winced at the noise.

"Sorry, he's got more energy than common sense," I mumbled.

Toko hummed then reached into his basket of goodies and pulled out a small piece of wood and handed it to me. Then he grabbed a whittling tool and handed that to me, too.

I took them both into my hands and watched him maneuver the tool into the wood and tried to copy his movements.

"Tell me of the sadness in your eyes?" he asked while his gaze was on the owl and the indention he was carving.

I twisted my lips and sighed. "I'm not sad, exactly."

"Hurt?" He hit the nail right on the head.

I shrugged. "I wish I could have met you sooner," I whispered, letting the wind take the admission with it.

"Ah, you speak of Catori's choices." His words held no judgment, just facts.

Mentioning my mother's name sent a bolt of guilt to sear my insides and squeeze my heart until I had to suck in a big breath and let it out slowly.

"You have her letters?" he asked.

I nodded. "Yeah, but it's not the same as having her."

He hummed and whittled the owl's eyes. I dug into the side of my piece, noting the shape already looked a little like a small bear. I curved the tool around an edge to create a rounded ear shape on one side, thinking it felt much the same as peeling an apple of its skin with a knife. I was an expert at peeling an entire apple into one long, swirling piece. I'd have to show that trick to Hope. She'd love it. And I loved making her smile any way I could.

"You are mourning my Catori. She would not want this," he stated knowingly.

I licked my lips and had to push aside the hurt to hear his words and let them sink in. Though if I were being honest, I'm not sure if I cared that Catori wouldn't want me sad. She made her choices, and these were the ramifications for those choices.

"I would have liked to know her. Know you. Know my sisters."

He nodded. "You would not be the person you are today if you had. Think on this," he stated then continued to whittle.

I curved another ear in the top and did as he asked. If I'd had Catori in my life, Evie, Suda Kaye and Toko, would I be happier? I had amazing parents. An incredible best friend who loved me like a sibling whom I loved in return. I'd graduated school and knew exactly what I wanted to do with my life. None of that had been taken away by Catori's choices.

Holy hell.

"She gave me this life and made this choice because she knew I'd be happy and healthy without her. Evie and Suda

Kaye needed her and she wasn't there. My fathers were there for me every step of the way. I had a perfect upbringing."

Tahsuda nodded but didn't speak, just kept whittling wood.

"And if I'd had her in my life, I would have been stretched between two places. There and here. Always leaving someone behind. My fathers at home. Her, you and my sisters here. My God…"

The realization hit me so hard I covered my face, lifted up my knees and sank into myself at the visceral blow.

Catori wasn't better off without me.

I'd been better off without *her*.

Without the heartbreak of living half a life with her and half a life with my fathers. What she gave my parents, what she ultimately gave me, was a real chance at pure happiness.

It was divine.

Selfless.

I swallowed around the acid coating my throat and stared out at the dark desert not knowing how to feel, how to breathe, after this realization.

"Catori died with a piece of her heart missing." Toko spoke slowly, but his gaze was on me when I turned my head to look at him. "She would rather be broken from your loss, the loss of a child, than have you break because of her loss. The loss of your mother. It was her final gift to you."

I closed my eyes and let the tears fall.

Toko put away his tools and wood then reached out a weathered hand. I took it and he pulled me over to him. I dropped the piece of wood, and the tool fell to my knees. I pressed my head sideways on his lap, my gaze on the pitch-black desert. My thoughts just as dark as I mourned the woman who gave up her own happiness to ensure mine.

My grandfather ran his fingers through my hair as I cried. At some point he started singing softly in Comanche. I didn't know the words; I had no idea what they said or meant, but I *felt* them. Deep in my soul I felt every ounce of his love and soothing words. Every hitch in his breath I memorized so one day I could tell my children about it. Tell Hope about how my beautiful grandfather sang to me when I was hurting.

For a long time I let the sadness overwhelm me.

I let the beauty of Toko's song soothe me.

And instead of being angry with the woman who gave me life, I was grateful. Thankful that she chose my happiness over her own.

I spent Friday horseback riding, walking the reservation and cooking with Toko. I wanted to absorb every bit of this life, learn as much as possible about my Native American roots as I could. Jasper found horseback riding frightening. Said he was given two feet that were meant to be on the ground. Probably because as it turned out, Jasper's exuberance in all things made the animals leery and every time he tried to approach, they'd whinny and stomp their hooves. We finally found something that was averse to Jasper's charm—horses. Not one in the stalls seemed to appreciate my bestie. Instead, he spent those hours learning how to make jewelry with Lina, Milo's mother. This, unsurprisingly, he excelled at.

For the evening, the guys all headed to a bar and grill that was connected to a hotel. Milo made sure all the men had their own rooms. Since the wedding wasn't until tomorrow late afternoon, the men could tie one on then sleep it off if they desired. Jasper was all in for this plan as Lincoln and Kyson weren't set to arrive until noon tomorrow.

The girls and I were in matching pajamas, a present from Evie, and sprawled on the floor of Toko's living room with pillows and blankets everywhere. There was only one extra bedroom, so we dragged the mattress from the queen bed into the living space and put it on the floor in front of the couch. This way we could all sleep together, Suda Kaye and Evie on the bed, me on the couch. I thought it was brilliant. In all my years, I'd never had a sleepover with girls. My sleepovers always consisted of Jasper and me.

Toko sat in the single chair, wearing a robe and house slippers, his hair a black sheet raining over his shoulders.

"Tell us a story about Mom," Suda Kaye requested.

Evie entered the living space, holding four glasses of what else? Native American wine. I was hooked. The stuff was incredible, and you didn't feel crappy the next day even if you went a little overboard.

Toko took one of the glasses and waited until Evie had passed them around. On the table were all the treats that Toko and I made after dinner. It was an amazing experience cooking with him. He seemed genuinely pleased that I was able to cook so well. I explained that it was my schooling and he shook his head. Said it was the Comanche blood running through my veins that gave me a special knack for food. Something I apparently was genetically predisposed to have, since both he and my grandmother, Topsannah, were excellent cooks. I let it slide and accepted the compliment because it made me feel good to think that some piece of him and my grandmother had been passed down to me through my genetics.

He hummed and looked off into the distance. "When Catori was a young girl, she decided she would be a dancer."

Suda Kaye sat up taller and I lay down along the couch, elbow to the cushion, head in my hand. Evie nestled on the edge of the mattress close to the food where she was snagging a slice of the pumpkin fry bread we'd made.

"At school she learned of this dance called ballet," he said thoughtfully.

"Mom did ballet. No way!" Suda Kaye blurted.

Toko shook his head. "Not exactly. For weeks she pretended to be a ballet dancer. Jumping around, spinning in circles. Until my Topsannah decided she needed to take a class. I was not happy."

"Did you let her go?" Evie asked, holding the pumpkin fry bread close to her lips as if she didn't want to let it get too far from her mouth but couldn't wait for his answer, either.

Toko nodded. "She was awful. Broke her heart in pieces."

Suda Kaye pouted. "Poor *pia*," she said, using the Comanche word for mother.

Toko held up his hand. "She was very sad. This made Topsannah sad. I did not like my girls to have sad eyes and hearts."

I nodded and then sat up, reaching for my wine. "Then what happened? Did she keep trying and become an awesome ballet dancer?" I asked on a rush then sucked back some delicious wine.

He shook his head. "No. Ballet was not for her. Topsannah met a woman at one of her quilting events. The woman taught the art of Turkish dance."

Suda Kaye grinned wide. "Belly dancing! Woo-hoo!" She jumped up and did some hip rolls, bringing her arms above her head, then clapped her hands together.

Toko smiled softly. "Yes. She became a master at the dance. This talent paid her way through her adventures."

"Can you girls teach me?" I asked.

Suda Kaye made a pa-shaw sound and held her arms out for me to come toward her. "Get up, Evie. Let's show our sister Mom's dance moves!"

For the next hour I learned to dance. I even got pretty good at the series of moves they taught me. At some point Toko left us to our laughter and giggling in search of his bed.

Then on bottle number four of wine, Evie tugged the quilt off the bed and handed it to Suda Kaye. She went over to a basket in the corner and grabbed two more, handing me one in a gorgeous red, black and white print. I followed them as they wrapped them around their bodies.

"Come on, bring your wine," she whispered and shoved her feet into her pair of the matching slippers she bought all of us. "Shhhh. You don't want to wake Toko. He's not usually ever mad, but he does get a bit grouchy if he misses out on his beauty sleep."

I snort-laughed at the thought of Toko being grouchy.

Suda Kaye and Evie herded me out the front door, closing the screen as quietly as three super-tipsy women could. Which wasn't quiet at all. It also didn't help that Evie kept loudly demanding we "Shush!" This had the adverse effect of making both me and Suda Kaye giggle even harder.

We walked across the dirt expanse and headed toward a picnic table overlooking the dark pasture before the mountains. Evie climbed on top and sat down in the center. She waved us both over. I took one side; Suda Kaye took the other. I held my wine goblet as though it were the very nectar of the gods, because right then it totally was.

Evie looked up to the sky. "Have you ever wished on stars, Izzy?"

I shook my head, not having any idea what she was talking about.

"When we were little girls, Mom would bring us outside to star-gaze and wish on stars. It's one of my best memories of her. We did this before Suda Kaye got married and I wanted to share this with you. Then one day you can share it with your children."

I tried not to get teary as Evie put her arm around me. "Look up. Find a star that calls to you."

The sky was magical this late at night. The darkest blue, with millions of twinkling stars that could be seen so clearly out there in the desert.

"Wow," I gushed.

"Did you pick one?"

"Just one? They're all beautiful." I frowned.

She nodded. "Yep, but you have to choose the one that calls to you. Close your eyes, look up and then open them. The first star that holds your attention is *your* star," she whispered as if our conversation was a big secret.

I did as she said, opened my eyes and zeroed in on a twinkly little guy that was next to a bigger, brighter one, but I liked the small-and-mighty one better.

"Do you have one?" Suda Kaye asked.

I nodded.

"Okay, repeat after us," Evie said. "I wish I may."

"I wish I may," I said.

"I wish I might," Suda Kaye said.

"I wish I might," I repeated.

"Have this wish," Evie added.

"Have this wish," I followed.

"I wish tonight," they both said at the same time.

"I wish tonight," I finished.

"Now you wish on your star. But you can only do it once. And you can't tell anyone what you wished for or it won't come true. And you can't wish again, until it does come true. Understand?" Evie whispered.

I nodded. "I think so."

"Okay, close your eyes and make your fondest wish on your star. Send it out into the universe and one day it will come true."

I smiled, closed my eyes and thought really hard. If I could have had any wish, what would it be?

The wind rustled my hair, the smells of patchouli and earth filling the air around our small huddle.

It came to me like a comet shooting across the sky.

I opened my eyes, looked at my star and wished Hope could have a mother who wanted nothing more than to choose Hope's happiness over her own.

twenty-one

Evie spun around in a circle, dancing across the living room. "It's my wedding day! It's going to be the best day ever!" The joy surrounding her swirled in the air and became infectious.

I chuckled as Suda Kaye grabbed Evie and spun her around and around.

I popped up off the couch as Toko entered fully dressed but not in his ceremonial attire. "I'll make breakfast! Oooh, how about a coffee crumb cake?"

Toko nodded. "I will help. You will teach me."

My heart started to pound as I nodded. Teach my grandfather something in the kitchen? A gift I would remember always. "I would love that, Toko," I breathed.

He went over to Suda Kaye and kissed her forehead. "Morning, *Huutsuu*." I had since learned this meant *bird* in his language. Toko glided to Evie and did the same, but he held her cheek and stared into her eyes. "Milo is your match. You will be happy and have many children. He is the dark to your light, *Taabe*. Do not fear the dark as it is part of us all. Balance is beauty. Remember this."

She nodded and my throat went dry at the devotion in his teaching. And I adored how he called her *Taabe*, which literally translated to *sun*. And she was. Milo was dark. Black hair, brown skin, coal-black eyes with a sad past, where Evie was golden. Hair, skin tone, smile and light, icy-blue eyes. Milo had suffered a major loss when he married young to a woman who was carrying his child. They lost the child, and then Milo lost the woman as she put her career and desire for other men before her marriage. Evie was his second chance at having the love and life he wanted, and I knew that man would let nothing stop him from making her his.

"He will need you to shine your light in all things to find his peace throughout your life together. This is your job as his wife, his partner," Toko added.

Her voice shook as she said, "I will, Toko. I'll be his light."

He gave her a curt nod and a pat on the cheek before coming to me. I stood still as he curled a hand around my nape and pressed a kiss to my forehead. "Let us cook, my *Kasaraibo*."

For the rest of the morning we cooked, laughed and ate. The coffee cake crumble went over smashingly. Toko had three pieces he enjoyed it so much.

Later, I'd just come out of the bedroom in my pale yellow sundress with flirty little cap sleeves to find Suda Kaye in her brilliant, burnt-orange spaghetti strap dress. It looked amazing with her light brown skin tone. The colors would go well against the sunlight and the desert mountain view where Evie and Milo would be married. Evie wanted us to match with the view, not take from it. She planned on having lots of photos, too. So much so that she'd hired a local tribesman from the reservation to take candid pictures so none of us would be bothered and could simply enjoy the event.

The sound of a car approaching down the rock-and-dirt road had my heart skipping a beat and excitement pouring through my veins.

"Kyson's here!" I whooped and dashed out to the back of the house, hearing Suda Kaye's laughter as I went.

Lincoln pulled up in his red GMC and I bounced on the balls of my feet on the small back porch. Kyson exited the car wearing a pair of super-dark blue jeans and a button-up, short-sleeve yellow dress shirt that went amazingly with my dress. He held a brown leather jacket over his shoulder with one finger. Black aviators were on his strong nose, and his skin glowed a warm tan color that made my mouth water. His dark hair was swept back away from his face but still, there were stubborn, sexy layers falling down over his fore-head. On his feet were an espresso-colored, well-worn pair of leather cowboy boots. My man was utterly edible.

I squealed like a little girl and ran to him. He saw me coming and thankfully braced because I flew into his arms, my lips slamming against his so hard I felt his teeth. My guy did not care. He looped one arm around my waist, the other dove into my hair and he slanted my head so he could kiss me fully deeply. I tasted cinnamon gum and Kyson. The best flavor ever.

Behind me I heard a manly squeal I recognized. I pulled my head from my man and turned to see Jasper responding exactly the same way I did. Only when he got to Lincoln, he jumped up and wrapped his legs around his boyfriend's waist. Lincoln caught Jasper at his small booty without any problem, crushing their mouths together.

Both Kyson and I laughed, and I lifted my head to stare into his handsome face. "I missed you."

He grinned and butterflies took flight in my stomach. "I can see that. I missed you, too, but not as much as Hope. I thought I might have to bring her with me when she realized we were here for Auntie Evie's wedding."

I frowned. "Maybe you should have. We could have made it work." Now I wanted Hope to be there, dammit.

Kyson kissed me quick and nuzzled my nose. "This was a big moment for you. I wanted you to have it without either of us needing to be looking after a boisterous six-year-old. Besides, I like to take a lay of the land in new places before I bring my girl."

"Makes sense. Come on." I pulled back and took his hand. "I want you to meet Toko!"

He hooked me around the waist as we walked from the new parking area to the front of the house. The parking in front had been cut off and Milo's parents and sister were already in full decorating mode. Right in the center of the space sat a long line of three picnic tables complete with colorful bushels of sunflower-and-feather centerpieces, all on top of a stunning handmade beaded table runner streaking down the center. There were unlit torches placed around the area with additional seating for two here and there so people could chat one on one when we weren't eating. Native American blankets were laid over hay bales that were set in a circular shape around a fire pit that had not been there yesterday.

"Wow, this looks amazing." Kyson took in the large space.

Standing in the center with his arms crossed over his ceremonial attire was my grandfather. His gaze was set on the desert and mountains. He licked his thumb, put his hand out and scanned the space as though he were assessing the sun and the wind placement.

We approached just as he turned around. His hair was al-

ready braided perfectly, parted down the center with feathers
and beads dangling down his chest. He wore an ivory-and-
bone chest plate that ran in a chevron shape down his chest
over the burgundy ceremonial robe-like outfit. It was magnificent and seemed to come right out of a Native American
fairy tale, but this was real life for him. For all of them on
the reservation. Sure, they'd merged and comingled—the
kids now went to school off the rez, friends were allowed
to come and go with permission from the people who lived
there—but they held fast to their traditions. They had their
own cattle, horses, gardens and still hunted a lot of the desert
for food. They built their own homes. Most of the women
sold some type of handmade art, in order to bring in additional monies to their home. The elders of the tribes led
the community and were respected in all things. And my
grandfather, Tahsuda Tahsuda, was one of them. It showed
from the lines in his skin, the gray streaks in his hair and the
wisdom in his eyes.

"Toko, I would like you to meet my boyfriend, Kyson
Turner. Kyson, this is my grandfather, Tahsuda."

Kyson held out his hand and bowed as he did, much to
my surprise. "Elder Tahsuda, it is an honor, sir."

Tahsuda took Kyson's hand and gave it a good shake before nodding.

"Thank you for having me and my brother at your home,"
Kyson added.

Toko held Kyson's hand and focused his gaze on him.

Kyson didn't move a muscle, just stood there and took my
grandfather's lead and waited.

Toko gave a small smile then looked at me. "I see good
things in your future, *Kasaraibo*. Very good things. But you
must remember, all good things come with the bad. You

will need to be strong." He patted the top of Kyson's hand and let it go.

Kyson's head turned toward me and I shrugged.

Tahsuda looked over our shoulders to where Lincoln and Jasper were making out against the side of the truck. The two were going at each other as though they hadn't seen one another in a year, let alone two days.

I closed my eyes. "Dammit, Jas. Two days. You only made it two stinkin' days," I grumbled.

Toko's lips lifted into a barely there smile as he took in the wild pair. "He is who he is. And who he is, is honest. He does not hide himself. There is honor in this." Toko spoke but it felt like he was teaching me a lesson. A good one. Something I needed to remember.

People were who they were. You accepted them as they were or not at all. You couldn't have it both ways. And those who were free to be themselves were the ones who lived truly free.

"I will check on Milo. You check on Evie. She is getting ready in my room. The sun will be over the bluffs in less than two hours."

"Glad to meet you," Kyson said warmly.

"And I you. Take care of my *Kasaraibo*." Though the way he said it sounded more like a command than a request.

"Absolutely. Nothing will harm her when I'm near," he vowed.

This made Toko smile, which took decades off his face. "This is good," he said and then took his leave, headed toward Milo's father, Sani.

"What's *Kasaraibo* mean?" Kyson asked as I linked my arm with his.

"Angel."

"Angel." He made the word sound even more beautiful than it already was. "Fitting."

"You think?" I teased.

He stopped when we hit the stairs of the porch and turned me toward him. "You *are* an angel, Isabeau. Every night I thank God you walked into my and Hope's lives. With you, I feel like I'm truly living again when I hadn't been in years. That is your gift. The people around you can breathe easier because you're there. Helping. Supporting. Loving. Shedding your kindness all over the place. You *are* an angel, baby. Mine, his, Hope's, everyone's." He cupped my cheek, dipped his head and kissed me so sweetly I felt the love he poured into every sigh, every swipe of his tongue. With every breath he took, I felt his words ring true.

"I love you, Kyson Turner," I blurted because he needed to know. Every time I felt his love, I wanted him to know he had it in return.

He grinned. "I know, baby. You show me every time I look in your eyes." He lifted my hand and kissed my knuckles. "And I love you, too. Now, let's go find your sisters and see about getting one of them hitched."

I smiled so wide my cheeks hurt. "Yay! I love weddings!"

He chuckled and shook his head. "I am not surprised."

I mock-glared and dragged him up the stairs and through Toko's home.

When we got to Toko's room I knocked lightly and responded, "Izzy and Kyson," when they asked who it was.

Suda Kaye opened the door and pulled me a foot inside. She pointed at Kyson. "Hey, bro, can I tell you to find somewhere else to be without sounding bitchy?" She grinned.

Kyson laughed, kissed my shoulder and squeezed my hand. "See you outside whenever you are ready. I'll go make sure

Lincoln and Jasper haven't taken their shenanigans to the back of the truck."

"Oooh, good idea. You never know with those two." I smirked.

He let me go and I watched his ass in those scrumptious jeans as he walked away. Suda Kaye was leaning on the door frame doing the same.

"The man has a fine ass, sister." She whistled. I playfully shoved her into the room and followed behind her.

There was a petite, middle-aged woman sitting in the lone chair, sipping a glass of champagne. She had brown hair that was liberally mixed with streaks of gray, soulful brown eyes and a smile that could ease any tortured heart.

She waved as I entered. "Regina. Evie's assistant and surrogate mother figure," she boasted and sipped her champagne. "You must be Isabeau. Stunning redhead with the bombshell body gave you away, sweetheart. The cheekbones and the smile, though, all part of the family, I see."

I grinned. "Nice to meet you, Regina. You can call me Izzy."

"You can call me Reggie. Everybody does."

I nodded and turned my head to the corner of the room. In front of a tall standing mirror, Evie stood in her wedding dress. She looked like an ethereal goddess. Her hair was pulled back on each side, just off her face. A single sunflower somehow tied into the center. The beaded bodice formed perfectly over her breasts, rib cage and tiny waist. From there it flowed out into waves of shimmery chiffon that just barely skimmed the floor.

"Well, what do you think?" She swallowed and put her hands out to the sides.

Chills raced through my body, and goose bumps rose on

my arms. "You're more than stunning, Evie. You're a goddess."

Suda Kaye grinned. "Milo is going to lose his mind when he sees you!"

Evie smiled wide as there came a knock on the door. Tahsuda entered, holding a wooden box, one it looked like he may have whittled himself.

"From my Catori to her daughter on her wedding day." He held out the box and Evie's hands shook as she reached for it. He covered her hands with his own. "You are more beautiful than the sunrise. More lovely than the sunset. Catori would be very proud in this moment. I am very proud."

Evie went straight into Toko's arms and hugged him for a long time. Not Suda Kaye, Regina, or I spoke, wanting Evie to have this private moment with her grandfather and the mother she'd lost.

Eventually, she sniffed and Toko murmured to her, "I will wait outside. When you are ready, we will walk you to your new life."

"That's my cue." Regina stood, all of five feet and no change. "See you on top of the mountain, my dear. And don't you fret. I'll drag that hunk of man all the way up if I find out his feet are chilly."

Suda Kaye, Evie and I all burst out in laughter.

"I'm sure he'll be waiting rather impatiently for me to arrive. I have no doubt," Evie announced with extreme certainty.

Regina and Toko left the room.

"Do you want me to go and let you have a moment?" I hooked my thumb toward the door.

She shook her head. "No, my goodness. I need you here when I do this." She held the box to her stomach.

Suda Kaye put her hand to her sister's shoulder. "It's okay.

You know Mom always wanted things to be a surprise at the right time. So go ahead, open the box. We're right here, by your side, sissy."

Evie licked her lips and I went to Evie's other side and stood close.

Inside the box was a familiar pink letter with Evie's Wedding Day scrawled on the front. She lifted it, and under it was a pair of wedding rings. His and hers, looped through an elegant, thin gold chain.

Evie covered her mouth as she handed the box to Suda Kaye and reached in to lift the necklace. "It's Mom and Dad's wedding rings," she choked out, tears filling her eyes and falling down her cheeks.

"Here, let me." My voice cracked as I took the chain and she spun around. I looped it around her neck and let the two simple gold wedding bands fall over her chest, near her heart. "They go perfectly."

Evie nodded over and over as I pulled her into a hug. "She really would be so proud of the woman you have become. I've only known you three months and I already know you're a beautiful woman, a great sister and will make an incredible mother one day."

Suda Kaye started sobbing before she, too, pulled Evie into her arms. "Mom knew you'd find the only man that could handle your light. You shine so bright, sissy, you needed a strong, good man that would bask in it, not try to cover it up. And now you can build the family you've always wanted. The family Mom would have wanted you to have."

Evie cried harder, the envelope clutched in her hand. I reached for the tissues I noticed on the dresser and handed her a few. Then grabbed a few more for me and Suda Kaye.

"Damn, now my makeup is a mess." Evie pressed the tissues under her eyes to sop up the tears.

Suda Kaye smiled. "Milo wouldn't care, but sit down and let's fix you up." She led Evie to the bed and sought about getting the blusher, concealer, mascara and lip gloss. Evie didn't wear a ton of makeup naturally, but every bride wanted to look their best on their special day.

I stood to the side. "Do you want some champagne?"

Evie shook her head then handed me the pink letter. "I want you to read the letter to me. Out loud."

"Um, are you sure you don't want to read this when you have time alone? I mean, Suda Kaye's fixing up your makeup and you need to go," I reminded her.

She swallowed, firmed her jaw and let Suda Kaye work on her face. "Please read it to me. I'm okay."

I took a full breath in and let it out slowly. Evie copied me so I did it again. She followed again. Okay, we were calming down. I could sense the room was starting to get back to light and airy instead of thick and emotional.

With careful movements I opened the letter and pulled out the single pink sheet of paper. I cleared my throat and read the first line.

Evie, my golden *Taabe*,

Today on your wedding day, my wish for you is to marry the man that feeds your soul and helps you chase all your dreams. You are grounded, loyal and responsible—everything a man would adore in a wife, a friend, a partner. I have no fear that you will be a perfect mate, and one day an even better mother than I could have ever dreamed of being.

The day you were born, the sun shone down on you and it never stopped shining for my golden daughter. Share that light with your husband, and never let it be dimmed.

When I married Adam, I thought I would never know such happiness.

Until you.

Every time I looked into your eyes, I saw joy and love. Hope and peace. You bring joy to so many with your essence, simply from standing in the same room. I can't imagine the man you choose wouldn't want to drown in your glory the way I did every time I looked at you. Every time I held you in my arms. Every time I came home to your golden light.

Though on this day, I will share one of my secrets.

You know why I never feared leaving for my adventures? Because I knew no matter what, you'd be okay. You'd make sure your sister was okay, too. You're the strongest woman I have ever known. The most loyal. And the most forgiving.

When I would return from an adventure, I knew you were hurt, but every single homecoming, you forgave. You loved. You were loyal. The man that wins you will have those gifts for eternity. Make sure he knows how lucky he is. And if he doesn't, I'm sure Suda Kaye will make it so.

And remember, I'm never really gone. I'm there with you now, watching over you reading this letter and wishing I could be there in person.

I love you, my Evie, and I'm so proud of the woman you've become.

Be happy in your new life with your mate.

From the stars and beyond,

Mom

I swiped the tears from my cheeks and folded the letter, placing it back into the envelope. Evie closed her eyes and twin tears fell down her cheeks. Then as if proving how strong she truly was, she took in a deep breath, let it out and stood. "Fix me up fast, sissy. I've got a man to make my husband."

The sun was just cresting over the bluffs as Evie and Milo said their vows. The wind blew her dress and hair magically. Milo stood tall, proud and more serious than I'd ever seen him. His hair was parted at the center in two braids, with golden yellow-and-brown feathers hanging down alongside them. He had a leather choker with a single turquoise stone in the center that caught the light beautifully. The couple held hands the entire ceremony, Milo sweeping his thumb along the tops of Evie's fingers, sometimes bringing them up to his mouth for a kiss.

Evie beamed. The sun shone off her skin as though she called it forth.

I sat in the front row, Kyson on one side, Suda Kaye on the other, Camden next to her. Behind us were Jasper and Lincoln. I was surprised that there were chairs for the small number of guests way out here, but somehow Milo's mother made it happen. I got the feeling that there wasn't much Lina wasn't capable of, especially when it came to her only son's wedding.

Standing next to Evie was Tahsuda. Next to Milo was his father, Sani. They both wore full Native American celebratory dress. Tahsuda looked straight out of a history book with the massive headdress made of black-tipped white feathers. Around his forehead was a band of red beads with two stars on each side near his temples. Feathers intertwined with beads and leather hung down alongside his braids over the burgundy cloth. His chest plate gleamed a brilliant ivory, making him look fierce and stoic. He stood as still as a statue, his gaze never leaving the happy couple as they said their vows and kissed.

The backdrop was magnificent. The sun just disappearing over the mountain as the ceremony ended.

As if we'd rehearsed it, the small congregation stood up and whooped and hollered when the couple turned around and faced us.

Milo lifted Evie and plastered her to his frame then roared, "My wife! Evie Chavis!"

Evie tipped her head back and laughed with pure, unfiltered glee as he held her aloft, spun around and then set her back on her feet.

"Now we feast!" Tahsuda boomed in that deep, commanding timbre that shook the very earth under my feet.

I turned toward Kyson and he looped his arms around my waist, resting them at the small of my back. "I'm glad I was here to see this." He smiled.

"Me, too."

He kissed me just as the photographer clicked a couple pics of us and dashed over to take photos of the happy couple.

I laughed, pure happiness filling my entire being. Kyson and I joined the rest of the people walking the ten-to fifteen-minute trek to Toko's.

Kyson swung my hand as we walked. "What kind of wedding do you want?"

"One with a huge cake," I answered honestly.

He laughed. "Leave it to my woman to be more worried about a wedding cake than anything else."

"I want good food, too. Everyone always talks about the food after the event, and I'm a chef." I nudged his shoulder.

"Okay, good food, big cake. Got it," he repeated.

"I believe I said huge cake."

He snickered. "Huge cake."

"Don't worry, Jasper will make it. He's a master."

"I have no doubt," he added. "Are you scared, me talking about marriage? You usually start to freak out when I talk about our future," he taunted.

I shook my head and inhaled a sharp breath. "No. You know what? Every moment of your life can't be planned out. My mother married a man she met after only a weekend together. Evie and Milo have been a couple for less than half a year. Suda Kaye and Cam fell in love as teens, separated for ten years then married quickly after coming together again. Love has no time limit. It just is."

He put his arm around me and pulled me closer so he could dip his face toward my neck. "This is good, because I was going to ask you to move in with me while on the ride back home on Monday."

I stopped where I stood and pressed my hands to his chest so I could look up into his gorgeous eyes. "Really?"

He grinned. "Isa, I want you in my bed. Want you teaching Hope how to make breakfast every day. Want you bringing home treats from the bakery that I have to work my ass off in order to keep those abs you love so much."

I ran my hands over said abs. "They're pretty awesome, honey." I did not hide the sexiness in my tone.

He tunneled his hand into my hair at the side of my head. "Want these wild red locks all over my pillow at night. Want to hear my girls chatting it up, giggling and laughing after a hard day on the job."

"Ky..."

"Want you in my life *every day*, Isabeau. *Every day*. Not when we have time. The time is now. I don't want to wait for my happiness anymore and I'm not going to."

"Okay," I said softly but he kept going.

"Want to make love to you every... Wait. Did you say okay?"

I smiled wide and lifted my arms up to the sides of his neck. "I'll move in with you."

"You will? When we get home? Not three months from now when you think enough time has passed." He squinted as if to assess I wasn't about to pull any fast ones.

I shook my head. "I'll move in with you when we get home, *after* you've talked it over with Hope. Made sure she's comfortable with the idea. Deal?"

He grinned. "Deal. Perfect fuckin' woman," he whispered against my mouth and then took said mouth in a heated, absolutely indecent kiss. So indecent his hand had traveled down my back and over my bum where he gripped hard enough to make me moan.

"Um, excuse me, kids. I believe that kind of display is inappropriate," Jasper teased.

"Yeah, get a room!" Lincoln hollered as they walked by, heading farther down the path hand in hand.

Kyson kissed me once, twice and then three times in quick succession. "You made me happy, baby."

I smiled and he took my hand as we followed the rest of the group. "Um, Ky, can we go back to the part where you said you want to make love to me?"

He shook his head. "I'll tell you all about it, when we're alone, in our hotel down the road after the reception."

"But I'm supposed to be staying at Toko's and..." The words dropped from my mouth as Kyson sent me a searing look so filled with lust my lady parts throbbed in response. "Okay."

He smirked. "Perfect fuckin' woman."

twenty-two

The wedding reception was a blast! Milo's parents got so drunk on Native American wine they started singing and dancing in front of the bonfire. Evie did not care one iota. She got up, dragged her husband to where they were boogying and danced slowly alongside them.

We drank. We danced. We feasted. We celebrated Evie and Milo. We celebrated being a family.

One of the best days of my life to date. The only downside was neither Hope nor my parents were there. If I'd had that, then it would have been perfect.

We spent Sunday showing Kyson the reservation, took another horse ride and had a family dinner outside. This one made by me, Jasper and Toko. Jasper and I pulled out the big guns. Making bacon-wrapped, blue cheese-encrusted filet mignon, risotto and a seared kale, spinach, arugula side dish that we sprinkled with crunchy prosciutto and olive oil. Toko made his world-famous fry bread and an antipasto platter of mixed cuts of dried meats, fruit, cheese and the like.

Sani and Lina were nursing major hangovers, so they left us girls and our men, including Jasper and Lincoln, to our own devices.

We ate under the stars and later roasted s'mores over the fire pit.

Toko told us more stories of our people and his upbringing, along with when he met Topsannah and married her.

The wedding and the time spent connecting as a family this weekend was magical. I'd remember it the rest of my life, and I couldn't wait to call my fathers on the way home to tell them all about it. They knew I was worried about meeting Toko and attending a family event here on the reservation, but they also told me I was a "Collins Woman," which was supposed to remind me that I shouldn't be afraid, and taking risks were part of learning. I was taught that there were no greater rewards than the ones that were taken after letting go of fear.

They were right.

Now it was Monday and we stood in front of my SUV, bags packed in the back of the truck, ready to head home where we'd pick up Hope. She should have just gotten out of school since she had half days as a kindergartner and was being picked up by Kyson's mom. We were going to take the three-hour drive straight to her house, where I'd meet his mother for the first time. She had dinner planned out and all her boys were set to be there. Which meant that Lincoln and Jasper were also saying their goodbyes and heading back in Linc's truck.

I passed Kyson my keys as I heard his phone ring. He pulled it out of his back pocket and lifted it to his ear. "Hey,

Mom…" he said, and I turned around and tugged Evie into my arms.

"Gorgeous wedding. I'm so happy I was here to see it." I pulled back. "You're staying another day and then heading to Denver?"

"Actually, Milo has a major meeting we couldn't pass up on Thursday, so we changed our plans. We're going home for a few days, then heading to Turks and Caicos for fun in the sun! Milo scored us this private cabana, sitting right on top of the water. There's a see-through window in the floor so you can view all the fish and ocean life swimming around. And you can jump right off and into the ocean from our deck…"

"What do you mean she was picked up by her mother!" Kyson roared into the phone.

Everyone turned to see my man pacing the desert floor, scowling. Anger radiated from his every pore as I approached.

"They let her take my daughter?" he barked. "She doesn't have any parental rights!"

Oh, no. Oh, no. This was not good.

I put my hand to Kyson's shoulder and found his body so hot it warmed the center of my palm immediately.

"Did you check my house?" he bit out. "Fuck!" he thundered. "Call the fucking police. She's kidnapped my daughter. I'm on my way! Get Dad's boys out…now!" He hung up the phone and whirled around. He lifted his head to the sky, the veins in his neck bulging frighteningly as he roared at the top of his lungs.

I whimpered and reached for him, but he put his hands behind his head then folded his body over his waist, panting. His body oozed a furious rage the likes of which I'd never known.

Lincoln was to his side in a nanosecond.

"Speak to me," he demanded. "Pull it together, bro, and speak to me." He put his hand on Kyson's back.

Kyson stood up, his eyes tortured, his facial expression ravaged.

Lincoln cupped both sides of Kyson's neck, forcing him to be steady. "Calm down and tell us what's going on."

Kyson's gaze flicked to me, and my heart ripped into a million pieces, tears hitting the backs of my eyes and falling down my cheeks. I knew it was bad with that single look.

Toko wrapped an arm around my shoulders and stood strong next to me.

"Veronica ransacked my house. Found Hope's birth certificate and went to the school. She presented her ID and the certificate as proof that she's Hope's mother to a new admin in the office they hired last week. She told them she was picking her up for a dentist appointment. The aide let her take my daughter before Mom could get there, even though she wasn't on the approved list! She's gone, Linc. Not at my house. Not at the school. She took my baby." His words left his mouth as though they were ripped straight from the depths of hell.

"Let's roll." Lincoln pointed to his truck.

"I need to call her, try to get her to see reason. Reach her somehow," he muttered.

I stepped in front of him and put my hands to his chest. "We'll get her back, baby."

He stared into my eyes for a full minute. I gave all my strength, love and conviction so that he could soak it up and turn it into the drive to get his daughter back.

Kyson clenched his teeth and nodded.

"Are you safe to drive? You're pretty upset, honey. I'm happy to take the wheel," I offered.

He shook his head and firmed his jaw. Then he inhaled in and out three times slowly. I watched as his demeanor softened and the tension in his shoulders, arms and face relaxed. "Nah, I'm good. Let's go."

"Call us when you know what's going on!" Suda Kaye called out, Camden holding her in his arms.

Toko watched as we four jumped into the two separate vehicles. He closed his eyes, put his hands together in front of his chest and dipped his head in prayer.

I closed my eyes and prayed right along with him.

"Try it again," Kyson growled out, his eyes glued to the road ahead, his foot heavy on the pedal going eighty-five. Being pulled over for a ticket was the last thing we needed, but I was in no position to demand he slow down. In fact, I was fine with him going faster if it meant we'd be closer to finding Hope.

I picked up his cell phone and hit Redial on the last number Veronica had called from, keeping the phone on speaker so he could hear. It went to voice mail. He'd already filled it with increasingly angrier messages until it was full. Every few minutes, he would demand I'd call again.

It was as if we were in our own circle of hell. He drove. I dialed. We listened to the sound of the robotic voice telling us the mailbox was full. Wash. Rinse. Repeat.

We were an hour and a half outside Pueblo when his phone rang from an unknown number.

"Answer it," he clipped, and I clicked the green button. "Turner," he growled.

"Is this Kyson Turner? Emergency contact for a Veronica and Hope Turner?"

My entire body went ice cold and I shivered in my seat. Dread coated my nerve endings and a fear unlike any other stifled the air in the car.

"Yes," he grated.

"I'm a nurse calling from Denver Health. I'm sorry to inform you that your daughter, Hope, and your wife, Veronica, have been in a very bad accident."

Kyson's nostrils flared and his voice was tight and reedy when he responded, "Are they okay?"

"I think it's best if we discuss that when you get here, Mr. Turner."

"Is my daughter okay?" His words were calm and clear, but I heard the ravaged need behind them.

The nurse took on a professional tone when she answered, "She's in surgery now. Should be out in an hour and we'll know more of her prognosis. She sustained several injuries in the car accident that have us concerned. One being a compound fracture of her right arm. The good news is, she was wearing her seat belt…" Her words fell away. "I'm sorry to say, Mr. Turner, but your wife…"

"Ex-wife," came out of his mouth as though it were covered in acid. "She kidnapped my daughter from school today. I don't give a fuck about her unless you're about to tell me she's been arrested by the authorities," he ground out, then clicked the blinker and took the exit heading toward downtown Denver.

Thankfully, we were closer to Denver than Pueblo.

"I think it's best if we discuss this in person," the nurse stated.

"We'll be there in twenty. Please call this number if there are any updates about my daughter." He reached over and clicked the button to end the call.

I put my hand over his and he gripped my hand so hard I winced at the pain but didn't let go.

"She's going to be okay. She's alive with a broken arm being fixed up. Let's focus on that, okay? Now, breathe with me." I inhaled for four beats and he followed. Then I exhaled and he did the same.

The entire rest of the way to the hospital we breathed together, holding hands and praying that Hope would be okay.

We entered the waiting area for the Pediatric Intensive Care Unit where Kyson's dad told us they were waiting. Turned out that Razor and his brethren had ridden out the moment Kyson's mom told him about Veronica taking Hope. They caught up with her an hour outside Denver and a car chase ensued. Half of the club, consisting of fifteen motorcycles, to one beat-up car.

Apparently, Veronica didn't slow down when she saw them. She started to swerve violently so the guys held back far enough to let the cops get involved, after Kyson's mom had called in the kidnapping. The cops chased Veronica down the streets of Denver. Veronica ran a red light, and turned to avoid oncoming traffic, but ultimately hit the car on Hope's side. The car flipped over and wrapped around a light pole.

Veronica wasn't wearing a seat belt. Her head had smashed through the windshield, her body left hanging half out and half inside the car.

All Razor knew was that Hope had to be cut out of the car with the Jaws of Life. She was bleeding from her head and her arm, unconscious when the paramedics arrived.

I met Carol, Kyson's mother, after the update. She had shoulder-length curly hair, incredible, kind blue eyes just like Kyson's and a singsong voice. She looked nothing like a biker babe in her fashionable dark stretch jeans and flowery short-sleeve top. Though she did look a lot like a grandma just scratching the surface of sixty, who was scared out of her mind for her grandchild.

I stood close to Kyson, who refused to sit, preferring to pace back and forth down the hall of the ICU.

"Izzy!" I heard called from behind us and there were Suda Kaye and Evie, holding hands, rushing down the corridor, their husbands following from behind them.

"What's going on? Is Hope okay? What happened?" Suda Kaye asked, pushing hair out of her face.

"What are you all doing here?" I choked out, my emotions all over the place.

"Your stepdaughter was kidnapped and in an accident. Where do you think we'd be?" Evie jolted her head back as though offended. "Lincoln called. We raced over as soon as we found out Hope was hurt."

Tears welled up and I opened my arms and cried in their hold. "Thank you. It means so much to Kyson and me that you're all here."

Suda Kaye rubbed her hand up and down my back. "Whatever you guys need. Coffee, food, someone to vent to, you've got it. We're here."

Kyson came over and wrapped his arms around me from behind, resting his chin on my shoulder. I wiped away my tears on my shirtsleeve and tried to be strong for my man.

"Means a lot that you're here," he said softly.

"What can we do?" Camden asked.

"Pray. Pray for my baby girl," he croaked out, emotion taking over.

I turned around and wrapped my arms around him as he buried his face against my neck.

After a good, long while, a man in surgical attire came out the doors to the ICU. "Turner family?" he called out.

Kyson and I held hands as we went over to the medical professional.

"Yeah, I'm Hope's father."

"And Veronica Turner?" He looked at his clipboard. "You're the Kyson Turner listed on her emergency contact?"

He nodded but didn't say anything.

"I'm sorry to have to tell you this." The surgeon's brown eyes were kind and gentle. "Veronica suffered significant head trauma and is currently brain dead and breathing through a ventilator."

Kyson closed his eyes as his mom let out a sob. I wrapped my arm around his waist, and put my other hand to his chest, right over his heart.

"My daughter?" he whispered.

"She's alive, but..."

The entire room let out a collective relieved gasp. "Thank the good Lord," came from Kyson's father.

"Mr. Turner, you have some very difficult decisions ahead of you," the surgeon spoke. "Your daughter not only sustained two broken ribs and a compound fracture to her arm, but also her head slammed against the car window during the accident. We've fixed the arm and repaired the superficial head wound but there is some concern due to the swelling in her brain. We want to put her in a medically induced coma in order to let the swelling go down and minimize the trauma."

"Whatever you need to do that will give her the absolute best chance of recovery," Kyson announced instantly.

"I'll need to go over the risks with you, which I think is best to do so privately."

Kyson nodded.

"And your wife..." the surgeon started, his mouth tipping into a frown.

"Ex-wife," he stated flatly.

"Be that as it may, you are listed as her next of kin and have power over her medical care. She's not listed as an organ donor on her medical record. Even though she was intoxicated, and her toxicology report showed a mixture of prescription drugs in her system, she is young. Her organs could save many lives."

"Do it. I'll sign whatever you need. The Roni I knew and loved would have wanted to save lives if she could."

The doctor nodded and informed us that the agency that handled donor procurement would come speak with him soon. Then he took Kyson aside, away from most of us waiting, and whispered the concerns and risks about putting a small child in a medically induced coma.

I zoned out and just held on to Kyson, praying under my breath that Hope would be okay.

"When can I see Hope?" Kyson's question broke me out of my prayer.

"Once she's in recovery, we'll let you come in two at a time." The surgeon glanced around the room and saw how big the crew was waiting. "Two at a time," he repeated.

Kyson nodded.

"I'll send a nurse out to get you once she's settled."

For what seemed like forever, we waited, and Kyson paced. The man was going to wear a path in the ugly white hospital tiles if he didn't stop, but I left him to it. I made sure I stood close enough for him to have me in his vision or stand next to me if he wanted the support.

Razor told the bikers to head out, promising to give an update when he could. Kyson made the horrifying call no parent ever wanted to hear, to Veronica's family in Missouri. He also told them he had offered Veronica's organs for donation and updated them on Hope. They were devastated, naturally, and planned to be at the hospital tomorrow to handle what was necessary for their daughter and be there for their granddaughter.

When the nurse finally came out and told Kyson he could see Hope, he reached out his hand to me.

"Honey, maybe your mom…" I glanced over at Carol, who was crying into Razor's chest.

Kyson shook his head and took my hand.

Hope looked like she was asleep when we entered the room. Her little body was hooked up to so many machines. A breathing tube made the realization that she was in a coma and not technically asleep all too real. I had to tear my eyes away and focus solely on her sweet face. There was a bandage at the top right side of her forehead, and her arm was in a complex-looking brace. Her face was littered with small cuts, which the doctor said were likely from the shattered glass during the accident.

I held down a sob that wanted so badly to tear through my lungs and out my mouth. I had to grit my teeth and clench my fists to hold it back. I watched as Kyson went to the side of his daughter's bed, put one hand to her cheek and the other to her free hand.

"Hey, bug, Daddy's here and you're okay. The doctors are taking real good care of you, sweetheart, and I'm right here. Me and Izzy are by your side, baby. You just sleep and get better, yeah? We'll be here when you wake up. We love you," he promised our sleeping angel.

"Isa?" He gestured to Hope, stood back, but kept his hand to the top of her head.

"Hi, little miss. You gave your daddy and me a real scare, but you're safe and sound and getting excellent care. Like your daddy said, we love you baby, and we're right here, waiting for you to get better." I couldn't stop the tears from trailing down my cheeks.

Kyson pulled me into his arms and together we cried, wrapped in one another's embrace. We stood there desperately holding on to one another, letting out all the fear the past few hours had brought, and breathing in the reality that his daughter was hurt but alive.

The forty-eight hours of Hope's induced coma were a nightmare for Kyson. The man wanted, no, *needed*, to look into his daughter's eyes. Thankfully, at the beginning of the third day, the doctors announced she'd had a dramatic improvement in the swelling around her brain and they were going to remove the tube and wean her off the medication.

Hours passed as Kyson and I sat by Hope's bed. He held her hand as the doctor and the nurse checked in on her. I stood in the far corner, trying to stay out of the way and be still as a mouse so no one kicked me out.

The prettiest sight in the entire world was when Hope blinked open her glorious blue eyes, frowned, turned her head and smiled when her gaze made contact with her dad. I swallowed down the emotion coating my throat that made it dry.

"Daddy," she whispered, her voice hoarse from being intubated for three days.

Kyson's eyes filled with tears and he picked up his daughter's hand and kissed her fingers over and over. "How are you feeling, bug?"

She frowned. "My head hurts. And I can't feel my arm. And it's hard to breathe here." She tried to move her injured arm then realized that wasn't happening. She turned her head and saw her arm.

"Baby, you were in an accident. The doctors are going to look you over really quick and make sure everything is good." Kyson's tone was gravelly.

Hope nodded as the doctor stepped forward and did his checks, wrote things down. He told Kyson everything looked excellent so far but she'd need to be monitored in the hospital for two or three more days, which would also be around the time they would x-ray her arm again to ensure the setting of her bones was good to cast.

The doctor and nurse left as Kyson kissed his daughter's head.

"You're gonna be okay, Hope. Daddy promises." He brought her hand to his cheek and held it there.

Hope's eyes filled with tears as if she'd just remembered something. "Daddy, the mean lady, she said she was my mommy and was taking me away from you and Izzy."

Kyson shook his head. "That was never going to happen. And you will never see that woman again."

Tears fell down her cheeks. "She was drinking from this big bottle that was clear and stinky. She drove crazy. I was so scared."

Kyson's lips tightened. "You're okay. You're not going to see her again."

"I cried a lot and told her I wanted you and Izzy. She said I was never going to see you again!" Her mouth twisted up and she started to cry harder.

I covered my mouth and cried into my hand as I watched my man console his baby girl.

"I want my mommy!" Hope sobbed.

"Baby, that woman…" he started but she cut him off.

A tortured cry left Hope's lips. "Not the bad lady! I want Izzy. My new mommy!"

"I'm h-here, baby. Right here, honey." I jetted over to the same side of the bed as Kyson and leaned over her, bringing my face close to hers.

Hope reached out to my cheek and started to take deep breaths, her eyes lasered on my face as her lips trembled.

I held her hand to my cheek the same way Kyson did. "I'm right here, baby. Not going anywhere."

"Never?" she whispered on a hiccough-like sob.

I shook my head. "Not ever."

"Are you gonna be my mommy?" she asked between ragged breaths.

I nodded. "If you want me to. I'd love nothing more than to be your mommy, Hope."

"I want you to," she said clear as day, and my heart filled with such love, I thought it might burst.

Tears slipped down Hope's cheeks and mine. Kyson tunneled his hand through my hair and curled it around my neck.

"Izzy's moving in and we'll be getting married soon. You can be a flower girl and everything. Would you like that, bug?"

Hope nodded and then smiled. "Can I help make the cake?"

I grinned so big and Kyson laughed out loud. "Girl after my own heart."

"I'm going to be a baker, just like my mommy." She smiled but her eyes started to droop. She had to be tired. All of us were exhausted but her words, the fact that she was awake and didn't seem to have any brain issues, was everything I prayed for. I'd take tired and exhausted if it meant Hope was on the mend and would be coming home soon.

I leaned forward and kissed her forehead. "You sleep, little miss. We'll be here when you wake up. And the next day, and the next day after that."

Hope yawned and closed her eyes and whispered, "I'll frost the cake," before slipping into dream land.

Kyson and I stared at our girl for a long time before he stood up and took my hand.

He brought us to the small futon-sized bed we'd been trading off using since she'd been admitted. He lay down with his back to the wall and patted the small space in front of him.

"Curl up next to me."

I eased down onto my side and pulled up my knees. My kneecaps hung off the edge, but I didn't care. Kyson wrapped me up in his warmth and held me like I was his world, when we both knew his world was lying in a hospital bed a few feet from us. I was good with being second in this scenario.

Kyson yawned and tightened his hold, pressing his face into the back of my hair so his chin rested in the crook of my neck.

"So it looks like you earned a new title," he murmured.

I smiled. "Yep."

"How does it feel to be someone's mommy?"

"Beautiful. Scary," I answered honestly.

"Hold on to that feeling because it doesn't really change as the days go by." He chuckled softly.

We held one another as the exhaustion started to take over. My eyes drooped and I closed them only for a second before he spoke.

"How's about adding another title. That title being *wife*?"

"Kyson…"

"Don't you dare say it's too soon. I don't give a fuck about soon or the amount of time we've had together. I only care about what I feel for you. What Hope just proved she feels for you. And there is no way on God's green earth that you are not going to be ours. So why wait?"

I inhaled full and deep and evaluated my feelings and thoughts on everything that had happened the past three months. Finding out I had sisters. Inheriting money from a man who didn't know me, but felt a kinship to me. Learning about my birth mother. Meeting Kyson. Falling in love. Building my dream job with my best friend. Growing my family to include a grandparent, sisters, brothers-in-law and becoming a mother to a motherless little girl I loved more than my own life. I'd lived five years in the past three months, and I didn't want to waste another day being uncertain.

Kyson and Hope were what I wanted. Pueblo was where I chose to live. The bakery was my dream job. I wanted to be close to my sisters and watch them grow their families right alongside my own.

"Okay," I finally said. "I'll marry you."

His entire body trembled around me. "I'm thinking Vegas, first chance we get. When Hope's cast comes off. You, me, Hope, your sisters, their men, your parents, mine, my brothers, Jasper and his parents. Family trip to Vegas."

I grinned, thinking how much fun it would be for the entire crew to go to Vegas. It could have worked but something about it didn't feel right.

Out of nowhere, in a glass-enclosed room with no windows to the outside world, I felt a breeze flutter my hair, and the scent of bergamot and patchouli tickled my nose.

"Do you smell that?" Kyson asked and my heart started to pound.

I grinned. "Yeah. And I've got an idea about our wedding."

"Anything, baby. All I want is you," he murmured into my hair.

"Instead of Vegas, I'm thinking Atlantic City. Gordon Ramsay owns a restaurant there. And even better...the Cake Boss's bakery is in Hoboken, New Jersey, and it's always been on my bucket list."

Kyson laughed and the sound was music to my ears. "Like

I said. Anything you want. Anywhere you want. I just want you."

My heart was in my throat as I closed my eyes and thought about how my mother went to Atlantic City and found the man she loved her entire short life. And that choice was the beginning of everything. My sisters. Me. The family I now have. She married that man after knowing him a single weekend. I was planning to marry Kyson after knowing him such a short time. Funny how things came full circle.

I fell asleep in Kyson's arms, our daughter healing in the bed close to us, knowing with my entire heart that my mother would be proud of the life she gave me.

epilogue

Three months later…

The blindfold that covered my eyes made my hearing acute. Kyson's hands were holding me at the biceps as I was led to what I thought was a door. Hope was holding on to my skirt, giggling herself silly.

"Don't peek, Mommy!" she teased and laughed.

Hearing her happiness settled my soul. We'd been through a rough and yet still wonderful three months. A week after the accident, Hope was officially released from the hospital. Jasper and I put all work on the bakery on hold. We both had an inheritance to fall back on; we could wait to start our dream until everyone in our lives was healthy. Kyson and I wanted to be with Hope while she healed at home, and Lincoln had to pick up the slack on the rest of the work that had built up while Hope was in the hospital. Jasper hung out with me and Hope during the day after the first couple weeks, dealt with all of our vendors and made sure everything would be ready to start in three months' time.

During that period, Hope recovered. It was amazing how fast children bounced back after a trauma, though those first few weeks of nightly nightmares, anger of not being able to use her arm and the headaches she continued to have were trying. Still, she persevered.

Last week, she got her cast off, the headaches were gone, her ribs healed up and she was now a boisterous little girl again. In celebration, the three of us, along with the rest of our family, bought plane tickets, made hotel reservations and jetted off to Atlantic City. We were married in the same little wedding chapel overlooking the ocean where Catori and Adam were married.

Toko wore his celebratory dress, which moved me to tears. After we said our "I dos" he thanked us for giving him the experience. He appreciated seeing where his daughter had married her husband and said it made him feel closer to her. At our wedding he gave me a wooden box, similar to what was given to Evie on her big day. In it was a blue turquoise hair comb that he said Topsannah wore when she married him fifty years ago. There was also a letter from my mother. In that letter she spoke of how she hoped my life was filled with unending happiness as that was her greatest intention all those years ago when she left me with my fathers.

We had a reception and dinner at Gordon Ramsay Steak in Atlantic City. The next day we all trekked our way to Hoboken so I could see Carlo's Bakery. We gorged on so many treats, there were bellyaches all around. Absolutely worth it.

Now it was a week later, and I was blindfolded and being led somewhere by Hope and Kyson for a surprise.

"Okay, Isa, you ready?" His deep voice rumbled in my ear.

I nodded. "Ready as I'm ever going to be." I laughed but

it turned into a gasp when he whipped the blindfold off my head and I was staring at my bakery.

My completed, perfectly beautiful, sparkling and shiny bakery.

Jasper held his hands up in the air from behind the gorgeous display counter and cried out, "Welcome to On the Sweet Side!"

"Oh, my God!" I covered my mouth and looked around, then turned and saw my entire family.

My dad Casey, my papa Ian, Toko, Suda Kaye, Camden, Evie, Milo, Lincoln, Razor, Carol, Vince and last but certainly not least, Kyson and Hope. They all started clapping and cheering.

I couldn't hold back the tears that fell down my cheeks. "What did you do?" I focused on Kyson.

He pulled me into his arms and cupped my cheek. "We had a job that needed to be delayed another week. So we've been able to bust ass on the bakery since the day after we got back from Atlantic City."

"You weren't supposed to start until next week and my God…" I glanced around, tears falling. "It's all done."

I turned in his arms and took in every detail. The incredible wooden saloon doors that separated the bakery and the kitchen. The quaint wrought-iron seats and tables we chose from a catalog weeks ago all set up, ready for guests to sit back and enjoy a tasty treat. A glass vase with a single peach carnation sat on each table. The walls were a peachy tone with the words we chose to use as decoration all etched in gold. Cream boxes with gold-and-peach ribbons were stacked up on one side near the electronic cash register. Above the back wall was a chalk-written list of the various treats we planned to have available and prices we'd set.

"Check this out!" Jasper pulled a cord over on the right

side of the board and the chalkboard slowly eased down to a level where we could erase and write on it without having to stand on a chair or ladder. "Kyson built this!"

"Honey." I choked on my words and faced him. "You did all this?"

He nodded and wrapped his arms around my waist. "My wife and her brother had a dream that was put on hold. It was necessary to do that, but I didn't want you to wait a minute more to live your dream. You gave me mine when you married me and signed the papers to adopt Hope. I wanted you to have yours."

I couldn't handle it. Everything was too much.

Too much joy.

Too much happiness.

Too much love.

I burst into tears and buried my head against his chest, letting it all go. He held me while I cried and rubbed my back until I felt a tug on my skirt.

"Mommy, we have another surprise, and I helped!" Hope exclaimed, her excitement not contained in the least.

I sniffed against my husband's chest and brushed at my tears. "Okay, little miss, show me your surprise."

She took my hand and led me to the very back of one of the cases where there were small saloon doors for the staff to get to the other side of the service counter. We pushed through and I let my hand slide along the handmade wooden display. Lincoln was standing by it with his arms crossed over one another.

"You guys did incredible, Linc. Thank you."

He grinned. "Anything for the woman who not only brought me the love of my life, but also made my brother the happiest man on earth. I figure I still owe you."

Jasper beamed. "Oh, you are so getting some later for that awesome compliment."

Lincoln smirked. "I always get me some."

"What do you get, Uncle Linc?" Hope asked, totally oblivious to the sexual innuendo.

I squinted at Lincoln with a look that clearly stated, "Be careful what you say to my kid," but he smiled and said, "I get all of Uncle Jasper's treats, of course." He grinned playfully. Lincoln had already moved into the apartment above the bakery with Jasper. My bestie felt he hit the motherlode with the antiques and was not ready to leave it. They agreed they would save up for a home together before moving.

Hope frowned. "Nuh-uh. I get some, too." She pursed her lips into a pout.

"Of course you do. You're right," Lincoln answered. "Don't you have a surprise for Izzy?"

Her eyes widened and she grabbed my hand and tugged me toward the kitchen. Everyone slowly followed us into the large open space.

She went over to the huge, four-tier wedding cake that sat in the center of our island and screamed, "Surprise!"

My mouth dropped open in awe. There were real peach roses on every tier liberally mixed with frosting. The leaves next to the roses were gold and made with an edible sugar coating Jasper had mastered. On the top of the cake were a porcelain man and woman holding on to one another. The cake was dripping in elegant decoration, swirls of frosting and fondant everywhere. And it smelled divine.

"It's beautiful. Better than anything I could have made myself," I whispered in complete awe.

Jasper had his hands on Hope's shoulders, a smile on his face so big it could have brought peace to the world.

Hope raced over and pulled a step stool out from under

the table. "And look, Mommy! My very own stool. Uncle Linc made it for me," she breathed, and bounced on the balls of her feet, which were covered in none other than rainbow Converse. Courtesy of one Uncle Jasper.

I smiled. "Amazing, sweetheart."

Hope skipped over to me and wrapped her arms around my waist, her chin to my stomach as she looked up at me. "Are you happy, Mommy?"

I cupped her little cheeks as I felt Kyson's warmth at my back, his chin going to my shoulder.

"Yes, baby, I'm the happiest I've ever been."

"Good!" She squealed. "Can we eat the cake now?" She licked her lips.

"Absolutely. Cake for everyone!" I laughed and felt Kyson at my back, his arm going around my waist as I watched our girl prance over to Uncle Jasper, who got the serving set out to cut the cake.

"We're going to need another one of those soon," Kyson murmured against my cheek close to my ear.

"A child?"

"Mmm-hmm," he rumbled, his hand going to my stomach. "Want to see a red-headed little girl running after her big sister."

I leaned against him as he wrapped his arms more fully around me. "Give me a year to make my business a success and you're on."

"Deal," he rumbled against my neck before dragging his lips along the column to kiss my cheek. He squeezed me once and then let me go.

I went over to my dad first and he wrapped me in a hug. "I'm proud of you, Izzy. The bakery is amazing and your family is wonderful." His voice sounded a little ragged and emotional.

"Thanks, Dad. I wouldn't have been able to do any of this without your and Papa's support, love and belief in me throughout the years."

My papa wiped a tear from his eye and pulled me into a fierce bear hug. "We love you, sweetheart. We only ever wanted you to have a beautiful life."

"And I do. The best!" I confirmed.

My papa rubbed his hands in front of him. "And, uh, we have a bit of exciting news of our own to share."

I pulled back and grabbed his hand. My dad Casey took my other hand and Ian looked at him then at me. "We're moving to Colorado!"

My mouth fell open and a wall of sizzling electricity hit my body, jolting me into action. I jumped up and down and dragged them closer. "Seriously? You're not fibbing!"

My dad chuckled and shook his head. "When you left and told us you were building the bakery here, we had a sit-down. We didn't want to be without you, only having short phone calls to check in. Plus, Ian wanted more time with Suda Kaye. It just made sense in the end. We're investing the money you saved us on our house and expanding your father's landscaping business to start one out here. I told my company I needed to move to Colorado, and they agreed to let me work from home."

"When?" I gasped.

He grinned. "It will take a little time, maybe two or three months for everything to be ready, but once we get home, we're going to pack up the old house and put it on the market."

"I—I—I don't know what to say." So many emotions swirled around me I could barely see straight.

"Say you're happy, silly!" Suda Kaye hooked her arm around Papa's waist and set her head on his shoulder.

"I'm beyond happy. It's a dream come true. To have my parents and my siblings, my bakery with my best friend, and my husband and daughter in the same place." I screeched out a, "Woo-hoo!"

Hope did the same from behind me, not having any clue why, but she never let an opportunity pass to make a lot of noise.

"Um, since we're all sharing a bit of good news…" Evie spoke up from behind me so I turned around as all eyes went to her.

Milo stood behind his wife, beaming, his long black hair fanned out and mixing with Evie's as he kept her close. He had his wife's back pressed to his front, and his large hands over her stomach. I narrowed my gaze and focused on those big hands.

"No. Freakin'. Way." I gasped.

Suda Kaye looked at me, then looked at Evie and Milo's hands, and then back to Evie, who nodded.

"No. Freakin'. Way," Suda Kaye repeated and brought her hands up to her chest in fists, her body positively vibrating with excitement.

"We're pregnant!" Evie said out loud and then covered her mouth as though she'd been holding on to this secret for a while.

Suda Kaye held her arms in the air, twirled in a circle and then ran to Evie and stretched her arms around both her and Milo.

Toko approached Evie after Suda Kaye, put his hand to her belly and smirked. "There is more news."

The smile on Evie's face made the entire room feel as though we were looking at the surface of the sun.

"We're having twins!" she cried, and my jaw hit the floor.

"Oh, my God!" I raced over to her and bounced on my

own feet, waiting patiently for her to stop hugging Toko as I could barely contain my excitement.

I went to her, cupped my hands to her cheeks and let the tears fall. "You're going to be a perfect mother."

Evie sniffed and tugged me into her arms. Suda Kaye got in on the action and we hugged, laughed and whispered our own sisterly excitement about being aunts for the first time, Evie being a mom and how happy we were for her and Milo.

Later, once the monster cake was cut and passed around, Razor went to the store down the street and picked up beer and champagne. The women sipped champagne and ate cake, except for Evie. Suda Kaye unearthed a bottle of Toko's favorite wine from her store, which he enjoyed thoroughly, and the guys drank beer.

I leaned back against the wall, one hand holding a glass of champagne, the other a second slice of delicious lemon and raspberry cake with vanilla buttercream frosting and realized I was happier in that moment than I could have ever imagined being in my wildest dreams.

My parents were moving to Colorado and would be in my life regularly.

Evie and Milo were having twins.

Suda Kaye could finally get to know her real father. She and Cam also got a golden retriever puppy so she could practice taking care of a living creature before attempting motherhood. She was having a blast with it and would often bring "Captain" to work with her.

I owned a bakery with my best friend in the entire universe.

Jasper was in love and living with grumpy Lincoln, who really wasn't that grumpy when you got to know him. I adored Linc because he loved my bestie to distraction and made efforts to show it.

I was married to the man of my dreams and a mother to a daughter I could dote on, love and spoil rotten with the hope for more children in the future.

My life was just like the name of my bakery: *on the sweet side.*

I smiled as I thought about how much Catori would have loved this day. "Mom, thank you for choosing my happiness over your own," I whispered as soft as a prayer while I took in the beauty around me. Jasper and Lincoln joking with my fathers. Kyson shaking Milo's hand and giving him tips on babies. Evie and Suda Kaye already talking about planning the nursery and a baby shower. Carol, Razor and Vince chatting up Toko and learning words in Comanche. Hope bouncing around to the beat of music only she could hear, going around and around the island, skipping as she liked to do.

"You may have believed I was a gift from God, but as it turns out, you were a gift to us all. Ultimately, it was *you* who brought all of the people I love most in the world together. Thank you for giving me life. Thank you for giving me this family. I love you, Mom." It was the first time I'd ever said those words out loud.

And as I took a bite of my incredible wedding cake, and sipped my champagne, a subtle breeze lifted my hair. I grinned as I watched Evie move into Milo's arms then stop and look to the side, her hair lifting off her shoulder. Then my gaze went to Suda Kaye, who turned around, inhaled deeply, looked at me, then at Evie and smiled.

The scents of bergamot, patchouli and the earth filled my nose as I kicked off the wall and went over to celebrate with my family.

★ ★ ★ ★ ★

note to readers

Hello, new friends,

On the Sweet Side is a standalone novel that is connected to the first two books in the Wish Series. However, if you have already read the first book, What the Heart Wants, you will have learned the story of Suda Kaye Ross. If you've read the second in the series, To Catch a Dream, you will have experienced Evie's story. This story is about Isabeau Collins but I won't give away how she connects with the Ross sisters.

In What the Heart Wants I explain how I developed the idea for this story after my dear friend and long-time personal assistant, Jeananna, told me her family history. I loosely based the first novel off her mother, the real Suda Kaye Ross. Her aunt is also Evie Ross, though everything that happens in To Catch a Dream is pure fiction.

This series is based on the sisters' Native American heritage. Through Jeananna's account of her mother's rich history, and her family line extending through the Comanche and Wichita Native American lines, I couldn't help but come up with my own story of what life could be like for a woman who grew up on and off a Native American reservation.

Much of what I've included here is the result of hours of research, including a great deal of focus on the Comanche and Navajo languages in order to be as accurate as possible with the few words I've used. Jeananna also shared some of her family's personal experiences, which allowed me to spin multiple fictional tales that I believe will resonate with women everywhere.

Still, as a fiction writer I took a lot of liberties and would never wish to offend anyone. I know how rich and diverse the Native American culture and tribes are, and I'm thrilled to have been able to shed a little bit of light on such beautiful people.

Isabeau is a woman after my own heart. She chooses to uproot her life in order to learn about an entire side of her family she didn't know she had. If you've ever been, or felt abandoned by someone in your life, you'll likely feel a deep connection to Izzy and her journey.

My greatest hope is that a small piece of these women, their adventures, their love stories and the lives they live resonate with you, and you finish this story feeling more connected to yourself and the sisterhood around you.

#SisterhoodFTW

Audrey

acknowledgments

To my husband, Eric, for supporting me in everything I do. I love you more.

To the world's greatest PA, Jeananna Goodall, I'm starting to realize we are super codependent on one another in our work lives and the worst part... I don't even care! You make sitting at the computer every day worth it. Knowing there's another person who wants these books in the hands of readers everywhere is such a special connection. Thank you for just being you. You are one of my best friends and I'm blessed to have you in my life every day, even if you live two thousand miles away. Let's do this book thing forever!

To Jeanne De Vita, my personal editor, for literally dropping everything to read this monster-sized manuscript and helping me through the highs and lows of the process, I can't begin to thank you. You are a true expert and I don't fear your edits, even when the manuscript is bleeding red. You always have a kind word and a generous spirit when working on my novels and I'm truly grateful for it.

To my alpha beta team Tracey Wilson-Vuolo, Tammy Hamilton-Green, Gabby McEachern, Elaine Hennig and Dorothy Bircher, for being the absolute best cheerleading beta team in the world. I'm always shocked that you are happy to read raw drafts chapter by chapter and share your thoughts. It's such a gift and a beautiful part of my process on writing each book. Thank you for always being there for me.

To Susan Swinwood, lead editor on this project, I am so thankful to be part of the HQN family. This series is my heart and soul and you've been so considerate and compassionate about it. Thank you.

To Lynn Raposo, for giving me so many awesome things to review and consider in the second round of edits. You have a way with words, my new friend! And Kathleen Mancini, for that extra pair of eyes to make this book sparkle, thank you!

To my literary agent, Amy Tannenbaum, with Jane Rotrosen Agency, you wholeheartedly believed in me when I told you I wanted to challenge myself and write sexy women's fiction. Your support is a blessing. Your friendship a treasure. Thank you for finding the right publisher for these stories. Mad love, lady.

To my foreign literary agent Sabrina Prestia, with Jane Rotrosen Agency, you are amazing, spreading the love for the Wish Series abroad. I can't wait to see all the translations in the future!

To the Readers, I couldn't do what I love or pay my bills if it weren't for all of you. Thank you for every review, kind word, like and share of my work on social media and everything in between. You are what makes it possible for me to live my dream. #SisterhoodFTW

about audrey carlan

Audrey Carlan is a No. 1 *New York Times*, *USA TODAY* and *Wall Street Journal* best-selling author. She writes stories that help the reader find themselves while falling in love. Some of her works include the worldwide phenomenon Calendar Girl serial, Trinity series and the International Guy series. Her books have been translated into over thirty languages across the globe.

She lives in the California Valley, where she enjoys her two children and the love of her life. When she's not writing, you can find her teaching yoga, sipping wine with her "soul sisters," or with her nose stuck in a sexy romance novel.

NEWSLETTER

For new release updates and giveaway news, sign up for Audrey's newsletter: https://audreycarlan.com/sign-up

SOCIAL MEDIA

Audrey loves communicating with her readers. You can follow or contact her on any of the following:

Website: www.audreycarlan.com

Email: audrey.carlanpa@gmail.com

Facebook: https://www.facebook.com/AudreyCarlan/

Twitter: https://twitter.com/AudreyCarlan

Pinterest: https://www.pinterest.com/audreycarlan1/

Instagram: https://www.instagram.com/audreycarlan/

Readers Group: https://www.facebook.com/groups/Audrey-CarlanWickedHotReaders/

Book Bub: https://www.bookbub.com/authors/audrey-carlan

Goodreads: https://www.goodreads.com/author/show/7831156.Audrey_Carlan

Amazon: https://www.amazon.com/Audrey-Carlan/e/B00JAVVG8U/

BOOKS BY AUDREY CARLAN